Praise for *The House at the End of the Moor*

"No one writes action and page-tur[...]
Filled with danger, romance and faith[...]
sure to captivate readers everywhere."

—Julie Klassen, bestselling author

"Filled with intrigue, danger, and toe-curling romance, *The House at the End of the Moor* is a masterful tale of redemption, forgiveness, and the beauty of restoration. A story to cherish!"

–Tara Johnson, author of *Where Dandelions Bloom*
and *Engraved on the Heart*

"An eerily, wonderfully written tale from master storyteller Michelle Griep. This book deserves a place of honor on your shelf!"

–Elizabeth Ludwig, *USA Today* bestselling author

"She must learn that love is stronger than fear. He, that forgiveness trumps rejection. Griep never disappoints, and she's penned another winner in this heartfelt tale of vengeance and grace!"

–Shannon McNear, 2014 RITA® finalist and author of
The Cumberland Bride, *The Rebel Bride*, and *The Blue Cloak*

"Another masterpiece by Michelle Griep; *The House at the End of the Moor* is hauntingly beautiful and a must-have for every home library."

–Ane Mulligan, Amazon bestselling author of
the Chapel Springs series

"The moors come alive in this tale of hidden souls, dangerous secrets, and burgeoning love. With echoes of the Brontë sisters and the deviousness of Dickens, Michelle Griep has spun a masterful tale of survival and love. I was captivated and did not escape until long after the end."

–Jaime Jo Wright, author of *Echoes among the Stones* and
Christy Award–Winning *The House on Foster Hill*

"I couldn't put this novel down. It has everything I want: a richly detailed and atmospheric historic setting, robust characters who grow from one chapter to the next, and timeless truths convincingly and naturally portrayed. Not only does *The House at the End of the Moor* sparkle with wit and wisdom, but the spiritual insight is seamlessly and powerfully delivered. Another impressive offering from Michelle Griep. I can't wait for her next!"
—Jocelyn Green, award-winning author of *Veiled in Smoke*

"Michelle Griep is my go-to author for heart-throbbing hunks; independent, feisty heroines; and a story that not only warms but keeps my adrenaline raging. *The House at the End of the Moor* is no exception. Danger, suspense, mystery, and romance all wrapped up in a masterfully written historical novel that not only entertains but teaches a spiritual lesson you'll not soon forget."
—MaryLu Tyndall, award-winning author of *The Legacy of the King's Pirates*

"How can a tale be both eerie and yet filled with such light and hope? *The House at the End of the Moor* pulls you into another time and place, completely atmospheric and full of everything that is great about Gothic-style fiction. Griep uses meticulous research as well as her signature wit to craft a tale that will leave you feeling as if you have trod the moors and scaled the tors of southwest England with Oliver and Maggie."
—Erica Vetsch, author of *The Lost Lieutenant*

"This sharply clever adventure captured me from gritty opening to brilliant finale! Griep has crafted a wonderfully terrible plight for her characters with a stunning conclusion and a romance that warms right through the pages. A true masterpiece of vivid creativity!"
—Joanna Davidson Politano, author of *Lady Jayne Disappears* and other historical mysteries

THE
HOUSE
AT THE END
END
OF THE
MOOR

MICHELLE GRIEP

SHILOH RUN PRESS

An Imprint of Barbour Publishing, Inc.

© 2020 by Michelle Griep

Print ISBN 978-1-64352-342-2

eBook Editions:
Adobe Digital Edition (.epub) 978-1-64352-575-4
Kindle and MobiPocket Edition (.prc) 978-1-64352-576-1

This book is a work of fiction. Names, characters, places, and incidents are either products of the author's imagination or used fictitiously. Any similarity to actual people, organizations, and/or events is purely coincidental.

Cover Design: Kirk DouPonce, DogEared Design

Published in association with Books & Such Literary Management, 52 Mission Circle, Suite 122, PMB 170, Santa Rosa, CA 95409-5370, www.booksandsuch.com.

Published by Shiloh Run Press, an imprint of Barbour Publishing, Inc., 1810 Barbour Drive, Uhrichsville, Ohio 44683, www.shilohrunpress.com

Our mission is to inspire the world with the life-changing message of the Bible.

ecpa Member of the
Evangelical Christian
Publishers Association

Printed in the United States of America.

In honor of Jocelyn Pagano, a stalwart warrior of the faith who fought a brave battle for her life against a sinister enemy—cancer. And as always, to the One who holds the power to vanquish *any* enemy, no matter how malevolent, Jesus Christ.

Chapter One

March 1861
Dartmoor Prison, Devon, England

Death prowled the cellblock like a dark animal seeking prey—especially the weakest. But Oliver Ward would be hanged if he'd let the beast devour the man in the cell beside him. It wasn't fair. It wasn't right.

When the next spate of coughing ended, Oliver scooted close to the wall separating him from Jarney. "Listen, when Barrow comes by, lay low. I'll tell him you're not fit for work today."

"No, I cannot let you, my friend." Jarney's ragged voice leached through the stone blocks. Whenever a fever raged, his French accent grew thicker—and today it was viscous enough to blend the words into a syrupy mess.

Boots thumped. Keys jangled. Cell doors swung open and Barrow's barks permeated the perpetually damp air. Oliver clamped his mouth shut. Speaking when not spoken to by an officer was asking for a lashing, and half the time Barrow didn't even need a reason to strike.

A second later, the hinges of Oliver's door groaned. Officer Barrow's broad shoulders filled the doorway. His arms were a little too long. His mouth just a bit too wide. And if he had a neck, it was buried beneath a thick scruff of black whiskers.

"Out!" Barrow bellowed. "Daylight's a-wastin'."

Oliver's gaze climbed the grimy walls, slick with mould and stained to an oily brown by the guilt of men. Near the top, a barred open space let in cold air and light as grey as his evening gruel. Daylight? Hardly.

Even so, Oliver shoved to his feet. Tarrying would earn him a crack in the skull—not that what he was about to do would merit a lesser punishment. Chains clanking from the shackles on his wrists, he strode out of his cell and swung into place at the back of the line of other prisoners.

As soon as Barrow reached for Jarney's door, Oliver wheeled about. "Officer Barrow, sir! Jarney's ill. I'll take his share of work today."

"That so?" A slow smile slashed across Barrow's face.

The hairs at the nape of Oliver's neck stood out like wires. Barrow *never* smiled. Oliver swallowed against the tightness in his throat. "Yes, sir."

The three prisoners behind him turned, the whites of their eyes catching lantern light and flickering with interest. Anything, even something as mundane as a few words to an officer, generated curiosity. Boredom was as real a killer as the pox.

"Huh." Barrow grunted, his brows arching to his hairline—which wasn't far off. Crazed locks of bristly black shot out in all directions from beneath the man's hat. "I don't recall asking you about Jarney." Those same brows lowered, drawing into an ominous line. "But now that I know you're capable of doing more, I shall expect it. Oh, and Ward? No talking unless spoken to."

Barrow's fist shot out. Knuckles slammed into cartilage, which gave way with a sickening crunch. Oliver's head snapped back. He stumbled, barely catching himself before knocking into the man behind him.

Laughter bounced off the walls, mocking without words.

Blood dripped onto his lips. Oliver swiped it away with the back of his hand, then once again faced Barrow, undaunted. "For pity's sake, man! You'll get no work out of Jarney today. Let him rest, and he'll live to work tomorrow."

Barrow chuckled. "Never learn, do you, Ward? Just can't keep that pretty mouth of yours shut."

Oliver raised his fists, ready to parry—but too late. Barrow yanked out his truncheon and whacked away, driving him to his knees as if he were naught more than a railroad spike to be pounded into the ground.

Blackness closed in. Sound receded, save for a bothersome buzzing and the muffled growl of Barrow ordering Jarney out of the cell.

Breathe. Just breathe.

Slowly, Oliver's vision crept back. Pain banged around inside his skull, radiating from crown to jaw. Turning aside, he spat out a mouthful of blood, then rose on shaky legs. One day Barrow would pay for his brutality—and Oliver could think of a hundred ways he'd like to see that justice served.

Jarney lurched out of the cell, shoring himself up with a hand on the wall, the chains on his wrists scraping against the rock. His hair hung in strings, hiding half his face, but he stood, thank God. He stood on his own. If he fell, Barrow would show no mercy.

Barrow slapped the end of his club against his open palm, the harsh sound making a point. "Let the thief no longer steal, but rather let him labour." His dark eyes drilled holes into Oliver and Jarney. "Therein shall ye find salvation."

Oliver blinked to keep from rolling his eyes, which would only invite another clout to the head. Officer Barrow fancied himself as the vicar of Dartmoor Prison, spouting scripture with as much gusto as a stiff eastern wind. He never got it quite right, though. A missing word. An added phrase. His own doctrines colouring God's precepts to a cadaverous shade. On the longest, coldest nights, Oliver often spent the black hours wondering if the man were Eden's snake come in human flesh.

"Move it!" Barrow smacked his club against the wall, the echo urging the five of them to turn about and tramp through the bowels of the prison.

It was a blessing, this broken nose of his. The stench in his own cell was putrid enough, but the reek in the passageways was worse. This time of day, when prisoners were yanked from their dark holes and hauled outside for manual labour, the opening and closing of doors stirred all the noisome stinks and collected them into one big, eye-watering vapor trapped in the corridor. It used to gag him. Now it just annoyed.

As they mounted the stairs, he whispered over his shoulder. "Grab hold, Jarney. I'll pull you up."

Chains rattled. Fingers dug into his shirt. Hopefully Barrow wouldn't notice Jarney's grip on his shoulders.

The stairway opened into a large hall, a hub of activity. Convicts of worse crimes than his shuffled about in leg irons. Those who'd committed lesser offenses wore nothing but the wrinkled clothing they'd arrived in. But all had been issued shoes with nails pounded into the soles in the shape of an arrow—a dead giveaway should someone be reckless enough to escape, leaving a trail so obvious a blind bishop could follow. Oh, they were easy enough to take off, but running barefoot in the wild could mean death. If not from the nip of an adder, then from the bite of rocks and gorse on the moorland, which could cut through the toughest of flesh or callus.

And nothing but miles upon miles of moor surrounded the prison.

Oliver trudged along. Around him, guards prodded prisoners, some destined for meaningful work such as oakum picking, but most were headed for rock breaking. Only God and Barrow knew how Oliver and his cohorts would spend the long hours of this day. Personally, he hoped for oakum. It was hand-shredding work, but at least it served a purpose.

Before they turned down the passageway, a crab-like man, ruddy-skinned and hunchbacked, scuttled sideways over to them. One of his legs was shorter than the other, giving him an off-beat gait. It was a wonder Officer Whimpole was yet on the payroll.

"Hold up there, Mr. Barrow."

As much as Oliver—and no doubt the rest of them—wanted to turn around and watch the exchange, to do so would mean time added to their service. And time was oft more brutal than the actual work.

Oliver strained to hear. A belch of damnation spewed out of Barrow, then he stomped to the front of their line and faced them. "Sorry, girls. There's another matter to which I must attend posthaste. Officer Whimpole and Mr. Piggins will oversee you today." He aimed his index finger at the prisoners like the muzzle of a gun. "And if I hear that any of you give either of my colleagues so much as a crossed eye, I'll send you to your Maker. Understood?"

"Yes, sir!" they shouted in unison.

Barrow stalked off. Whimpole took his place, making sure to handle the revolver at his side. He was an arthritic old coot, but no less deadly with that firearm loaded and ready to go.

"Outside." He tipped his head towards the front door. "The lot o' ye. Piggins has a wagon ready."

So. . .no oakum or rock breaking, then. And best of all, no Barrow. Oliver resisted the urge to make eye contact with Jarney, though the man had to be thinking what he was. Any little twitch might give him away—give *them* away—and this was too momentous an occasion for error. This might be it, though. The day. The show. The single moment Oliver had been counting on since he'd arrived in this hellhole.

Escape.

Whimpole pivoted and led the way. Mistake one. No guard should turn his back on his prisoners. Oliver flattened his lips to keep from smiling.

Outside, a cold blast of air drove misty rain sideways, cooling the hot throbbing of his nose. He hoisted Jarney into the back of the wagon while eyeing the big blob on the driver's bench, reins gripped in hands the size of mutton roasts. Mistake two. Piggins was as dull-witted as Whimpole was arthritic. The warden never should've paired them up. Surely this was a sign from God.

Oliver climbed into the wagon bed and sat beside Jarney, opposite the other three prisoners from their corridor. Snooks, Badger, and Flayne ignored them. Ignored each other. Ignored anything other than the sound of their own breathing. It was safer that way. Oliver had learned early on that self-containment could save your life, though he broke that rule for Jarney, a man as unrighteously accused as himself.

As soon as Whimpole pulled himself up and hunkered next to Piggins, the wagon rattled forward, and they left behind the grey hulk of Dartmoor Prison. Not that the surrounding countryside was any less forbidding. Unforgiving moorland stretched farther than the eye could see. Desolate. Dangerous. Whoever thought to put a prison in the middle of this godforsaken terrain was a genius.

As they bounced along, Oliver leaned towards Jarney. "Today's the day," he whispered.

"*Oui*, for you."

He narrowed his eyes. Was Jarney having second thoughts? "For us," he encouraged.

The wheels hit a rock, jostling them all. Oliver shored up Jarney with a grip to his arm.

His friend faced him, his skin as colourless as the pewter sky. "I will slow you down. I am not worth your getting caught."

Oliver slipped a glance at the other men. None looked their way. Not that they would've understood Jarney's accented words or heard his own above the rumble of the cart, but even so, Oliver lowered his voice to barely a whisper. "Don't be ridiculous. Every soul has value."

"Even Barrow's?"

He sucked in a breath. That stung. Of course Barrow was one of God's creatures—but so was a rat.

The wagon rattled onward and didn't stop until Whimpole shouted, "Ho!"

They halted near a breach in a sheep fence on the farthest reach of the prison grounds, where Whimpole turned to Piggins. "I'll take this one. Next break is bigger, near a half mile on. Ye'll see it. Swing back this way when ye're done, aye?"

Piggins's big head bobbed, and Whimpole lowered himself to the ground, a hammer in hand. "Ward and Jarney, out!"

Oliver gripped the wagon's backside and hauled himself over, chains clanking, then offered up a steadying grip as Jarney descended. His friend swayed when his feet hit the uneven turf. Oliver anchored him with a hand to his shoulder.

Whimpole threw the hammer at their feet. "Have at it, boys." Then he hunkered next to where the wall was yet whole, gun in his lap, protected from wind and rain. Mistake number three. Oliver hid a grin.

He retrieved the hammer and nodded for Jarney to follow him to the other side of the fence. A nearby cluster of sheep complained at their presence. Good. Their bleating noise combined with the occasional whoosh of wind off the moorland would cover up a whispered conversation. He turned to his friend. "This is it. You fetch rocks. I'll pound them, taking care to break my shackles as well. Then we'll switch places and you—"

"No." Sorrow etched lines in the grime on Jarney's brow. "I cannot make it. I will only slow you down. Once you are free of your chains, I will distract Whimpole and you run."

"I'm not going without you. You deserve justice every bit as much as I."

"And God will see to it, my friend." He gripped Oliver's arm in a weak hold. "Never lose hope."

"But we can do this! We can—"

The hammer of a gun ratcheted. So did Whimpole's voice, both overriding the noisy sheep. "Quit yer jawin' and get to work!"

"Yes, sir!" he and Jarney shouted and turned. Sweet mercy! Whimpole stood on the other side of the breach, three paces away. How had he drawn so near without a sound? Then again, it made sense the deadening whoosh of wind and baa-baaing sheep could just as well work against them as for them.

Jarney advanced a step, stumbling as the next gust nearly took him down. "Permission to haul rocks, sir?"

Whimpole lowered his gun and flipped up his collar against the rain, a growl rumbling in his throat. "Reuse what's fallen."

Oliver gained Jarney's side, mind whirring. If they weren't allowed to range farther into the moor, he'd have to come up with a different plan of escape, and, Lord, but he did not want to use violence. He motioned towards the ground. "Look for yourself, sir. The rocks here are nothing but crumbles. We use those and we'll be back out here next month, guaranteed. Plus it'll take twice as long, since we'll have to—"

"All right! All right." Whimpole turned aside and spat. "Just get it done, but only one o' you retrievin' at a time. Understood?"

"Yes, sir!"

Apparently satisfied, Whimpole shambled back to his post against the wall. Jarney plodded off, shoulders wilting. From relief or from his fever? Oliver lifted his face to the rain, letting the fine spray wash away the blood left from Barrow's fat fist.

God, grant Jarney strength enough to leave this place behind—or grant me the power to carry him.

Stanchioned by faith alone, he set to work. Jarney hauled him a rock. He broke off the edges to fit snug against those on the wall—taking care to strike the iron hasp on his shackles every other swing. By the fifth stone, he'd added a layer to the fence and cracked the cuff-pin on his right wrist. Four more rocks, and the other was nearly freed.

But each successive trip cost Jarney more than the man could pay. Sweat dripped from his brow. Heat radiated off him in waves. His eyes sank deeper into the sockets, and blue rimmed his lips. This had to stop.

When Jarney handed him another rock, Oliver leaned in close. "We'll switch places after the next one, then you free yourself. I'll take on Whimpole, and we'll run."

Jarney nodded. . .or did he? Hard to tell when his friend shook so much from cold and exhaustion.

"You are a good friend, Ward. Truly. But I cannot make it. You know I cannot."

"But if we—"

"No!" Jarney's voice rang out surprisingly sharp.

Oliver tensed. That one little error could bring their wild attempt crashing down upon their heads. They both glanced in Whimpole's direction.

The man sat like a lump of coal, hat brim pulled down, shoulders hunched. Had he dozed off?

Oliver unlocked his clenched jaw. "Jarney, listen to me."

"No, you listen." His friend's grey eyes burned into his. "Promise me you will run. Fast and far. Clear your name, then come back for me."

Oliver shook his head. "I cannot leave you. I *will* not. It isn't right."

"Yet it is the only way." Years and tears and lines carved deep into Jarney's face. "You'll not get another chance like this, and you know it."

A sigh ripped out of him. Blast! Was nothing ever right or good on this side of heaven?

"Get yer lazy backsides to work!" Whimpole growled, his head rising just enough to skewer them with a cancerous gaze.

And that was it. No more time to argue. To plan. To think.

Oliver gripped Jarney's arm. "I'll come back for you. I vow it."

A sad smile lifted half of his friend's blue lips. "Of course you will. Godspeed." Then he turned and staggered off.

Oliver's throat ached as he watched his friend pick his way over the mounded scrub, clutching his belly with one arm. How wicked the ways of men, when the poor must suffer while the rich wallowed in their wealth. He ought to know. He'd seen both sides.

White-hot fury rose up from his gut, choking him, and he swung the hammer. Hard. The wearied metal cracked and the shackle broke free.

"Stop!"

He froze. Heaven help him. Whimpole had seen.

But no. The guard shot to his feet and leveled his gun at the scarecrow shape edging across the desolate landscape. "That's far enough, Jarney. Get back here."

Jarney didn't so much as glance over his shoulder. He lumbered on, stumbling ahead, until the mist draped his form like a burial shroud, and he disappeared.

Whimpole heaved out a string of curses, then slip-ran in a cockeyed gait after Jarney.

Godspeed, indeed.

Oliver yanked the bonds off his wrists, gouging flesh and not caring, then threw the chains to the ground. A minute later, his shoes lay beside them. Though he hated to take the time to do so, he ripped off the bottom half of his shirt and hastily tied the shreds around his feet, then picked up the hammer and took off at a dead run.

He followed the wagon trail. Ahead, the wall curved. He'd cut right, then tear onto the moor and—

A gunshot boomed. Flaming pain cut into his arm, and his step hitched. But he couldn't stop now. Not ever.

Sooner than he liked, he veered off into the rugged wasteland, a single burning prayer pumping hard with each heartbeat.

God, have mercy. God, have mercy!

Hopefully He would, for it would only be a matter of time before Piggins and the dogs were set loose after him. Or worse. Constable Barrow.

And then there'd be no mercy.

Chapter Two

Three days later
The edge of Dartmoor, near Lydford

Nights like these, when the wind shivers the bones of the great old house, ghosts of my past waft about unmoored. Inevitable, really. One can never fully leave behind the souls of those held dear.

Oh Papa, are you well? Are you safe? Do you even think of me?

Enough! Giving myself a mental shake, I shift in my chair and tilt my worn volume of *Jane Eyre* to catch more of the lamplight. The familiar words are my truest friends. Though I've read the thing countless times, the story never fails to thrill. As a girl, I anguished with Jane and longed for my own Mr. Rochester. But not once had I imagined that like my favorite heroine, I would be shut away here in an isolated house with secrets locked behind the doors. An eerie coincidence, that. Yet the comparison ends there. Jane had her Mr. Rochester to love. I have no one.

And never will.

A touch to my shoulder jolts me from my thoughts, and I peer up from the page to a peaked face. My maidservant, Nora, is every bit the timid little bird as Jane, standing there silent in her black gown and starched white apron. How she manages to keep so pristine even at this late hour is a testament to her ethics. The woman is driven beyond all distraction. Always tidy. Forever precise. Even the way she holds out the cup of tea for me is elegance perfected.

I lay the book in my lap and take the cup with a smile. "Thank you, Nora. Don't worry about the dishes. You've had a long day, so retire early if you like." I nod towards the scruffy sheepdog sprawled near the fire. "Malcolm and I shall be going to bed shortly."

At the mention of his name, Malcolm lifts his head. After a cursory glance to discover if any bones or mutton fat are involved, he plops his jowls back onto his paws and closes his eyes.

Nora nods, then leaves as quietly as she arrived. She belongs here, on the moor, appearing and vanishing like a mist.

Wind howls in through the loose windowpane near my elbow. The low moan garners an open eyelid from Malcolm. I turn my back to the draught and drink my tea in a few gulps, then rise. Better to curl up with my book beneath a warm counterpane than suffer the chill of a rousing spring tempest.

Bending, I collect my novel and saucer, then trade the warm sitting room for the cool of a dark corridor and head for the kitchen. The passageway twists, but no matter. I can roam it with my eyes shut now.

Paws pad behind me. I am Malcolm's sheep—the only one he herds and cossets. I found him on the moor that first week I arrived. He was half-dead, savagely beaten by a shepherd's rod. Whatever the crime, no dog deserves such a thrashing. To this day he favors his left foreleg, but it never stops him from racing over rocks and heath. I fancy we are a lot alike. Wounded but not overcome. Braver than anything life throws at us.

But that's a lie.

With a sigh, I pick my way to the washbasin. The first drops of rain pelt the window as I set down my empty cup, the clatter of porcelain against soapstone adding to the percussive beat. Malcolm brushes against my leg, and I pat him on the head. "Come, boy, off to bed with us."

A growl rumbles in his throat, and he tenses beneath my touch. My pulse quickens. Something's not right, not if he—

The door bursts open. I slap my hand to my chest, a strangled scream flying past my lips. My book plummets to the floor.

Wind and rain usher in a dark shape. Malcolm bounds ahead, greeting the intruder with a sloppy lick to his hand. I wilt against the sink, catching my breath.

"Steady on, Mrs. Dosett. Din't mean to give ye a fright." My man-servant pulls off his hat and dips his big head. "My pardon to ye."

"No pardon required, Dobbs." I retrieve my book and shake it in the air, blaming my skittishness on a novel. "I ought not be filling my head with such vivid imaginings on a stormy evening." Malcolm circles back and rejoins my side, and though he leans hard against me, I am grateful for his watchful care.

Dobbs hangs his hat on a peg and shrugs out of his coat, sucking in a breath as his arthritic shoulder catches on the fabric. Despite his age and ailments, he is a tree. A bit bent, but an ancient, sturdy oak, as hardworking as Nora.

But that doesn't stop me from verifying his tasks are completed. "You took care of the burn pile?"

"Before the rain started."

"The barn door is secured?"

"Tight as a cork in a bottle."

I step away from the washbasin. "Only after the animals were settled, though, yes?"

"Aye, but I don't mind telling ye I had a hard time of it, especially with ol' Black Jack, the rascal. I've yet to meet a giddier pony." He secures his greatcoat on a peg next to his hat, then faces me. "Not that I blame the beast, mind. There's a wicked wind coming off the moor-land, more than just blowsy. Got an edge to her, the sort that curdles the blood. The Whist Hounds'll be roaming tonight, and that's for certain."

I press my lips flat. Dartmoor residents are steeped in superstition, inmates of their own fearful penitentiaries. But are we not all captives to our singular peculiarities?

I grip my book in both hands and lift my chin. "Good thing we are snug in the house then, hmm? And with that thought, I bid you good night."

I retrace my steps past the worktable, but as I reach the door, Dobbs calls out. "Might I have one more word, missus?"

I turn. So does Malcolm. "Of course."

"Been meanin' to speak with ye since this afternoon." Dobbs draws near, his boots falling heavy on the stone tiles. "When I were in the village today, old Nacker gave me a note from my sister o'er in Thorndon Cross. She's ailin' and asking me to stop by. Wondered if ye could get along without me for a week or so?"

Absently, I reach for Malcolm's head and twine my fingers in his fur. "Is it that serious?"

"Dunno 'til I go."

"I suppose you are right." My brow folds, and I'm glad the shadows hide it. It won't do to have him reading my thoughts. I hate the idea of Dobbs leaving. A manservant is a necessary evil—one I am loath to part with.

I relish the silky feel of Malcolm's fur, a solid reminder that he will be here for me, no matter what. "When would you leave?"

"First light, weather permittin'."

"I see. Well. . ." It's rude to hesitate. Offensive to even consider denying his request. But do I have enough supplies on hand until he returns to avoid making a trip into the village? Or—for shame! What am I thinking? I release my hold on Malcolm, heat burning up to my ears. Have I become as self-centered as those I fled from in the first place?

I flash him a smile. "Go then, and with my prayers for your sister's speedy return to good health."

He bows low. "Many thanks. I'll be back a'fore ye know I'm gone. I wager ye and Nora will be safe enough without me. Oh, and missus?" He dares a step closer, and Malcolm immediately wedges his body between us. "I know yer penchant for walking, but leastwise while I'm gone, take a care and stay close to the house, aye? Many a man has met his end in a bog or a crag or a'followin' a pixie. I won't be near 'bouts to help should ye cross a patch o' trouble."

True. I've heard the tales of those lost and ruined on the moor. I turn, calling over my shoulder as I tread into the shadows. "Thank you, Dobbs. I shall keep that in mind."

And I will. . .but honestly, it is not the moor that I fear.

Chapter Three

Some days are meant for running free. Hiking your skirts and bounding over tufted grass in an expanse larger than your imagination. Such is the draw of a morning washed fresh by rain. The earthy scent of damp dirt promises so many possibilities.

But as Malcolm and I venture onto the moor, Dobbs's ominous warning of the night before slows my steps. Not that I care a fig for enchanting pixies or hellhounds. No, the real danger is turning my ankle on a hidden rock or inadvertently venturing into a quaking bog. Yet none of that stops Malcolm. His long black fur flies in the air as he races circles around me. A smile stretches across my face at his unhindered romp. Oh to be so carefree.

Unbidden, *La Traviata*'s "Brindisi" pops into my head. For a while, I hum along with the swell and fall of the orchestra—for it is as real now as if I were once again standing on stage. Before long, I break into song. It is a glory to lift my voice to the blue sky, my audience God alone.

Ahead, Bray Tor rises from the ground. The dark granite crags stain the spring's tender green. Climbing to the top strains muscles and breaks a sweat. One false foothold guarantees a tumble, inviting a ripped gown or torn skin at best. At worst, a snapped bone.

But there is no greater view than at the crest.

I gather my muddy hem and tie the fabric into a knot, freeing my legs, then shout, "Come, boy!"

Malcolm trots ahead. His black eyes seek me out now and again as I pick my way from rock to rock, following a narrow sheep trail. At one point, my shoe slides on a patch of moss saturated with water. I fling out my hand, grasping for purchase on the jut of another slab. As I heave myself upward, the rough surface grazes my palm. It will sting later when I soak my hands in warm water, but there's no turning back. Not this close to victory.

At last I clear the final ridge and stagger to my feet. Wind gusts, knocking the bonnet from my head. I let it ride the current and bang against my back, tethered by a ribbon. Stretching wide my arms, I embrace the vast ocean of rolling hills draped in green and brown. But I am a fickle lover. No doubt I will curse the very same landscape on the trudge back home.

In the distance, two men hike together. Long poles with sharp iron blades rest against their shoulders. Peat cutters. A bit early in the spring, but with the ground softened by rain, I cannot blame them for wanting to try to harvest a patch or two. One of the pair throws his head back and faint laughter carries on the wind, mingling with the bleating of sheep. The men's camaraderie stirs an ache in my soul, tainting my triumph at topping the tor. I cannot remember the last time I shared such lightheartedness with a friend. Will I ever again?

Frowning, I reset my bonnet atop my head and tie the ribbons tight. It's necessary, this loneliness—but that doesn't mean I have to like it. Or pretend it doesn't hurt. Because it does. A hollow in my chest stretches out as vast and empty as this barren countryside. God Himself declared it is not good for man to be alone. I don't think it is for a woman, either.

But there's nothing to be done for it now.

As if sensing my plummeting spirit, Malcolm lopes over to me. He cocks his head, his pink tongue drifting past white teeth. My faithful companion always knows when melancholia settles upon my shoulders. He never fails to shore me up.

I pat him on the flank. "As usual, you are right, my friend. There is not one reason in the world I cannot laugh with you, hmm?" I ruffle his fur and am rewarded with a sloppy kiss to the back of my hand. "Shall we go home, boy?"

Without further encouragement, he ambles off and pads his way down the tall heap of rocks. I follow, though at a sluggish pace in comparison. Sure-footed Malcolm has a long wait at the bottom until I join him, and even then I make him tarry while I catch my breath.

I push away from the rocks and arch my back, preparing for the arduous trek back to Morden Hall. "Ready, boy?"

Malcolm jerks his head to the west—the opposite direction of the house.

"No, silly. We are done with our adventure for the day— Malcolm? Malcolm! Come back!"

No good. The dog tears off across the rugged flats, chasing a flash of grey fur. A rabbit, no doubt. I huff. While I don't relish going after him, neither do I want him getting lost. Bother!

I dash after the rogue, but he is too fast. The best I can do is trail the runaway, keeping an eye on his route and praying he'll tire of his doggy antics sooner rather than later. But then I see my chance. Malcolm dodges to the right, circling in a big arc. If I forge quickly ahead, I can catch up with him.

Gathering my skirt higher, I bolt into a patch of green grass. Moisture seeps into my shoes. Alarm creeps up my spine. The farther I go, the more my feet sink. Stopping is certain danger—but so is going ahead. Wildly I glance about and spy a nearby tussock. Can I make it?

There is no choice.

With as much momentum as I can gain from my slow speed, I leap. If I miss, the sodden murk hiding beneath the guise of vegetation will gladly pull me in, and I will be stuck. There is no telling how deep the swampy water is beneath the thick layer of muck.

Thankfully, my heels dig into a hump of solid ground. I flail my arms to keep from pitching forward. For now, I am safe—and trapped twenty paces inside a quaking bog with Malcolm nowhere to be seen.

Overhead, fluffy clouds amble by, ignoring my plight. Would that I could reach up and ride one all the way home. It is too far to jump to the solid ground from whence I came. Even now, my footsteps disappear as the waterlogged grasses close around them. I should've listened to Dobbs. Walked the road a ways or strolled along the river instead of coming out here. Will I forever be doomed to act without thinking? And yet if I stand here thinking for the next day and a half, my thoughts will not get me out of this predicament.

God, You have rescued me before. Will You do so again?

Slowly, I pivot, searching every possible route. Behind me, another tussock is close enough to jump to without a running start—but farther away from the edge of the bog than I am now. So, it is of no use. Unless. . .I narrow my eyes. Past that is another hump, and another, slowly arcing towards solid ground. The distance is farther than going back the way I came, but it is a sounder wager.

Working up my courage, I roll my shoulders, then leap—and land on the next mound. There. Not so bad.

I crouch and spring again, making the following one as well. Three to go. This isn't as hard as I imagined. On the contrary, my blood races with the exhilaration of it. Another hop and triumph is close at hand.

But as I fly through the air once more, I fall short. My forward foot breaks through the tentative layer of vegetation and sinks. A great slurping noise combines with my scream—and my whole leg disappears beneath the deceptive layer of grass. As I continue to plummet, I spread my arms and grasp the edge of the tussock. Between this and my other leg that is still on the surface, I stop myself from further immersion. A putrid odour arises. I turn aside my face and gasp, but fresh air is only a dream. My disturbance releases marsh gasses of a most hideous sort.

"Help!"

Tall grass and gusty wind squelch any hope of the men I'd seen earlier hearing me. I am on my own. With one leg yet free, I kick with all my strength and attempt to swim through the muck. No good. My sodden skirts weigh me down.

I dig my fingers into the mound of grass and pull until my arms shake, moving me an inch—maybe—and loosening a great tuft so that my left hand loses purchase. I scramble to grasp a new hold yet grab nothing but stinking mud.

No! Will I die here with no one to know how I met my end? Unacceptable. Unfair. Fetid water rises up my neck. How painful will it be when it seeps into my lungs?

God, is this it? Am I done hiding? Is the running over?

Just then a glorious sound rings out. Barking. Never again will I scold Malcolm for such a wonderful deep-throated noise.

"Here, boy! Over here!" I holler again and again, until my voice turns shrill. He cannot see me, nor I him, so tall is the grass where I lie. But no matter. He would not let a sheep go under, and I am the only sheep he has. The thought slams into me, and I suck in a breath despite the stench. How like my great Saviour, rescuing me time and again though I cannot see Him.

Soon, my furry friend thuds onto the mound nearest me. His nose nuzzles my hand. Oh sweet heavens. What if he thinks this is a game?

"No, boy. Pull! Get me out!"

He continues to rub against my hand—and then my fingers feel his collar. I understand his method. "Good boy, Malcolm. Good dog." I shove my whole hand beneath the leather strip and immediately he pulls. My shoulder wrenches from the strain. Pain burns along my arm. But ever so slowly, I ease out of the mire, until at last I stagger to my feet.

Malcolm leaps to the next—and last—tussock before the end of the bog, then looks back at me. Expectant. Waiting. It is close, closer than the others, but now my gown is lead and my muscles quiver.

Malcolm barks an encouragement. He believes in me, this dog. I dearly hope his faith is not misplaced.

I wring out my skirt the best I can and retie the hem, freeing my legs. Both are covered in black slime. Even so, I lift a prayer and leap. Malcolm springs at the same time. I land on the tussock, Malcolm on the moor. He sits and cocks his head, one brow lifting.

I cannot help but smile, and before I lose my nerve, I take my last jump. My feet hit the ground next to him, and he barrels into me.

We roll to the ground—the blessedly solid ground—and despite my fright and angst and anger at him for running off in the first place, I laugh.

"What an adventure, eh boy?"

I rise, not bothering to brush off the dirt from our tumble, and turn my face towards home. Nora will not be happy with me. La! I can barely stand the reek of myself. My poor maid will have to work long and hard to rid my gown of the malodour clinging to the fabric.

As I draw closer to Morden Hall, I scheme how to avoid Nora until I can wash at least some of the sludge off the fabric. At times like this her muteness is a blessing, for I can only imagine the terse words I should rightfully receive. Her scowl will be punishment enough.

I shiver the rest of the way home. The cold from my sodden skirts leaches into my bones. It is not soon enough when I finally hike down the small rise leading into the backyard.

Near the kitchen door, I shove my hand close to Malcolm's face, palm up, indicating he must wait for me. He's as filthy as I. "Stay, boy."

He drops to his haunches. I ease open the back door, thankful when the hinges don't squeak, and slip into the kitchen.

Then freeze.

Nora stands near the worktable, gripping the edge, white-faced and with a wild glaze to her eyes. She is as disheveled as I. No, worse.

For it is blood that coats her hands, her arms, and smears in murderous swipes across her apron.

Chapter Four

"Are you hurt?" I rush to Nora's side and circle her. Her hem is ripped ragged, and though she's not as soaked as I, the bottom of her gown is wet. But no cuts mar her skin. No abrasions graze her flesh. My prim little maid doesn't appear to be injured at all.

I stop my crazed circling. "What has happened?"

Nora grabs my hand, compelling me to follow. Her cold fingers are steel, unrelenting in their grip. Never has she touched me so forcefully. Alarm rises, rushing as fast as the blood pumping through my veins. Even more disconcerting, Nora doesn't lead me out the back door. She pulls me through the house, heedless of the trail left by my muddied skirts, a trail she'll have to clean up later.

My first thought is that Dobbs has been hurt—until I remember he left hours ago. . .unless he's returned? Taken a fall from his horse, perhaps? Maybe he even now lies in a heap near the gate. Nora shoves open the front door, and I brace myself for the sight.

The drive is empty. The gate stands open. No tragedy stains the sunshiny brilliance of the glorious March afternoon. Nora drops my hand and beckons me to follow, then hikes her skirts and takes off at a brisk clip.

I catch up to her as she turns onto the road. Casting her a sideways glance, I begin a round of our guessing game—the only way Nora communicates save for writing.

"Are we going far?"

She shakes her head.

"Is someone you know hurt?"

She shakes her head again. That rules out Dobbs.

"But someone *is* hurt, correct?"

Her wide eyes turn to me. Fear etches her brow. It is answer enough—one that frustrates. Did she not have sufficient work to mind her time at home that she must go seeking trouble?

"Why were you out on the road? Why did you leave the house?"

Nora scowls.

Drat. In my haste, I've broken a cardinal rule of the game. Only questions that can be answered by yes or no are allowed. I touch her arm. "Sorry. Clearly something obliged you to leave. Something important, no doubt. Am I right?"

She nods, then turns off the road and hikes a route through flattened grass. Hoofprints churn up the ground at regular intervals. Ahh. No wonder my maid ventured this far.

"Black Jack got out again, didn't he?"

Nora nods over her shoulder.

Naughty pony. Too smart for his own good. I sidestep a pile of manure and huff a sigh. I'd once seen an escape artist work his way out of leg irons and wrist cuffs, all while submerged in a great glass case filled with water. Black Jack could've beat the man's time.

"You followed," I think out loud, "hoping to bring him back, and came across someone who needed help. A woman?"

Her white cap shakes along with her head.

So, a man then. Of course. Who else would bring such a difficulty into my life?

The path widens, opening onto a strip of cotton grass and milk-wort that follows the edges of the river Lyd. As I pull up next to Nora, she lifts her arm and points downstream.

Twenty paces away, Black Jack nibbles at fresh shoots where they're greenest at the water's edge—not far from where a body lies deathly still on the bank.

"Oh dear." I rush ahead and drop to my knees on one side of the man. The pony rips grass and munches as if a human soul isn't about to depart into eternity.

A strip of cloth is tied around the man's head, explaining Nora's torn gown. Blood saturates the material and oozes out above the fellow's left eye. His legs are yet in the water. Long legs. He is a strapping man—leastwise, he might've been once. For now, his cheekbones stick out sharply. Mud covers half his face, matting in clumps on the dark growth of his beard. Raven hair, long and unruly, clings to his brow. His eyes are closed, but thankfully, his chest rises and falls.

"Sir?" I nudge his shoulder. "Sir!"

He doesn't stir. Nora's worried gaze meets mine, looking to me to make a decision.

I sink back on my heels. What am I to do? I cannot take a strange man into my home, even if Dobbs were present. Too risky. Too dangerous in too many ways. I've worked overly hard to protect my anonymity. I cannot lose it now.

But neither can I leave a man to spill out his lifeblood on the riverbank. He'll die. Someone will find him. People will question, and questions will exhume all I've sought to bury these past nine months.

Oh God, what do I do?

The prayer lifts gooseflesh on my arms, for it rises from the grave of nearly a year ago. It is the same plea I whispered the night I left my former life behind.

A chill breeze sweeps in off the end of the moor, just beyond the river. I shiver. The man groans. Nora pleads with her eyes. The price may be high, but I cannot leave the stranger here.

I fix my gaze on Black Jack. His jaws work, his halter strap riding along with the movement as he chews. I toy with the idea of getting the man onto the pony's back—then discard the notion. There is no way my petite maid and I can lift such a broad-shouldered man, malnourished or not.

There's nothing to be done for it, then. It's up to Nora and me alone. I shall have to send her back for the pony later. "Take off your apron."

Nora's lips ripple as if she questions my sanity, yet she complies.

Once the fabric is free, I scoot behind the man and plant my feet, then look to Nora. "I'll shore him up. You wrap your apron around him, supporting his back, and hike the straps through each armpit. I don't think the straps are long enough to tie him to Black Jack, and Dobbs never did finish fixing that dogcart, so you and I will have to drag him back to the house, using your apron as a litter."

One eyebrow arches, and the same question rises in me. Are we strong enough to haul him from the river, through the grass, along the road, and finally into the house?

My lips twist. We shall soon find out.

"Ready? Go." I speak with more enthusiasm than I feel, then shove the upper half of the man off the ground. He smells of moss, muck, sweat, and blood. I can only wonder how long he's lain here. How long he's been in the elements.

Nora snaps into action, trussing him with all the gusto she uses to twine up a goose for the oven. Once she's finished, I ease the man back to the ground and rise. I gather one end of the sash, Nora the other.

Then I meet her gaze. "On three. One. Two. Heave!"

I tug with all my body weight. So does Nora. The fabric strains, but it holds. Slowly, we work the man up from the bank, then pause to catch our breath where the ground straightens out. His head lolls to one side, but he appears no worse off than lying in a bloody heap on the banks of the brook.

And so a pattern begins. We heave. We drag. We pause. We breathe. Bit by bit, we get him to the house. With shaky arms and the last of our strength, we heft him onto the sofa in the sitting room, both of us too weary to care about the resulting stains to the upholstery. I drop into the adjacent chair, breathing hard.

"Go change your clothes, Nora. You'll catch your death. I'll wait here in case the man rouses, then when you are able to attend him, I shall remove my wet things."

She hesitates, but I shoo her off with a flick of my fingers. "Go. I'll be fine."

Nora disappears into the corridor, and I swing my gaze to the stranger on the sofa. Uneasiness prickles the hairs at the nape of my neck. I don't think I have seen him before, yet in an uncanny way, he is familiar. My throat closes with an unsettling premonition.

Is this the beginning of the end for me?

Chapter Five

There were two things Oliver Ward couldn't tolerate. No, three. Helplessness. Hopelessness. And the pungent stink of an egg poultice. Currently, he suffered them all without even opening his eyes. Better he were dead. . .unless, perchance, he was?

He blinked—then winced. Blast! How could such a small movement hurt so much? Groaning, he turned his head, willing the double shapes to stop spinning and meld into solid forms. A hard enough task were it daylight, but, judging by the dark shadows just beyond the reach of firelight, night was well advanced.

Several deep breaths later, he scanned the room from wall to wall, focus sharpening. It was a cozy space, rather homely, one that harboured a dog, a woman, chairs near the hearth, a table with a tea set, and a rug. A sitting room, then. But where? And how?

Skirts swished. The dark-haired woman lowered to his side, concern etched into her brow. A pretty face, but one to appreciate later. His gaze swung to the beast anchored at her side. The hackles on her dog's back stood at attention. White teeth glistened in the lamplight. No wonder the woman didn't fear to come so near a stranger.

"You are awake." The woman's voice, while quiet, filled the room like a song. This was no harsh fishwife. "I was beginning to wonder if you would rouse at all."

"Where am I?" His own voice rasped in comparison.

"Morden Hall. End of the moor." She bent closer, the fine fabric of her black gown rustling. "How do you feel?"

Like death. He cleared his throat. "I've been better."

"No doubt." She crossed to the table, the dog never leaving her side, then circled back and knelt once again. This time she held a cup to his mouth. "Here, drink this."

One swallow of the tepid liquid was enough. The foul concoction would be better used to fertilize the woman's garden. He turned away his head. "No more."

Disapproval flattened her lips, but she nodded and set the cup aside. "Very well."

In the brief moment her gaze was not upon him, he studied her closely—or tried to. A man might get lost in those doe-brown eyes of hers. How many had? She was a beauty, her movements cultured. A lifetime ago he'd encountered many such women at London dinners and soirees. What the deuce was a woman like that doing out here in the wilds?

He angled his head for a better look, then grimaced as pain seared across his temple. "Who are you?"

"I might ask the same of you." Like the flash of a spring tempest, the brown in her eyes darkened, then suddenly faded. "But let us talk in the morning. You need rest. Your injuries are severe, and I fear you could still develop a fever. How long were you out on the moor?"

Too long. Barrow's dogged pursuit had made sure of that. The man had nearly caught up when he'd paused shortly after escaping to scavenge a change of clothes and a decrepit pair of boots from a shepherd's caravan.

He shifted his shoulders against the cushion and clenched his jaw, biting back a groan. "Days, maybe," he answered. Or was it weeks? "I don't know." Hang it! He sounded like a babbling idiot. He clamped his mouth shut before he could shame himself further.

The woman angled her head, lamplight riding the curious tilt. "I suppose it is no wonder you are confused. You must've slipped crossing the brook and cracked your head on a rock. The wound was fresh as of this afternoon when my maid found you. She's since stitched it up."

Carefully, he lifted a finger and probed a fat wad of bandaging wrapped around his crown. Bulky but serviceable, and entirely necessary. He owed the woman, both of them, his life. Only God knew what would've happened had anyone else found him.

"Thank you—and her." He lowered his hand, then grunted as his arm hit the side of the sofa. Sweet mercy! He'd forgotten about that wound, such was the distraction of the banging in his skull.

"Take care." She needn't have pointed at it, but her slim finger aimed at his bicep anyway. "I don't know how or when you managed such an awful abrasion, but by the looks of it, it's not healing well."

He glanced at his arm, and for the first time noticed his shirt sleeve had been cut at the shoulder seam, where a poultice pressed tight against his skin. That explained the stench. Though Whimpole's bullet had only grazed him, it still might be his death.

Discarding her advice, Oliver pushed up to sit. "I appreciate your accommodation, but I must go."

She leaned forward, planting her hands on his shoulders, and shoved him gently—yet forcefully—back. "You'll do nothing of the sort. As much as you and I both desire you be on your way, you won't get far on that ankle of yours."

His gaze followed the length of his leg to where his left foot rested high on a stack of cushions. Yet another padded bandage was wrapped around his ankle, making it twice the normal size. Egads! How many other damages had he sustained? Quickly, he scanned the rest of his body, from his muddy and torn trousers to his bloodstained shirt. Lord only knew what had become of the waistcoat and overcoat he'd pilfered.

"I've left a bell within reach." The woman tinkled a small silver chime in front of his face, jerking his attention back to her. "Ring if you want for anything, but for now I think your most pressing requirement is sleep."

He stifled a snort. Sleep was the least of his needs. No sooner did the thought cross his mind than an incessant banging carried in from the corridor. Someone at the door. Oliver's gut clenched.

God, no. Not when I've come this far.

The woman set down the bell and rose. In one fluid movement, she grabbed a woolen wrap from the back of a chair and draped it over him. "Good night, sir. Malcolm, come."

Without a backwards glance, she swept from the room. The dog hesitated, his black eyes gleaming a threat, then he turned and trotted after her.

Gritting his teeth, Oliver shoved off the wrap and once again pushed up, this time swinging both feet to the floor. The room spun. When it stopped, he stood and hobbled to the door, sweat beading on his brow, grunts catching in his throat. His head, his arm, his ankle, all throbbed white hot. Only the cold plaster wall he leaned against held him upright. It was too soon to be standing, and far too soon to run if the woman opened the door to Barrow.

"Thank you, Nora." The woman's voice traveled like a shadow on the night. "I'll see to it."

Footsteps padded nearer. Sucking in a breath, Oliver eased away from the door, molding his body against the blessed wall. Thank God for sturdy bulwarks.

The footsteps stopped just past the threshold. He clenched his teeth. If the woman—this Nora—peeked in, what was he to say of prowling about like a common thief? And if she accused him as such? He squeezed his eyes tight, staving off ugly memories.

But the footsteps padded onwards. Oliver edged back to the opening just in time to hear the grind of hinges from an opening door.

A man's voice. Bass. Commanding. Yet so removed and low, it was hard to distinguish what he said. Oliver dared a step nearer to the corridor.

"I am." The woman answered in her resonant tone, the same she'd used when speaking to him. "What is this about?"

Oliver leaned closer to the passageway, listening with his whole beat-up, broken body.

"Not to alarm you, but I have reason to believe an escaped convict is in the area. Inch or two taller than I. Dark hair. Brownish-green eyes. Wounded in one arm, leastwise had been. Have you seen such a man hereabouts?"

Oliver's heart stopped, his skin suddenly clammy. That gravelly voice belonged to Barrow. One word from the woman, just one, and he'd be dead.

Shoving away from the wall, he gasped. Darkness closed in. Pain screamed and muscles quivered. He pushed through it all, lurching towards the sofa. Then the table. Finally, to the window. He gripped the sill, summoning the last of his strength. How long of a drop would it be? How loud the thud of his body? How far before hounds or bullets or both ripped out another piece of him? No matter. He had to get out of here.

Now.

He is a hairy man, this beast at my door. Constable Barrow's black side-whiskers blend into a moustache then twine into a beard that scruffs against his blue collar when his jaw moves. I don't like it. I don't like him. Nor does Malcolm, judging by the low growl in his throat. It's ironic, really. Why should I feel safer in the presence of the injured stranger—who is perhaps a criminal—than I do with this man of the law?

"A convict?" I wonder aloud. Is it true? Could I be harbouring a prisoner? Not a far-fetched idea, especially since the man made it very clear he wished to leave. And there had been a certain caginess in those hazel eyes of his. Indeed, a very real possibility. Goodness. Must trouble follow me everywhere?

Then again, how do I know Mr. Barrow speaks truth? I've been lied to before by those in authority.

"Aye, missus," the constable rumbles. "Ran off nigh a week ago now."

Gooseflesh rises on my arms as I meet his gaze. "Is he very dangerous?"

The constable shifts his weight, loosening a spray of droplets from the brim of his hat that have condensed from the pervading night mist. "No saying what a desperate man might do. So, you've seen him then? When and where?"

"I. . ." I clear my throat, stalling. What if the man in my sitting room is desperate? Regains his strength and lashes out at me or Nora? We are two women alone out here at the edge of the moor. Of all the inopportune times for Dobbs to be away! I grip Malcolm's collar all the tighter. "Excuse me, Constable, but if this runaway is potentially volatile, ought I hire extra protection until he is caught?"

"Probably no need for such extreme measures, missus. I am all the defense you should require. However, I cannot protect you unless you tell me everything."

I bite my lip. Perhaps I should tell him. Lawmen are discreet, are they not? There's no reason anyone should know the convict—if that's the stranger's true identity—was found here. Maybe I should let Mr. Barrow have a look at the man.

I open my mouth to say as much, but the constable's voice rings out before I get a chance.

"More than that, Mrs. Dosett, you'll be a hero. All of Lydford will sing your praises if it's your information that leads to the capture of this wily fellow."

A sour taste rises up at the back of my throat. While it is right and good to comply with the law, to turn in a criminal and see justice prevail, I cannot risk the chance of my name getting out. One word, just one, and I will be worse off than before. I will not go back—I *cannot* go back—not for the sake of one runaway offender. I'd rather take my chances with the bedraggled man on my sofa. Besides, for all I know, the fellow might be an innocent farmer caught unaware and turned around by the harshness of the unforgiving moor.

I lift my chin and don a stage mask perfected by years and applause. "If I discover anything I believe you ought to know about, Constable, I will be sure to inform you. I wish you all the best in your search."

A tic near his left eye twitches in a rhythmic pulse. His dark gaze narrows. "All right," he concedes, yet it is a strained concession, pushed through a sieve of distrust. Part of the job. . .or part of the man? "But if you should happen upon him, send word to town. He's not the sort you ought to invite in for tea, if you get my meaning."

I reach for Malcolm, my rock, my comfort, and take courage in the feel of his coarse fur against my fingers. "Yes, I understand. Thank you."

The constable dips his head, releasing more drops from his hat onto his beard. "Good night, missus."

"Good night." I shut the door, then lean against it, second-guessing myself. The lantern on the vestibule table flickers from the rush of air. Shadows dance as wild as my pulse. What if the man lying in my sitting room is dangerous? Dobbs is gone. Nora can't even scream should she be attacked. No one would know if the stranger finished us off in the dark of night.

Pah! What am I thinking? The man can hardly sit upright without swooning, and he certainly cannot make any swift movements on that swollen ankle of his.

Malcolm pushes his nose into my hand, and I stoop to pet him. "And there's always you, eh boy? My keeper and protector. I think we shall manage just fine."

Even so, I straighten and collect the lamp, then stride down the corridor to the kitchen. I bypass the table, taking care not to crack my hip against the corner, and grab the meat cleaver from the shelf. It is heavy in my grip. Too heavy. Fine for the breaking of bones but not light enough to offer any real protection. I put it back and finger the handle of the boning knife. Light cuts a line along the sharp edge of the blade. Perfect.

I turn away, armed, and debate my next move. Sleep with the weapon beneath my pillow or confront the man and find out the truth—*if* he speaks truth? A great sigh bellows out of me. It is ludicrous to think an escaped convict would actually admit he's a fugitive. No, better to just douse the light in the sitting room and let the man sleep, then send him on his way in the morning.

Malcolm glances at the larder, likely hoping for a late-night bone, but soon joins my side as I slip out the door and make my way down the darkened passage. Light creeps out in a triangular swath from the sitting room door. My throat tightens as I near it. A ridiculous response. He is the one at my mercy.

Hiding the knife behind my back, I hold up my lantern and enter the room—then frown. The woolen wrapper lies in a heap on the floor. So do two cushions. The sofa is empty. But where? My stomach turns.

I grip the knife tight as I raise it high. Never again will I be caught unaware. My gaze darts around the room and lands on a curtain pulled from the rod. Setting down my lamp, I creep towards it. I skirt the sofa, round the side of the high-back chair near the hearth—then lower my knife and rush ahead to where Malcolm has already darted.

The man sprawls on the edge of the rug, in the cold space between carpet and moulding. I drop to my knees. He doesn't move. Sweet merciful heavens. If he's expired, how am I to explain a dead man in my sitting room?

"Sir?" I press my fingers against his shoulder. Malcolm paws his leg.

No response.

Dread hammers loud inside my head. "Sir?"

I lift my hand to his nose to feel for breath, praying, hoping, and... Warm air, albeit faint, clings to my skin.

I sink back on my haunches. So does Malcolm, looking from the man to me, then back again. The man lives, praise God. That danger is past, but its removal does nothing to lessen the doubt incited by Constable Barrow.

"Who are you, Mr. Stranger?" I whisper. "And why were you out on the moor?"

Chapter Six

Some nights, sleep comes hard, like a long and grueling wrestling match, the sort that outweighs and outmaneuvers you by worries and fears and what-ifs. Ahh, but when slumber finally does seep in, gifting body and mind with blessed relief, it is a welcome boon, a treasure—one that is rudely snatched from me by a nudge on the shoulder.

Gripping my knife, I bolt upright, bed frame creaking from the sudden movement. My heart bangs hard and fast against my ribs. Nora's eyes widen in the grey light of early morning, and she retreats a step.

I lower my weapon but do not lessen my grip. If that vagabond has hurt her in some way, he'll feel the slice of my blade. "Are you all right?"

By now, Malcolm has left his rug near the hearth and stands at my maid's side, looking from me to her.

She reaches for my arm and pulls me from my bed, head vigorously nodding. If not her, then. . . ?

My gaze slides past her, as if the stranger might suddenly appear in the doorway. "It's the man, isn't it?"

Once again she nods, then leads me out of my chamber. Malcolm trots ahead of us both. Thank God last night I'd been so worn as to flop atop my counterpane fully dressed—though the nip of my corset is sure to leave a lasting mark. For at least the hundredth time since Dobbs left, I repent of allowing his absence. It is a foreign feeling, this desire to have a man present—one that swells as I enter the sitting room. I have no idea what I'll face from the stranger.

The curtains are drawn back, casting the first ray of sunshine onto the sofa where the man lies. His eyes are closed. His face is flushed. Unnaturally so. Has the fever I feared come calling?

I hurry ahead, and when I press my fingers against the thin line of brow peeking out from his bandage, a putrid stench hits my nose. His skin burns, but even more alarming is the greenish-yellow liquid oozing from the plaster on his arm. Clearly the egg poultice isn't helping.

"Oh dear," I breathe out. My stomach sinks with the inadequacy of my words. This is obviously more than an *oh dear* situation.

I rise and cross to the bookshelf, running my finger along the spines until I happen upon *Buchan's Domestic Medicine*. The cover is frayed at the corners, but the information inside matters most. I page through until I reach the chapter on inflammations and abscesses, then scan the paragraphs. No wonder our simple egg and vinegar mixture didn't work. The man needs more than a homespun remedy. I snap the book shut and glance across the room at Nora. "Have we any lixivium?"

Nora shakes her head.

"Bran?"

She shakes it again.

Drat! My shoulders slump. Defeat never comes easy, but I will not give up. There's too much at stake. A man's life. Nora's safety. My anonymity.

Malcolm joins my side as I pace from bookshelf to door, then back again—and again—weighing the possibilities. If I do nothing, the stranger might die. If I send Nora to town, she will more than likely be taunted and pelted with gravel just like the previous time I sent her. And if I go myself, my identity could be compromised. All rocks. All hard places. I lift a silent prayer to the ceiling.

What am I to do, Lord? Which one of us do I sacrifice?

My flesh tells me to leave the man be. Clean the wound as best as possible and consign him to heaven's arms if God so wills it. . . But my heart constricts at the thought. I have no idea to which eternity he might be headed.

Nora blocks my path, ending my pacing. She holds out her palm and angles her head towards the front door, indicating her willingness to go to town. I am tempted to grab my reticule and supply her with the coins, and I take a step closer to the door to do so—until a horrid image flashes in my mind. Nora, cheek cut and bleeding. Hands scraped from a hard shove to the ground. She is a favorite plaything of the cruel pack of village boys—and an even crueler man—which was the reason I'd chosen her in the first place to serve me out here at the end of the moor.

I glance past Nora's shoulder to the man lying still and sweaty on the sofa. *Are you worth this much trouble?* The thought barely surfaces when I stifle a gasp. How often might God think the same of me?

It's settled, then. I face Nora. "I will journey to town. Clean the man's arm as best you can and keep him cool until I return."

The fine lines on her forehead smooth, and she nods, clearly relieved she won't be required to venture into the village after all. But my own brow tightens as I ready myself and head to the stable to outfit Black Jack. If anyone recognizes me, all the care I've taken to conceal my identity these past nine months will be in vain.

As the pony eats up miles on the way to Lydford, I attempt to give my anxiety to the Lord, yet like the persistent breeze howling off the rugged landscape, my worries do not go away. Quite the opposite, especially as my horse rounds the last bend and we trot into town. I've not been here since the day I stepped off the coach and secured my lodgings at Morden Hall.

This time of morning, people are out and about. I refrain from meeting the stares of a few women near the dressmaker's, tuck my chin to avoid the gawk of a serving girl who shakes out her apron into the street, and I turn my face completely away from the glimmer of interest in the eyes of a sandy-haired man taking a draw from a pipe as he leans against a doorframe. It is not soon enough that I find the apothecary shop and slip inside.

A bell tinkles as the door shuts behind me. I cross to a long slab of a counter, breathing in the tang of mint oil mixed with the sweet, earthy scent of licorice root.

Behind the counter, the apothecary turns and wipes his hands on his stained apron, a Mr. Blandin, according to the sign out front. White hair sits like an afterthought atop his head, as if the straight ends whisking out at all angles might just get up and walk away. White eyebrows bush into a thick line above his spectacles. For all his crazed hair, however, he is clean shaven, his face lean and stretched over high cheekbones. "Good day. How may I be of service, madam?"

"I should like to purchase a lixivium and bran poultice."

With the lift of one finger, he shoves his spectacles closer to his nose, then studies me closely. "Suffering an inflammation, are you?"

"Yes—n–no," I stutter. What kind of woman does he think I am? "It is not for me personally, but someone I am caring for."

"I see." He peers at me over the rim of his glasses. "You'll be needing a bottle of laudanum to go with it, I suppose?"

"Yes, I suppose I do. Thank you."

"Give me a moment."

He turns his back and begins pulling out drawers and bottles and other ingredients that *Buchan's Domestic Medicine* never mentioned. Still, he ought to know his business. I wander the aisle nervously, then bend and gaze into an enormous carboy filled with yellow liquid. The bell tinkles once again, and I inadvertently turn to the sound. A woman in a green cape with a plaid ruffle enters, a young boy at her side.

The apothecary glances over his shoulder. "Be with you shortly, Mrs. Porchdale."

"Thank you, Mr. Blandin." The woman's green eyes sweep over me. The boy turns his whole head and gapes. "Pretty lady, Mama."

"William!" She whisks him to the other side of her skirt, scolding as she does so. "It is vulgar to stare. Don't be rude."

I turn away, as saddened as his mother by the boy's response, though for different reasons. His breach of etiquette doesn't concern me nearly as much as the lusty man he might grow into.

Once again the bell tinkles. Goodness. Must half the population of Lydford be in need of medicines today? I stand resolute with my back to the door.

"Ah, good day, Mrs. Porchdale." Another woman's voice, this one more of a soprano, albeit in an off-key tone. "Don't tell me little William's ear is troubling him again?"

"No, this time it's Betty. She's too poorly to. . ."

The women's chatter continues, but I pay it no heed. The only voice I want to hear is Mr. Blandin's announcing my order is ready. I work my way to the far end of the shop, but as Mrs. Porchdale sucks in a gasp, I cannot help but be drawn back in to hear what made her react with so much shock.

". . .to think such a person of ill repute might be here in our little corner of the world. Scandalous! Not to mention the reward that's sure to draw an unsavory sort."

My ears tingle. Are they speaking of the man who is even now laid up in my sitting room? I sidestep down the counter, feigning interest in the tins on a shelf as I draw closer to the women.

"How much is offered?"

"Fifty pounds."

"Fifty! Are you certain?"

My thoughts exactly. What on earth has the man done to merit such a price on his head?

"I saw it with my own eyes." The soprano's voice pinches tighter. Without looking at her, I imagine the pride radiating off her stiffened shoulders. Her words lower, making it hard to hear and forcing me to turn towards the pair. As I suspected, indignation ripples her lips as she speaks. "The paper's there for all to see, right on the wall of the Castle Inn, though I suppose other coach stops along the route are plastered with it as well."

Mrs. Porchdale harrumphs. "I don't feel safe anymore, what with criminals running hither and thither. Why, who knows when one might—William! I said quit staring."

My gaze drops to the boy. So does the other woman's, but just as quickly, her eyes narrow on me. Her head angles. Her lips part. One brow edges higher.

I turn away, biting my lip. *Please, God. Please don't let her recognize me.*

Mr. Blandin pivots and lays a paper sack on the counter in front of me. "Here you are, madam. That'll be one shilling."

"Thank you." I yank out some coins and shove them towards him with one hand while snatching the parcel with the other. "Good day."

I dart away without a second look, waving off Mr. Blandin's "But your change!" as I pull the door shut. Outside, I fill my lungs with deep breaths, slowing my pulse. Of course the woman couldn't know me. It is an irrational fear. Is not the fact that I may be housing a fugitive worth fifty pounds not a more pressing concern? I bypass Black Jack and cross the road, making my way to the Castle Inn. There's only one way to positively identify the stranger, who may even now be stepping across death's threshold.

Outside the inn, a public coach with six high-steppers parks in front of the door. Three women chatter together as they leave the confines of the carriage, a servant loaded with hat boxes and packages trailing them. A tall gentleman puffs on a cigar then belches out smoke like a chimney while he waits for his portmanteau to be handed down from the pile of luggage atop the coach. Two other men chuckle their way through the inn's front door, speaking of pints and pies. The exchange of all these travelers kicks up road dust. Good. I shall be only one more face in the scurry. Nondescript. A nobody in a sea of humanity.

I edge sideways around a particularly rotund man who shoves the last of a pastry into his mouth. Once through the inn's front door, I cling to the side of the wall. The lobby is cramped. The ticket seller at the podium collects money in a flurry. Did no one think to purchase their tickets *before* the coach arrived? No matter. It is easier to slip by unnoticed to read the parchment nailed to the wall at his back.

The words are large and bold at the top, then shrink in size and contrast. I drink them in, thirsty to know if the stranger is Constable

Barrow's escaped convict and what crime he has committed.

£50 **Reward**
Breach of Contract

The further I read, the more I choke, and my hand flies to my throat. I cannot breathe. The information is far worse than I expected. At the bottom corner of the paper is a hand-drawn likeness of the person of interest. Expertly crafted. One I did not want to see.

Mine.

Chapter Seven

Sebastian Barrow should've been a preacher. Everyone said so, from the first time he'd stood atop a crate as a four-year-old to convert the likes of his Skudge Alley playmates. And they were right. Every last one of them. But he'd shoved his arms into the blue woolen coat of the constabulary at twenty. Now instead of saving souls, he shackled and locked them away.

He jammed on his hat as he stalked through the inn's public room, angry he'd overslept. Angrier still at the hole in his left boot. All because Oliver Ward had given him the slip for nearly a week. The blackguard. He had to be close. Sebastian felt it in his gut—and his gut was never wrong. He'd covered most of the hidey-holes in Lydford, even skulked about the old dungeon ruins at Lydford Castle on the off chance Ward was crazy enough to shelter in a former prison. But he'd not yet torn apart St. Petroc's. Churches were notorious for housing castoffs. A soft-hearted reverend might even have tended the criminal's wounds, nursed him to strength, especially if Ward had spun some sorrowful tale of woe. Sebastian would turn the place inside out.

"You be needin' a room again tonight, guv'nor?"

"I need it indefinitely," he growled, without sparing a glance at the paunch-bellied innkeeper. Though he had nothing to go on other than the maybes and might-have-seens from two men out on the moor yesterday, he harboured a hunch that Ward was here. Somewhere. Tucked in a crevice like the snake he was. Sebastian's hands clenched into fists as he neared the lobby. He'd find Ward—the scoundrel—and teach him what was right and good. That's what preachers did.

Leaving behind the odour of sausage and ale, he entered the space between public room and front door, where two women and a boy huddled near the now-empty clerk's station. He smirked. Stupid women. Could they not read a timetable? The next coach didn't arrive until tomorrow morning.

"No!" The shorter of the two frowned at the other. "We cannot get involved in such scandal. Look, there's a constable. Better he should handle this."

Heaving a sigh, he averted his gaze and blew past them. He didn't have time for jabbery women and their petty stolen hair combs or other such trivialities. He should've taken the time to remove the duty band from his sleeve—though officially, he was on duty and would continue to be until he finally hauled Ward back to prison.

He stalked out the front door, then spit a curse as sunlight blinded him. A pox on the sun. Hunting was always easier in the monotone greys of a cloudy day. Fumbling in his pocket for a match, he retrieved one, then lit his cigarillo and inhaled a few puffs before he set off for the stable. He'd find that scoundrel Ward and haul his sorry backside to prison even if he had to—

Blast! He roared as pain drilled into the sole of his left foot. Hobbling over to a bench near the stable door, he sank like a rock and lifted his foot for inspection. A nail head peeked from the center of the hole, blood leaking around the edges.

Gritting his teeth, he pinched the nail and yanked it out in one swift movement. Blood flowed freely then. Enough to wash out an infection? By all that was holy, he didn't have time for this!

He growled as he limp-walked to his horse and cast a wild gaze about the stable. Where the blazes was an ostler when he needed one? Was the world full of nothing but layabouts and incompetents? He reached for his tack, and by the time he saddled his horse, his whole sock was squishy on the bottom. Good thing the apothecary was just down the road.

After a short ride, he dismounted and swung open the door of Blandin's Dispensary. The bell annoyed him. So did the scowl on the shopkeeper's face when Sebastian lifted his leg and thwunked his boot on the counter. Why such dismay? Surely the man had seen blood before.

"I need this fixed." Sebastian spoke slowly, in case the fellow wasn't truly the apothecary but some underling clerk.

The man frowned. "I am not a cobbler, sir."

"Not the shoe! The wound."

The man narrowed his eyes. "I am not a surgeon, either."

"I don't need a surgeon." The words barely made it past his clenched jaw. Precious minutes were being eaten away with this folderol. "What I need is a bandage and a poultice to keep infection at bay. Is that something you can do?"

"Of course. You're my fourth poultice in the past hour." The man sniffed, his spectacles bouncing as his nose wrinkled. "Now, if you wouldn't mind bleeding somewhere other than atop my counter"—he lifted a finger—"there is a chair."

Sebastian limped over and sat, then once again inspected his wound. The red flow had stopped, mostly. Satisfied, he lowered his foot and studied the apothecary's back as the man worked. He appeared to know what he was about, reaching now for a glass vial and then a canister of some sort of powder.

"You said four poultices," Sebastian thought out loud. "Is that an unusual number for the space of an hour?"

The man squinted at him over his shoulder, almost as if he'd forgotten he wasn't alone. After a huff, he turned back to his work. "Somewhat, I suppose. I don't generally do so many in such a short time."

Interesting. Why the uptick? Sebastian leaned forward in the chair. "Who were they for?"

"Mrs. Porchdale, Mrs. Graves." He spoke in time with the grinding of his mortar and pestle. "And some woman I've not seen before. Wearing mourning garb. I didn't have the heart to tell her the poultice she purchased would be too late if she's already taken to wearing black."

An image of a black gown rose up like a spectre in a graveyard. Sebastian's gut pinged, suspicion rolling around with the porridge he'd eaten for breakfast. "Other than the woman's clothes, what did she look like?"

"Rather striking." Grind. Grind. "Dark hair. Luminous eyes." A quick stir. "A particularly lilting voice, quite melodious."

"She give her name?"

"No, but judging by her fine gown and the fact that she overpaid without a care for her change, I'd say she's not from around here. Seemed to be in a hurry to leave, as well."

Sebastian scratched his jaw, fingers rasping against his whiskers. It surely did sound like the high-and-mighty Mrs. Dosett had made a visit to town. "What was the poultice for?"

"An infection of some sort—which is exactly what you'll have if you do not take a care with that foot." The apothecary doubled back to the counter and set down a white roll of cloth and a small jar. "Here. Use the paste twice a day with a fresh bandage each time. Naturally I recommend you first wash the foot. Now then, that'll be twelve pence, please."

Sebastian paid the fellow and grabbed the items, then took care striding back out to his horse. He'd have to make a quick stop to his room for a fresh pair of stockings and to apply the salve, but then it was off to hunt for Ward. And if he wasn't at the church, then perhaps a revisit out to Mrs. Dosett's might not be a bad idea. Either someone in her house ailed, or she was sheltering someone who did.

And after days out in the elements, that someone very well could be Oliver Ward.

∞

Nora is a miracle worker. By late afternoon, the stranger's fever had broken. He is still unconscious of our movements, yet he looks better than this morning. His skin holds colour and there are no more oozings or odours from his wound. Perhaps he's lived through the worst of it and can be on his way in a day or two.

I smile at Nora, who collects the basin and the last of the rags to be washed. "Thank you. As usual, your work is exemplary."

She dips her head, and a hint of pleasure sparks in her dark eyes, then completely disappears as a knock echoes from the front door. Two callers in as many days? It is more than in all the months I've lived here.

I stay Nora with a touch to her arm. "I'll get it. You finish here."

With each step down the passageway, my pulse quickens, despite the reassuring cadence of Malcolm's paws behind me. Has someone seen the likeness on the handbill at the Castle Inn and connected it to me so soon? By opening the door, will I usher in a past I have no wish to entertain? I blow out a slow breath, expelling my irrational fears. Save for the apothecary and the two women in his shop today, I've had no contact with anyone in Lydford, and none of them know where I live. The thought soothes, and I reach for the knob.

Yet as I open the door, once again my heart pounds. The blue-coated constable fills the doorway, the same as last night. In the afternoon light, however, his black beard is much bushier and his eyes are set far deeper beneath his great sweep of eyebrows than I first credited. He smells of tobacco and horses.

"Mrs. Dosett." He touches the brim of his hat in greeting.

"Good afternoon, Constable Barrow."

He says nothing more, though I suspect he cannot. He's too busy studying me. His dark eyes memorize and catalogue each aspect of my face, from hairline to chin. He squints a bit and leans closer, as if he's reading a mystery novel and cannot skip fast enough to the last page to discover the true felon. So unnerving is his stare, a shiver creeps across my shoulders. Has he seen the handbill?

With effort, I force my voice to a calm contralto. "I assume you have not yet found your convict?"

A small laugh rumbles in his chest. "Not yet. Might I come in? I have a few more questions for you."

"No!" The word flies out too harshly, and I instantly curve my lips into a pleasing smile. "I am sorry, but my manservant is away. It wouldn't be seemly for me to entertain you alone."

"I am a constable, missus. You've nothing to fear from me." He advances, his broad shoulders about to shove past me, when Malcolm—my blessed, fierce boy—immediately fills the gap and growls.

Constable Barrow looks from Malcolm's bared teeth to me. "Call off your dog, if you please, madam."

"He's just doing his duty, as are you." I reach for Malcolm's collar and hold him in place at my side. "I assure you, Constable, any questions you have for me can be as well spoken here as in my sitting room."

A storm darkens the muddy brown in his eyes. "Are you hiding something, Mrs. Dosett? An injured man, perhaps?"

Little prickles tingle along my arms. I set my jaw and stare him down. "If I wouldn't let the likes of you inside—a fine, upstanding man of the law—do you really think I would harbour a criminal?"

"I've seen stranger things, madam."

Malcolm rumbles another growl, and I shush him before once again facing the constable. "What is it you wish to know?"

"Why did you buy a poultice today?"

My grip tightens on Malcolm's collar. How on earth would he know that? "I do not see how that signifies."

Once again his gaze sweeps over me. "You appear to be hale, so clearly you are caring for someone who is not."

"Just because my manservant is away does not mean I don't have other servants in attendance."

He narrows his eyes to suspicious slits.

"Constable Barrow." I clip out his name, refusing to be cowed by his interrogation. Never again will I fall victim to an intimidating man. "Plainly state your charges against me, and I will answer them in a court of law. Until then, I refuse to provide any more information pertaining to me, as is my right."

Slowly, a gleam of white teeth grows in size as his smile widens.

"Well, well. . . You are a well-educated woman, more so than most Dartmoor widows hereabouts."

I arch a brow. "I shall take that as a compliment."

"Take it any way you like, yet now that we have your intelligence established, I can only assume you are smart enough to know that should you in any way aid an escaped convict, you will be indicted as well."

"I understand."

"Very good." He nods.

Whew. At last the harrowing conversation is over. I release Malcolm's collar and reach for the door. "I bid you good day, Constable."

"Tut, tut. Not so fast." He holds up one hand, halting my hasty retreat, and the other he shoves into his pocket. A scrap of fabric emerges, and he holds it out to me. "Have you anything to say about this? Found it not far down the road, next to a trampled area of scrub by the brook."

I flex my fingers before retrieving the tattered bit of grey cloth. Reddish-brown bloodstains blemish the strip. It is part of Nora's gown. Guilt rises hot up my throat. Should I tell this man everything? Come clean about the stranger in my sitting room? Be done with thinly veiled accusations and innuendo?

I lift my face to Constable Barrow's coal-black eyes and hard-lined face, and my stomach twists. There is no mercy in that cold gaze. No quarter would be given to the stranger—*if* he is indeed the convict. And if he is not, revealing the man now would only add to the constable's questions of my character. I cannot afford a full-blown investigation into my identity.

Squaring my shoulders, I nod. "Yes, I know this fabric. It belongs to my maid."

"Oh?" He cocks his head. "She took quite a fall, I'd say."

I clench my teeth. What to say? While I am certainly not beholden to the bloodied man we rescued, I feel an inexplicable need to protect him, especially while he is in such a vulnerable state. But there's nothing for it. I must tell the truth—yet maybe not all of it.

"My maid was chasing my runaway pony. Black Jack is notorious for his roamings."

He grunts. "Is she badly hurt, then?"

"Nothing I cannot manage. Thank you for your inquiry."

For a moment, he says nothing, just stands there, staring at me. "Very well, then. Good day, Mrs. Dosett." He drawls the name unnaturally long.

"Good day." Easing Malcolm aside, I shut the door, clutching the scrap of Nora's skirt in my clammy hands. Clearly the constable suspects me, and as I bolt the lock, my shoulders sag. How much time is left until the world crashes down upon my head?

Wild to escape the answer to that question, I seek out my ragged copy of *Jane Eyre* and settle into the worn wingback in my room. Better to focus on someone else's problems—even a fictional character—than dwell on my own. And it works for a while. I trade Morden Hall for Thornfield, lose myself in the intrigues of the mysterious manor home, until the swish of fabric and the light step of Nora pulls me from the story. She stands paces away from me, eyes wide and face pale. Her fingers ball up the edges of her apron.

Something is wrong.

I shoot to my feet, setting the book aside. "Is it the man? The stranger?"

She shakes her head and beckons me to follow. And so begins another round of the guessing game as I trail her downstairs, through the passageway, towards the kitchen.

"Is something wrong with you?"

Again she shakes her head.

I sigh. "Don't tell me Black Jack has escaped again."

Another shake. By now Malcolm trails my heels. It can't be him, then.

"Has Dobbs returned? Is something wrong with him?"

Her head wags from side to side as we cross the kitchen floor. She leads me to the window. I am no closer to distinguishing what has her so vexed—until I peer through the glass.

Across the yard, Black Jack runs nervous circles in his pen. The stable door is cracked open, and near the rear corner of the barn, the tail of a dark blue coat flutters wild in the wind where a man dashes behind it. A big man. A hairy one.

Constable Barrow.

Anger flares hot in my chest. Has he been skulking about here all this time? I frown at Nora. "Did he speak to you? Was he rude?"

Once more she shakes her head and withdraws a carrot from her pocket.

Sudden understanding dawns. "You were going to give Black Jack a treat, and on your way out, you noticed the constable?"

This time she nods—victory!

"And you came and got me, yes?"

Her head bobs frantically.

I smile. "Good work, Nora. I'm glad you didn't face the man alone. Did he see you?"

She shrugs.

I purse my lips. Of course he did, if he's any sort of worthwhile officer, which likely accounts for his hasty disappearing act to the other side of the stable. Well, we'll just see who's faster. I reach for the doorknob and glance at Malcolm. "Ready, boy?"

Two grey-scruffed ears perk, and he cocks his head at me.

I yank open the door. "Go!"

He bolts. So do I. Nora's feet pound the ground behind me.

The dog tears around the back of the stable. By the time Nora and I reach it and gain a wide view of the horizon, the last of day's light paints the world with a bluish brush. The constable straddles a grey gelding that gallops down the road, a trail of dust rising behind him. Malcolm gives chase, barking, but as fast as he is, he is no match for a horse. Why would Constable Barrow run off like a marauding ruffian caught in the act of pillaging?

Gathering up my skirt hem, I dash to the open stable door, which is now banging against the jamb from the wind. I stop just inside—and scowl.

Two barrels are overturned, lids off and oats spilling onto the ground. A few stacks of hay and straw are forked through and strewn about. Lord knows what's been done to the supply in the loft. Both pen doors gape open, more straw falling out of them. The saddle rack is tipped over and has knocked into the bench, toppling the tools to the dirt. Clearly he was searching for his convict, but his careless investigating has left me with quite a mess. No wonder the constable ran off before I discovered what he was about. I'd serve him more than a piece of my mind, and if we ever cross paths again, I still will. Must it always be a man who upends my world?

Disgusted, I huff and turn to Nora. "I suppose we'd better roll up our sleeves."

She nods and reaches for a hay rake. I pivot and head towards the house for an apron. Clearly the constable believes I am concealing his convict.

Am I?

Chapter Eight

A haunting sound beckoned Oliver from the depths of darkness. Soft. Rich. What? Where were the curses? The howls? The guttural cries of his fellow inmates?

His eyes popped open and he shifted his head, freeing up both ears to listen. Quiet humming floated on the air, making him feel almost human again.

Across the room, the dark-haired woman stood with her back to him, her hands busy with something on the table, her black skirts swaying with her movements. Was she in mourning? Maybe. So much emotion vibrated in her voice. Rossini, if he were correct. Or maybe Wagner. He frowned. What the deuce did a Dartmoor widow know of opera?

He pushed up for a better look at her, gritting his teeth lest the movement steal his breath. Surprisingly, though, the pounding in his head had mellowed to a simple dull ache. How long had he been out? Quite a while, if the fuzzy coating on his tongue was any indicator.

The woman paid him no heed, so lost was she in her music, which suited him. This time, without the fog of fever or acute pain, he studied his redeemer—for his redeemer she was, in more ways than she could possibly know.

Though curved in all the right places, she was a slender woman. Not sickly. Not delicate. Judging by the steel in her spine and what he'd experienced thus far of her spirit, she could hold up the sky had she a need to do so. Deep brown curls tinted with copper piled atop her head. A few tendrils dared to spiral down her long neck in a graceful afterthought. Still, for all her elegance, there was a certain wildness about her. An undefined wariness. Hidden beneath that black gown was a woman as changeable and unpredictable as the moor. He'd bet on it.

Her aria swelled. He could take it no more. Curiosity would ever be his downfall—a curse laid on him by his father. "Rossini," he croaked, then swallowed and tried again. "Is that Rossini?"

The humming stopped. Her shoulders stiffened. The woman turned and crossed to his side, neither confirming nor negating his query. "You're awake." She bent over him, concern folding her brow.

Her gaze roamed over his face, her brown eyes familiar. Was it the cut of her jaw that kindled reminiscence? Or the line of her fine, proud nose that birthed a vague recollection? He'd swear in front of God and country he'd seen her before. Somewhere. In his life before blood and torture.

She pulled back before he could think further on it. "How do you feel?"

"Better." Indeed. The word rang true. No more sweat dotted his skin. No violent chills shook his bones. Perhaps after a crust of bread and chunk of cheese, he could be on his way again.

"Good." The woman retreated and reached for a bellpull.

He pushed to sit up—attracting the attention of the scruff-haired beast near the hearth. The dog lifted its great muzzle and eyed him intently. Oliver tensed. But the animal merely plopped its maw back down on its paws. Apparently he was no longer a threat.

The woman gathered a teacup and once again swept over to him. He scowled at the offering, the bandage on his forehead pulling the skin. He could still feel the swampy grit of the nasty concoction she'd last served.

"Don't worry." She smiled. "It's only Bohea this time, and a weak brew at that."

A pang stabbed his arm as he reached for the cup. Would the blasted wound never heal? Still, had that bullet lodged, he'd not have made it this far. He tossed back a mouthful of tea, summoning up a measure of gratitude for small blessings, such as infection instead of amputation.

A somber-faced maid entered on silent feet. She stood just inside the door, a spectre in a crisp white apron.

"Some broth, please," the woman instructed. "More hot water as well, I think."

The maid nodded and disappeared as quietly as she'd come. Not a word passed her lips, not even a "Yes, mistress" or an "As you wish."

Either it didn't bother the woman or she didn't require her servants to acknowledge her, for she returned to the table and picked up a pair of shears. As she set about clipping the last of a few sprigs of dog violets and arranging them in a vase with some pennywort, another queer riffle of familiarity niggled in a corner of his mind. Her lithe actions flowed like a dance. A performance.

He slugged down the last dregs of his tea and set the cup on the floor. "Who are you?"

The woman spoke over her shoulder, hands never once stilling from arranging the greenery. "I am your hostess, for now. My name is Margaret Dosett."

Dosett. Dosett? He turned the name over, feeling the weight of it, measuring the value—and came up short. He'd not known a Dosett in all his thirty years. He must've cracked his head harder than he credited. . .unless Dosett was her married name and he'd known her before she wed?

He glanced about the sitting room, well lit with lamps, drapes drawn. As well apportioned as the house appeared to be, homey in a spartan sort of way, what kind of man had dragged such a fine woman out to the wilds of the moor?

His gaze drifted back to her. "This house belongs to you, then?"

"No." She angled her head one way then the other, studying her floral creation. A poor bouquet, but the best available from this land—and well did he know it after days of cold and rain.

Apparently satisfied with her handiwork, she turned to him. "I am only a tenant here at Morden Hall."

Only a tenant? She made it sound as if that were a bad thing. Did the woman not realize how fortunate she was? "At least your husband left you with funding for such a fine shelter. Many other widows in your situation want not only for a roof but scraps to eat."

Her eyes narrowed. "I owe my means to no man."

Though her tone remained pleasant, fire sparked in her gaze. He'd hit a nerve.

He lifted his hand towards her gown. "I assumed by your mourning garb your husband had passed. But perhaps it is your father you grieve?"

"Assumptions are the devil's handiwork, are they not?"

A smirk twitched his lips. A question for a question, a tactic he oft employed.

Once again the grey-skirted maid flitted in, this time carrying a tray. She set it on the table nearest the sofa, just within his reach. Mrs. Dosett offered her a small smile. "Thank you, Nora. That will be all for now."

The maid left, and Mrs. Dosett turned back to her clippings, gathering them into a pile.

A rich, meaty scent drifted off the bowl, and his stomach clenched. How long had it been since he'd eaten real food? He grabbed for the spoon, but after shoveling in a few mouthfuls, he tossed it down and reached for the entire bowl, not caring if he looked like an animal. The liquid burned his lips, his throat, but ahh. . . The pain was worth it. Of all the fine meals he'd eaten in his day, none matched this glorious broth. Then again, even grubs and grasshoppers would suffice after days of starvation. He drained the dish and set it down, sinking back with a new warmth in his belly.

Mrs. Dosett—finished now with collecting her clippings—pushed the vase to the center of the table and wiped her hands on a nearby cloth.

He puzzled over the sight. She worked as if he were naught but a shadow relegated to a corner of the room, one to be ignored, careful to watch her step around, but not feared. What manner of woman did that?

He leaned forward, cocking his head. "I am surprised you stay on here alone. The moor is a wild place."

"You ought to know, I suppose."

Taking care not to smack into the cut on his brow, he smoothed back his hair. He must look like a grizzled wild man himself. Lord only knew what this woman thought of such a rough-edged nomad like him.

She snatched up the shears and the cloth, then turned and crossed to him. "Suffice it to say I have my reasons to be here as much as you do."

Aha! Was that her roundabout way of inquiring about him? He snorted. Women. Even the best of them were too timid to strike a matter head-on. "And you are curious about my reasons, are you not?"

She stared down at him. "You may keep your secrets, sir."

He couldn't help but chuckle. In all the universe he'd never thought to meet a woman who would stay her hand from turning over every rock to peek beneath. "You are a rare one, Mrs. Dosett. Why did you not tell the constable about me last night? Are you not the least bit curious if I am the man he is looking for?"

She shifted the shears to her other hand then tucked up a stray piece of hair, matter of fact, as if they discussed nothing more than a new scone recipe. "That was two nights ago."

Two? He blinked. He'd been out for that long?

"And no," she continued. "I prefer not to know anything about you. It serves no purpose, as you'll be gone in a few days."

He smirked. He'd be gone by tomorrow. Even so, she was a brave woman for putting him up. "Are you not afraid I might attempt to murder you in your bed?"

Her own lips mimicked his wry twist. "I have bigger fears than an incapacitated vagabond."

The lift of the stranger's brows satisfies in a peculiar way. Even so, a shiver runs across my shoulders. Not from his manly quirk of curiosity, but from the dimple carved deep near his mouth when he'd smirked. It's impossible, but I know that dimple, and somehow I know this broken and disheveled man. But from where? And when?

Questions fly to my tongue, but his head sinks back against the cushion and his eyes slowly shut, saving me from a potentially fatal blunder. I blow out a long breath. It is better not to ask. If he is someone from my past, it is far more prudent to leave him buried in the graveyard of my previous life. Thank God his fever is broken. The sooner he is out of here, the easier I will breathe.

I turn on my heel and collect the tea chest, balancing the shears and cloth atop the small wooden box. It isn't likely the man will jump up and stuff his pockets with my precious supply, but all the same, I stride out of the sitting room and wend my way down the corridor with my cargo.

I stop in front of a cupboard tucked beneath the stairway. After a covert glance over my shoulder to make sure Nora isn't creeping about, I shove my fingers into the space between collar and neck and fish for a chain. On it, a silver key is tethered. I unlock the door in one swift movement and dart inside, leaving the door cracked open for light.

On one side of the tiny space is a line of shelving, where I deposit the tea chest next to an unsent letter to my father. Was it only two weeks ago I considered sending it, thinking it might finally be safe to do so? Thank God I had not. If those seeking me were willing to place a fifty-pound bounty on my head, who knows what they would do to Papa should they find out he had such a letter in his possession?

I turn away from it, and the ruby-red gown on the opposite wall grabs my attention. How could it not? The accompanying necklace sparkles in the triangle of light seeping in. This costume is the last link to Daisy Lee.

I should've burned it the night I arrived at Morden Hall.

Clutching the shears in one hand, I lift the other and stroke my index finger along the cold fabric, disturbing a faint scent of violet still clinging there. Strains of Rossini and the aching vibrato of a violin crescendos across time, and though I fight the siren call, suddenly I am back in Ambrose Corbin's ballroom. Women laughing. Men teasing. And towards the rear of the crowd is a dark-haired man, passionate in conversation, cutting one hand through the air, brandishing a book in the other. I strain my mind's eye. Does he have a dimple?

The swish of Nora's skirts ends the moment. Heart pounding, I jerk away my hand and immediately retreat, slamming the door and locking it.

Would that I could so easily shut out the ugly memories that will not go away.

Chapter Nine

Fruitless. Pointless. Done.

Sebastian dug his heels into his horse's belly, upping the animal's pace. Over the past three days he'd turned Lydford and the surrounding area upside down on Ward's account, but the man just wasn't here. Not now, at any rate. Likely the rogue had already moved on—and so would he. Tomorrow. Before dawn. Leave behind this nowhere village and head north, towards Bristol. If Ward had any sense, that's where he'd run.

Sebastian tugged on the reins, veering off at the Castle Inn's stable. A muscle knotted in his shoulder, and after he dismounted and handed over the horse to the ostler, he rubbed the offending area. He was getting too old for this. Chasing criminals cross-country. Wrangling them back to prison. How many more souls must he bring to justice before his own was set free?

Just outside the door, he pulled out a cigarillo, lit the thing, then glanced at the heavens, where twilight's deep blue-black spread like a bruise. "What's it to be, God?" he whispered between puffs. "Is Ward enough? Is he the last?"

He waited, but no answer came. As usual. Apparently God was not yet satisfied with his penance. But he'd not quit. He'd never quit, not until the Almighty once again smiled upon him.

Sebastian dropped his smoke and ground out the burning end with his heel, then strode towards the inn. The sole of his foot was still tender. Next payday, he'd buy some boots.

As he neared the door, a boy carrying a tray approached him, blocking his path. "Partridge pie, sir?"

Stupid boy. Couldn't he see he wasn't to be bothered? He side-stepped the urchin with a growl. "No."

He'd not taken two strides before the boy caught up to his side. "Better 'n what ye'll find inside."

Sebastian ignored him.

The boy sped up and once again darted in front of him, a chip-toothed grin slagging lopsided on his face. "Get yerself a tasty morsel here and now, and avoid the crowd o' the taproom. I'll give ye a cut price too, bein' yer a man o' the law and all."

A frown weighed heavy on his brow, the hairs of his eyebrows hanging like a black cloud over his vision. Clearly this boy wasn't raised properly. A child ought to be trained in the way he should go, which was clearly not to get in *his* way. The lad needed discipline. Now. Where was the urchin's father?

He glanced about, and seeing no one, his irritation flared. Must it always be up to him to right the wrongs on this godforsaken planet?

"I said no." He swung back his arm then struck hard and fast, smacking the tray from the boy's grip.

The lad stumbled. The pies flew. The tray cracked on the ground. Sebastian stomped off and yanked open the inn's front door. By God's grace and his hand, hopefully the lad had learned something.

Men's laughter and women's chatter wafted out of the taproom along with the scent of turnip soup. Bah, but he hated turnip soup! He scrubbed a hand over his face. Apparently, the evening was to be no better than his long day of scouring the countryside for Ward.

Hesitating near the door, he debated turning in with an empty gut or. . . The debate faded as his gaze snagged on a handbill hanging behind the porter's podium. What was this? In one quick swipe, he snatched the paper from the wall and held it in front of his eyes. Normally, he couldn't care less about some woman breaching a contract, but the likeness on this one twinged his gut more than the thought of turnip soup. He shifted his gaze to the description.

Margaret "Daisy" Lee
Aged 25 years; height 5 ft. 3 in.; brown eyes, straight nose,
curly chestnut hair, small mole on right cheek;
of stately mien and resonant voice; native of Bath.

Wanted for absconding months before the end of a legally binding contract with a certain Mr. Groat, her manager, also of Bath.

Well, well. Sebastian sucked in air through his teeth. Though the name be wrong, he'd wager Mrs. Dosett and this Daisy Lee were one and the same. Now there was something that would taste good going down—bringing the uppity Daisy Lee or Maggie Dosett or whoever the blazes she was to justice. He'd telegraph this Mr. Groat tonight. At least one man in this world should have the scoundrel he sought sooner rather than later, and the finder's fee would earn him a finer pair of boots than his paltry wages could afford.

Lighter of spirit, he shoved the handbill into his pocket and strode into the taproom. He'd not discovered Ward—yet—but he had taught a valuable lesson to a lad and would restore a runaway client to her manager. A small return for his time in Lydford but not a bad one.

Behind the long slab of a wooden counter, the paunch-bellied innkeeper waved him over, the rag in his hand flapping in the air. "Pardon, guv'nor. A word, if you don't mind."

Sebastian frowned, his good feelings quickly waning. If the man tried to sell him some turnip soup as doggedly as the boy had his pies, it would take all his restraint to keep from popping the fellow in the nose. He wound past occupied tables, now and then edging sideways between two-fisted drinkers. "Yes?"

The innkeeper sniffed, his red-tipped nose bobbing with the movement, and set down the mug he'd been drying. "Two men were in here earlier, askin' after you. Said I din't know where you were but that you'd be back."

Hmm. What the devil would they want with him? He narrowed his eyes at the barkeep. "And?"

The man reached for another mug and swished the rag around the inside of it. "Said you told 'em the other day that should they find anything of value hereabouts on the moor to bring it to your attention." After a last swipe with his rag, he set the mug down next to the other then reached beneath the counter. He pulled out a small, bone-coloured object and handed it over.

Sebastian lifted the thing eye level. The bowl of a clay pipe rested on his open palm, the stem broken off. A faint scent of brownstalk tobacco clung to it, so did a smudge of reddish dirt. All in all, it was a nondescript pipe. Cheap. As common as the one lying on the bed stand in his room. There was nothing valuable about it. Still, he'd learned long ago not to dismiss a lead—*any* lead—so abruptly.

He lifted his gaze to the barkeep. "Where exactly did they find this?"

Finished with his mug duty, the man tossed the rag into a nearby bucket while he answered. "Not far from Bray Tor, near Morden Hall."

Sebastian rubbed his thumb over the rough edge of the broken stem, thinking hard. Pipes weren't allowed in prison, so Ward wouldn't have left with one on his person, yet that didn't rule out he'd stolen it. Still, being on the run and all, would he really have taken the time to pack a bowl and pause for a smoke? Doubtful. But he definitely would've taken the time to lift a change of clothes, shucking his telltale convict's coat. The pipe could've fallen out of his pocket, unbeknownst to him. Sebastian frowned. Or it could've fallen out of any man's pocket who'd happened across that rugged stretch of land. This trinket could mean nothing at all—or everything.

The pad of his thumb hit an embellishment on the heel, and he turned the bowl over to peer closer. A raised circle enclosed two letter *B*s. A maker's mark, and a familiar one, if he weren't mistaken. Only one way to be certain, though. He shoved the broken pipe into his pocket and eyed the barkeep. "Send up a crust of bread and some cheese. A mug of ale too, and this time," he lowered his voice to a deep grumble, "make sure it's not watered down."

The barkeep's Adam's apple bobbed, but to his credit, he didn't retreat or go red in the face. "Aye, guv'nor."

Sebastian pivoted and threaded his way across the rest of the crowded taproom, then took the stairs two at a time. He might be onto something. He might not. Such was the game. Good thing he was an adept player.

He tromped into the room, leaving the door open for light, and without sparing a minute to doff his hat, snatched up his pipe from the small table near his bed. A slow smile twitched his lips. Pulling out the broken bowl, he set the two down on the bed stand and squatted, peering from one to the other. The circles matched. So did the double *B*s. Even the flattened end of the spur was identical. These two pipes came from the same craftsman—Benjamin Black of Princetown, Devon, the closest village to HM Prison Dartmoor.

He rubbed the sore spot on his shoulder, grimacing. If the men found the pipe stem near the house at the end of the moor, and he'd not found Ward in the stable there, then that left only two options. Either the rogue had scented him and fled, or he was holed up in that house, sheltered by Maggie Dosett—just as he'd suspected all along.

Rising, he yanked out the folded paper in his other pocket and shook it open, then stared at the image. "Well, well, madam," he gruffed. "Could you possibly be breaking the law in more ways than one?"

He eased onto the mattress, bed frame creaking along with his bones. Perhaps he oughtn't leave tomorrow morning. He could simply arrest the woman. Haul in two criminals. But. . .bah! That'd be one more criminal to keep track of. No, the woman was worth more monetarily than the cost of the effort it would take to haul her in. It would be a boon to return to Dartmoor Prison with Ward *and* a pocket full of coin.

Holding firm to the handbill, Sebastian shoved to his feet. A telegraph now would bring this Mr. Groat to Lydford either on tomorrow's coach or the next day's.

And in the meantime, he'd search that house of hers whether she liked it or not.

Oliver hobbled over to the draperies and pulled them open. The last light of day bathed the moorland in an ashen hue. He frowned. Had he seriously slept the day away? He didn't have time for such luxuries. Every minute he spent here was one more minute in which Barrow might snare him.

But pain still shot from his ankle to his shin. He ignored it, mostly. Boxing up agony and stowing it in a corner to be disregarded was a skill he'd quickly picked up in the dank cell of Dartmoor Prison. He'd open those boxes one day, remove each hurt one by one and lay them on the altar of justice—then rain holy vengeance down upon the head of the true criminal who'd stolen the jewels for which he'd been indicted. Soon, God willing.

Are You?

He peered up at the darkening sky outside, then blew out a long breath. Lately his faith was as vaporous as the mist on the moor. . .just one more thing taken from him the day he'd been locked in shackles and despair.

"I see you're feeling much better."

He turned—carefully. He'd already shamed himself one too many times in front of Mrs. Dosett. He'd not add falling flat on his face to the tally. "I am, thanks to your hospitality."

She held a lamp in one hand, the light of which highlighted a swiftly rising look of horror. Without a word, she dashed to his side and yanked the drapery shut, curtain rings screeching in protest. An odd task to complete with such obvious haste, yet it gave him the opportunity to hop-step over to the sofa without her scrutinizing his awkward footing.

She whirled back to him as he sank onto the cushions. "Mind that you keep the curtains drawn until you are able to leave, which may be as soon as tomorrow, judging by your apparent mobility." She tipped her chin, eyeing him. The endearing upturn to her nose hinted she possessed a certain impishness—a mix of playful cunning and particular intelligence. But it was more than that. It was familiar. Why? For the hundredth time, he sorted through possibilities and came up short.

She strolled over to the mantel and collected a small book, her dulcet voice filling the room like a song. "I shall have Nora remove the bandage on your head in the morning. She can fix that sleeve on your shirt as well. I believe she's already repaired your coat. The pocket was nearly torn off. Hopefully the contents weren't valuable, for whatever you carried is now likely somewhere out on the moor or washed downstream."

Once again she glanced at the draperies, as if they might spring open of their own volition—and he could stand it no longer. Such skittish behaviour was obviously for a reason. Had she discovered his identity? "Why?"

Her lips pursed as she faced him. "Do you not wish to leave here fully clothed?"

"No—yes. That's not what I meant. Not that I object, but I am curious as to why you have such a sudden need to keep the draperies drawn?"

She clutched her book in both hands, almost like a shield to hide behind. "I'd rather not provide the constable any reason to search my house as he so thoroughly upended my stable the other day. Catching sight of you through the window would certainly give him cause to do so."

Oliver frowned. Her caution didn't quite ring true. "But he's already been here, has he not?"

"Twice, actually."

His gut turned. *Twice?* Blast that Barrow! The man was a bloodhound circling for a kill. Absently, Oliver rubbed his thumb over the raised scar on the back of his hand—a little gift from Barrow's blade the day the man had pinned his arm to the cell's doorframe. But if Barrow truly believed his quarry was holed up in here, he'd have busted open that front door long ago. Why was he still sniffing around. . .unless it had nothing to do with himself?

"Tell me, Mrs. Dosett." He stared at her, keen to detect the slightest tic or twitch. "Why would you not let the constable inside?"

She held his gaze with a fierce boldness. "Suffice it to say, sir, that I am a very private woman."

"Oh you're more than that, I think." He leaned forward, suddenly suspicious. "What is it you're running from?"

Her lips curved, and in the depths of her brown eyes, something sparked, belying that smile. Fear? Maybe. But something more glinted there. Something hard. Something hurtful.

"Perhaps"—her voice lowered to a near-whisper—"the real question is what am I running to?"

"Fair enough." He nodded, fascinated by her twist of the conversation. "What is it you are running towards?"

She padded across the carpet, pausing next to the sofa yet refusing to look at him. For a long time she said nothing. The mantel clock ticked. Outside, wind rattled the windows. And the longer she stood there, the less surprised he'd be if she simply walked away without another word on the matter.

But she not only held her ground, she clearly enunciated an answer. "Isolation. Anonymity. A life no man can alter. That is all I seek."

He cocked his head. What kind of woman consigned herself to a loveless existence? Did not all females run hard after matrimonial bliss?

He traced the outline of her profile, searching for a tinge of humour—any tinge—but she stood statuesque, neither smirking nor smiling.

"It bears repeating, you are a rare one, Mrs. Dosett. I assumed every woman wished to know and be known by others."

"I used to think so."

"What changed?"

She stiffened. "Me."

She faced him then, rewarding him with a full smile. "You have quite the silver tongue, sir. You'd make a fine politician. Perhaps that is what you should be running towards."

He shoved down a bitter laugh. She had no idea how close she'd hit. "Politicians are a penny a stone. I seek something far more uncommon."

"Such as?"

"Justice. Nothing more. Nothing less."

She chuckled, the sound merry, warming the growing chill of evening. "Let me know if you find it, will you?"

"You don't think it possible?"

"You may as well be chasing pixies." She shook her book at him. "Or reading of such."

He shifted on the sofa, fully drawn in by her unorthodox dismissal of what most women deemed virtuous. "That's rather cynical of you."

"I prefer to think of myself as a realist." She clutched her book to her chest and strode towards the door. "And with that I bid you good night, sir."

Everything in him yearned to coax her back, to explore the other unique bends of her mind and words. His lips parted—then he snapped them shut. What was wrong with him? He had a mission to carry out, one that didn't involve conversation with a fascinating woman.

He turned his face away from the door. "Good night."

But her footsteps doubled back and her voice—this time steely edged—traveled from the threshold. "There is one more thing you should know now that you are up and about. I do not sleep unarmed."

He snorted as her shoes clipped down the passageway. She was plucky, he'd give her that, and altogether too intriguing. Margaret Dosett was a woman he'd like to get to know better.

Too bad he'd be leaving in the morning.

Chapter Ten

Morning sun pours through my chamber window as I collect my breakfast tray, and for a moment, I soak in its warmth. But storm clouds draw a black line on the horizon, stark at the edge of the blue sky currently overhead. By afternoon, another tempest will shake the house.

I whirl and stride out of my room, feeling as contrary as the April weather. All the man's talk of justice last evening still chafed. Poor, misguided fellow. His mission is a fool's errand. I suppose he'll have to learn the hard way—just as I did—that righteousness belongs to God alone. It will not be found at the hand of man.

At the bottom of the stairs I turn right, though my mind goes the opposite direction, towards the sitting room. Is the stranger up and about? Has he kept the draperies drawn as I asked? How has he bewitched my dog so thoroughly that Malcolm now prefers his company to mine? For no paws pad behind my skirt hem. But no, surely my faithful companion is merely keeping an eye on the man lest he get out of line. . . Isn't he?

The scent of ginger reels me into the kitchen, banishing all my bleakest thoughts. Nora flattens a large circle of biscuit dough on the big table, the rolling pin ridiculously large in her petite hands. The spicy scent makes my mouth water. Since hiring her, I've gained at least half a stone.

"Breakfast was delicious, Nora." I set the tray next to the basin. "Has our guest already taken his?"

Without slowing her cadence of rolling one way, then back the other, Nora nods. Of course she's served him, and likely already cleared away his dishes as well. *What have I done to deserve such a gem in a flour-dusted apron?*

I set my own dishes in the washbasin and replace the tray on the storage shelf, then turn back to her. "Perhaps you can finish mending his shirt today?"

She rolls, and rolls, not missing a beat, but her face lifts towards a peg on the wall where the man's coat hangs—*only* his coat. The white shirt sleeve is gone.

"You've already repaired and returned it to him?"

She nods and sets down the rolling pin, fingering a tin biscuit cutter instead.

"My, you have been industrious." I retrieve the woolen coat and drape it over my arm. "I suppose he may as well have this now. Oh, and by the by, being it's been four days, I think we may safely remove those stitches from his forehead and—"

Nora lifts a hand—the other studiously cutting circle after circle—and points across the room. On the far wall, atop a cupboard counter, rests a pair of scissors. The remains of a bandage coil in a wire basket on the floor.

I smile and face the maid once again. "You are always one step ahead of me. His gash is healing well, then, I take it?"

She bobs her head.

"Good. Maybe by tomorrow he'll be able enough to use that ankle of his and we can see him on his way."

Leaving Nora to her baking, I enter the coolness of the corridor. After a few twists and turns, I stroll into the sitting room—but freeze just past the threshold. Across the carpet, the man leans heavily on his uninjured leg. He stoops over a washbasin, his back towards me, yet I can see half of his face in the mirror propped atop the table. He scrapes a blade along his jaw, removing white lather. It is an intimate scene, this mundane act of manliness, one an unmarried woman should not witness. But though it's indecent of me to be so mesmerized by a man shaving in naught but his shirtsleeves, I am helpless to turn away. My eyes are fixed on the stranger in the mirror.

His gaze lifts suddenly and bores into mine in the reflection. Instant heat rushes to my cheeks. I've been caught.

The man's mouth quirks. "You may come in, Mrs. Dosett. I daresay you've already seen me at my worst. Surely a bit of soap won't put you off."

"I was. . .I mean to say. . ." Words stagger around on my tongue like little drunkards. What is wrong with me? I jerk my face away from the mirror and stride over to the sofa, scrambling to regain my composure. "Here is your coat. I think you'll find Nora's needle skills second to none."

The man goes back to scraping off the lather, the rasp of blade against whiskers overly loud in the quiet room. "Agreed. She did a fine job on my brow. Once healed, I doubt there'll be a scar of which to brag."

"I should hope you'd have better things to boast about." I lay the coat over the back of the sofa and smooth out the wrinkles.

"Ahh. . ." The scraping stops. "Is the lady finally curious about the mysterious man in her sitting room?"

Once again warmth flares across my face. Of course I'm intrigued, but the less I know of him, the easier it will be to keep from getting entangled in his life. "My apologies, sir. What you choose to speak of is none of my affair."

A low chuckle rumbles in his throat. "I wonder if your husband appreciated what a rare woman you are."

I straighten and absently run my palms along the black silk of my gown. Hosts of epithets bombard my mind. *Liar. Deceiver. Fraud.* Guilt sprouts a fine sheen across my forehead. It is wicked to allow this man to believe I am a widow, but so be it. It is the role I must play.

I motion towards the dog. "Come, Malcolm. Let us leave the gentleman to finish his work in peace."

Malcolm lifts his head, looking from me to the man, but does not rise.

"No need. I am done," the man mumbles as he dries off his face, then tosses down the towel and turns to me with a smile.

All the blood drains to my feet. No, it cannot be. It cannot *possibly* be! Now I know why those hazel eyes are so familiar. Clean shaven, the man's square jaw is unmistakable, as is the cleft in his chin. And so is the dimple on the right side of his mouth. His dark hair is combed back, framing a face that is altogether too memorable. Too startlingly handsome. Though the name escapes me, I know this man.

He was there the night I fled from society.

I grab hold of the back of the sofa to keep from falling.

"Mrs. Dosett?" He hobbles towards me. "Shall I call for your maid? You look rather ill."

"No need. I am fine." I inhale deep and long through my nostrils. Thus fortified, I straighten and arrange my mouth into the semblance of a smile—a pleasant one, hopefully. "Rather it is I who should be inquiring about you, though you appear to be well mended. How's the ankle?"

"Stiff. Sore. But serviceable, as long as I don't put my full weight on it."

"I am glad to hear it." More pleased than he can know. While another day or two of rest would no doubt benefit him, he cannot stay. Surely he will piece together who I am as aptly as I've finally identified him, yet why has he not already? Has the isolation of the past nine months rendered me as drably indistinct as the rugged moorland?

I turn from his watchful gaze and backtrack towards the door. Pausing at the threshold, I refuse to look him full in the face, but rather cut him a sideways glance. "Would you like a cup of tea before you leave this morning?"

His brows raise. "How did you know I'd be leaving today?"

Ah, good. At least we are agreed. I flutter my fingers in the air. "Clearly you are in a far better state than when you arrived, and I assume you have somewhere else to be other than in my sitting room."

"Indeed." He reaches for his coat. "And yes, I'll take that cup of tea, thank you."

I scurry down the passageway. Malcolm's paws *tip-tap* behind me. One cup of tea—just one—and the man must go. I fumble with the key at my neck, the chain snagging a piece of hair as I yank it off. Pain stings the nape of my neck, but it is a small inconvenience compared to what will happen if the man recognizes me.

Fanning my face with one hand, I unlock the cupboard door with the other. Light pours into the small enclosure, dazzling the ruby necklace into brilliant red sparkles and painting vivid the scarlet silk of the gown—and that's when the fuzziness finally clears. Without the fancy dress and painted face, no wonder the man didn't know me. Who would expect the famed Daisy Lee to be shut away in widow's weeds in a far-off corner of England?

The tension in my shoulders eases—then instantly knots back up when a line of fur on Malcolm's back stands erect. A growl vibrates low and throaty.

"What is it, boy?" I whisper.

The dog takes off towards the kitchen, where a man's harsh command barks.

"Move aside! Now!"

Clenching my jaw, I give the door a shove and follow in Malcolm's wake. As familiar as I am with the man in my sitting room, I also know the bass voice accosting the solitude of Morden Hall. Constable Barrow. The nerve of the man, sneaking in the back door!

I storm into the kitchen, where the constable's arm wraps around Nora's neck in a choke hold. He uses her as a shield against the snapping of Malcolm's jaws. His black eyes burn into mine. "Call off your dog, or it'll be the worse for your maid."

Nora's face pales to parchment. Her fingers desperately claw at the constable's thick arm.

I have no choice. "Malcolm! Leave it!"

Malcolm continues to bristle, but he circles back to my side. I grab his collar—for now, anyway. "What is the meaning of this? Unhand my maid at once!"

"She needed a bit of discipline, Mrs. Dosett." A wicked grin slashes across his face, yet he releases his hold and shoves her aside. "She doesn't know her place."

"Nor do you know yours, sir. This is my home, and you have not been invited inside. I thank you to leave at once." I point towards the open door.

Nora gasps and splutters as she works her way to stand behind Malcolm and me.

The constable doesn't budge. "Hospitality is a trait of the godly. I'd say you're a bit lacking. Now, step aside."

I lift my chin, defiance emboldening me. "I will not. Either you leave or I will release my dog."

Sensing my threat, Malcolm strains against my hold.

In one swift movement, the constable pulls a gun and cocks the hammer, aiming the barrel at the dog's head. The gleam in his dark eyes negates any doubt he's hesitant to use it. "Don't make this harder than it has to be."

Nora whimpers at my back. It is a pitiful sound and completely unfair that fear alone gives her somewhat of a voice. Slowly, I step aside, pulling Malcolm with me, for I am out of options. The stranger in the sitting room will have to fend for himself.

"Good choice." Constable Barrow plows past me and stomps down the corridor. I follow, never once loosening my grip on Malcolm's collar. He growls the whole way.

The officer must've noticed the drawn drapes in the sitting room, for that is the room he stalks towards, a lion on the hunt. My heart pounds loud and sickening in my chest. How to explain the stranger? Is he the man the constable seeks? And if he is, how do I escape a terrible indictment? Harbouring a criminal is surely a felony of the worst sort.

Oh God, please, let this all be a mistake.

Constable Barrow swings through the sitting room door. Sucking in a deep breath, I charge after him.

The room is empty.

Taking care to ease the fabric over the wound on his arm, Oliver wriggled his hand through the sleeve of the coat, then guided on the rest of it. Thank God for dutiful housewives and washing lines to air the laundry, or he'd not have made it this far. It felt good to be fully clothed again, even if the garment stretched too tight across the shoulders and threadbare patches thinned at the elbows. Hopefully the owner wasn't missing the thing too much, but it would be well worth the man's temporary discomfort. Oliver would return it to the fellow along with two new sack coats sporting a guinea in each pocket.

But even so, he bowed his head. *Forgive me, Lord, for resorting to thievery. May it not be necessary to—*

His head jerked up. His muscles clenched. Voices, muffled yet clearly angry, crept in from the corridor. A woman's—Mrs. Dosett's—and a man's. Bass. Harsh. Demanding. And far too familiar.

Barrow. Hang the cursed cully! Would he never give up?

Oliver snatched the straight razor from off the table and shoved it into his pocket, his lips twisting. Oh, how soon a sin once confessed could be repeated.

God, have mercy.

Wheeling about, he hobble-ran to the door, where the toe of his boot hit the uneven threshold, knocking him off balance. He stumbled into the corridor, barely catching himself. Instant pain stabbed his ankle, rising hot and sickening clear up to his gut. Sweet blessed heavens! How was he to outrun a constable on a gimpy leg? The ugly truth punched him hard.

He couldn't. Blast!

But what to do? Think! *Think!*

He jammed his hand into his pocket and fingered the folded razor. Flight was out of the question, but fight? Pivoting, he limp-sprinted down the passageway, discarding that idea as well. A blade was no match for a pistol.

Grinding his teeth, he hobbled on. There was nothing for it, then. As much as he hated to take the coward's way out, hiding was his only option. But where?

The constable roared. Bootsteps thudded closer. Time was running out.

The corridor opened into a small hall of sorts, where two other passageways connected, and a stair led upward. His gaze traveled the length of it. He'd never make it out of sight if he tried to shamble-step his way up those steps—but no need, perhaps. Below the stairs, a door gaped slightly open, leading into what was hopefully a cupboard large enough to house him. He could hide there for now, then when the footsteps passed, make a limp-gaited escape out the back door and hole up in the stable. Barrow had already searched there. He'd be a fool to do so again... And thus the fool would be fooled, God willing.

Are You?

Boots pounded. Skirts swished. Oliver dashed into the cramped space—then stifled a roar of his own. Rage boiled from head to toe as he yanked the door closed and turned the latch, shutting him in with a scandalously low-cut scarlet gown...

And the ruby jewels he'd been convicted for stealing.

Chapter Eleven

My gaze darts from corner to corner in the sitting room, faster than Constable Barrow's long legs can carry him to the shadowy nooks. No man-sized shape billows out from the draperies. No leg or arm appears as the constable lifts the ruffle at the bottom of the sofa with the tip of his gun. Nothing scurries from hiding, either, when he rudely shoves my chair aside. How had the stranger vanished so quickly and thoroughly on his twisted ankle?

For now, I push away the question and pop my fists against my hips. "I don't know who or what you expected to find, sir, but as you can see, there is nothing here to interest you."

A gravelly chuckle accosts the quiet room. "You cannot begin to know what interests me, Mrs. Dosett."

He tucks away his gun and grasps the edges of the thick curtains, yanking them open. The brass rings screech in protest. Then he moves to the other set of windows and does the same. "Why are these closed?"

The growl of his question is more of an accusation than a query.

I clutch Malcolm's collar tighter. I can't very well admit my intent was to shut out the likes of him—but neither can I lie. So. . . what to say?

"Not that it signifies," I drawl, stalling for time, for words, for truth—and thankfully, brilliantly, an idea comes to mind. "But ofttimes I suffer from a headache. Light intensifies the pain." It's true. I do battle such agonies from time to time and frequently have Nora draw the drapes for just such a reason.

"Oh?" He turns to me, his bushy brows climbing up his forehead. "Have you a headache now?"

I scowl. Indeed. The man *is* a headache. "Yes."

He smirks, but it quickly twists into a glower as his dark gaze lands on the washbasin. He crosses to it in two strides. "What is this?"

Little needle pricks run down my spine. The bowl is exactly as the stranger left it, the towel balled up at its side. Holding my breath, I scour the tabletop with a sharp gaze. The razor could be my undoing, but there is no flash of silver. I blow out a quiet *thank You* to God then skewer the constable with a piercing stare. "You can see for yourself what it is, can you not?"

He does not look away. "A woman's sharp tongue is an abomination to God."

Automatically my jaw tightens. I will *not* be subject to twisted scripture. If I am to be condemned, it will be by merit of my true sins. "I believe the correct wording of Proverbs six lists that abomination as a *lying* tongue, not a sharp one. And it does not single out women as the sole bearer of such wrath."

Black fury ignites in his eyes, almost demonic in its force. I plant my feet to keep from retreating. Malcolm strains against my hold.

With a sneer, the constable shoves his hand into the basin then pulls it out, rubbing leftover soap scum between his thumb and forefinger. Lifting it, he sniffs the mess and his gaze narrows on the filmy lather.

Then he flicks it aside, the droplets splatting against the arm of the sofa. "A darkened room is a curious place to shave."

I force a small laugh, praying to God it comes across as ludicrous instead of jittery. "Quite the misguided idea, Constable. If you are going to indict me, then have at it. Otherwise, I will thank you to leave at once. I grow tired of your baseless insinuations."

"Baseless?" His boots pound across the floor, intimidation thudding in each step. He stops just short of Malcolm's lunging reach. "Then how do you explain the whiskers in the water, Mrs. Dosett?"

I freeze, a doe before the hunter. One false word—nay—one false movement stands between me and a cold gaol cell.

"They are hairs, Mr. Barrow," I admit. "*Dog* hairs. My maid has not yet emptied the basin after washing down the baseboards."

My stomach heaves as the lie passes my lips. The very abomination I spoke of seconds ago now convicts me.

Oh God, forgive me. No more will I deceive. Please, have mercy, and send this man—

Constable Barrow huffs and shoves me aside, knocking me into Malcolm. The dog growls, yanking against my grip, but I hold tight as I right myself, then turn us both around and flee the sitting room.

For the next twenty minutes, I traipse after the man as he storms into every room in Morden Hall. At each doorway, a fresh wave of fear steals my breath. I do not take in air until I scan from wall to wall and am satisfied the stranger is not secreted away. Where he's truly gone, I do not know—nor do I want to. I only hope he is gone for good.

All possibilities exhausted, Constable Barrow finally trots down the stairs and stops in the hall. Slowly, he pivots in a circle, as if some new corridor will appear that he might exploit.

I toy with the idea of releasing my grip on Malcolm's collar and allowing his snapping teeth to shoo the man out. "Are you quite finished barreling through my home, sir?"

Without so much as a glance my way, he stomps to the cupboard door beneath the stair.

My heart stops. So do my lungs. There was no time to lock the thing an eternity ago when the constable rampaged into the kitchen.

His podgy fingers grip the knob.

I swallow, throat impossibly tight. Sweet blessed heavens! Is that where my unwanted houseguest is hidden? And if not, how am I to explain the gown without revealing my identity or succumbing to deception once again?

The constable yanks—but the door does not open.

What? I stagger, grateful the man's back is towards me, for surely it is a giveaway of my confusion. Had I locked the thing after all?

Constable Barrow pivots and hitches a thumb at the closet. "What's in here?"

"My tea chest." It's a half truth, but a truth nonetheless.

He glowers. "Open it."

"I will not! I have been more than patient with you, sir, and I am through with your rude antics." I whirl, running from him, running from falsehoods. Is this what my life will be from now on, doomed to forever and always run?

A grip on the upper part of my arm yanks me back. The constable shoves his face into mine. His hot breath defiles my cheeks.

"You're through when I say you are."

Malcolm lunges, and I am sorely tempted to let him go—a highly gratifying prospect, but a temporary one. It will do nothing to keep the bully from shooting him or from returning. No, it is time to wield a gun of my own, though in doing so, I offer a glimpse of who I really am. Still, I have no choice.

"If you do not unhand me at once," I seethe, "I shall see you squirm beneath the thumb of Lord Greenham."

"Greenham?" Mr. Barrow narrows his eyes. "You're bluffing."

But his lips flatten with a slight ripple of doubt—enough that I wrench from his grasp. "Do you really wish to find out for the sake of opening a tea closet? One word from me in Lord Greenham's ear and you will find yourself not only fired but arrested for the brutality of your assault on my maid. And do not think for one minute that he won't listen to me. The judge and I go way back."

His nostrils flare. A direct hit—yet he doesn't retreat. How much more incentive does the man need?

As a last resort, I yank out the chain from my bodice, revealing my key. "And if you must know, *I* am the only one with access to the space. Your disrespect to a lady of standing will not be well met, so tell me, Mr. Barrow, how exactly will you explain your groundless suspicions of me to a high court judge?"

He stands motionless, huffing like an ox. The hatred in his gaze is a living monster.

"This isn't over, Mrs. Dosett." He spins on his heel and stomps down the corridor, limping just a bit. Seconds later, the slamming of the front door shakes the bones of the house to the rafters.

I peel my fingers from Malcolm's collar. Instantly, he tears off in the wake of the constable. On shaky legs, I lean against the wall then sink to a heap on the stairs. Never again will I take in a stranger from off the moor, half-dead or not. It's nearly been my undoing.

Malcolm lopes back. Apparently satisfied the danger is well and truly gone, he snuffles over to me with a great lick to my cheek. I cannot help but allow a tremulous smile as I swipe the moisture away. I bury my face in his fur. "That was close, eh boy?"

"Closer than you think."

I jerk upright, heart hammering against my ribs. Hazel eyes stare down at me, green flecks waging war with gold and brown. Slowly, I rise. "Where were you?"

"I might ask the same question." His jaw hardens. "Where were *you* the night of June eighth? And don't tell me here at Morden Hall, because I think we both know better than that, don't we. . . Daisy Lee?"

∽

A skirt? He'd suffered in the hell of a cold stone cell all for the sake of a thieving woman? So much rage coloured Oliver's vision he nearly didn't detect the blanching of Margaret Dosett's face—and when he did, it only served to stoke the fire in his gut even more. But of course. Why not a skirt? Was it not a woman's teeth that first pierced the flesh of the apple in Eden, bringing down all of mankind?

He advanced, hating that he had to hobble-step like a cripple to close the distance between them. By the time he reached her, she'd risen to her feet.

"Why?" The question ripped ragged past his lips, and it took all he had and then some to keep from shouting. "Why let me bear the blame for your crime? Have you no soul whatsoever?"

She wilted against the wall, shoring herself up with a hand flat against it. "I—I don't know what you're talking about."

"Margaret Dosett. Daisy Lee." He spit out the names like curses and shoved the jewels in her face. "Or is it more fitting I should call you thief?"

A low growl rumbled in the dog's throat as the animal stationed his body between them. Oliver hitched back a step—but only one. He'd see this through come teeth marks or not.

"I am many things, sir, but I am no thief." Her spine stiffened to a ramrod, and she shot out her open palm. "That necklace is mine, and I will thank you to hand it over at once."

"Sweet merciful heavens, woman, but you are a bold one!" Bitter laughter bubbled up to his throat—the sort he'd heard one too many times leaching out from behind locked doors. This was insane. Shameless, even. He jammed the jewels—no, the *evidence*—into his pocket.

The woman narrowed her eyes, her voice coming out in breathy puffs. "Who are you?"

"Someone you never should have thought to cross." Sighing, he plowed a hand through his hair, not heeding—and even welcoming—the stinging pain on his forehead when he accidentally brushed against his gash. "I am Oliver Ward, member of the House of Commons and wrongly convicted for the theft of the jewels you stole."

The barest flicker of recognition lit in her gaze, then she shook her head. "I don't understand, and clearly you do not either. That necklace is nothing but a bit of paste and metal made to look genuine. Why would you be condemned for rubies that are not real?"

Her brown eyes blinked, confused, like a rabbit staring down the muzzle of a rifle and wondering if she ought to run or freeze until the trouble went away. For a fraction of a second, his heart wrenched. Did she speak truth? Were the jewels in his pocket truly not genuine, and he was blaming an innocent woman? But. . .no. His lips twisted into a wry grin. How easy it was to fall victim to the wiles of an accomplished stage performer.

"A very pretty act, miss, but an act all the same." He snorted. How many other men had she lied to so prettily? "Of all those I've blamed these past months, never once did I think to accuse you. I daresay you duped us all. I can't wait to see their faces when this comes to light, Corbin's especially."

The woman swayed, and despite the growling dog and duplicity of the woman herself, Oliver reached for her, propping her up as best he could. A full-out swoon might take them both down, but thief or not, she had cared for him when he'd been in need. He could do no less.

Hardly a breath later, she rallied and pulled away from his touch. "If you seriously think I am to blame, why did you not call out to Constable Barrow when he was here?"

"Pah!" That unrighteous hellhound? The woman could have no idea. "Barrow would've shot first and listened later—and then not believed a word I might say. No, I will bring you to justice myself and see you convicted of the crime for which you are clearly guilty."

Her chin jutted out, her proud little nostrils flaring. "The only crime I know of is your harsh accusation against me. That gown is mine, as are the faux jewels, made for my last performance. I am the rightful owner. But if that worthless necklace means so much to you, take it. Take it and leave! You'll find my pony in the stable. Send him back with a boy." Looking past his shoulder, she called out, "Nora!"

"If you think I'm leaving without you, madam, you are sorely mistaken." He stared her down.

She held his gaze, unflinching. "I am not going anywhere."

The mettle of the woman! Astounding. Though admittedly, one would have to be spirited to buck convention and lead such a public life. . .which birthed a whole new question. Besides the value of the necklace, what had driven her to forsake a wildly popular operatic career? As precious as the jewels were, the amount once sold wouldn't support her for the rest of her life, especially not in the style to which she was surely accustomed. No, something else must've prodded this brown-eyed woman to run off to the wilds of a moor.

But what?

At his back, footsteps tapped down the corridor and entered the hall, drawing Margaret Dosett—Daisy Lee—or whoever she truly was to attention. "Nora, see Mr. Ward to the stable. He may have use of Black Jack, nothing more."

He gaped. Did she really think she'd get off so easily? Grabbing her arm, he guided her away from the stairs and down the opposite passageway, towards the sitting room, and steeled himself for a bite to his backside from the dog. Surprisingly, the animal merely followed, albeit growling all the way.

"Let me go!" She wrenched sideways.

"Not until we settle this." He held tight, though at the cost of a misstep, putting pressure on his injured ankle. Fine beads of sweat broke out on his brow, and he bit back a groan.

"Settle what?" She shot him a sharp glance—one that could cleave flesh from bone.

Without a word, he led her over to a brilliant beam of sunshine streaming in through the window. Releasing the woman, he retrieved the necklace, then held the largest jewel up to the light, angling it one way. Then another. Then. . .there. Near the bottom of the teardrop shape, a flaw. A small one, but a darkened, dull spot nonetheless.

Still holding the thing aloft, he edged aside, making space for the woman. "Take a look. See?"

She frowned at him first, then reluctantly peered at the gem. "What?"

"The flaw on the bottom, the dark spot. Perfection is a sure sign of paste, and this one is clearly marred."

She backed away, eyeing him as if he were a lunatic. "That proves nothing."

"All right." He grabbed the small mirror he'd been using earlier to shave and dragged the ruby over the glass, then offered it to her. "What do you see?"

Her nose scrunched. "Nothing."

"Exactly. A true gem leaves behind no colour whatsoever. Paste jewels always do."

Something behind the woman's eyes moved. Conscience, perhaps? Was she finally realizing there was naught to be gained by keeping up this charade? Behind her, the maid stood silent, wringing her hands. How intertwined were the two?

She set the mirror down on the table. Her white teeth toyed with her lower lip for a moment, then she lifted her face to his. "How would you, a professed member of Parliament, know so much about rubies?"

"Prison was an education, in more ways than one." His free hand curled into a fist. Nine months of that nightmare had taught him the depravity of man. He'd learned of vices and crimes and things he'd rather not have known from the boasts and confessions of fellow inmates.

She set her jaw. "I still don't believe you."

"Nor I you. Have you a diamond?"

"Real or fake?" The lift of her brow mocked.

He ignored it, bent on proving he was right—the one thing that'd kept him alive thus far. "The only thing strong enough to cut a ruby is a diamond."

"Well, I am sorry to disappoint, but I have no diamonds, genuine or otherwise."

"Fine. This will have to do." He shoved his hand into his other pocket and produced the straight razor, then flipped out the blade and ran the steely edge across the gem.

The woman gasped. The maid drew near. The dog moved to sit at his side. Oliver held out the ruby—the *unmarked* ruby.

She bowed over the thing, as did the maid, then straightened and folded her arms. Her lips slanted into a defiant line. "Again, that proves nothing."

Blast the stubborn woman! "It proves these are real!"

Silently, the maid fumbled at her neck, both hands at her nape. She unclasped a tarnished chain and pulled out a small, golden ring tethered to it. Her dark eyes bored into his as she held it out to him. A question? Or a threat?

Either way, he took it from her. The thin band was worn. Old. An heirloom of some sort. Her mother's, perhaps? At the center, a tiny flake of diamond caught the sunlight and bounced it back. Was it big enough?

Worth a try. Holding the ruby in one hand, he sliced gem across gem, then held the ruby aloft. A clear, thin line ran diagonal where he'd scratched the surface near the edge in the most inconspicuous place possible. No sense willfully ruining such a valuable piece. Vindicated, he handed the maid back her ring and speared the little thief with a glower. "Now what have you to say?"

With a jaunt to her head, the woman unfolded her arms and reluctantly peered at the cut ruby, then frowned at him. "I'd say a diamond could as well cut paste as it could ruby."

Blast! But the woman had a quick mind. He suppressed a grunt, hard-pressed to know if it stemmed from admiration or irritation. "Fine," he conceded, then angled his head toward the window. "Follow me."

He hobbled over to the glass panes, the rustle of women's skirts just behind him, then swiped the ruby across the glass. A deep line etched where he ran it. Victory!

"Well?" He turned to her. "Can a paste replica do that?"

She backed away, shaking her head, until finally she reached for the sofa arm and eased herself down. "But. . .how can it be? How can it possibly. . . ?"

Oliver gritted his teeth. Either this was an amazing act, or she was telling the truth. And, God help him, he was beginning to believe the latter.

But if she wasn't the real thief, then how the deuce had the stolen necklace ended up here with her?

Closing his fingers over the jewelry, he hobbled to the adjacent chair and sat. "I think it's time you tell me everything, Mrs. Dosett, or Daisy Lee, or whatever name you're going by—and I mean *everything*—that brought you here to Morden Hall."

Chapter Twelve

I turn the key over and over in my hand, avoiding the terrible stare of Mr. Ward. If the sofa were not holding me up, I'd surely be prone on the floor, such is the weakness his revelations have wrought. Is it true? Have I been hiding a necklace of immense wealth in a rude little closet smelling of tea?

"I hardly know where to begin," I whisper.

Mr. Ward sighs, long and low. "How about we start with your name. Your *real* name."

Slowly I rub the pad of my thumb along the smooth metal on the key's shaft. Dare I unlock my true past to this man? Is it safe? Is *he* safe—a convicted felon? But. . .does it really matter anymore? He's identified me. Perhaps safety had only ever been an illusion.

I lift my face, meeting the challenge head-on. "I am Margaret Lee, Maggie to those who know me best. Dosett was my mother's maiden name."

"And Daisy?"

The name rises like a spectre, and a shiver runs across my shoulders. I never liked the flower or the name. It was too flimsy. Too transient. Here today, gone tomorrow. My lips twist. Fitting, though. Just like my career. My family. My life. Had my manager been some sort of prophet to have called me such to begin with? Or in promoting me as the capricious flower, had he saddled me with a curse?

I wrap both hands around the key, willing my nerves to calm. "Daisy was a moniker for the stage, a nickname of sorts for Margaret."

"Ahh...I see. *Marguerite* is French for daisy." He nods, and a hank of his dark hair falls forward, covering the gash. He swipes it away, his hazel eyes catching the light and flashing more green than brown as he gazes at me. "I'm guessing you are not a widow, either."

Fumbling with the chain on the key, I duck my head into the loop and secure the necklace back to its rightful resting place. "You are correct. I am not married and never have been."

"Why the charade?"

"People pry less when they see a widow's weeds."

"An astute observation." Once again the green flecks in his eyes flash, but this time not from sunlight. Is that gleam admiration or condemnation?

"But go on." He shifts in his chair. "How is it you came to be here?"

I regret tucking my key back beneath my bodice. Now what am I to hold on to as I try to navigate the uncharted waters of his questions? How much should I tell? Or more importantly, how much should I leave out?

The beginnings of a true headache throb in my left temple, and I rub the ache while evading with a question of my own. "If I am not mistaken, you were present the night of my final performance, were you not?"

"I highly doubt it." A bitter smile ghosts his lips. "The last social gathering I attended was at Ambrose Corbin's estate, and that was some nine months ago now."

"Yes. *That* was the night I fled."

"Interesting." He cocks his head. "Why do such a thing?"

His query drives me back in time, grabs me by the throat and forces me to witness that dangerous June evening when my world ended. I hold my breath, but though it's been months, I can still smell the cloying scent of vanilla tobacco and too much cognac—Ambrose Corbin's signature scent—one to this day I cannot seem to completely wash off my skin. Nor can I rid myself of the feel of him.

I cannot stop the coldness that hardens my tone. "You intimated of your time in prison, Mr. Ward. My former life was no less hellish."

Both his brows shoot skyward, followed by a wince. "I highly doubt it, but please, explain."

Of course he doesn't believe me. Who would? By all accounts, I led a charmed existence, far from the deprivations suffered by paupers, and well I know it. I was not born to silver cutlery and porcelain china, but to the smell of old books.

"You think me mad, no doubt. Perhaps I am." I suck in a breath and shake off the dismal thought. "Beautiful gowns, adoring audiences, invitations galore to opulent affairs. . .I do not deny my public life had its allure."

I rise and skirt the sofa, putting the bulk of it between me and this man. "Yet it is an ugly truth that when a woman goes on stage, it is not her talents that are seen, leastwise not by men. I spent more time dodging pinches and stolen kisses than actually singing."

Sorrow darkens his face. "I am sorry to hear it."

I ignore his pity, for it is too little, too late. "The night of Mr. Corbin's soiree was no different, save for the power of the man making the advance. Before my performance, he—" My throat closes. If I give voice to what happened, speak the threat aloud, it will breathe life into the monster all over again.

Mr. Ward rises, the lines of his jaw hardening to steel. "Did he hurt you?"

What's this? A man actually caring about me? Laughter tastes bitter in my mouth. "Does it matter?"

"Of course! I meant it when I said justice means everything to me, and if you were harmed, then Corbin must be held accountable."

I grip the back of the sofa to keep from tipping over, but just as quickly, my astonishment pales in the burning brilliance of reality. Powerful men like Ambrose Corbin will never be found liable, not for the likes of a woman.

"Suffice it to say, Mr. Ward, that I did not linger long enough after the concert for Mr. Corbin to enact his threats, and so you find me here."

"No, there is more to it than that, I think. By your own admission, untoward advances are regrettably commonplace. One more would not cause you to flee." He rubs the back of his neck before his gaze locks onto mine. "Exactly how did that scoundrel Corbin threaten you?"

A slow smile ripples across my lips. This man must be a force to reckon with on Parliament's floor. "You are very perceptive, sir."

"And you are evading the question. What did Ambrose Corbin say? What power does the fiend wield over you?" Ever so slightly, his fists shake at his side, keeping time with the pulse throbbing in a vein on his neck.

"You bear the man animosity yourself," I observe.

"Perception is one of your virtues as well." A small smile flickers, then fades. "But continue, if you please. I would know the truth."

I pace the length of the sofa, running my fingers along the back of it to keep myself steady. It is better to focus on that than the words coming out of my mouth.

"The night of Mr. Corbin's house party, he gave me an ultimatum. Either I accept his invitation to warm his bed, or he'd ruin my reputation *and* that of my father. That would mean not only the downfall of my father's business, but a quick trip to the workhouse, which would be the death of him."

Whirling, I pace back the other direction, shoving down the horrid image of my grey-headed papa locked in a cold stone institution. Though our relationship had never been marked by great affection, neither did I wish him such a horrid fate. Nor do I now. My self-inflicted exile has been worth the cost. May God continue to protect him and me despite the bounty for my return, the stolen jewels in my possession, and the hazel-eyed man whom I don't know how much I should trust.

I push the melancholy thoughts aside and continue. "I figured if Mr. Corbin couldn't find me—if I ruined my career before he had the chance—he'd leave my father alone. I fled that night with all haste, stopping only to retrieve my life savings."

"Why come here? Why Morden Hall?"

"Why not?" I shrug. "It's far from Bath. Remote. Isolated."

"So is Siberia. You could've chosen anywhere in the world, and so I repeat, why here?"

I sigh, slightly irritated. The man is more determined than Malcolm with a mutton bone. "Very well, if you must know. My mother—God rest her—grew up not far from here. She painted such a vivid picture of the moor with her stories that, well. . .the pull of it was irresistible."

There. I've said more than perhaps I should, but it is the truth, and here will I stand—which I do. I plant my feet and face Mr. Ward.

He folds his arms, tucking his fingers gently beneath his injured arm. Yet the harsh thrust of his jaw is anything but gentle. "Why should I believe such a tale?"

The irony of it all bubbles up inside me and spills out in a small chuckle. I have finally confessed, out loud, what I've been so desperately hiding these past nine months, and the man doesn't believe me?

"Take it as truth or leave it for a lie, sir. It matters not to me what you think."

"It should." He narrows his eyes. "For I have the power to reveal that the jewels in your possession belong to Ambrose Corbin's wife. And once he finds out, it will be more than the ruin of your reputation at stake. It will mean time in gaol. Or worse."

⌒⌒

It didn't matter how many times he'd seen it. When a woman's brow crumpled with despair, it never failed to stab Oliver in the heart. And the horrified look on Maggie Lee's face—all because of his stark words—added an extra kick to his gut.

He sank onto the arm of the sofa and studied Miss Lee's transformation from confident woman to frightened young lady. Either she was a consummate actress and quite possibly the most accomplished liar he'd ever met, or she was telling the truth. And knowing Corbin, that was a distinct possibility. If the blackguard had actually carried out his wicked intent on this woman. . . Well, may God have bestowed mercy on the man's soul, for Oliver surely would not have.

But was she telling the truth? He hadn't made it into Parliament by nurturing a penchant to be duped. More often than not, it paid to be wary, especially of those who appeared to be trustworthy, a lesson he'd learned well at the hand of his father.

Like the sudden drawing down of a shade, Miss Lee once again schooled her features to a pleasant mask and resumed her seat on the sofa. "Mr. Ward, whether or not you believe me, I have been more than forthright with you. I expect the same courtesy in return. How is it I found you broken and bleeding in the wilds of Dartmoor, escaped from prison? Why were you accused of thievery in the first place?"

He couldn't help but snort. "Trust me, if Corbin could've staked me through the heart with a heftier charge, he would have done so."

"Oh? At odds with your fellow representative?" She leaned back against the cushions. "Do you not both serve the same constituency?"

"Yes, but I earned my place. His was bought through devious means."

"How can that be? He fills an elected position."

"Your profession has its ugly truths. So does mine. Ambrose Corbin bought, bribed, and stole his way into his position." Rising, he hobbled over to the side table and poured a glass of water. He held it up, an offering. Despite the tension between them, ladies should always be served first.

She shook her head. "That's quite an indictment, though knowing Mr. Corbin, one I am hard-pressed to doubt. But that is not the matter at hand. Tell me, how could Mr. Corbin have possibly charged you with theft when the jewels were not in your possession?"

He downed the glass in three big swallows, then refilled. "As you've experienced, Corbin is a duplicitous snake. Lord knows how much he paid—or perhaps threatened—the two servants who accused me. They gave false witness to purportedly seeing me swap his wife's real jewels for paste before the gala."

"Yet that does not account for the fact that you did not have the necklace on your person at the time."

"No, but between those two testimonies and what I suspect was quite a hefty bribe to the judge, it was enough to put me away. . . which is exactly what Corbin and his cronies have wanted since the day I joined the House of Commons."

"Why?"

He grimaced. How many times had he asked God the very same? How was he to explain that to which there was no easy answer other than the greed and wickedness of man? Were it not for himself and a handful of other men fighting to tear down Corbin's slums, Ambrose would continue to live at the expense of the less fortunate. Removing Oliver left one fewer opponent to threaten Corbin's ill-gotten security.

Clutching the glass, he eased back to the chair. "It's a story best left for another time, perhaps. The point is that I was a most convenient scapegoat to be found that night."

"Hmm. . ." Her finger tapped against the arm of the sofa. Only God knew what went on behind those brown eyes of hers, because she wasn't seeing him now. She stared right through him, as if the chair adjacent her were unoccupied. "I remember that night clearly. Entering the ballroom, the crush of so many suits and gowns gathered in the warm space, the hum of too many voices, and—" Her eyes cleared, her gaze pinned on his. "Yes. You were there, across the room, involved in a rather heated discussion, if I don't miss my mark."

"Indeed." He remembered her as well, leastwise once she'd begun to sing, for her sweet voice could woo the hardest of hearts and induce them to melt. A hush had fallen hard and sweet with her rendition of Rossini's *Tancredi*—no wonder her humming had sparked his memory when he'd awakened from the fever.

"If you and Mr. Corbin were so at odds, why on earth had he invited you?"

"He didn't. I came with someone he'd not dare to embarrass publicly. Lord Shaftesbury."

A small smile curved her lips. "He's a good man, a rare commodity." And just like that, the smile vanished. She leaned forward, spearing him with an arched eyebrow. "But why the insistence of attending in the first place when you knew you'd not be welcomed?"

Hah! Were politicians ever truly welcomed anywhere? He tossed back the rest of his drink, washing down the snide remark, then met her gaze. "There was an important piece of legislation I've been championing, one that's languishing for support. Are you familiar with the Viscount Palmerston?"

"Of course. He is the Prime Minister."

"Then you can imagine the importance of gaining his backing. I'd been trying to meet with the man but to no avail. It was rumoured he'd be in attendance that night."

Her slim shoulders lifted. "What has this to do with you being accused of stealing the jewels?"

"Corbin knew if I could gain the ear of the viscount, then I could likely get my piece of legislation passed—an act he is patently against, for it would demand the tearing down of the very slums he owns. He needed to shut me up, figuratively and literally." He gripped the glass so tightly, he was sure to add more wounds should the crystal break.

Rising once again, he hobbled to the table and set the thing down, then turned to Miss Lee. "Shortly after your performance— which, by the way, was stunning in every respect—Mrs. Corbin screamed, drawing everyone's attention. The ruby necklace she'd been wearing had fallen apart, proving it was an imposter. Naturally, that abruptly ended the party. Each guest was searched, but to no avail. The real jewels were not found. I was arrested the next day."

"But you didn't have Mrs. Corbin's necklace." Her hand cut through the air, her eyes flashing fiery. "Apparently I did."

She was plucky, he'd give her that. He stifled a grin. "Corbin saw his opportunity and he took it." He paused, connections forming in his mind. "That must have been why he never hunted you—surely you would have been suspected, disappearing like that. But locking me up was more valuable to him than discovering the truth or finding his wife's jewels. Unless. . ."

More pieces fell into place. He clenched his hands lest he smack his forehead. Stupid! Why had he not thought of this sooner?

"Unless what?" she prodded.

"It may be that Corbin swapped the necklaces on purpose, premeditating my incarceration and intending to recover the true gems later that evening during his tryst with you. When you didn't show, he simply claimed the insurance money and satisfied himself with the knowledge that I was out of the way for good."

Miss Lee gaped. "How devious!"

She had no idea. Corbin was a true spawn of Satan himself.

"But by your own admission, Mr. Corbin did not know you'd be in attendance." She frowned and rose. "I don't see how he could've possibly premeditated such an act."

True. He inhaled deeply, willing his swirling thoughts to coalesce. Perhaps he was being a bit hasty.

Miss Lee paced to the windows and once again drew the drapery. "You are an escaped convict, Mr. Ward. I'd be a fool to believe you without question, especially since you've taken possession of the necklace."

She turned to him. "Tell me, what's to keep you from absconding the second I turn my back?"

This time he did smile. Plucky, indeed. "Besides my ankle, you mean?"

"Within a week, you'll no longer be so impeded."

"Well then, Miss Lee." He rose and met her stare. "I suppose you shall have to wait and see the true content of my character—as I will yours."

Chapter Thirteen

Moonlight lands in a swath of rectangles on my bedroom carpet. Even when I close my eyes I see white squares. And no wonder. I've been staring at them long enough. Tonight, sleep is as elusive as truth. Though I'd spent the better part of the day discussing possibilities with Mr. Ward, I am no closer to figuring out how Mrs. Corbin's necklace came to be locked up in a dark closet of Morden Hall. By this point, I'm sick of thinking about it.

I fling off the counterpane so suddenly Malcolm jolts awake on the rug. "Come, boy," I whisper as I shove my arms into my robe. Perhaps a mug of cider will make me sleepy.

Padding down the stairs, I listen for any movement from the sitting room. Which is ridiculous. Surely Malcolm and I are the only ones creeping about the shadows at this late hour.

The kitchen is a solitary island at the back of the house, quiet and empty. I retrieve a mug and pitcher of cider, then absently set them down and stare out the window.

The backyard is ethereal. Fickle moonglow highlights only the topmost half of things. Darkness shrouds the dips, the hollows, the deepest, most hidden crevices. An aching sadness wells up my throat. The scene beyond the glass is far too much like my life; merely the things on the surface are exposed. I show the world only the facets of me that men wish me to be. Papa grooming me to be a clerk in his bookshop. My manager driving me to outshine all other opera stars. Not that I didn't enjoy those things, and, truth be told, I still yearn to perform onstage at the Royal Opera House in London, but for the most part I've spent so much time living up to others' expectations that I hardly know who I am.

A sigh deflates me, and I bow my head. *What did You make me to be, Lord?*

"You look as if you bear the weight of the planet on your back."

Whirling, I slap my hand to my chest. The broad-shouldered silhouette of Mr. Ward enters the kitchen. Malcolm sits unperturbed at my side. So much for my watchdog alerting me to trouble.

I inhale deeply, willing my pulse to slow. "Your ankle must be doing much better. I didn't hear your footfall."

He half limps to the table at center and pulls out a stool, sinking to it before he answers. "Indeed. Thanks to your care and Nora's, I am on the mend. I owe you my life several times over."

My brow crumples. I've done nothing more than anyone else with a heart would do. I push away from the counter. "Are we not to care for our fellow man?"

"Most people say so, though when it comes down to it, few are willing to act upon their convictions, especially when it is an inconvenience."

An astute observation. I lift the pitcher towards him. "Would you like some cider?"

He nods, and I reach for another mug.

"You couldn't sleep?" His deep voice curls over my shoulder.

I shake my head as I pull out a stool for myself.

"It's contagious."

A milky beam of light angles in through the window, dull yet bright enough to wash over his square jaw and flash of a smile. Now that Oliver Ward is cleaned up and once again vibrant with life, it is easy to see why a woman might fawn over him. He is strikingly handsome. How many London socialite hearts has he broken?

I snap my gaze down to the mug in my hands, heat flooding my cheeks.

"Care to tell me what troubles you so? Though I think I can

guess." His tone is soft, genuine, the sort that woos and encourages all at once.

I roll the mug between my hands, unwilling to look up. "I've been over that night at the Corbins' a hundred times in my head, conjured all the possibilities I can think of as to who swapped those jewels, but I still cannot rightfully pin the blame on anyone."

Pausing, I swallow some of the sweet cider, scrambling to collect my pell-mell thoughts into something coherent. "One of the servants is the most likely thief. But any number of them could have had access to my trunk. It'd been delivered to the estate that morning, and I didn't arrive until late afternoon. All someone needed to do was pick the lock and trade necklaces. Then when I changed from my costume, replacing it in the trunk, that same servant could've simply repicked the lock late in the night and made off with the necklace. But how to uncover the true criminal?" I lift my face to his. "And why has that person not tried to find me? Surely the guilty party realizes I ran off with the treasure. Unless. . ."

A chill shivers across my shoulders. Ambrose Corbin knew I'd been wearing a replica of his wife's necklace. Did he know it was the real thing and was even now looking for me, or had he paired up with Mr. Groat's search? And if my manager discovers me, will he make my location known to Ambrose? With such a high bounty on my head, it's a logical conclusion.

Setting down his mug, Mr. Ward scrubs at his jaw, then laces his fingers on the table. "I have a gut feeling that Corbin himself is tangled up in this. That there was some other plot underway that night, and when you vanished, I was the most expedient scapegoat."

His words echo my own thoughts, yet I cannot help but ask, "A plot such as what?"

"I don't know, but I do know this—wealth means everything to Corbin. Whether or not he really believes me to be the thief, it doesn't make sense he was so satisfied with my incarceration that he never pursued locating his wife's jewels. Unless he has been, of course. At any rate, we can thank God he hasn't tracked you here."

Despite the warmth of my woolen robe, I shiver and pull the fabric tighter at the neck. The possibility is a recurring nightmare. But what to do now? How to navigate the murky waters of restoring Mr. Ward's good name without attracting attention to myself?

"We could box up the necklace and send the package to Mrs. Corbin by post," I think out loud, and like the chugging of a great steam engine, the idea picks up speed. I meet Mr. Ward's gaze across the table. "It could work. No one would suspect such a valuable item would be sent in a plain box by coach. Once she receives it, there is nothing to keep you from appealing your case. If there is no stolen property, there can be no conviction, and your name will be cleared while I maintain my anonymity. You may stay here until then, of course, safely out of Mr. Barrow's reach."

His mouth twists into a wry smirk. "Though I thank you for your offer, I am not a man given to hiding behind a woman's skirts. And while I admit your plan does restore the stolen property to the rightful owner, it does not mete out justice to the real culprit."

"I do not question your valor, sir, but is it not fair enough that the lady will have her rubies returned and your honor will be restored to you?"

A stranger stares out through Mr. Ward's hazel eyes. A hard man. Frightening. I lower my hand and dangle my fingers, coaxing Malcolm to my side.

"Someone must pay for my nine months of torment." His voice is more threatening than one of Malcolm's growls. "For Jarney's—" His lips clamp shut.

I want to look away, to run, to hide from the rage etched in harsh shadows on his face. But I cannot. It is too familiar. I've battled the same anger towards Ambrose Corbin since that night in June.

So I offer him the question I frequently ask myself. "Are you speaking of justice or vengeance?"

"Touché." He lifts his cup and drains it dry, then slams it back to the table. "But do you really want Corbin free to terrorize other women? What's to stop him from discovering your whereabouts in the future and threatening you all over again?"

True. More than anything, I want that man locked up. Put away. Far from me and other unsuspecting women. Ambrose Corbin is a lecher. A monster. . . But is he also a thief? For what purpose? He's one of the wealthiest men in Bath.

I frown into my mug. "Why would a man arrange to have his own wife's jewels stolen? Once that necklace turned up, you—or any other accused—would've been freed."

"Unless he never meant to let anyone know he'd taken the necklace back and—wait a minute. Of course! Corbin could very well have planned to have the real jewels sold so he could pocket the money, leaving his wife none the wiser."

"Plausible," I murmur. "Yet how can you be so certain he is involved?"

"I can't. It's just a gut feeling. But something's not right about this whole thing. And if there's one thing I've learned in politics, it's to trust my gut."

And there is the crux of it. Trust. Such a necessary evil. He trusts his gut, but do I trust him? His opinions? His conjectures? I know nothing about the man other than he serves in the House of Commons and is on the run from the law—poor evidence on which to convict Ambrose Corbin. Still. . .if there's a chance to put that villain away—even the smallest chance—the risk of revealing who I really am is worth whatever consequence I might face from breaching the contract with my manager.

I nibble my lower lip. It is a precipice upon which I stand, toes over the edge. Either I step back now or commit to falling headlong into what might be danger, for me and for Papa. But truly, there is only one choice to be made.

I lift my chin to meet Mr. Ward's gaze. "What is our plan?"

A small chuckle rumbles in his throat, and he shakes his head. "There is no *our*, Miss Lee. This is something I must do alone. I will not have you exposed to Corbin again."

"You won't make it to Bath on your own. You won't even make it to Lydford, not with Constable Barrow sniffing about, and he strikes me as one not to cross."

He leans forward, a jaunty jut to his jaw. "Are you so concerned for me?"

What's this? Flirting? Or genuine curiosity? Hard to tell in the dark. Either way, I sidestep the question. "With God's help, I brought you back from the brink of death. I do not wish to do so again. Besides, taking me along is to your benefit. I know a thing or two about stage makeup and performing. Done right, no one will pay us any mind."

He leans back on the stool, a slow smile flashing white in the shadows. "I suppose traveling with you has its merits. Barrow won't be looking for a couple."

"It's settled then. I'll pack tomorrow and set things right with Nora. We can leave the following day, if your ankle allows for it." I rise and collect the mugs. "Oh, what exactly is our plan once we arrive in Bath?"

"That, Miss Lee, is a very good question." His answer follows me to the basin—yet it is no answer at all.

"And?"

"I'm working on it."

"Do you mean to tell me we shall travel to Bath and indict the most powerful man in town, yet you don't know exactly how we'll accomplish that?"

His grin broadens. "Yes."

∽

By the time dawn seeped through the gaps in the drapery, Oliver gave up the pretense of sleep. He'd dozed for three hours—maybe—but it was enough. Lord knew he'd oft survived on less, and that with having to break rock all day with little more than a bowl of pea-grey soup to go on. Fortified by a thick slice of bread and a hefty chunk of cheese, he could conquer the world.

But apparently not a dogcart.

Huffing out a growly breath, he tossed down a two-inch screw and traded it for a three. Then scowled and dropped that one as well. The stable workbench looked like a war zone after all his rummaging, though admittedly, it hadn't been pristine when he'd ambled in there earlier that morning. Iron parts, some old, some new, lay heaped in piles. Likely they were ordered in some sort of rhyme and reason, but not one that he could figure out—and he desperately needed to if they were to take the disassembled vehicle to town tomorrow.

"How is it coming along?" Miss Lee's sweet voice and even sweeter lilac scent entered through the open door.

Resorting back to the two-inch, he swiped up the screw and faced her with half a smile. "I may be better suited to arguing legislation than wrangling with a dogcart, but all in all, it will be ready to go by tomorrow. Did you never use the thing?"

"Not really. My manservant usually walked to town when needed. He'd been meaning to fix it, and as you can see, he acquired the new parts and started the job. But then he got called off to visit his ailing sister, and. . ." Her trim shoulders rose and fell. "Well, at least you're gaining a fresh confidence. If your career as a politician should fail, you'll have a trade with which to support yourself."

"Right." A smirk twisted his lips. "I can see the shingle above my door now." He swiped his hand through the air as he spoke. "Oliver Ward, dogcart repair."

Laughter bubbled out of her, rich and musical. "For an escaped convict, you are quite a likable fellow, Mr. Ward."

He grinned. "I have my moments."

So did she. She was a picture, this woman, one he couldn't easily pull his gaze from. Even without stage makeup and garbed in her bleak black gown, her chestnut hair pinned into oblivion atop her head, Maggie Lee's beauty would not be tamed. She'd chosen well, moving to this desolate house at the end of the moor. Anywhere else she'd attract too much attention—which could be problematic as they traveled to Bath. . .and was certainly a problem now, with the way she distracted him from his work.

He swung back to the bench and grabbed a few more screws,

shoving them into his pocket. "Have you squared things with your maid, then?"

"Yes. I've left sufficient funds with Nora to keep things running for the next several weeks. I hate leaving her here alone, but she will have Malcolm. And hardly anyone ever stops by this far out on the moor."

He snorted. "Until recently, you mean?"

"Until you arrived, yes."

Indeed. Morden Hall had been a very wise choice for her. Leaving behind the workbench, he crossed to the small carriage and measured the screws against the width of the splinter bar, speaking as he worked. "I am sorry to have broken your solitude, yet I cannot help feeling it was God ordained."

"You are a man of faith?"

The wonder in her voice turned him around. But of course she would be surprised. A half-dead convict. An avowed politician. Neither role was known for piety. He arched a brow, the pull against his gash nothing more than an annoying ache now. "I'd never have survived prison without God, Miss Lee."

Her brow puckered, and she ran a finger aimlessly along the workbench he'd just abandoned. "I wonder, sometimes, how anyone survives anything without Him."

"They don't. They perish."

She jerked her gaze to his, hand dropping. "You are very singular, Mr. Ward. Sometimes prudent with your words, other times harshly blunt."

"Likable *and* singular? How ever do I manage that?" He winked and turned back to the puzzle of the dogcart—but not before catching a rosy hue spreading over Miss Lee's cheeks.

He expected to hear her skirts swish out the door. Instead, her footsteps padded over to him. "Have you thought yet of how we will proceed once we reach Bath?"

Frowning, he dodged the question and the quizzical look on her face by stooping to pick up the screwdriver, where he'd left it on the ground. He'd invented and discarded as many plans as there were carriage parts to join together. None ever quite fit, though. Not wholly. Not yet.

Breeching tee in place, he stepped back and surveyed the rest of the parts that yet needed to be reattached. "Just working out the finer details, Miss Lee."

"Hmm, well. . .I suppose if we are to be traveling companions, you may call me Maggie. I was thinking we ought to pose as brother and sister."

Her words drove all thoughts of iron rings and wooden shafts from his mind. She was a bold one, he'd give her that. Bold *and* practical. Admirable qualities. No wonder she'd been able to manage on her own way out here.

Slowly, he turned, flipping the screwdriver around in his hand. "Good thinking, *Maggie*."

She beamed. "I am happy you approve, *Oliv*—"

Her mouth slammed shut. Panic widened her eyes. Heavy footsteps pounded the gravel outside, drawing closer.

With one sweep of his uninjured arm, Oliver directed her behind his back and advanced a step, screwdriver gripped pointed end out, like a dagger.

If Barrow's ugly mug darkened the doorstep, this wouldn't be pretty.

Fear tastes sour at the back of my throat. How has the past nine months of peace splintered into so many pieces all in the space of six days?

Mr. Ward plants his feet, one in front of the other, and stands somewhat crouched, hand coiled back and ready to strike. He is a lion, poised to pounce.

But where is Malcolm? Why has he not barked a warning?

Boots pound closer. A shadow grows larger on the ground outside the door. Man-shaped.

My breath hitches, and I shrink back, glancing wildly around for a weapon. If there is to be a fight, I will not be the fainting flower. My fingers wrap around the handle of a hammer that lies next to an overturned bucket. Thank God for Dobbs's careless ways.

"What's this?" A voice booms from the door, one that is blessedly recognizable. In steps my ruddy-faced, barrel-chested manservant.

I drop the hammer, pulse slowing to a normal beat.

But Dobbs snatches up a small hatchet from the workbench. "Let the missus go. Now!"

Mr. Ward lifts his screwdriver all the higher. "Who are you?" he snarls.

I sidestep Mr. Ward and hold out my hands, one towards each of them. "All is well, gentlemen. Mr. Ward, meet my manservant, Dobbs. Dobbs, this is my guest, Mr. Ward."

Neither of them moves.

"Truly, there is no danger here for either of you. Please, put down your weapons."

Mr. Ward lowers his screwdriver, yet he does not release it. Same for Dobbs and his hatchet. I suppose it's to be expected. Alley dogs don't warm to others until a plate of fat is offered.

I cross over to Dobbs and rest a light touch on his coat sleeve. "Come. Let us speak outside." I head for the door, calling over my shoulder as I go, "Carry on, Mr. Ward."

Dobbs grunts, yet his boots grind the gravel behind me, and he grumbles with each step. "What were ye thinkin', missus, takin' in a stranger, and you here alone with naught but a mute maid?"

The afternoon sunshine is brilliant—a direct contrast to the dark scowl etched on Dobbs's face. "Nora and I found Mr. Ward near death out on the moor—tut, tut!" I wag my finger at him, nipping off the sure rebuke about to launch from his lips. "I remember your warning, yet the man needed help. You'd have done the same."

His lower lip shoots out, as petulant as the wiry hairs sticking out from his flat cap. "Mebbe, but that be a man's risk to take, not a woman's."

Instantly, my own hackles rise. All my life I've been told what is acceptable, what is not. I am done with it. I toss back my shoulders and stare down the old man. "What's done is done, and I remind you that it is you who is in my employ, not the other way around."

His jaw grinds for a moment, then a reluctant "Aye" grumbles out of him. "But seein' to yer safety *is* part o' my work."

I sigh. A cool gust sweeps across the yard, pulling hard off the end of the moor. Brushing back a loosened bit of hair, I search for the right words to mend and heal. "I appreciate that. Truly. And I am happy you've returned. Now tell me, how is your sister?"

He humphs and folds his arms. "Well enough to talk the ear off a parrot. She was still abed when I left, but like as not is kickin' her heels about town by now."

"I am glad to hear it."

Dobbs nods at the stable. "How long is he stayin,' this guest o' yers?"

"Only until tomorrow, at which point I shall leave with him for Bath. I expect to be gone several weeks."

The old man's grey eyes widen. "I know it be lonely out here on the moor, missus, but this?" He shakes his head. "This just ain't right."

Hah! I choke on his assumption. He has no idea how hard it was all those years on the stage to stay one step ahead of grasping libertines. "I assure you, Dobbs, all is not as it appears."

He eyes me silently for a moment. "O' course. My pardon. But are ye sure ye know what ye're about, then?"

His question slaps hard. "No, not at all. Are any of us?"

"Some more 'n others, I s'pose. Just take a care, aye? For all yer bluster, ye've a soft heart. Guard it well, lass, from that man in there"—he hitches a thumb over his shoulder—"and any other."

I stifle a very unladylike snort. Of all the dangers I face, losing my heart is the least of my concerns.

Chapter Fourteen

Morning sunshine made Sebastian queasy, especially in the spring. It might have had something to do with his sister's tears on that life-changing April morning twelve years ago. The scream of the scoundrel who dared sully her. The gunshot. The blood. Or maybe not. Could just be he preferred the solemn dark of winter nights.

Leaning back against the doorpost of the Castle Inn, he dug in his pocket and flipped open his watch as coach wheels rumbled closer, grinding against gravel. Nine o'clock. Right on time. Good. His feet itched to be back on the road. Blast that Mr. Groat for taking a full two days and then some to arrive. Every passing hour was one more in which he'd have to play catch-up to Ward, though in all likelihood, the blackguard couldn't have covered too much ground. Not injured. And he was. Though there'd been little evidence of the man holing up at Daisy Lee's, Sebastian would bet on it.

He snapped shut the watch's lid and stuffed the thing into his pocket, then pulled out a cigarillo and eyed the passengers as they alighted. A fat man, jowls waving like a bloodhound's ears, breached the door first. The coach sprang back as soon as his feet hit the ground, springs creaking a sigh of relief.

Next, two young girls popped out, followed by a shrew-faced matron with a scowl that could blister paint. Sebastian cocked his head, studying her as he took a drag of his smoke. Swap out that gown for a pair of trousers, stick a truncheon in her hand, and the woman would make a fine prison guard.

His gaze snipped back to the coach the instant a man carrying a satchel descended, blinking into the sunshine as if he cursed the light as much as Sebastian did himself. The man's legs were long. Skinny. Poked into an oval-shaped body, not barrel-chested, per se, but distinctly solid. His black-sheened coat gave off an iridescent sort of glow. Kind of purplish. Sebastian looked closer. Sweet blessed heavens! Had the dandy seriously traveled in a brocade tailcoat?

As soon as the man spied him, his feet skittered across the rocks, heels clacking. "Excuse me, but might you be Officer Barrow?"

Though he bested the man by at least three stones and a hand span in height, Sebastian retreated a step. Something wasn't right about the fellow, and he didn't like it. Not the vacant stare or the whiff of newly turned dirt that wafted about him. And particularly not the queer way the man's teeth clicked when he spoke.

"I am Officer Barrow." He tempered his tone, giving no hint to the unease prickling his scalp, and flicked aside his cigarillo.

"Good to meet you, sir. I am Wendell Groat, manager to Miss Daisy Lee." He shot out his hand.

Sebastian stared at it, abhorring the freakish reluctance paralyzing him, then shoved out his own hand. His fingers wrapped around cold skin—smooth yet hard—as if he gripped a large beetle fresh from the soil. He yanked his hand away.

Groat smiled, a knowing gleam in his little eyes. "I understand you have information as to my missing client's whereabouts?"

Rubbing his palm along his greatcoat, Sebastian scowled. "I do, but it ain't for free."

"Of course not." A slight chuckle scuttled out of him. "Like my advertisement said, you shall be rewarded fifty pounds for her return."

"Huh," he grunted. "Let's see it."

"Pardon?" Groat stepped closer, angling his head as if he hadn't heard correctly.

Sebastian shifted his weight to keep from retreating. The urge to do so was annoying. So was having to explain himself. "I want to verify you have the money before I tell you where the woman is."

"Cautious fellow, are you?"

Pah! He'd be a dead man a hundred times over were he not. Tugging down the brim of his hat, he stared at the fellow from the blessed shadow. "You learn to be in my line of work."

"I see, well. . ." Groat cleared his throat, the sound as repulsive as his click-clackety way of speaking. "I mean this in the best possible light, Mr. Barrow, but what is to stop you from simply grabbing the note and absconding once I show it to you?"

A small bit of admiration crept out from a corner in Sebastian's heart. He could—possibly—respect a man, who like himself, took precautions. God smiled upon the circumspect. So did he. "You'd make a fine officer yourself, Mr. Groat."

His smile faded as quickly as it arose and—unnerved or not—Sebastian advanced and grabbed the man by the collar, lifting him to his toes. "Yet I insist. Show me the reward money."

He released Groat, who coughed and clacked and ground his jaws but, to his credit, did not complain or strike back. He merely reached into his valise and pulled out a banknote.

The paper waved just beyond Sebastian's reach, flapping in a lusty breeze. "Happy?"

"I will be, once that money's in my pocket. You'll find the woman at Morden Hall, the house at the end of the moor." He held out his hand. Easiest bit o' coin he'd made in a long time. Just thinking about a new pair of thick-leathered boots eased the remnant of pain leftover from the nail he'd stepped on.

But before he could blink, Groat tucked the money back into the valise and snapped shut the clasp. "No payment until I receive my goods. Take me to her."

"That wasn't part of the bargain," he roared—apparently a bit too loud. Near the inn's door, the glowering matron shot him an evil eye.

"Now, now, Mr. Barrow. The handbill distinctly stated the reward would be paid once the woman is in my custody. And clearly"—the man's head swiveled, taking the upper half of his body along on the ride—"she is not."

"You're quite the stickler for details, aren't you?" Sebastian scratched his beard, fingers tangling in the curly weave and pulling his skin. He didn't have time for this. He ought to be out searching for Ward. Still, it would be a pleasure to see Daisy Lee put in her place, restored to the care of a man who could bring her back into line. A real pleasure. The same sort of zing that charged through him whenever he dragged a criminal through the iron jaws of the prison's front gate.

He dropped his hand. "All right. I can work with that. Follow me."

Sebastian sidestepped him and headed across the road to the stable. Behind him, footsteps snick-snacked against the gravel and caught up to him surprisingly fast. He glanced over at Groat as they strode side by side. "Not that I balk at the price, mind you, but I am curious... Why so much recompense for a mere breach of contract? I should think you'd simply move on. How can one woman possibly be worth so much trouble and coin?"

Groat peered up at him. "Opera singers are a rare breed, Mr. Barrow. One doesn't *simply move on,* as you put it. Daisy Lee brings in more money in one week's ticket sales than I daresay you make in a year."

"Aha." He grunted. "Missing your golden goose, are you?"

"In a word, yes."

"So you'll drag her back to the stage, and then what?" He stopped just before the stable door and turned to the man. "You can't very well force the woman to sing, and she strikes me as one to dig in her heels."

"Not to worry. I have my ways."

Simple words. Innocuous. Almost bland. But all the same, a cold shiver spidered down Sebastian's spine. Daisy Lee obviously needed a firm hand. But was Wendell Groat the one to provide it?

Bah. The man was her manager. Groat's job was to know how to handle her. Just like Sebastian's job was tending to Ward.

"Wait here," he ordered, then spun on his heel.

A strong waft of manure smacked him in the nose as he entered the stable, and he bypassed a great pile dumped from a mount who'd recently been brought in. Across the open area, his horse, already saddled, waited where he'd tethered her. Next to her, another horse—likely the one just arrived—waited to be untacked and brushed. Down near the tack room, the ostler was busy pulling the saddle off another patron's bay. Providence!

Sebastian snagged both horses' leads and led them towards the door.

"Hey! What are you doing? You can't take that horse." The young ostler's voice cracked. Why could inns never afford to hire real men?

"I'm not." He kept walking. "I'm borrowing it."

"That's the same thing!"

Fingers gripped his arm from behind. Oh no. That would never do. Such disrespect could not rightly go undisciplined. Sebastian dropped the lead and grabbed the hand, jerking the ostler's wrist backward as he whipped around. The boy-man howled. His knees hit the ground with a satisfying crack.

"Only the wicked borrow and do not pay back, boy." He upped the pressure. "Are you calling me wicked?"

"N—no, sir." Girly whimpers gurgled out the ostler's throat.

"Good."

And good thing he wouldn't be staying any longer at this inn. With a snap, he forced the fine bones until they splintered, then let go.

The ostler shrieked and folded into himself, nursing his injured hand. Sebastian crouched and barked into the boy's ear to be heard above his caterwauling. "The horse will be returned by noon. And a word of advice, boy, always be prepared. A sharp knee to the groin would've stopped me."

He rose and grabbed the horses, then handed off one to Groat, who stood at the door with a dark gleam in his eyes.

"I admire your style, Officer Barrow."

He snorted. "I suspect you have a style all your own, Mr. Groat."

An enigmatic smile slid across the man's mouth, then vanished as two burly men stalked towards the stable from across the road, one of them waving at them.

"What's the rumpus? Billy get kicked by a horse?"

Groat swung up into the saddle, then leaned low, speaking for Sebastian alone. "I think now might be a good time for us to leave."

Sebastian followed suit, hefting himself upward and leading them both out to the road. It wouldn't do to have to explain why the stable boy wouldn't be able to buckle up harnesses for the next several weeks. Groat's horse kept pace with his, even when he upped his speed to leave behind the shouts and chaos at the Castle Inn.

But just before clearing the edge of town, he slowed and squinted into the distance, where a dogcart rattled along. Two shapes— women—huddled together on the seat, the older one holding the reins in gloved hands—*large* gloved hands. In fact, everything about the woman was oafish, from the breadth of her wide shoulders to the length of her long arms. The long brim of her bonnet hid most of her face except for the square cut of her jaw. Gads! What rock on the moor had she crawled out from?

"Is everything all right, Mr. Barrow?" Groat drove his mount closer to his and glanced over his shoulder. "Not to be an alarmist, but those two men at the inn have turned onto the road behind us."

"Mmm," he grumbled, noncommittal. His gaze drifted to the other woman. She wore a grey veil—indicating her face must be so pock-ridden as to be a terror. She was definitely slighter than the other, hunched over as she was. Yet her body swayed like a green willow with each jolt of the carriage, as if a young woman lived inside that cocoon of thick wool. The dogcart rolled closer, and he narrowed his eyes, studying the crones.

Then he tugged on the reins and stopped smack in the middle of the road.

∞

Of all the roads in all of England, this had to be the one Barrow chose?

Oliver gritted his teeth, praying he was wrong—but no. The closer he drew towards Lydford, the less chance of mistaking the black hulk of iniquity perched atop his horse, staring at him and Maggie like a rider of the apocalypse about to rain down destruction. And this time he had a partner. He was a dandy of a fellow, but that didn't mean he'd be any less dangerous.

Though everything in him screamed to turn the dogcart around, Oliver forced his hands to hold the reins loose. Amble along. Play the part of an old woman conveying her friend to town. One wrong move from him, one stray gasp from Maggie, and all would be lost. Thank God she'd not yet recognized the danger—nor would she, if he could help it.

He turned towards her, taking care to keep his face hidden in the shadow of the ridiculously long-billed bonnet. "The wrap on my ankle loosened. Can you tighten it?"

"What?" Even behind the thickly woven veil, sunshine caught the rise of her brows. "Now?"

"Yes. We can't have me stumbling out of the carriage when we get to the inn, drawing attention to us. Can we?"

"I suppose not." She bent and fumbled with freeing his foot from the hem of his gown.

And not a moment too soon. Barrow lifted a hand, shading his eyes, and craned forward for a hard look.

This was it, then. Oliver's pulse pounded fast and loud. If Barrow got a glimpse of his face, the bonnet and dress wouldn't matter. He tucked his chin and reached for his knife, just in case.

Barrow's mouth opened, likely about to order him to stop, when the other fellow leaned aside and tapped him on the arm. Sweet heavens! That was a mistake. Barrow *never* let anyone touch him, and those who did got their fingers broken.

Barrow whipped aside, about to snap some bones, when something caught his attention. For a moment, he went slack in the saddle, then cut a glance to his companion and kicked his horse into a gallop. The two tore past the dogcart, hooves spewing up divots of dirt. Oliver gazed over his shoulder, watching their retreat. What in the world?

By the time he turned back, two mounted men rode hard down

the High Street, apparently in pursuit, for they raced past him and Maggie as well. A smile quirked Oliver's lips. Were Barrow's sins about to catch up with him? Ahh, but he'd love to see that bit of justice carried out.

"—better?"

He faced Maggie, who now sat upright, head tilted and waiting for an answer to a question he hadn't heard.

"Pardon?"

"Your ankle." She pointed at his foot. "Is the wrap better?"

"Oh yes. Much." A guilty pang nicked his conscience, may God forgive him. Truly, his ankle only bothered him when he chanced a full-weighted misstep onto it. "Thank you."

Facing forward again, he stared down the road towards the Castle Inn. People buzzed around a stagecoach, a few preparing to board, others embracing loved ones with their goodbyes. It would be a packed ride, but it was easier to hide in a crowd.

"Looks like the coach is being readied." He slid his gaze to Maggie. "Your timing is impeccable."

"More like Nora's. She's the one who knows this town inside and out."

Hmm. If the woman were accustomed to the busy pace of village life, why had she moved out to the desolate moor? He urged the horse onward, yet kept his gaze fixed on Maggie. "How did you come by her in the first place?"

"I met her when I visited the solicitor's office to inquire about housing. She worked for him—Mr. Tuttle—a miserable man in all respects." Just then, the wheel dipped into a rut, and Maggie flung out a hand, gripping the side of the carriage before she continued. "I was tightening up my reticule after paying for a year's lease on Morden Hall, when out in the corridor, Nora tripped on the edge of an up-curled rug. The huge coalscuttle she was carrying spilled. Mr. Tuttle flew into a frenzy and struck her, even though she ought not have been carrying the thing in the first place. She didn't so much as whimper, not even when he terminated her employment right then and there. I remarked on such a merit when he returned to the room, and that's when I found out she was mute. He taunted her mercilessly for being a freak of nature."

Maggie's voice took on a sudden hard edge, and though her veil hid her face, no doubt a mighty glower creased her brow. "Mr. Tuttle might as well have kicked a puppy in front of me. I determined to offer Nora employment. And I did. She wasn't hard to find. The village boys apparently thought it great sport to harass her as much as Mr. Tuttle had."

For a moment, Maggie fell silent, and when she spoke again, it was so quiet Oliver had to lean towards her to pick out the words.

"Thank God that is behind her now. Nora has been a blessing to me ever since, and I like to fancy I've been one in return."

"I have no doubt that you are."

"Are you so quick to compliment a thief, sir?"

He grinned, admiring her wit. Admiring even more the gentle soul that he sometimes glimpsed beneath her guarded exterior. Not many women of means would look so kindly on a defective maid.

He eased the dogcart to a stop, not far behind the public coach, then turned to her, voice lowered for her alone. "You can still back out, you know. I am more than willing to take on the risk of exposing Corbin and returning those jewels by myself."

Laughter sang out from beneath her veil. "What, and miss all the fun of seeing the illustrious Mr. Oliver Ward act the part of an old woman?" She swept a hand towards his dress. "If Parliament could see you now."

He snorted. "Get your fill, because next stop, we pose as brother and sister and this gown is gone. How you women even move about is beyond me." The truth of his words hit home as he swung to the ground. Skirts swirled. He teetered. Maggie laughed again.

But both of their good humours faded as they approached the door of the inn. Oliver tugged his bonnet brim as low as he dared and spoke under his breath. "Keep your head down. Stay in the shadows. I'll do the rest."

She reached out a tentative hand and squeezed his arm. "Be careful."

"Don't fret. I've done harder things than purchasing a few coach tickets." True. But he'd never had to do such things while garbed in linsey-woolsey and employing an old woman's voice.

He pushed open the door, nodded for Maggie to wait for him in the corner, then approached the podium.

"Two for Bath," he rasped, pitching his tone up a few octaves. Not bad. Believable, even.

But evidently not comprehensible, not the way the ticket seller eyed him. "Sorry. What's that?"

He cleared his throat and tried again. "I need two tickets for Bath, please."

"Ahh, that'll be five shillings, madam." The clerk set about stamping some papers while the door behind Oliver ushered in fresh morning air and the grumbling growl of a patron.

Oliver fumbled with the drawstring of the bag hanging off his wrist. The thing swung like a pendulum as his big fingers dug into the pouch. Maggie had given him coins enough to purchase the tickets, making it hard to fish out—

"Hurry it up, old woman," a man rumbled at his back. "I ain't got all day."

Frowning, he finally pulled out a half sovereign and shoved it across the podium. Without so much as a glance, the clerk passed back two tickets and three half crowns. Oliver stared. The clerk, in his hurry, had overpaid him.

"You've got yer tickets, so move!" Hot breath wafted over his shoulder, stinking of sardines and—oddly enough—marmalade. "That coach is about to leave. I'll not miss it for the likes of you."

Irritation burned a trail up Oliver's neck. The big bully. One swift pop in the nose would put the man in his place—and also draw unwanted attention. So instead, he simply collected the tickets and pushed back the coins. As much as the extra could be a blessing down the road, it wouldn't be right. "You gave me too much change, sonny," he squeaked out.

"Did I? Let's see..." The clerk scooped up the money and fingered through it.

Curses pelted Oliver right between the shoulders. "For the love of a three-legged sheepdog!"

As if conjured, in from the taproom strolled a dog-faced man, carrying a ledger and a frown. As he surveyed the scene, the lines at the sides of his mouth deepened, then he faced the clerk. "What's the problem here, Jones?"

"This lady here says I gave her too much change."

"Oh?" The manager's brown eyes swung his way, then narrowed.

Blast! Just what he needed. Oliver tucked his head.

The man behind him shuffled from foot to foot.

Finally, the manager broke the silence. "She's right. God bless you, madam, for your honesty." He held out a crown.

"Thank you." Oliver snatched the money and was just about to turn away when he remembered one last item of business. "Oh, I've a dogcart outside. Will you keep an eye on it till my manservant picks it up?"

"The deuce with your dogcart!" the bully behind him roared. "It'll be fine. Now leave."

"Sir! If you don't mind." The manager looked down his nose at the man, then smiled sweetly at Oliver. "Yes, madam, actually there has been a bit of foul play here at the stable today, so you are quite wise in making your request. I'll send a boy now to retrieve your bags if you like."

"Ahh, yer a real gent, sir. A balm to this old lady's soul." He patted his chest. "God bless ye."

"Are you quite done?" The words were razor sharp, harsh enough to draw blood. Was this how the man always treated his elders? How many old women had he browbeaten in his day?

Clutching his tickets in one hand, Oliver whipped around and drove his elbow into the man's kidney as he passed, then rumbled under his breath, "Yes, sonny, I'm done."

A gasp and a groan followed him and Maggie outside.

"That was. . .impressive." Maggie peered at him through the lace of her veil. "I daresay he had it coming. But I am curious. You could've just walked away sooner, you know. Pocketed that extra bit of money the clerk handed you instead of making a to-do about it. Many people would have. Why didn't you?"

Most of the time Oliver scorned his father's values—yet one truth he fully and rightfully agreed with. "If we are not faithful in the small things, we will not be found faithful in the large." He turned towards the coach, fighting the strong urge to offer her his hand and help her into the carriage. A lady—especially one purportedly as old as he currently masqueraded—simply wouldn't do such a thing.

Instead, he merely swept out his hand. "Now then, ready for an adventure?"

Chapter Fifteen

Riding in a public coach is a peculiar kind of torment. Crammed in with strangers, elbow to elbow, thigh to thigh. I breathe through my mouth, trying not to inhale the reek of stained leather mixed with the cloying scent of cheap perfume.

Worst of all, I hate the way my breath catches every time Oliver cranes his neck to stare out the window. He is on edge. Alert. As if at any moment, he expects Officer Barrow to pull the carriage over at gunpoint and demand us to stand and deliver ourselves.

Sighing, I lean my head against the wall. I cannot wait for this journey to end, yet it's been only a quarter of an hour since we left Lydford.

So I close my eyes and shut out the cramped quarters, visually at least. Would that I could stop up my ears as well. The old man next to me snores with an open mouth. On the other side of him, his wife chatters about the high price of camphor oil as if he hangs on her every word. Across from me and Oliver sits a young couple with a squalling baby. The child's cries shake my bones as violently as the bounce and sway of the coach. And as if the noise inside weren't enough to bear, the passengers seated outside on the roof break into a boisterous taproom song.

What *am* I doing here? Have I done the right thing by leaving Morden Hall? Should I have allowed Oliver to sort out the mystery of the jewels on his own? The questions, combined with the juddering of the coach, ignite a throbbing pain in my temple, and I reach up to massage the offense.

"Are you all right?"

Oliver's question brushes light and low against my ear. I nod, and a smile curves my lips. Even through the haze of my veil, he looks ridiculous. A proper parliamentarian in a shawl, a bonnet, and skirts with a tufted hem? Not many men would be confident enough to pull off such a farce. He is a rare breed, this man. . .I'm not sure what to think about that. He's put me off kilter since the day he arrived. But in a good way—nothing at all like my former manager.

Thankfully, the next half hour passes in quieter fashion. The babe stops wailing. The old woman drifts to sleep. I even grow accustomed to Oliver's tense surveillance. It is to be expected, I suppose. After breaking out of prison, looking over one's shoulder surely must be a habit hard to control.

A shout from the coachman breaks the monotony. "Cheriton Bishop!"

The great wheels grind to a stop. The couple across from us bundle up the babe and exit. I watch their departure, wondering what sort of life they go to meet. A sweet little cottage nestled in the hills, perhaps? Or a cold wreck of a shack that will ruin the child's health and bend the shoulders of the young woman? Only God knows—an uneasy comfort, that. I have yet to reconcile why the Creator allows some creatures pleasure and ease while others suffer years of cruelties.

"Excuse me." Oliver shoves past me, his falsetto voice just a little too high.

"Where are you—" I press my lips shut. He's already out the door. What in the world? We'd agreed to remain inside the coach until we reached Exeter. The less we are seen, the better, unless. . . Has he spied some sort of danger so urgent he must meet it head-on?

My heart trips, and I scoot over to the now empty seat, gaining a clear view out the open door. I can't hear his words, but Oliver's voice warbles as he converses with the couple. Surely they cannot pose us any threat. Can they?

He holds out a glove. A smile lights the woman's face as she collects it. The man pats him on the shoulder. I sink back in the seat.

Oliver risked his own well-being for the sake of a forgotten glove? I move over when he climbs back in, marveling at the strange act.

As he settles beside me, the old man across from us leans forward. "That were a kind act, missus."

"Oh, you know. . . A lady needs both of her gloves." Oliver trills an off-key laugh that is more haggish than ladylike.

I cannot help but chuckle and am glad for the veil hiding my face as I study him. With all his unpredictability and compassion, I could learn to like a fellow such as this. And even in the outmoded bonnet, he is a handsome man.

He peers over at me, a single brow raised beneath the brim. "Something amusing, dearie?"

My grin grows so wide my cheeks hurt. When was the last time a man made me smile so much? The question immediately douses my humour, and I avert my gaze, more on guard than ever before. A man who can make me laugh is a hazard to my heart, and I have enough peril in my life at the moment.

Once again I settle into the rhythm of the coach. Two stops later, we all exit. Even those who'd paid lesser fares and were seated up top climb down to the ground. Horses must be changed, and the driver needs a bite to eat. I'm not so hungry, but surely Oliver is. I turn to ask him, but he is gone.

Gone?

I spin in a circle, searching the milling people for a broad-shouldered, tatty-gowned old woman. Where could he have—ahh. Bag in hand, Oliver darts rather unladylike behind the inn, no doubt heading to the privy for a quick change. I am surprised he lasted this long in petticoats.

The sun peeks behind a bank of clouds while I wait, and I gaze to the west. Rain could drag our thirteen-hour trek into fifteen or more. A pewter blanket heads my way, tucking the blue beneath it as it lazily edges across the sky. At least it's not black. Riding in a coach with the windows closed against rain does not rank high on my list of preferences.

Near the front door of the inn, a patch-haired mongrel sits in the dirt. Ribs washboard at his sides as he breathes hard, tongue lolling. Poor thing. Though he is not nearly as bad as Malcolm when I'd found him, still my heart lurches, and I cannot stop from cooing kind words as I approach him.

"There's a good fellow." Stooping, I reach out my hand. "There's a good boy."

Liquid brown eyes stare up at me. Tentatively, a fuzzy muzzle sniffs my fingers. And just like that, we are friends. I scratch behind his ear. He leans into it, one hind leg kicking with pleasure. I'd love to bring this dog to Morden Hall, give him a good home, steady meals, and a faithful companion such as my Malcolm. Perhaps if he's still here on my return trip, I will see about coaxing the coachman into allowing him to board.

"Replacing me so soon?"

I rise, turning towards Oliver's deep voice, and my breath catches. He is a man of extremes. He made a hilarious old woman, with his shambling about and critchedy voice, but now garbed in an old suit of Dobbs's, nipped and tucked by Nora's able fingers, he is a dashing gentleman, albeit a bit shabby around the edges. Dobbs is no fashion plate.

I give the dog a final pat on the head. "I gave the matter some thought, but I suppose you will do."

"I am happy to hear it." He leans close, near enough to smell the leftover scent of rosemary soap on his skin. "And I'm even more happy to be rid of those miles of fabric. Shall we?"

Oliver offers his arm and ushers me inside the establishment. After ordering at the bar, he escorts me to a table in the corner. Once he is settled on the chair opposite, his body blocks me from any curious onlookers as I remove my veil. Admittedly, his position is a boon for him as well, since he faces away from the other patrons.

It is surprisingly bright without the thick lace in front of my eyes, and I blink at him. "While I've no doubt you are more comfortable in trousers, I must say you managed your costume with finesse. Do you have sisters, perhaps, that you learned to mince about so proficiently?"

"No, though I admit to a keen study of the fairer sex." He winks, and the effect is altogether too attractive. "And you? What of your family?"

"There is only my father. Mother died in childbirth, along with my younger brother."

"My condolences." Pity softens his tone.

I wave off his concern. "It was long ago. Papa and I learned to get on."

Just then the serving girl arrives, handing a plate of mutton and mash to Oliver and a bowl of stew to me. I take a sip, then peer over at Oliver. "What of your family? Your mother and father?"

"My mother passed on when I was ten, at which point I was promptly trundled off to boarding school." He trims the fat from his meat into a neat pile on the side of his plate, then pops a bite into his mouth.

The stew warms my belly, but after a few more mouthfuls, I set down my spoon. Traveling always steals my appetite. So I go back to querying Oliver while he eats with gusto. "And your father?"

Muscles work at the sides of his jaws, and he spears another piece without glancing at me. "He lives."

I lean back in my chair, ignoring the scrapes of forks and knives and chattering patrons around us. "Your father must have been devastated when you went to prison."

He slams his fork down, and the fierce stranger I'd glimpsed once before stares out at me through Oliver's eyes. "Must he?"

I suck in a breath. "Forgive me, I—"

"No, forgive me." He pinches the bridge of his nose, inhaling deep and breathing out long and low. By the time he looks at me again, a sheepish, lopsided smile quirks his lips. The man is as changeable as an April wind. "I'm afraid all that time in a gown has made me quite snappish."

I stare. Something deeper is at play behind those hazel eyes of his, and it has to do with his family—his father. But far be it from me to broach that inflamed subject again.

I return his half smile. "I shall take that into consideration when planning our disguises in Bath. Speaking of which, have you solidified our plan of action?"

"Just about."

Hmm. His noncommittal answer means either he is unwilling to share his idea or he doesn't actually have one yet. Neither appeals. I open my mouth to protest when a great bellow from the front of the public room turns everyone's heads.

"Coach is boarding! Five minute warning."

"Time to go." Oliver pushes back his chair and rises. I do the same. Once again he offers his arm, all civility and with the best gentlemanly manners—except out of the corner of my eye, just before I lower the veil over my face, I catch him palming the fat off his plate and hiding it in his fist.

What in the world?

⚭

Sore ankle or not, it was sheer freedom to stretch one's legs instead of fighting against the dead weight of petticoats. And who wouldn't wish to have a beautiful woman—despite her veil—hanging on his arm? A man could do far worse. Oliver should be in a banner mood, and he knew it—which only irritated him all the more.

Jaw clenched, he stepped outside. He'd prided himself on controlling his emotions, caging his anger, hiding his innermost thoughts. Not anymore. Was it the doe-eyed probing by Maggie Lee or a latent rage left over from prison that'd nearly tipped his hand about his estranged relationship with his father? He hadn't thought of the man so passionately for years. Why now?

Bah! He ground his teeth. Cassius Ward wasn't worth a second thought. No man was who didn't show up for his own son's trial—especially a father who'd worked in the legal profession for decades.

Shoving down the raw sentiments, Oliver surreptitiously held out his hand as they passed the dog by the door, revealing the fat from his chops on an upturned palm. A cold nose brushed against his skin as the animal mouthed the treat. No doubt the morsels were gone in one gulp, though he didn't slow to look. No sense getting too friendly with the mongrel. He'd done all he could for the beast. His step hitched. Was that perhaps how his father felt about him?

Interesting concept, that. One he'd tuck away and revisit later in the dark of night when no one could see the anguish on his face.

He helped Maggie up into the coach, then paused on the step before entering. Taking advantage of the slight elevation, he gazed down the road towards Lydford—leastwise as far as he could see before the lane cut off into a curve. He squinted, keen on spying any horseman riding hell-bent after them, but no cloud of kicked-up dirt or lathered horse bolted their way. Perhaps Barrow was yet tied up with whoever had tailed him. It was only right the pursuer got a taste of what it was to be pursued.

Satisfied, he ducked inside the coach and sank onto the cracked leather seat next to Maggie. It didn't sit well that by occupying the place at the window he exposed her to the discomfort of being jostled into the old man seated beside her, but truly it was a necessary evil. He might save them if he spied Barrow in time to escape the bully. How exactly he'd accomplish that, though, was as frustrating as coming up with a plan to take down Corbin and return the jewels—a plan he had yet to conjure.

"I saw what you did." Maggie's resonant voice pulled his face from the glass.

Blast! He'd lingered too long on the step, stared a little too hard down the road, and now that she'd picked up on his concern, she'd worry as well—a fate he'd hoped to spare her.

"Truly you needn't—"

"Don't be so modest, sir." She wagged her finger. "It was a kind thing you did, feeding that poor dog." She leaned closer, her breath warm, her voice low against his ear. "You are a very kind man for a convict."

The muscles in his shoulders loosened, and he relaxed against the bouncing seat. Either the woman was hiding behind a mask without him sensing it—and she very well could be, judging by her fame on stage—or she still didn't know Barrow had spied them coming into town.

Despite his vigil, the next hours passed uneventfully. Never once did Maggie let on she suspected the threat that at any moment might gallop up behind them. Nor did she complain of the monotonous ride or the influx of passengers forcing them into tighter and tighter quarters. Even when they stopped for dinner, she graced him with pleasant conversation instead of sniping about the rain that seeped from the heavens in a bone-chilling drizzle.

How many women did that? A few saints, perhaps, but none of those who ran in his usual circles, where a perfected pout was considered a beauty mark.

They pulled into Bath just before midnight, stopping in front of a gas-lit coaching inn. The Saracen's Head was a cheery beacon on this wicked eve of cold and damp. A warm mug of mulled cider and a soft mattress would be a welcome respite after thirteen hours on the road. Too bad they wouldn't be staying.

Oliver edged past Maggie and the old couple who'd managed the grueling ride mostly by snoring, then opened the carriage door and planted his feet on wet cobblestones. Reaching up, he assisted all three out. The coachman was too busy hailing a porter to help him unload the baggage.

After a thorough handshake and a "thank you," the elderly gent and his lady shuffled off. Maggie sighed as she watched them go.

"In an odd sort of way, I shall miss them—"

The crack of a whip turned her head towards the front of the coach. "Off with ye!" the coachman roared. "Ye grime-faced little weasel!"

Footsteps slapped the wet pavement. Careening around the horses, a dark shape darted their way and didn't stop until just the other side of Oliver.

A young boy lifted his face. He might be eight, maybe nine, or perhaps seventy-two. Judging by the wary, hard-edged glint in his eyes, the lad had already lived a hundred lifetimes on the streets. Too much knowledge sharpened that gaze. Too much hunger and need sculpted those cheekbones.

"Any ha-pennies to spare, sir?" His teeth—one of the front missing completely—chattered as he spoke, and no wonder. A ragpicker would turn up his nose at the gauze-thin shirt draped over the boy's bony shoulders.

Oliver's heart twisted. The poor. The downtrodden. The weak and vulnerable. These were who he'd been fighting so hard for in Parliament when Corbin had stolen his voice and locked him away. He shoved his hand into his pocket, only to finger nothing but fabric. He'd spent the last of Maggie's coins on their dinner.

"I said off!" the coachman barked again, closer, louder.

Oliver spun, catching the man's arm just as he was about to once again wield the whip. "Leave him be. He's just a boy."

Sneering, the fellow wrenched from his grip. "That's no boy. He's a thievin' cully who'll lift yer purse and slit yer throat before you can take a breath." He reared back his arm.

"I said leave him be," Oliver growled and struck.

An elbow to the gut was enough to slacken the coachman's grip. Oliver snatched the whip and threw it aside, nearly stumbling when he landed full force on his sore ankle.

The coachman grumbled curses, an amazing feat considering how he sucked air in through his teeth. "Fine," he spit out and pivoted. "But don't go blamin' me when the by-blow robs ye blind."

Oliver smirked. He didn't have a thing of his own the boy could pilfer. Turning back to the lad, he peeled off his sack coat and wrapped it around the boy's shoulders, then stooped, face to face. "I've not a penny to give you, boy, but you can have my coat."

"Caw, sir!" Wonder lit the boy's face, erasing years, restoring his rightful youth. "I'll not forget this. Thank ye."

"Thank God, boy. I'd not have had a coat to give you were it not for Him." He tussled the boy's hair and stood. "But were I you, I'd make a run for it. That coachman's in a foul mood, now more than ever."

The boy dashed down the street, coat hem swinging at his knees, and disappeared into the misty darkness. It was only one small lad. One used piece of clothing. But after the horrors and degradation of nine months in prison, the act did much to restore a measure of humanity to Oliver's soul.

Satisfied, he turned and faced Maggie, who stood with a hand pressed to her chest and a gape so wide, he could see the shadowy silhouette of it beneath her veil.

The full reality of what he'd just done hit him hard in the belly. She'd given him that coat, begged it off her manservant, and now without it, he was in a state of woeful undress. Shame burned white hot up his neck. The coat was never his to give, nor would she wish to be seen with a man in naught but shirtsleeves and a waistcoat.

"I. . ." What was he to say? She had every right to be angry. He cleared his throat and coaxed the most soothing tone he could manage. "Forgive me. Once my freedom and fortune are restored, I vow I shall replace Dobbs's coat, and as soon as humanly possible, I shall borrow a replacement."

She shook her head. "When will you stop doing that?"

Puzzled, he rubbed the back of his neck. Did she really think he'd give away more? "Soon, hopefully. I'm only a waistcoat and shirtsleeves away from indecency."

"No." She stepped closer. "I mean when will you stop surprising me?"

"Oh, that." Relief tasted sweet, and he grinned. "Well, probably not tonight. Come along. I'll grab our baggage."

He turned to go, but her hand on his arm stayed him.

"The porter can get it. Come. Let's go inside."

Though he hated to refuse her, he shook his head. "No, we are not staying here."

"What do you mean?" Her chin angled like a curious tot's. "Where will we go?"

"If I tell you all my secrets, then you won't be surprised anymore, hmm?"

"But it's so late." As if on cue, she lifted a hand to her veil, stifling a yawn—and the sight grated against his resolve. So did the fatigue fraying her usual dulcet tones. "Might we not stay here just the one night?"

He ground his teeth, debating. It would be safer to lodge elsewhere, someplace less public, away from prying eyes. But her shoulders drooped and there was no denying the weariness in her voice. And all the long way here, he'd not seen one sign of Barrow.

Shoving down the last of his doubt, he offered his arm. "Very well. One night cannot hurt, I suppose."

Chapter Sixteen

Sebastian had two problems: an overwhelming desire to stop for a smoke and nod off for a few minutes, and his damp trousers. Every blessed step of his horse, each sway and creak of the saddle chafed the inside of his thighs raw. Gads, but it'd been a long day yesterday—first wasting time in dodging the inn's men bent on retribution for his rough handling of the ostler. Then the problem of finding Morden Hall empty save for the servants. By the time they hired a suitable horse for Groat to ride, night had fallen. Yet soon this would end. Likely today. Maybe even within the hour, for he was close—*very* close. He could feel it in his bones.

Midmorning, the streets of Bath were a riot, teeming with costermongers, housewives, and drays hauling barrels and lumber and loads of manure. Sebastian shifted gingerly on his mount and scowled. Cities were rife with noise and sin—which was why he preferred the quiet life at Dartmoor Prison. Oh, a few howls and curses cut into the peace there, but nothing like the droning humanity on these streets.

The Saracen's Head was no less busy. Sebastian dismounted near the front door, just past a gaggle of women tittering on about who knew what. Wendell Groat followed suit, his shiny leather shoes clattering onto the pavement next to him. Not one of the man's black hairs was out of place. He'd ridden surprisingly well throughout the night, as if he were used to damp cold and darkness, and looked no worse for the wear after the hard ride.

Sebastian pulled an extra pistol from his pocket, keeping his larger, double-action Adams for himself. "Here." He held it out. "Ward's a desperate man. This could get ugly."

"I'm not here for Ward." Groat pushed the barrel away with a bony finger. "And I don't need a gun."

No, of course he didn't. A line of gooseflesh paraded down his arms just thinking of the way Groat had coerced Daisy Lee's whereabouts from her manservant at Morden Hall. Applying pressure was one thing. Groat struck so fast, so unexpectedly, it was anybody's guess if the old manservant would ever see properly again, and he did it all with a devilish grin that said he *relished* having an excuse to strike.

"Suit yourself." Sebastian wheeled about and stalked into the inn. An apple-cheeked serving girl directed him to a man in deep conversation with a woman in an apron near the kitchen door. She clutched a wooden spoon in one hand and tucked her head, nodding now and then, clearly repentant about something. Pish. His business was far more significant than the state of some overcooked potatoes or underdone pork.

He advanced and poked the man in the shoulder. "You the innkeeper?"

The man turned and looked from him to Groat, then back again. "I am. Can I help you gents?" Seizing on his distraction, the woman behind him scurried off.

Sebastian threw back his shoulders. He had no way of knowing for absolute certain if Ward and the woman had been on last evening's coach, but it was always better to play a hand with confidence. "I'm looking for some people that were on the coach from Lydford. A man and a woman. Or two women, perhaps."

The man's eyes narrowed. "Well, which is it?"

The words were snipped short, the tone harsh, as if the innkeeper had better things to do than stand here talking to him. An affront of the highest degree. There was nothing more important than to bring justice to Oliver Ward.

But God was merciful—and so was he. "Doesn't matter. The point is I'm looking for a pair." He stepped close, as graciously as his own Lord might, and smoothed the innkeeper's lapels with his fingertips.

Then snugged the man's cravat knot tight—*very* tight. "There now." He retreated a step. "What say you?"

The innkeeper spluttered, his fingers desperately tugging to loosen his neckcloth. Finally, he cleared his throat and glowered while edging back and gaining space. "If you must know, most of those passengers have checked out by now. I believe there is only one couple left."

Perfect. "Room?"

"Four. Just down the corridor. But I will not have you harassing my guests. Understand?" He puffed out his chest, a rather bland show of courage, but one that Sebastian could respect.

"My good man." He smiled, and when he reached out to pat the innkeeper on the shoulder, the man flinched—just as the manservant had when Groat had pressed him. Of course, this was entirely different. "I assure you harassment is not at all what I am about. As you see, I am an officer of the law." He waved his arm in front of the man's eyes, duty band yet on his sleeve. "So go about your business, and I shall go about mine. Am *I* understood?"

The fellow's face drained of colour. "My pardon for the misunderstanding, Officer. Had you stated your profession first off, I'd not have questioned you so. This is a law-abiding establishment. I don't want any trouble here."

"No trouble at all. Carry on." He turned to Groat. "Why don't you step outside and cover the back door, in case they slip past me. Not likely, but it pays to be cautious."

Groat scuttled away without a word, and good thing too. The eerie clack of his teeth every time he spoke was starting to crawl beneath Sebastian's skin.

Setting off in the opposite direction, he entered the corridor, then pulled his gun, keeping it low and at the ready. Door four was at the end of the passageway, near a window. He'd have to keep an eye on that. Convicts would as soon jump through glass than go peaceably.

Near door three, he slowed and padded the rest of the way on soft feet. At door four, he stopped and pressed his ear against the wood. A woman's voice leached out, followed by a bass reply.

Sebastian eased back, heart pumping fresh waves of blood hard and strong through his veins, exciting a rash of little tingles up his legs. It was always like this moments before a catch. Right before he pounced. It was a heady feeling, like sipping a dram of good Scottish whisky, and for the space of a few breaths, he savored the rush of warmth and anticipation.

Then he cocked his gun and kicked in the door.

The woman inside screamed. The man stumbled backwards, eyes wide, clearly caught off guard. Both of them had grey hair—*real* grey. Not wigs. Not fake.

Even so, Sebastian barreled in and scanned behind the door, then lifted the bed skirt, and finally trotted over to the window and glanced out at the stable yard where the iridescent coat on Groat's back caught sunlight and bounced it back. Bah!

Whirling, he tipped his hat at the old couple. "Your pardon, ma'am. Sir."

A host of emotions propelled him out the door, down the passageway and across the taproom. A small bit of confusion. A boatload of irritation. Rage and fury and some disgust. But not one shred of chagrin or humiliation surfaced. The old couple could flap their jaws all they liked to the innkeeper about his abrupt entry into their room, and he'd still not apologize. He'd only been doing his job. No...*God's* job. Bringing justice to this wicked world was godly work—a calling and a curse, that.

Outside, he stomped down the cobbled stretch to where it opened into a back courtyard. He waved Groat over, then leaned against the wall and pulled out a cigarillo and a match. A few short puffs later, he inhaled a soothing mouthful of smoky tobacco.

Groat drew up beside him. "Well?"

He turned, sucking in a drag and blowing out a small cloud. "It wasn't them."

"I told you there was no guarantee they were even here to begin with. That manservant said Bath, he never said this particular—"

"Any ha-pennies to spare, sirs?" A tug on the back of Sebastian's coat accompanied the rude interruption.

A tug? Someone seriously dared touch the hem of *his* garment? This was not to be borne.

He pivoted, about to strike, then stopped midmove. A boy stood before him, about waist high, smudgy-faced and stringy-haired, and wearing a sack coat that came to his knees.

Sebastian squatted to eye level with the lad. "Tell me, where'd you get that coat, boy?"

"I didn't kipe it." He lifted his pointy little chin. "It's mine!"

"Hmm. . . You know what happens to liars, boy?" Like a strike of lightning, he snatched the little urchin by the collar and yanked him close. Then slowly, he lifted his cigarillo, burning end facing the brat, and rolled it between his two fingers, driving home the possibilities as he edged it a hair length away from the lad's cheek. "Liars burn, boy. They burn forever."

The boy squinched his eyes shut, but didn't move, not a jot. Smart lad.

"I—I swear I din't steal this coat, sir," he squeaked out. "A man gave it to me, he did. Just last night."

Even without touching the burning end to the boy's flesh, a red mark grew. A little closer and a slight sizzle would be heard, followed by a white hot circle of miniscule bubbles. His grin grew in anticipation. . .and he froze. Groat had grinned too, as he had struck the manservant.

"Let him go," Groat rumbled. "We don't need him."

Sebastian jerked his cigarillo away from the boy yet didn't loosen his grip. "But he might know something. It's Ward who gave the boy this coat, I know it. It's the same fabric as the old man's pants back at Morden Hall."

"No matter." Groat flicked his fingers, batting aside his objections, teeth clicking with each word. "I think I know where they are."

"How can you possibly know that?"

"Women are sentimental creatures, and there's a particular

keepsake Miss Lee left behind at the theatre. If she is indeed in Bath, she'll eventually show up there. Your man may still be with her, and if he's not, well. . .I'm sure you can persuade her to talk."

Sebastian released the boy and stood, not caring that the urchin sped away. Groat was right. He could be *very* persuasive.

∽

We are shadows, Oliver and I. Keeping to the sides of buildings. Walking neither too slow nor too fast. Heads down, we refrain from eye contact with those we pass. I am as eager to avoid running into Wendell Groat as Oliver is Constable Barrow. Though I'd scanned a morning newspaper, dreading to read an article calling for my arrest, the only missing person mentioned in any depth was some French marquis. Apparently, Oliver and I weren't newspaper material.

Yet.

Still, I keep my head down, as does Oliver. But as we cross Milsom Street, I look up. The pull of glancing down booksellers' lane is too much, the call of the past too overwhelming. Even were I blind, the smell of books and ink permeating the air would lift my head. A girl may leave her home, but home never leaves the girl. Good or bad, childhood marks the heart indelibly.

I turn my face and pick out the faded blue sign five shops down. The door of Rag and Bone Books stands open. Even without peering in, I see in my mind's eye the grey-tufted head of my father shelving a copy of *Oliver Twist* or *Fordyce's Sermons to Young Women*, completely engrossed in his work. The bookstore is his breath. Anything outside of it may as well not exist, even his only daughter. That is why I didn't hurry to send my letter, assuring him of my safety. I doubt he knows I left the stage, left the city, left his life. The bitter truth ought to smother any love I may feel for him. But it doesn't. My little girl heart still yearns for his embrace.

"Is there a problem?"

Oliver's low words warm my ear, and I jolt to the present. Gracious heavens! How long have I been standing still, gawking down Milsom Street?

"No." I force a small smile. "No problem at all."

Skepticism flashes in his eyes, but thankfully he turns and continues down the pavement. I follow, and just like ten years ago, I am both relieved and melancholy to leave my old neighborhood—yet that soon changes to horror when we turn south. The farther behind we leave the city center, the closer I press to Oliver's side.

Despair walks with us on Avon Street, bending men's shoulders where they skulk in doorways, hanging women's heads as they shuffle past, carrying baskets of laundry to be delivered. Want and poverty drape a sooty mantle over everything. The ramshackle buildings cram together and lean over the streets, blocking out light and hope. This bleak slum is a stark contrast to the creamy stone buildings that make up most of the great city of Bath. But no wonder the poor are relegated to this rat maze. It hurts the sensibilities to witness such poverty. Those with means would not wish to feel guilt for their pleasures.

Next to me, Oliver carries my bag of belongings. It's not much, but even a change of clothing, some tooth powder, a hairbrush and combs are a vast wealth compared to what these people own. Though I come from humble beginnings, I never had to scrape and scrounge for a bite to eat, not like the scavenger children we pass who pick their way through a refuse pile. Why has Oliver brought us here? Surely this cannot be the safe place he intends for our lodgings.

I peer over at him to ask as much, but he veers down a narrow space between two buildings where I must follow at his back. My shoes squish into greenish muck, releasing a stench worse than a quaking bog. I hike my hem and swallow a rise of nausea.

The passageway opens into a dismal courtyard. A mossy well stands at center, rocks falling off the side of one wall, a bucket green with scum clinging to the edge of another. I feel eyes upon us, staring out from darkened doorways and rag-covered windows, yet Oliver strides on, undaunted, as if he's fully at home here in this place of filth and gloom. Puzzling, that. Politicians usually only deign to set foot in such squalid quarters when votes are to be had.

He swings right and pounds on a door, offering me a reassuring glance over his shoulder before the door jerks open.

A man in a purple velvet tailcoat answers, and I shrink closer to the safety of Oliver's broad back. Great patches of the man's coat are threadbare, giving him the appearance of a mangy whippet. He is as lean as one too, his cheekbones sticking out like handles on his face. His nose is sharp, his chin pointy, but none of that is as off-putting as the knife he grips. One swipe and Oliver will be cut down.

Oliver chuckles. "Is that any way to greet your old friend, Filcher?"

The man's eyes narrow to slits. "Ward?"

"One and the same."

"Well, I'll be. . ." Slowly the knife lowers, and the man—Mr. Filcher, apparently—advances and grips Oliver's shoulder. "Yer alive?"

"For now. May we come in?"

"O' course! O' course. Make yerselves t'home." Mr. Filcher steps aside and sweeps his arm towards the open door. Then he dips a deep bow towards me. "My lady."

I put on my best stage face, refusing to curl my nose at such hospitality even though he smells of gin, sweat, and burnt beans. I bid him rise with a lift of my fingers. "Please, this is your home, and I am your guest. No need for such formalities."

He straightens, brows arching clear up to his greased-back hair. "Aye, miss. As you like."

Inside, my stage face falters. The place is hardly larger than my tea closet at Morden Hall. In front of a hearth that holds maybe two pieces of coal sits a woman with a babe to her breast. She watches me without a word, but her pale eyes say it all, such is the fury crimping the skin at the sides. She hates me, this woman. Hates my gown, my earbobs, the shoulder cape secured at my neck with a ribbon. And that loathing grows when Mr. Filcher bustles in after us and lifts her by the shoulders.

"Get on with ye! Can't ye see there's a lady present?" He snatches the chair and delivers it to me as if I am Queen Victoria herself. "Here, miss."

"Oh no! No, I couldn't. Please let your wife—"

"Pah!" The woman spits on the floor. "T'aint no wife o' his."

Mr. Filcher grabs a broom and shoos her towards the door. "Off with ye now, luv. I've business to attend."

Through it all, Oliver frowns. He says nothing, yet the green flecks in his eyes deepen—a sure sign much goes on in his head.

Mr. Filcher nudges the chair closer to me. "Don't mind Mary. She needs to get her lazy backside off to the factory anyway. If she's late to work one more time, she'll get the boot, she will. So go ahead, miss. Have yerself a little sit-me-down."

I glance at Oliver, who nods ever so slightly, then lower to the seat and offer Mr. Filcher a smile. "Thank you, sir."

"Think nothin' of it, miss." Then he turns to Oliver, shaking his head. "Gotta admit, Ward, I din't expect to see you gracing the streets o' Bath again. Nine months nibbed in with bludgers and cutthroats would finish off most gentle folk. Course ye ain't known for yer gentleness when punching about for a new law now, are ye?" Coarse laughter rumbles out of him.

Oliver smiles. "It'll take more than that to bring me down."

"Heh, heh! Course it will! But now that yer done servin' yer time, I reckon yer scrappin' to get back in the fray, eh? Bloody up those priggish fops a'settin' pretty down in par-ley-ment. Still. . ." Filcher cocks his head, light landing on his torn earlobe. How many fights has this man been in? "What ye doin' here, and in yer shirtsleeves no less?"

Oliver steps away from the wall he's been leaning against and folds his arms. "I need lodging, Filcher. We both do, the lady and I. A few nights. Maybe more, but hopefully not."

"What? Wantin' to stay here in Corbin's fine palaces?" He swings his arms wide, smacking a wooden mug off a shelf in the process. "And with yer fine lady to boot?"

My brows rise at the innuendo—especially when Oliver says

nothing to negate the man's assumption.

"Yes. This is the last place Corbin would expect to find me. I'm here to bring him to task, to mete out justice where justice is due."

Mr. Filcher whistles. "What do ye intend?"

I suck in a breath and lean closer, ignoring the stink of the tiny room. Oliver has not yet shared our plan. Will he do so now?

His jaw hardens. "I shall find who was really to blame in the stealing of that ruby necklace and bring it to light—while hopefully bringing down Ambrose Corbin along the way."

"Well, ye better hope that rotten swell don't get wind yer here in his fine courts. You shine a light under some rocks and snakes'll bite. Corbin ain't gonna like this thing revisited, especially not if you find them jewels in all yer rock turning."

"Why not?" I cannot help but ask. "It is his wife's keepsake after all."

Mr. Filcher scratches his chin, his dirty fingernails rasping against the dark stubble. "Why, I heard he already spent that insurance money—wasted it all at a gaming table over at The White Horse." His hand drops and the angles on his face sharpen to a glower. "While he wines and dines, we suffer and die."

"Insurance?" Oliver unfolds his arms, fists bunching at his side. "I rotted in prison while that fat bullock preened and pampered about on insurance money?"

"Aye. Every last farthing. He's got gaming fever, he has. Any money what crosses his path don't last more 'n one night. Generally happens every first o' the month when his bully-boys come in col-lecting the rents. Instead of using our hard-earned pennies to clean up that plague-pit o' a well out there or stopping up the roofs from leaking on our heads, Corbin wagers it all at the table. Devil's teeth! But it's a black heart beating beneath that fancy waistcoat o' his."

"That's atrocious!" I shake my head, horrified, and glance at Oliver.

But it is not Oliver I see. The feral man, the one I've glimpsed before, once again stares out from his eyes, primal and deadly. A shiver skitters across my shoulders. Were Ambrose Corbin in the room, I have no doubt he'd be bleeding out on the floor. Jaw clenching to tight lines, Oliver stalks to the door and stares outside.

"Aye." Mr. Filcher nods. "And that's what yer man there was aimin' to stop." He hitches his thumb towards Oliver. "He were working to pass a bill to tear down this warren and build a whole new neighborhood. No, more 'n that. A whole new life for us here on Avon Street. 'Tis his leadership of a few fine fellows in the House what fights fer me and my people. Aye, you can be mighty proud o' yer man there, miss. We are."

My man? I swallow. I should correct the fellow, let him know Oliver and I are naught but acquaintances thrown together to right the ills of Ambrose Corbin, but a queer knot blocks my throat. For a single, dizzying moment, I almost wish it were true. That the man standing vigil in the doorway, steeling every muscle against the injustice of the world, was my man.

"Well, enough o' that blackguard." Mr. Filcher crosses to Oliver and cuffs him on the back. Brave man. "You want housing, Ward, I know of a little hidey-hole you and yer lady can bide in." He chuckles. "If only Corbin knew ye were stayin' in his—"

"No!" Wheeling about, Oliver grabs the man by the coat. "No one can know."

Mr. Filcher's mouth twists, but finally he nods. "All right, though I wager half the slum already knows yer here, man. But don't ye worry none. No one'll breathe a word. We owes ya that and more, and we knows it. Still, I'll make sure tongues don't wag a twitch."

Heaving a great sigh, Oliver releases him and sets him back on his feet. "I appreciate that, Filcher."

"Like I said, we owes ya." He glances at me. "Come along, miss. It won't be much, but it'll do ye."

I press my lips flat. I can only imagine what he means—and it is not a pretty picture.

Chapter Seventeen

At least they wouldn't have to worry about rats. No self-respecting rodent would step a paw across that rotted threshold. Closing his eyes, Oliver pressed the heel of his hand against the bridge of his nose, an insane hope flickering that such a small act would make the world around him disappear.

But when he dropped his hand and blinked his eyes open, black mould still climbed the stone walls. Cobwebs hung just as thick overhead as before, and jaundiced light continued to leak through the single window. Surprising, really, so coated was the glass with greenish-brown film.

Blowing out a long breath, he scanned the small room. Over in the corner, a three-legged table was propped up on some rocks with two overturned half barrels to serve as chairs. All were rife with an unknown oily substance. And that made up the sum of the furniture in the small room—for surely the stained mattress in the corner could not be counted as a bed.

Oliver bit back a groan. Filcher's place was a castle compared to this cesspit. Come to think of it, so was his prison cell.

Behind him, Maggie stifled a cough. A small sound, but one that ignited a hot rage in his belly. She shouldn't be here. *No one* should be here. How Corbin could allow fellow humans to live in such abominable housing was a testament to the man's stinking rotted soul.

Oliver turned to Maggie, who yet stood near the door—and he didn't blame her. Even he wanted to make a run for it.

"I apologize for this." He swept out his hand. "You deserve far better."

Her lips curved into a brave smile. "Borrowing from your own words, it will take more than this to bring me down."

He clenched his jaw to keep from gaping. He couldn't name one man who would bear such wretched lodgings with nary a complaint. Yet there she stood, head held high, shoulders back, ready to take on the world if she must. Ahh, but he could love a woman like this.

Love?

No. He raked his fingers through his hair, discarding the bizarre notion. The timing couldn't be worse to play such a wild card. Maybe someday, God willing, but not at the moment.

"If all goes well"—he batted away some of the cobwebs as he spoke—"we won't have need of this place for very long."

"I am happy to hear it. So, what is the plan?"

For a moment he hesitated, concentrating instead on clearing off the low ceiling. His idea sounded good in his head, but would it make sense spoken aloud? And even if it did, would she mock it? Not that he wasn't used to such criticism on Parliament's floor, but this was different. This time he actually cared what she thought. A dangerous position. One that could leave scars—a bitter lesson he'd learned as a boy. Father had often dissected his notions, leaving nothing but an empty shell to be discarded.

"Oliver?" She stayed his arm with a light touch. "Your plan?"

He flinched away, annoyed at his own foolishness. What his father thought no longer mattered.

"Very well. Here it is." He puffed out his chest in a show of false bravado. "Corbin and a magistrate will meet for lunch. While they dine, I shall place the necklace in Corbin's barouche while you approach the two and accuse him in front of the magistrate, and voila. Corbin will try to talk his way out of how the jewels ended up in his coach, and he might very well do so, but he cannot escape from having to pay back the insurance money—money which I doubt very much that he has. At the very least, he'll be gaoled for fraud, and trust me, he will not survive such an experience."

Her brow furrowed. "But he is the richest man in all of Bath!"

"He used to be, but his appetites have pared that wealth down to nothing. You heard Filcher."

"Still. . ." Nibbling her lip, she paced the small room. Four steps one way, then back, and again, until she stopped in front of him, her big brown eyes searching his. "What if you're wrong that he has no money? How can you be so sure?"

"I can't, not without help from Filcher."

Once again, her brow scrunched—an endearing trait, one that made him curl his fingers into his palms to keep from smoothing those fine lines.

"I fail to see how Mr. Filcher can help with finding out how much money Ambrose Corbin may or may not have."

A small laugh rumbled in his throat. Of course she didn't. The most powerful men were usually the most underestimated. "Don't let Filcher's shabby coat or the neighborhood he lives in deceive you. On the contrary, those trappings work in his favor. Filcher is the most connected man in all of Bath. Take me, for instance. He sought me out when I was first elected. Exchanged promises for promises—all of which he's kept. And that's earned him the trust of rich and poor alike. If something needs to be done above or beneath a table, he not only knows who can do it, but holds their ear as well. Bank records won't be a problem for him to uncover."

She thought on this a moment, then nodded. "All right, but how do you know Mr. Corbin and a magistrate will be taking lunch together? And where?"

"Because we will orchestrate it."

This time only one of her brows arched, followed by a smirk. "Let me guess, Mr. Filcher again?"

"No. I'm afraid this part is on us. We'll send an invitation from Corbin to a magistrate, and another from the same magistrate to Corbin. Each will think the other is inviting him to luncheon." Bypassing her, he strode to the door and looked out at the dismal courtyard while working a knot in his shoulder. If all went right, this would soon be naught but an ugly memory.

Footsteps padded behind him. "Are you a forger, Mr. Ward?"

"It's Oliver, remember?" He turned to her with a smile. "And no, I am not an off-market scribe, but I am intimately familiar with Corbin's signature from having fought against him for years."

"Hmm." She frowned and folded her arms. "And what of a magistrate? You know one well enough to render a passable signature as well?"

"Unfortunately, no, but I am gambling that Corbin won't either."

"I see."

Did she? Did she truly understand how many ways this whole scheme could backfire? She shouldn't have come. Shouldn't have—

"Would it help to have a copy to look at?" Her head tipped inquiringly, both the question and the innocent quirk robbing him of thought. "Of a magistrate's signature, that is."

"Of course."

"Well. . ." She flashed a smile then edged past him, strolling into the courtyard and calling over her shoulder. "I know just where to get one."

※

The Beauford Square entrance to the Theatre Royal is a forgotten stepchild, overshadowed by the ornate arches and gilded plasterwork of the front door on Saw Close. Only stagehands and performers venture back here. And this early in the afternoon, none of them will be about.

Still, I pause in the alcove before entering. I've not been entirely truthful with Oliver. Coming here could be a mistake, but it is one I am compelled to make. Besides garnering a magistrate's signature, I desperately hope to retrieve a small locket I'd been forced to leave behind in my dressing room—a locket with a miniature of my mother's face.

"Is there a problem?" Oliver's voice rumbles low at my back.

I bite my lower lip. If Mr. Groat happens to be inside and sees me, Oliver's plans for justice will be upended, and I've not yet shared with him that possibility. He has no idea there is a price on my head. It will do him no good to get tangled up in my legal issues when his are not yet resolved.

I turn to him. "Wait here. It's better if I go in alone."

"No." He shakes his head. "It's too risky. Someone needs to watch the door while you rifle about for the magistrate's box seat registration form. I won't have you getting caught and accused of theft."

Green flecks blaze in his eyes, a stark contrast to his dark hair. There's a flinty set to his jaw, and he squares his shoulders. Though I've not known him long, I am familiar with this stance. He will not be moved no matter what line of reasoning I attempt.

Stubborn man. Frustration rushes from me in a sigh. "Very well, but there are a few things I should tell you before we enter."

"Such as?"

"I need to stop at my dressing room."

His brows knit. "Why on earth would you have a magistrate's signature in there?"

"I don't. I am after a locket."

Oliver shakes his head. "Do you really think now is the time for such a triviality?"

Heat rises up my neck as quickly as a host of reckless words. "There is nothing trivial about the only keepsake I have of my dead mother." My tone is terse—one I instantly regret.

The flecks of green in Oliver's eyes pale, stricken, and he holds up a hand. "Forgive me. I had no idea."

Of course he didn't. What is wrong with me? My surge of anger cools to embarrassment, and I offer him a sheepish smile. "It is I who should apologize. I've been angry with myself ever since I left it behind, a regret I will rectify today."

"Agreed." He frowns. "But do you think your things will truly be there after all this time?"

For a moment I still, my heart tightening as if I'd been splashed with cold water. I hadn't considered that possibility. But, no, if Mr. Groat is willing to pay such a reward for my return, he hasn't moved on. "They'll be there."

My confidence seems enough to convince Oliver. He shrugs. "Very well. That's one thing, but what's the other? You said there were a few things I should know."

"Yes, well. . ." Hmm. Where to begin with Mr. Groat? "It's about my manager. You see, well. . .he's. . ."

Words fail me. Even coherent thought fails me as I think on the peculiar cruelties I've witnessed towards others at Mr. Groat's hands. Only once, when I'd first sheltered beneath his tutelage, did I displease him. I still bear the scar on my thigh where he'd jabbed me with a letter opener—an act that cured me of any future rebellion.

A breeze eddies into the small space, tugging loose a curl. I tuck it and my black memories away, then meet Oliver's gaze. "Suffice it to say Mr. Groat is not the most pleasant of fellows if you cross him."

"Don't fret. He need never know it's you who's broken into his office and taken a receipt. And if you like, we'll replace it as soon as this is over."

"No, it's not that. I have already crossed him."

"Oh?" Oliver's gaze sharpens. "How so?"

There's no hiding it anymore. Not even from myself. As much as I've wanted to pretend my manager's search for me is nothing but a triviality, that his threat isn't nearly as ominous as Ambrose Corbin's, the truth is that Mr. Groat is every bit as ruthless—especially when it comes to money, and my absence has sorely cut into his income. My stomach twists, and I press a hand to it, quelling the dread building there. Sooner or later I will have to deal with the consequences of breaking my contract.

I opt for later and force a carefree tone to my voice. "There is a bounty on me. My manager put out a fifty-pound reward for anyone who informs him of my whereabouts."

Oliver rocks back on his heels. "What the devil did you do to warrant such an amount?"

"By running away that night, disappearing to Morden Hall, I breached the contract I signed."

For a while Oliver says nothing, just stands there rubbing the back of his neck, until finally he shakes his head—and suspicion narrows his eyes. "I'll grant you breaking a contract is no small thing, but fifty pounds? There's got to be more to it than that."

His doubt cuts deep, and I'm not sure why. Countless other gentlemen have called my character into question. Such is the nature of being a stage performer. But this time, with this man, it hurts like a festering sliver.

And I don't like it.

I lift my chin, shoring up my dignity. "I assure you, sir, that is the sum of my guilt."

His stare bores deeply into mine, so intent it steals my breath.

Then just like the slamming shut of a finished book, the intensity fades and a half smile plays across his lips. "Seems we are both on the run then, eh? But—hold on. You knew your manager was looking for you, yet you came to Bath with me? Why take such a dangerous risk?"

He's right. It is a dangerous thing I do, all because of Ambrose Corbin. Had he not compelled me to hide in the first place, I'd not have reneged on my legal duty to Mr. Groat. I would've ridden out the rest of the year and never signed over any more of my life to him. Now I am at the man's mercy, and he has none. Fury rises to my throat, and I glower up at Oliver.

"Believe me when I say I want Ambrose Corbin put behind bars every bit as much as you do. It is worth any risk to see that through." My voice shakes. So do my hands, and I clench them.

Oliver holds up his palms, warding off my venom. "All right. I understand." He tips his head towards the door. "Lead on."

I fish about in my reticule and retrieve my key—thank God I thought to bring it along. Inside, shadows greet us, and I reach for Oliver's hand. His eyes widen as I entwine my fingers through his. No wonder. It is a brazen act, this intimate press of flesh against flesh, his strong and warm, mine suddenly going clammy, but it is necessary.

With my other hand I ease the door shut, and we are cast into utter blackness.

"Follow me," I whisper.

I lead him through the workroom. Each breath of piney sawdust and metallic twang of lead paint welcomes me back to the theatre. Only once do I crack my hip against a table. Oliver's strong grip rights me when I stumble.

I push open another door, and dim light from vigil lanterns paints the stage and the auditorium in a mysterious twilight. Since Mr. Groat's office is upstairs, he insists these lamps continually shine over his domain, that he may look down like a god to keep an eye on his little world. His arrogance is a fire hazard.

I drop Oliver's hand, and after a quick glance, I am satisfied there is no lamp lit up in Mr. Groat's office nor is there anyone about. Keeping to the shadows, I edge across the stage towards the spiral staircase on the other side. But halfway through I stop, my gaze irresistibly drawn towards the auditorium. A flood of emotion washes over me. Strains of music I love echo from the past. I know I did the right thing in giving this up. Still, I am grateful for the times music mended and healed my soul. Thankful for the transformation of a timid little book clerk into a poised woman of elegance. But oh! The jitters that shook through me that first night the curtain opened. How strained my voice was when I sang in *La Traviata*. How thunderous the applause that followed. I close my eyes, chest suddenly tight. How unwanted were the touches from gentlemen afterwards who assumed I was every bit as much the fallen woman as Violetta.

"We should make haste." Oliver's low voice snaps my eyes open.

I nod, then with a last look at the rows of red velvet seats, march to the spiral staircase. Up we go, curving into the higher realm of ropes and pulleys, gangways and storage—and more importantly, Mr. Groat's office.

Above the box seats is a passageway lined with three doors. Two are shut—the one for Mr. Groat's office and the one that hides a chaos of miscellany, everything from broken chair rails to leftover programs. It is the middle door that concerns me.

Light spills out from the small prop room. It's more than likely not my manager—he wouldn't stoop to such a menial task as sorting through costume accoutrements, but still. . . Should we turn back?

I exchange a glance with Oliver. He tips his head back towards the stairs. We turn.

And a shrill voice hits between my shoulder blades. "Public ain't allowed up here."

My step falters. If only I can make it to the stairs and fly down. I flutter my fingers in the air, waving off the house mistress. Hopefully she won't—

"Ho! Ho! That be you, Daisy, luv? Why, go on with ye! I can hardly believe my old eyes. I knew ye'd come back. I knew it! Been sayin' so ever since ye trundled off last summer."

My shoulders sag. Mrs. Threadneedle may be nearing sixty, but she's as foxy as she was in her prime. There will be no outmaneuvering her.

Oliver frowns at me, motioning wildly for the stairs, but I turn from his entreaty. He has no idea of the sway of the house mistress. She is only a step below Mr. Groat. If I can manage a word in edge-wise, I will convince the woman we are here for some triviality instead of a covert deed.

"Oh Mrs. Threadneedle"—my hand flies to my chest—"you gave me a fright."

"Sorry, luv. Just gettin' a chapeau for the next performance. Needs some new feathers. Can't have a dandy of a hero sportin' about in a brown-nap without a stitch o' finery on it, can we?" She rocks back on her heels, her grey eyes glinting. "My but it's grand to see ye. Like I said, I knew you'd be back. Mr. Groat's going to be so—"

"No! He cannot know you've seen me!" The words blurt sharp, startling us all.

Mrs. Threadneedle grips the hat, blinking, her lips rounded to a small O.

Oliver eases to my side, and for the first time, Mrs. Threadneedle's gaze drifts from me to him. He flashes a killer of a smile, and though it's not directed at me, my own knees weaken.

"What Miss Lee means to say—Mrs. Threadneedle, is it?—is that our little visit here is a surprise. A very special surprise for some very special people. We would be honored to have your strictest confidence on the matter." He reaches for her hand and bows over it, blessing her fingers with a light touch of his lips, and as he rises, he once again locks eyes with her. "But of course I need not beseech such a fine lady as yourself. Why, you must have superlative intrigues of your own, I imagine. All the finest ladies do."

She opens and closes her mouth, apparently lost for words. Stunning. The woman lives to spout monologues. Finally, she speaks, and it comes out all breathy. "O' course I do, have intrigues, that is."

Oliver dips his head, peering at her through his lashes. "*Je suis enchantée, madame. Tu es toute la grâce et la beauté.*"

Mrs. Threadneedle twitters like a lovelorn schoolgirl. And no wonder. His voice rumbles low, intimate, as if she were the only woman on the face of the earth. I cannot help but wonder what my own reaction would be should he ever speak to me in such a fashion—and for a breathless moment, I wildly wish he would.

Pulling her hand from his, Mrs. Threadneedle fans her face and mutters, "Oh my."

Oh mercy. At this rate, she'll faint clear away and we'll have to deal with a flattened house mistress.

I step forward. "Don't let us hamper your labour, Mrs. Threadneedle. You have many costumes to manage, and you wouldn't want to upset Mr. Groat with unfinished business."

The threat of displeasing the manager snaps the woman from her daze. "Aye. Yer right." She bobs her head. "Ahh, but it was good to see you, luv. You and yer fine gent. Hope all goes well with your surprise."

Oliver bows. "Good day, my lady."

She giggles as she passes between us, flourishing the hat in the air. "And a very good day to the both of you."

I lift my eyes to Oliver. "You're quite the charmer."

"You have no idea." He winks.

Oh but I do. My heart stutters at the gesture, and I spin on my heel and race towards Mr. Groat's office. I free a hatpin from my bonnet and have it at the ready by the time Oliver catches up.

Wordlessly, he works to pick the lock. How a member of Parliament knows such a devious skill is unsettling, yet this is no ordinary politician—especially not after spending nearly a year in gaol.

Finally the lock clicks, the door swings open, and I sweep in. Oliver posts himself near the threshold, ready to sweet-talk Mrs. Threadneedle should she return for another hat.

I yank open the middle file drawer and slide my finger along the alphabet, stopping at the letter *H*. Thankfully Magistrate Hunter's name should be towards the beginning.

Hart, Hillman.

"Make haste," Oliver whispers from the door. "Mrs. Threadneedle may be returning."

Hogard—

"Those aren't a woman's footsteps I hear."

My heart hammers and my fingers shake.

"Hurry!"

Hunter. I yank out the document and push the drawer shut, then scurry past Oliver. Thuds—two sets—pound up the stairs as he fiddles with relocking the door. My belly twists as I stare down the passageway towards the staircase.

An eternity later, Oliver grabs my arm and we dash for the prop room, just making it inside when feet land in the passageway. If anyone pops their head in here, we will be discovered.

A bass voice rumbles something too low for me to hear—but loud enough for me to distinguish the owner. Constable Barrow. I inch closer to Oliver.

But I edge even nearer when words that end with distinctive clicks draw close to the prop room. Though I desperately want to, I cannot tear my gaze away from the open door.

"A baseless concern. You'll find your man where the woman is. She'll come here. She left behind too many baubles in her dressing room. And with a little leverage, my theatre hands will let me know as soon as she shows up."

I sag against the wall and look back at Oliver—and that's when I realize we are not alone, for Mrs. Threadneedle stands wide-eyed and staring at us just past his shoulder.

Chapter Eighteen

Time stops. So does my heart. One cry—nay—one small shuffle of Mrs. Threadneedle's feet and Oliver and I will be exposed. Our lives are wholly in the hands of an overworked, underpaid, grey-haired matron who loves to talk.

Beside me, Oliver shakes his head at the woman while lifting a finger to his lips. Her eyes follow his movement—but her mouth opens. My lungs burn for want of air. Will she give us away?

Mr. Groat's and Mr. Barrow's voices continue to rumble. My name, Oliver's too, bandies about like a shuttlecock between them.

Mrs. Threadneedle's mouth gapes wider.

And I pray—or rather plea—for God to clamp her lips as effectively as those of the lions in Daniel's pit.

Oliver edges away from me, towards her, and whispers something in the woman's ear. The longer he speaks, the farther away the footsteps in the passageway travel, and the more Mrs. Threadneedle's lips draw together. By the time Mr. Groat's keys jangle and his office door swings open, Mrs. Threadneedle is grinning—and a blush deepens on her cheeks.

It's my turn to gape. What charms has Oliver worked to effect such a change?

He pulls back from her. She winks at him, flutters her fingers at me, then hustles out the door.

Straight toward Mr. Groat's office.

I whip my gaze to Oliver, a field of questions nettling my tongue, but before one can sprout, he hurries me out the passageway. Mrs.

Threadneedle's voice trills from inside Mr. Groat's office, loud enough to hide our footsteps. Oliver leads me to the stairs and we dash down. At the bottom, he makes to cross the stage. I plant my feet and yank him back, a sharp shake to my head. The manager's office directly overlooks the stage, and my dressing room is in the opposite direction.

Now I am the leader, winding through narrow corridors that are secret to the public. One more flight of stairs and we are beneath the stage—safe from the prying eyes of Mr. Groat and Mr. Barrow.

I fumble in my pocket for my key and shove it into the lock on my dressing room door. It doesn't click. It doesn't need to. The door is already unlocked—a door I *always* kept secure. Frowning, I enter.

We stand in a war zone.

The drawers on my dressing table hang open, a scarf dangling from one, a broken chain of beads on another. Cosmetic pots are tipped over. My wardrobe is empty, one door askew because the bottom hinge is broken. All the gowns are gone. A single silk stocking sprawls like a corpse on the floor. Whoever searched this room didn't care about me or anyone else noticing.

"Are you always this careless with your belongings?" Though humour lightens Oliver's tone, I am anything but amused.

I race to the dressing table to search the bottom drawer for my mother's locket, but my fingers meet only air and wood. My heart catches in my throat. Has someone stolen it? Why, oh why, did I not tuck my precious keepsake in my pocket that fateful night? Why did I leave it here? What was I thinking?

I grip the edge of the table and fight back hot tears. I hadn't been thinking, that's what. I'd been caught up in the thrill of performing. Of entertaining the masses. And now I must pay for that sin.

"Is this what you're looking for?"

Whirling, I face Oliver, who holds a fine chain with a silver pendant. I snatch it from him and clutch it to my heart, breathless. "Where did you find it?"

"Here." He points to the ground under an overturned chair. "It was snagged on the cushion."

"It must have gotten caught when they ransacked my room. Thank goodness they didn't see—"

"No time." Oliver cocks his head and his face hardens. "You've got your keepsake. Let's go."

He ushers me out the door, pulling it shut behind him, then whispers, "Lead the way, but make it a back way if possible."

I'm about to question his strange behaviour when I hear it. The same sickening thud of boots against stairs we'd experienced earlier.

I dart to the right, away from the staircase, and edge along a darkened corridor. It's a tight fit, meant only for theatre boys to pass messages between dressing rooms and the front reception office. My skirts are too wide and shush against the walls. The fabric on Oliver's broad shoulders does as well.

An eternity later, I open a narrow door, and we slip into the velvet and brocade room, where the privileged few take drinks on plush sofas before a performance.

"This way," I whisper to Oliver. Another corridor. More twists and turns, then we double back. Moments later, we are once again outside the Beauford Square entrance, but my heart doesn't stop pounding until we are safely inside a carriage that Oliver hails.

He heaves a great sigh as he sinks next to me on the bench seat. "Good work."

"Thank you." I smile as I catch my breath. "Tell me, what did you say to Mrs. Threadneedle? And how did you hear them coming so quickly? I didn't hear a thing until we were in the corridor."

"I told Mrs. Threadneedle to let him know we were in the building."

"You what!" I fling out my hand as the coach careens around a corner. The movement judders me to the core as deeply as Oliver's confession.

Worse, he has the audacity to chuckle. "You should see your face right now."

My hand shakes around the locket. The nerve of the man!

He reaches for my hand and lifts it to his lips, ever the charmer—and much to my chagrin, the action cools the flash of anger to naught but ashes. "Forgive me, please. I find humour soothing, though this time I fear my words were misplaced. There was no way we could keep Mrs. Threadneedle quiet, so I gave her something more productive to say." He looks at me as if he's just solved an intricate mathematical equation.

I shake my head. "I don't understand."

"I explained to Mrs. Threadneedle that our surprise was to pop out of the prop room in full costume, to astonish Mr. Groat, and what a jolly good laugh it would all be. But I needed her to keep him busy so we could accomplish that. I have no idea what she said to the man, but clearly she didn't hold his interest for too long. I knew your dressing room would be the first place he'd look after he discovered the prop room to be empty."

My mouth drops. "You are amazing."

"And you have a cobweb in your hair."

Smiling, he brushes away the offense—just as the cab hits a rut, knocking us both together. His cheek grazes mine, the rough stubble of his unshaven skin a reminder of his masculinity. Our gazes lock, and a queer tingle runs deep in my belly. His lips are a breath away. One more pothole and that fine, wide mouth will be hot against—

This is ridiculous. The stress of the morning—of the entire past several weeks—is surely getting to me. I pull back and lift my chin. "Yet that is not the full story, is it? What did you tell Mrs. Threadneedle that made her blush so violently?"

A rogue smile quirks his lips. "I merely said today is Wednesday and what a brilliantly sunny afternoon it is."

Hah! I narrow my eyes. Surely he doesn't expect me to believe such gibberish. "And why would that heat her cheeks?"

"I spoke it in French." He winks.

Despite our harrowing experience, I laugh. "There is never a dull moment in your presence. With your highly adept chicanery, I'm beginning to believe this really will be over soon."

"Indeed." He sinks back in his seat. "Very soon."

My laughter turns sour in my throat. As much as I am ready for this misadventure to be finished, there is a sudden sad realization burning in my heart.

I will miss this man.

∞

Shooting first and asking questions later wasn't usually Sebastian's approach, but sometimes exceptions had to be made—and after the not-so-merry chase Ward had led him on, this situation was particularly exceptional. As soon as the gilded letters of Daisy Lee's name on a dressing room door came into view, he tore past Groat and burst into the room with a roar.

"Got you now, Ward!"

His words bounced off empty walls. Lowering the gun, he made a quick search of the small chamber, then turned on Groat with a scowl. "You said they'd be here."

Slowly, the man pivoted from where he stood near a tilted mirror, his eyes glittering black beetles in his face. "They were. Look, the dust has been disturbed."

What the skip-nippity did he care for dust in this mess? Where the devil was Ward? "They can't have gone far. We'll turn this building inside out and shake them free like the pocket lint they are."

"Don't work harder, Mr. Barrow." Groat tapped a bony finger to his temple. "Think smarter."

"What are you going on about? They're within our grasp!"

"I think not. Daisy knows every passage in this theatre. They are long gone."

Blast! The woman was far too cunning—and Lord knows he couldn't abide a cunning woman. Releasing the hammer, he shoved his gun into its holster. "Running like the rats they are," he murmured. Made sense. Rodents always scurried to the darkest corners.

But where would they scuttle to next?

Turning from Groat, he paced the perimeter of the room, cataloguing what few contents remained. Nothing was helpful. So, what would be? *Who* would be? Who would Ward trust with not only his safety but his woman's?

And then he knew.

Sebastian snapped his fingers and wheeled about to face Groat. "Ward's family. Tell me of them."

Groat shook his head. "That's a wrong line of thinking. Too much bad blood there. Ward would never seek out his father—and neither should you."

"Why the devil not?" He threw out his hands. "It's the perfect lead!"

"Mr. Ward's father is the Hawk of Crown Court, a barrister with such lofty connections that not even I would dare cross swords with him."

Ward had the blood of a man of law running through his veins, one that might bend justice to his own whims? His own blood began to boil. "No one is above the law," he thundered.

"Now, now, Mr. Barrow. Cassius Ward wouldn't actually break a law. He would twist it, like a noose around your neck. If he desires a man be put away, the poor soul stands no chance. I suggest you stay far from him, just as your escapee will. They broke communication years ago, and there's not a chance in a million your convict will seek his father's aid. The safer bet is to keep an eye on the man who accused him. I'd wager that's who Ward's going after."

Despite the awful click of Groat's teeth, Sebastian had to know more. Keep the man talking—even if the sound burrowed beneath his skin. "And who is that?"

"Ambrose Corbin is your man. Find him, and you'll likely find Ward."

Perfect. In three long strides, Sebastian cleared the door, then popped his head back in to eye Groat. "Are you coming along?"

"As much as I'd like to witness your spectacular catch, I must decline. Daisy is holed up somewhere in this city, for now, at any rate. Not to worry, though. I have many connections myself. Go." He waved him off. "Find your Mr. Corbin, and I shall find my little flower."

Chapter Nineteen

Two days. Two days of looking over his shoulder, on edge. Not that Oliver wasn't used to it, but this time, knowing both Groat and Barrow were gunning for them, those two days dragged into an eternity. But now, finally, all the hardship and danger was nearing an end—and none too soon. He'd not see Maggie suffer one more evening in that hovel of a shelter, even though she'd spent some coin to have it cleaned and purchased fresh bedding. Nor did he relish another long night huddled outside against the door, keeping watch. The kink in his neck might never go away.

His pace slowed as he and Maggie neared the Royal Station Hotel. A lifetime ago he'd walked tall through those front doors. Sure of himself. Sure of the world as he knew it. How many meals had he shared in that opulent dining room, trying to persuade the powermongers, the rich, those in positions able to make a change in the lives of the needy? Change wrought by his ideas, his determination? And look at him now, slinking in the shadows, keeping to the edge of the pavement. Blast that Corbin!

"This is it." Maggie's sweet voice and a slight pressure on his arm turned him towards her. She stopped at the mouth of a narrow passageway near the end of the building. "Are you ready?"

He smirked. He'd been ready to see Corbin in fetters since the day his own wrists had felt the bite of iron.

But the longer he stared into Maggie's big brown eyes, the more his gut twisted. It was wrong, this plan of his, putting her in harm's way. What if it failed? What if he were caught, dragged off, forced to leave her behind to fend for herself just like he'd left Jarney in that rat hole of a prison? Corbin would show her no mercy. If anything, the scoundrel's appetite would be whetted for worse devilment than he had intended in the first place.

"Maggie, listen. You don't have to do this." Oliver grabbed her shoulders and gently eased her into the small space between buildings. "Wait here, where it's safe. I'll manage on my own and—"

She lifted a finger to his lips. A startling touch, one that licked a fire through his veins.

"We've been over this before. That dining room"—she tipped her head towards the hotel—"is my stage. I was made for this. I can do it. We carry out the plan as is, and it will all soon be over. You'll have your freedom, and in a way, so will I."

He brushed aside her finger, then wrapped her small hand in both of his. Fortitude sparked in her gaze. Resolve reverberated in the jut of her jaw. She was a fierce beauty, all confidence and strength. Quite the contrast to the childlike hand engulfed in his—the fine bones that with the slightest pressure could be crushed and broken.

Oliver shook his head. "I'll never forgive myself if something goes wrong, if Corbin hurts you."

"I've escaped his clutches before and can do so again if need be. Besides"—she shrugged—"it's a public place, a room full of people. Nothing will go wrong."

He frowned. Walking into a lion's den was no small thing, and if they were both being honest, that's exactly what he was asking her to do, facing Corbin like this. *Accusing* Corbin like this. He'd seen grown men driven to their knees by fear, and she had every right to buckle now. Yet there she stood without so much as a flinch, willing to face the man who'd threatened her and her father.

"You're a rare one, Maggie Lee," he breathed out.

"So you've told me." Her lips curved into an amused grin. "Several times."

And that was it. The smile. The gleam. The good-natured teasing and willingness to face whatever came her way. Though he'd known her a scant two weeks, deep down, an unstoppable urge to know her more welled up and flew out. "Tell me, when this is over, when I am a free man, would you do me the honor of allowing me to call upon you?"

The request filled the space between them, charging the air with possibility. Horrible timing on his part—but he wasn't repentant. Not one bit.

One of her eyebrows quirked. Other than that, though he tried to read the mystery behind her eyes, her gaze gave nothing away.

"I shall think on that, sir. For now. . ." She pulled back her hand. "God go with you."

And then she was gone, her skirts rustling past him, her feet flying down the busy street.

"God go with us both," he whispered as he peered around the side of the building and watched her disappear into the hotel.

Indeed, Lord. Keep her safe. Make this work.

Time stretched. Too long. Too thin. Each passing carriage that didn't stop was a taunt. Every dark-suited man who bypassed the hotel was a mockery. By now Maggie had surely been seated and served an aperitif. Where was Corbin? Had the sly fox figured out the trap set before him?

Footsteps crunched against gravel in the passage behind him—sort of. It was more like a *step-kick-skitter, step-kick-skitter*. A strange rhythm. An odd sound. Oliver had no choice but to pull his gaze from the street and glance over his shoulder.

Working his way down the narrow throat of the passage, a boy kicked a broken bit of glass as he went, zigzagging wherever the shard landed. The lad's hair—in need of a good clipping—hung like a mop in front of his face, and an oversized coat draped to the boy's knees. Oliver narrowed his eyes. Blast! It was *his* coat—leastwise the one he'd borrowed from Maggie's manservant.

Oliver snapped his head back towards the street and huddled closer to the building. Hopefully the boy wouldn't recognize him. A curious lad tagging at his heels would ruin everything.

Just then a black-lacquered barouche with an ornate gold *C* emblazoned on the door stopped in front of the Royal Station. As if on cue, a footman burst out of the hotel and opened the carriage, standing at stiff attention as a long-legged god in a meticulously tailored dress coat and trousers emerged.

Ambrose Corbin was a flash of elegance, an Adonis that mesmerized, turning the heads of several pedestrians. Wealth clung to him like an aura, as if he bathed in money. Drank it. Breathed it. The sort of man whom those afflicted by hunger and want tried in vain to draw near to, for the slightest touch of his trouser leg might shake loose a penny or two.

Just the sight of him raised bile to the back of Oliver's throat. He planted his feet to keep from tearing after the man. Revenge, hatred, rage, and a host of even baser emotions knotted his muscles until he was a blade—a steely, sharp-edged knife, ready to slice and gut.

"Why, it be you, sir! Thank ye again, for the coat, I mean."

Oliver stared a second longer, until Corbin vanished into the hotel, then he glanced down at the smudge-faced lad peering up at him. "Sorry, boy. I've no time now."

He sidestepped the lad and stalked down the street. Shoving his hand into his pocket, he fingered the velvet pouch containing the jewels. Slipping into the barouche unnoticed to plant the ruby necklace would take some skill, some timing, and a well-placed rock.

He scanned the road and scooped up a broken piece of cobblestone without missing a beat. Angling behind the carriage, he waited, then ducked out as soon as a wagon loaded with barrels rolled along. Then he struck. The rock hit the front lantern of the barouche, shattering the glass—and drawing a mighty roar from the coachman atop. Snatching his whip, the driver swung down to the street, ready for battle with the hapless wagoner.

Now was the time.

While the driver and coachman argued over the damages incurred, Oliver whipped around to the other side of the barouche and made a dash for the door. He yanked it open and—

"Stop right there, Ward!"

His heart froze. So did his breath. That growl was the stuff of nightmares.

Oliver wheeled about. Officer Barrow charged like a bull down the pavement—straight towards him.

God, no. No! He wouldn't go back. He'd *never* go back.

He broke into a dead run, dodging pedestrians, tearing for the gap between buildings. Hot pain shot up his ankle, and his step faltered. A grunt ripped out of him, but he pressed on. Thank God, he pressed on.

Barrow raged not far behind.

Clearing the side of the building, Oliver ducked into the narrow passageway and poured everything he had into a mad sprint. Sweat stung his eyes. His muscles screamed, but not as blindingly painful as his ankle. Still, he couldn't slow. He wouldn't stop, even if he had to run on nothing but bone against gravel. More than his life was on the line this time. He had to shake Barrow. Circle back to Maggie. Wave her off.

If she blamed Corbin of theft and the magistrate found the barouche empty, she'd be gaoled for falsely accusing a member of Parliament.

⌾

I dine with ghosts.

Too many memories fill this room. Light bounces off crystal goblets of wine, and I recall the first sweet taste ever to cross my lips at the table near the window. Men and women talk, smile, laugh—just like my first meeting with my manager in the overstuffed chairs by the entrance. My gaze drifts. The whole of the dining room spreads in front of me where I sit in the corner next to the servants' entrance.

And I thank God that Wendell Groat has not chosen this day to dine and laugh and coerce a potential new patron of the arts.

Sipping a glass of cucumber water, I fight the temptation to close my eyes and revisit Oliver's request, to remember the deep brown-green velvet of his eyes and hear his husky voice asking to call on me when this is all over. The man is becoming far too attractive, in more ways than one.

And that is something I dare not dream possible.

So I toy with the glass stem as I scan from table to table. In truth, I am not familiar with Magistrate Hunter, but there are three potentials who might be him. A gentleman with silver-streaked hair nurses a tumbler in a chair by an overlarge potted plant. Another fellow already spears a piece of meat, so it's probably not him. Or it could be a great ball of a man, waistcoat buttons about to pop, who picks at a fruit bowl, his gaze darting between a cluster of grapes and the door. I follow his line of sight.

And my skin crawls.

Long legs stroll across the threshold. Before I even catch a glimpse of the man's face, my heart pumps dread and fury. I press a hand to my stomach as he struts over to the table by the potted plant and the greying gentleman with the tumbler.

Ambrose Corbin is a tall man, turning the heads of those nearby, and no wonder. His golden hair is stylishly slicked back. His blue eyes startle, so pure and clear. Power drapes over his broad shoulders like a mantle. Everything about him screams success, from his snow-white high collar to the shined-leather tips of his black shoes. He is beautiful. Mesmerizing. An angel one is tempted to worship and fear.

But inside that expensive suit and flawless skin is the heart of a demon.

A flash of hatred burns up from my belly—but not for him. Hating Ambrose Corbin serves no purpose, for even were he to disappear, hundreds of other men could and would easily take his place. It is what he stands for—the lust, greed, and malice—that sickens me. It is not right that he walks free, spreading his poison, while men like Oliver are made to rot away behind bars.

The man with the silver streaks rises at Ambrose's approach. They shake hands. After a few words, a ripple of confusion moves from one man's face to the other. So, they've uncovered the ruse.

Inevitable—but far too soon. I swallow the hard lump of panic in my throat. If Ambrose leaves now, he'll catch Oliver in the act of planting the jewels, exposing him and ultimately me. I can only imagine the furious fit Ambrose would throw. . . And once again I and my father will be in peril.

Thankfully, the magistrate retakes his seat. But my alarm pounds harder with each beat of my heart when Ambrose remains standing.

Slowly, he pivots. His wintry gaze moves from table to table, person to person. In a few breaths, it will land on me. What to do? Dart out the servants' entrance? Duck under the table? Feign a sneeze and hide my face in the napkin?

That's it. I finger the white linen—

And a waiter steps up to my table, blocking my view, but best of all, blocking *me* from view.

Thank You, God.

He stares at me, confusion wrinkling his brow. Then the lines ease. His wide-set eyes flash with thinly veiled adoration. "Pardon me, but I must ask. . . Aren't you Daisy Lee?"

My breath catches, but I glance up at the waiter with what I hope is a pleasant chuckle. "The opera singer? You must be mistaken."

His eyes narrow. "Not likely. I remember all my best patrons, and you were ever the kindest."

Mouth dry, I lick my lips, hoping to coax out words that will deter but are not outright lies. "I am flattered, but I am sorry to disappoint."

His stare is terrible, but finally, he relents and shakes his head. "No, no, it is I who must beg your forgiveness for my boldness, madam. Such an uncanny resemblance, but I see now your hair is different, your eyes not as wide, and I remember Miss Lee wears a beauty mark."

And again, thank You, God, for the wonders of makeup—and the difference without.

"Well, there you have it. I cannot be Miss Lee."

He shuffles uneasily. "Even so, it is not my place to take note. Please, if you wouldn't mind." He leans closer, concern folding his brow. "May we keep this faux pas between ourselves?"

Relief unknots the muscles in my shoulders, and I smile. "I won't breathe a word."

"Thank you." He smiles too. "And may I say that though you are not the great Daisy Lee, you are every bit as gracious and beautiful."

"Thank you."

"Indeed. Well then, are you ready to order?"

I remove the napkin from my lap and place it on the table. "Actually, the water has quite refreshed me. I require nothing more."

"Very well." He dips a bow. "There is only a nominal fee for such a small service. You may settle with the front desk. Good day to you, madam." After a nod and a crisp pivot, he strides through the servants' entrance and the door swings shut behind him.

I duck my head and gaze through my lashes over to the magistrate's table, a combination of dread and hope throbbing in a vein in my temple. I don't want Ambrose to recognize me yet—but neither do I want him to quit the dining room.

He sits like a king on a throne across from the magistrate. Apparently he's decided to stay for lunch despite the ambiguity of the invitation.

I finish off the rest of my drink, gauging the time, minding the minutes. Surely by now Oliver has tucked the ruby necklace into Ambrose's carriage, but has he gotten far enough away? I wait a bit longer, then rise on shaky legs. As always before I give a performance, I inhale deeply and slowly blow out all the tension. Then I lift my chin.

It's now or never.

Chapter Twenty

It didn't matter what he ran from—the past, the present, a crazed prison constable fixed on dragging him back to a rat hole. Running was always the same, whatever the motivation. Oliver's head and heart pounded, breathing was a chore, and worst of all, he never quite knew what the outcome would be.

"Stop!"

Barrow's roar thundered like a cannonball down the narrow passage. Oliver didn't dare glance over his shoulder to judge the distance between them.

Instead, he pumped his legs all the harder, slipping once when his shoe hit a patch of rotting lettuce. Flailing his arms, he barely prevented himself from falling headlong. Sweat trickled into his eyes. Stung. Fire burned in his lungs, his thighs, his ill-healed ankle. Yet he pressed on.

No one in their right mind stopped for a hellhound.

Ahead, where the passageway opened onto another lane, a boy in bunched-up sleeves on a sack coat far too large for him turned. The whites of his eyes shot wide. No wonder. In a few breaths, Oliver would plow him into the gravel. To the boy's credit, he spun and tore off. Smart lad—especially since Barrow wouldn't have stopped for him either, and that menace raged all the louder behind Oliver.

"This ends now, Ward!"

So did the passage.

Oliver bolted into the next road, wildly glancing to the right and left. Which was the best escape route? Was there a place to hide? The lane was impossibly narrow. An old mews. Blast! A crowded street would've been a better place to vanish in plain sight.

"Go!" The boy yelled. A horse whip cracked. "Walk on!"

Oliver whirled. Behind him, parked at the edge of the opening, the boy urged a swaybacked mare hitched to a heaping manure cart into motion. The big wheels rolled. The cart jolted. Dung fell to the pavement. With another crack to the rump and a tug on the horse's headstall, the boy coaxed the workhorse to the mouth of the passageway and stopped when the big cart blocked it.

"Move this wagon!" Barrow blasted shocking oaths from behind the noxious load.

The boy scrambled away, waving towards Oliver with the whip. "Come on!"

He broke into a sprint. It wouldn't take long for Barrow to scale that load of horse droppings, and he'd be all the more furious because of it.

Halfway down the block, the boy swung aside and jumped down a short flight of stairs. So did Oliver, taking care to land on his good foot first. The lad dropped the whip and yanked open the rear door to the hotel, then darted inside. Oliver followed and was instantly hit with heat from a working kitchen.

A white-aproned mistress with a broad backside stood across the room, bent over a cauldron of some sort of savory broth. Two scullery maids glanced up from chopping carrots at a big table, brows raised. Oliver flashed them a smile and picked up a nearby crate, as if he were on an errand to deliver it somewhere else in the establishment. As soon as they lowered their faces to work, he set the crate down and tugged the boy into a corridor near the stairs. Perfect. This reprieve from Barrow gave him much-needed time to warn Maggie to abandon her mission—*if* it wasn't already too late.

But how?

He squatted to face the boy, hoping to come up with something that might work. "Thanks for your diversion out there. Now I need you to—"

"No vagrants in the kitchen!"

Thunderation! Must everything be against him today?

Summoning his fast-talking skills, honed from years of arguing with his father and politicians, Oliver rose and pivoted, facing a stern-jawed waiter with an impressive glower. He forced a pleasant smile and a small laugh.

"Ho ho! But you are mistaken, my good man. This boy here is helping me out of a sticky female situation. You see. . ." He leaned closer, as if he and the servant were long-lost friends, used to sharing the utmost confidences. "There are two women in the dining room, one I've barely escaped from and the other I'd like to escape with. Perhaps you've seen who I'm talking about? She's of yea height." Lifting his hand, he indicated Maggie's stature. "Has brown hair and eyes of a most striking hue, and she looks uncannily like the opera star Daisy Lee."

The waiter squinted, taking measure of Oliver. Not good. He could look no better than a dog's dinner, sweat stained and disheveled thanks to Barrow. Even so, Oliver lifted his chin. Would to God the man might lend a sympathetic ear despite his appearance. And quickly.

Please, God, for Maggie's sake.

"Yes, I've seen her," the waiter finally drawled. "What of her?"

"We were to meet for a tryst until I was found out. Any chance you could snag her for me? Let her know Oliver awaits and bring her down here so we can slip out undetected? I'd be ever so grateful, and there will be a coin in it for you. Maybe two. I was going to send in the boy here, but will you help?"

"I cannot—"

"Please." Oliver gripped his arm. "Time is of the utmost importance. I would spare that sweet lady from facing the wrath of the woman who thinks she owns me. You don't want a catfight on your hands in the dining room, do you? Bad for business. Bad for you." He inclined his head and lowered his voice. "Bad for us all."

Oliver released the man's sleeve and retreated a step, giving him space and time to consider the request, but hopefully not too much. If Maggie had made her move already, he'd have no choice but to come out in the open with the necklace and try to persuade the magistrate she'd been an innocent dupe in this failed scheme.

The waiter stood silent, lips pinching, looking from him to the boy and back again. Perspiration trickled between Oliver's shoulder blades. This was taking way too long.

"Very well. But if this is some sort of skullduggery, I'll see the two of you arrested." The man's words dangled in the air like a hangman's noose as he wheeled about and ascended the stairs. A tug on Oliver's sleeve drew his gaze away from the man's long legs.

"There a coin in it fer me too, sir?"

A shameless request, but all the same Oliver's heart squeezed. The boy's hollow cheeks and hungry gaze proved testament enough to his need.

"Yes, lad. I'm sure that can be arranged."

Minutes later, skirts rustled at the top of the stair and Maggie came into view, curiosity, worry, fear, and relief following one right after the other in the flash of her eyes.

At the landing, the waiter stayed her with a touch to the arm and tipped his head towards Oliver. "There, do you know that gentleman? Do you wish to leave with him?"

"Yes. Thank you, I—"

The words were hardly past her lips when Oliver rushed to her and pulled her into his arms. "Darling!" He spoke for all to hear, then whispered for her alone, "Sorry for the charade, but pay the man a coin."

He held his breath. It was a gamble, this bold move. Would she slap him for such an intimate advance? Wrench away and ruin his ruse?

"I thought you'd never come," she purred just loud enough for the waiter to hear. Without batting an eyelash, she sweetly kissed Oliver's cheek.

And the touch of her lips nearly drove him to his knees.

She pulled away, fumbling with the strings of her reticule, and retrieved several pieces of silver. On an open palm, she offered them to the servant with a brilliant smile. "For your trouble *and* your silence."

He dipped a bow and, doing so, swiped the money from her hand in one fluid movement. "Thank you, madam. But I suggest you both make haste. If Cook discovers you, you'll have more than one angry woman on your heels. Good day." After a quick nod, he bypassed them and strode down the corridor towards what was likely the hotel's wine cellar.

As soon as he was out of hearing range, Maggie turned to Oliver. "What happened? I'd just risen from my seat when the waiter told me you were down here."

"Thank God he got to you when he did, but there's no time to explain. The boy and I—" He swept his fingers towards the lad, only to swipe thin air. The boy was gone. But without his coin? Strange, that.

He reached for Maggie's hand. "Come on."

They dashed towards the kitchen—only to see the lad at the back door, motioning for them to follow. The scullery maids once again watched silently.

Not the cook. As soon as she caught their movement, she wielded a soup ladle like a sword. "Out! I'll put ye all to work—or worse!"

The boy scampered off first, Oliver and Maggie not far behind. But at the top of the stairs, at street level, the lad paused, his head turning one way then another.

"What do you see?" Oliver breathed out.

"That man, the big one what was chasing you."

Oliver swallowed. Would Barrow never quit? "Where is he?"

"Here," he whispered.

Oliver's heart stopped. Maggie's fingers turned icy in his. They all inched back down the stairway then flattened against the wall. One downward look from the constable and they'd—

"Constable!" Footsteps pounded, drawing closer. "Come and see. My whip's been stolen."

"I've not the time for—"

"Oy! What a stink! You smell like my load. Say. . . Don't tell me you're the one what's been mucking about with my horse and cart. T'aint proper, even for an officer o' the law. Come along now and set things aright!"

"That was your cart?" Barrow gruffed. "Why, I ought to haul your sorry carcass in for blocking the lane!"

While the two raged on, the boy edged up the stairway, too quickly for Oliver to yank him back. If the lad gave them away. . .

Oliver watched, trepidation pounding like a hammer in his head. Maggie gripped his hand all the tighter.

But as the voices barked louder, becoming more heated, the lad crooked his finger, beckoning them to follow.

Should they?

It was either that or remain at the mercy of one backward glance from Barrow. Slowly, painstakingly quiet, Oliver led Maggie up the stairs, easing one foot in front of the other. When his head was street level, he saw the heels of Barrow's beat-up boots, two—maybe three—yards to his right. His back was to the stairway, his arms flapping in the air, making some kind of boisterous threat against the hapless manure collector. This close, it would be a hazard and a miracle to sneak off unnoticed. But the boy was already a good measure down the lane, his hand cutting through the air for them to follow.

Oliver glanced at Maggie. Grim-faced, she nodded.

They padded up the rest of the stairs and quick-stepped it to the boy, then they all broke into a run.

God was gracious. God was gracious indeed!

But just as they made it to the corner, a roar ripped out of Barrow. "You can't run forever, Ward. Stop now!"

Oliver handed Maggie off to the boy. "Take the lady to Avon Street."

Maggie yanked her hand from the lad's and faced him. "But—"

"Go! I'll lose Barrow and meet you there."

Barrow's boots thudded hard against the cobbles, growing louder with every step. Oliver whipped about and tore off.

Running. Again.

And he still didn't know what the outcome would be.

⟨∞⟩

It is curious how squalor can feel like safety. But as the boy and I turn onto Avon Street, I welcome the choked passageways and shadowed nooks—and pray that Oliver will soon find sanctuary here as well. The alternative is far worse than a few nights in a slum.

"Here ye be, miss."

The boy peers at me, face smudged, ridiculous coat sleeves bunched up on rail-thin arms, making him look like nothing but a collection of bones and dirt. I pull out one of my few remaining coins and stoop to his level.

"Thank you for your help, my good man. If it is not too forward, may I know your name?"

A gap-toothed grin widens on his face as he pockets my offering. "It's Bodger, miss. But you can call me Bodge. I reckon you and yer man are my friends now, eh? What with the coat and the coin."

"Oh, he's not really my. . ." I clear my throat. Explaining the relationship between Oliver and me is no small task, and certainly not one for a young boy's ears.

"Yes, Bodge." I return his smile. "We are friends, and I thank you for leading me here. Now, being that we are companions of sorts, would you mind going to see if you can aid Mr. Ward in any way? It is a very bad man who is chasing him."

"Aye, I knows he is." Bodge rubs his cheek with the back of his hand, then whisks about and takes off. "See what I can do, miss!"

Gathering my hem, I sidestep all manner of refuse until I finally reach the door of the small room that's been my haven these past two days. I am grateful for the anonymous lodging where no one will think to look for me, but oh how I miss Morden Hall.

I unlock the latch, dart inside, then shove the door shut behind me. Fumbling with the ties of my bonnet, I cannot help but wonder—and worry—about Oliver's safety. There's nothing I can do but pray—

"You've been a very naughty girl, Daisy Lee."

A low voice behind me clicks out each word. It's a prominent sort of lisp. Unnerving in the way each word cracks like the crunch of a foot upon a beetle. My stomach drops, and I whirl. Wendell Groat's skinny legs stretch out from the shadows like a cockroach from a crevice.

I lean against the table, gripping its edge for support. "Mr. Groat, I . . ."

My excuse balls into a great lump in my throat. Truly, what can I say other than I am guilty of forsaking my contract?

"You know what happens to naughty girls, don't you?" A slow smile bares his teeth—all yellowish and somewhat pointy—which is more unnerving than his question. Only two things give this man such pleasure—profit and the anticipation that animates him right before a strike.

My stomach heaves as I calculate the distance between him and the door. Though the room is small, there is no way I can rush past him without his long arm snagging me.

I grip the wooden edge all the tighter. "You don't understand. I *had* to run. I had to flee. There was no time. It wasn't safe for me to get word to you."

"You think I care about your safety?" He advances a step, chuckling. Then all mirth fades and he stares at me with vacant eyes. A corpse couldn't look more dead.

"What I care about," he clicks, "is money."

"I—I know I wronged you. I have cost you ticket sales, appearance fees, and—"

A slap rings out. My head jerks aside, face stinging. Something warm oozes from the side of my mouth. The table wobbles as I stagger, then I let go completely and wipe away the blood.

Mr. Groat stands eerily still, as if he's not moved a muscle.

"Where is the necklace?"

I blink, dazed, pressing my cool fingers against my hot skin. "What?"

"Don't play the part of the dullard. It ill becomes you." The sides of his mouth pull down, carving a great half circle on the bottom part of his face. "Where are the jewels you stole the night of Corbin's party? I will have those rubies, and I will have them now."

I breathe deeply and lower my hand, desperately trying to make sense of why we are speaking of a necklace when we should be discussing my broken contract. "But those jewels are Mrs. Corbin's."

"They are mine."

"Yours? But..." Sudden understanding hits me as hard as his slap. "It was you? *You're* the one who swapped the necklaces? I thought Ambrose Corbin was to blame."

Mr. Groat's dark eyes blacken to two shiny shells. "Ambrose Corbin is a leech. A bloodsucker. A parasite who attaches himself to opportunity that is not of his own making."

"You're both tangled up in this?" I shake my head, then think better of it when the movement throbs in my temple. "How?"

"You always have been a little fool, hmm? Still, a very pretty fool at that." Mr. Groat closes the small distance between us, reaching out so that his finger snags a piece of my hair. He rubs it between his thumb and forefinger.

I daren't move.

"I arrived along with your trunk at the Corbin estate on the morning of your last performance. Bribing a disgruntled second footman for his livery was no problem. In fact, there would've been no problem at all had Corbin not discovered me in his wife's chamber as I traded the necklaces." He rubs my hair a moment more, then leans in close to smell it. When he exhales, his breath is hot against my neck.

My virtue is not in danger—and never has been with this man—but even so, fear breaks out in fine beads of perspiration on my brow. My manager harms in other ways...ways that leave permanent marks.

He pulls back and drops his hand. "Were it not for my quick

thinking and business savvy, I'd have been hauled in then and there. As it was, we cut a deal, Corbin and I. I was to sell the jewels off-market, and he was to get forty percent. He'd collect the insurance money, and in return I would remain silent. It was a larger profit for him but even at sixty percent, a tidy sum would be in my pocket and I'd have avoided a visit to Newgate...until you ran off with that necklace. Tell me, how did you know the one you wore was real? There was no way you could have unless..."

He steps toe to toe, nose to nose, his black eyes boring into mine. He smells of dirt, fungus, things that rot in the dark. "You didn't know, did you? Always the naive little lamb, eh?"

He chuckles, and tiny flecks of spittle coat my cheeks. I stiffen at the affront. He's right. Though I'd had no control over the first contract signed years ago by my father, I never should've signed the second when I'd come of age. La! I'd been more than naive. I'd been a stupid girl duped by this man's promises of security and wealth.

"Well, I suppose it's worked out for the good." Once again, he fingers my hair, this time tucking it behind my ear. His touch is unnaturally cold against my skin. "Corbin need never know about this little meeting. Now I may sell that piece and keep the entire yield to myself. So, hand it over."

I hardly dare breathe. He won't like what I have to say. "I don't have it," I whisper.

He clucks his tongue, the noise overloud in the tiny room. His finger probes from my ear down to my neck. All my blood drains to my feet, especially when he steps back and skewers me with a cool stare.

Ever so slowly, he pulls out a thin knife from inside his dress coat. No, I am wrong. It is a five-inch ice pick. My eyes instantly water. Old Graves, the set carpenter, has worked with an eye patch since his run-in with the same instrument.

"Give me that necklace before I split more than your lip."

I inch back—but there's nowhere to go. The table cuts into the back of my thighs. "I don't have it here." My voice shakes, and I swallow, summoning my stage persona. Fear will only entice him. "But I know where the jewels are, so if you kill me, I'll take that information to the grave."

"Kill you? Don't be droll." He flips the ice pick around—and around—his gaze following the circular movement. Then grips the handle, lifting it high. "Well? Where is it?"

"I'll get it to you if you don't hurt me. Two days. Give me two days and I'll meet you at noon at the Circus lawn. I'll hand it over there and then."

The lie tastes as nasty as the bile that's risen in my throat.

The ice pick hovers. Mr. Groat stares me down. Then tucks the weapon back inside his coat.

And smiles.

"All right. But do not think to inform the authorities, bring anyone along, or disappear altogether. I've found you once." He backhands me again, so hard my ears ring. "Next time I will not be so lenient."

Chapter Twenty-One

Winded, but blessedly free of Barrow, Oliver limp-trotted back to Avon Street. Thanks to an impromptu fishwife riot over some highly priced pikes and zanders in Market Lane, he'd lost the man. But even so, he glanced over his shoulder. A few scapegallows and chancers peered at him from doorway shadows as he passed, but in the slum, that was to be expected. At least no raging bull of a constable out for blood charged after him.

The tension in his shoulders slackened, and Oliver even allowed a small smile. It'd been a close one today. Ahh, but Jarney should've seen ol' Barrow covered in horse dung, garnering shouts and curses as he raced along. What a laugh they'd have shared—and still would, God willing, *if* Jarney could hold on to life until he returned for him.

But first he'd have to figure out a new plan to snare Corbin.

"Maggie?" Oliver tapped on the door a moment before opening it wide and slipping inside. "I've lost him. I've lost Barrow."

With her back towards him, she rose from where she'd been kneeling on the pallet bed, apparently praying. Dare he hope—for him? The thought did strange things to his heart.

She turned, pressing both hands to her stomach. "Thank God you're safe!"

So she *had* been fretting about him. A good-natured reply launched to his tongue, then turned to ash as his gaze landed on an angry red mark marring her cheek. Her bottom lip swelled on the same side, and her eyes were glassy from spent tears. Oliver's gut lurched as an ugly realization elbowed its way in.

She'd been hit. Hard.

In three strides, he pulled her into his arms, wildly searching her face for any further abrasions. Whoever had done this would pay dearly. He'd see to that bit of justice, Barrow on his tail or not.

"What happened?"

She winced, and no wonder. The fierce snarl that ripped from him would make a bear back down.

"My manager was here." Her voice shook slightly, but she held his gaze.

"*He* hurt you?" Oliver wheeled about, retracing his route to the door and yanking it open. Outside, the world was scarlet, shaded by such a hot rage he had to blink.

"Where is he?" he growled back at Maggie. "The theatre? Is that where the coward scuttled off to after hitting a defenseless woman?"

"Oliver, please." Her feet padded softly, her touch on his arm but a feather. "Tracking down Mr. Groat will do you no good. Do not waste the time. We need a new plan, one that includes him *and* Corbin."

Of course he had a plan—one that involved meting out justice at the end of his fist. But. . . He angled his head. What the devil did Groat have to do with Corbin? "What do you mean?"

"Come inside. We'll draw attention." Her fingers pressed into his sleeve, guiding him away from the door and gently closing it behind them.

Huffing a breath, he allowed her to lead him to the two half barrels near the ramshackle table. She was right. Avon Street had ears big enough to spread scandal faster than an oil fire.

Maggie straightened her skirts, then breathed a sigh. "Ambrose Corbin is not fully to blame for the theft of the jewels. Mr. Groat was in on it as well. It fact, it was his idea. He exchanged the necklaces on the morning of my performance, shortly after my trunk had been delivered to the Corbin estate, but Mr. Corbin caught him in the act. After some silver-tongued bartering on Mr. Groat's part, they ended up trading silences. Mr. Corbin would say nothing of the swapping as long as he was paid forty percent of the value when Mr. Groat sold the necklace. In return, Mr. Groat agreed to keep mum about the insurance money that Mr. Corbin would acquire illegally. Both would profit, and as long as they kept their pact, neither would go to gaol."

"Yet *I* rotted in a cell for nine months?" Slamming the table with his fist, Oliver shot to his feet and paced the tiny room, his pulse a primal drumbeat in his ears. Two men knowingly ruined his reputation, sent him to what could have been his death, and all for the sake of some coins in their pockets? "Blast!"

Maggie stiffened—and the sight cut straight to his heart. He'd frightened her. What a beast. Had she not suffered enough terror for one day?

He inhaled so deeply that his ribs ached, then slowly blew it out and resumed his seat. "Forgive me. I fear my manners are still fettered in Dartmoor Prison. Even so, I vow to contain myself for your sake. Now, tell me." He leaned back on the barrel and folded his arms. "How did Groat find you? Did he spy you and the boy on the streets? Were you followed here?"

"No. He. . ." She pressed her lips together, her gaze drifting past him to a shadowy corner of the room. "He was here when I arrived."

The news hit him like a hammer. If Groat knew where they lodged, it would be only a matter of time before Barrow found out—a very short time. Shoving away from the table, he once again took up pacing. They couldn't stay here, that much was clear. But where to go? Take the risk of calling on some of his friends, see if they would shelter two fugitives? Spend whatever money Maggie had left in her purse to hole up in a nondescript inn somewhere? Go rough and hunker beneath a bridge?

He tugged at his collar, desperate for air. None of those would work. Nothing would, not with Barrow and Groat on the prowl. No, they'd have to stay somewhere where those two bloodhounds would fear to tread. A place too dangerous to risk entering.

Oliver grimaced as the seed of a horribly perfect idea took root and grew—and the thought of it nearly doubled him over. There was only one refuge possible to hold the two at bay.

"Pack your belongings," he spat out before he changed his mind. "We leave at once."

"Where are we going?" She rose, hands flopping out at her sides. "There is no place to hide. Mr. Groat will stop at nothing to get that necklace back. And your Mr. Barrow is clearly not going to give up easily."

"True, but neither would dare trespass on the property of the most powerful barrister in Bath."

Maggie shook her head, clearly not convinced. "It is a very big assumption that either of them would personally be acquainted with some bigwig barrister."

"A man in Groat's position, with connections to society, would no doubt be familiar with the Hawk of Crown Court. And if Barrow isn't, Groat is sure to educate him."

"But you are a convict on the run, and I am still wanted for breach of contract. How will you convince a mighty man of the law to provide us shelter instead of tossing us both in gaol?"

Oliver gritted his teeth, hating that the only alternative was the one that would gut him more thoroughly than Barrow ever could.

"Because that barrister is my father."

∞

As the cab judders along a lane leading out of town, I swallow a wave of sickness. What a day. Mr. Groat. Mr. Barrow. Both seep in everywhere, slip through cracks, ooze into thin spaces where they are not wanted. Like a rising river unleashed from its banks, they seem completely unstoppable. Will Oliver's father truly be able to help us? And if so, why did we not go sooner?

I glance at Oliver. He sits silent, hands clenched on his thighs, head turned and staring out the window. The only thing carefree about him at the moment is the sweep of dark hair that grazes his collar. What will his father think of this shaggy-headed man? Will he even recognize him?

"Has it been very long since you last spoke with your father?" My question bounces in rhythm with the jiggling carriage wheels.

"Years," he murmurs.

Years? I huff out a breath, both from surprise and a particularly deep rut that dips the side of the coach. Clearly his brooding silence is valid. What does one say to a loved one after such a long void? My own heart squeezes at the prospect. Considering the circumstances, this will be no easy reunion.

"Well, then. . ." I infuse my voice with a lightness I don't truly feel. "I imagine your father should be happy to hear from you."

A snort rips out of him and he faces me, staring as if I'm a lunatic fresh from a ward at Bedlam. "Happy?" His voice strangles. "I wouldn't count on it."

Sadness lurks deep in that brown-green gaze, as if a little boy looks out from within, heartsick and needy. I have no idea what's transpired between the two in the past, what hurts fester, what wounds still bleed. But heedless of scars or resentment or hostility, deep down every son craves the love of his father—whether he admits to it or not.

I lay my hand on his shirtsleeve and press in what I pray he'll take as compassion. "People change, Oliver. Time can soften the hardest of hearts." It's an old adage, but heartily true. It took years to soften my bitterness towards my father.

He shakes his head, a raw chuckle in his throat grinding as harsh as the turn of the wheels. "I appreciate you wanting to make this easier, but truly, no amount of placating sentiments will make the situation any better. I shall just have to grit my teeth and get through it."

"Well, as long as you're gritting. . ." I sigh and pull back my hand. Averting my gaze, I finger the hem of my sleeve. Since there is no cheering him, I might as well let him know we have but two days to resolve the rift with his father and all our problems before I must meet with Mr. Groat. "I suppose now is as good a time as any to tell you."

"Tell me what?" His tone is deadly.

I pick at a thread, stalling. Perhaps this wasn't the best occasion to inform him after all, but it's too late now. "I—" I clear my throat and try again. "I promised Mr. Groat I would meet with him in two days to hand over the necklace."

"You what?"

The question slaps the air, as stinging as Mr. Groat's strike to my cheek. Oh, why have I come? I should've stayed at Morden Hall. Let Oliver manage everything. Yet deep in my soul I know that wouldn't have worked either.

My fingernail moves from thread to thread. Sucking in a breath for courage, I lift my face and hold Oliver's incredulous gaze. "I'm sorry. It couldn't be helped. Mr. Groat left me no choice."

His lips flatten into a hard-edged grimace. Reaching sideways, he stills my frantic picking, then blows out a long breath. "It seems we are both out of options at the moment." He squeezes my hand, then pulls back. "Don't worry. I'll think of something. You will not have to meet with that monster ever again."

The protective edge to his words releases a surge of warmth through me, but even so, I look away. I'm not sure what to do with this foreign feeling. It excites. It comforts and thrills. And it completely upends everything I've come to believe about men. Oliver Ward cares deeply about others—about *me*—and with no apparent expectation of a return for that compassion. It is too unsettling to consider, for to believe such a love exists, I would have to tear down the wall I've built to hide behind. And then I would be vulnerable—something I vowed never to be the day my father signed me over to Mr. Groat. That betrayal lived on in the young girl part of my heart, forgiven but not forgotten.

We roll through ornate wrought-iron gates, and my eyes catch a glimmer of a gilded *W* worked into the pattern. The road curves and a limestone manor looms larger as we near it. Wisteria climbs in green-frosted glory against the sand-coloured backdrop, its buds still tiny clusters but its vines embracing the two stories with the promise of beauty to come. Quite the contrast to the hovel on Avon Street.

Moments later, the coachman halts the horses beneath a front portico, and I descend onto a crushed shell drive and pay off the driver. Oliver leads me to the door and rings the bell. Tension radiates off him as we wait. His jaw clenches tight. So do his hands. He stares at the door as if it's a mountain to climb, one that could take his life.

A tall man in somber black livery appears. His dark hair is shot through with silver, his blue eyes are faded, and little creases crimp the skin near his temples. He is the quintessential butler, wearing his years as stalwartly as his pressed suit. I have no doubt he is as much a fixture in this home as the marble pillars or cut-glass chandelier in the hall behind him. Servants this imposing are the envy of any wealthy gentleman or lady. I creep back a step.

Oliver advances. "Foster." He gives the man a curt nod. "Is my father available?"

The man's mouth opens, then as suddenly closes. Emotion flashes in his eyes so briefly, it is hard to name it. Surprise, certainly, but something more. Sorrow? Anger? Sympathy?

"My pardon, Mr. Oliver." He dips a bow. "But the barrister is out at the moment. Would you care to wait?"

"Yes," Oliver answers without pause.

Foster leads us into a museum. Thick Turkish rugs cover the floor. Alabaster sculptures tastefully line the walls. Cherubs on pedestals. Grecian urns and Roman profiles. And at center of the grand space, right in front of a carved staircase, is a statue of a Virgilian mother, her young son beholding her with adoration. A shiver wriggles across my shoulders as we pass the symbol of familial love. Knowing what little I do of Oliver and his father, it is a stunning hypocrisy.

After depositing us in a sitting room, Foster leaves on silent feet. Oliver immediately stalks to the window and stares out as if he desires to leave already. Is he second-guessing his decision to come without even giving his father a chance?

No matter. We are here.

I wander the elegant space, running a finger along the mahogany back of a velvet-cushioned sofa. A black lacquer mantel clock ticks away our lives, one second at a time. My gaze drifts upward. Overhead, the plasterwork on the ceiling is an intricate design of palm fronds, rose petals, and intertwined vines, all tipped with gold paint. The whole room smells of lemon oil and beeswax. Not one vase or freshly cut flower is out of place. I've admired many opulent homes over the course of the years, but this one has its own special charm. What would it have been like to grow up here?

"It is a beautiful home," I think aloud.

"It is a beautiful cage."

I blink, taken aback, then angle my head. "What do you mean?"

"Had I become the man my father wished, taken on his mantle of representing none but the rich and privileged, I'd have been trapped here, locked in the chains of status and wealth." The words are low, monotone, as if he speaks to no one but himself. Finally, he turns from the glass and skewers me with a direct gaze. "Tell me, could you really live in a house such as this now that you've experienced abject poverty, known firsthand the deprivations and prejudice directed towards the poor?"

The raging bitterness in his voice steals my breath—a resentment I'm not sure I understand. I've lived in both humble and privileged circumstances, and each holds its own peculiarities. "In a way," I soften my tone, hoping to soothe whatever piques him so, "the wealthy suffer their own deprivations and prejudice, do they not?"

"Not to the point of starvation and death." The words are throaty, passionate—and altogether curious. This vehemence against his own roots burns like fire in his eyes. And then it hits me. He is proud—pleased, even—to cast aside where he's come from. . .to shun the family God placed him in simply because of its prosperity.

"I appreciate your compassion for the poor, Oliver. I really do. But I fear you judge the wealthy too harshly. Not all who are rich are self-centered moneymongers, just as not all who are poor are virtuous. Having lived amongst both the rich and the needy, I find it is the heart of the person that makes the man, not the amount of coin in his pocket."

His nostrils flare, and a muscle on his neck stands out like a cord.

I bite my lip. I've said too much. Pushed him at a time when he's already anxious about an audience with his father. I bow my head. "Forgive me if I've spoken too—"

His hand shoots up, cutting me off. "No need. You've spoken as a true diplomat, and your candor is refreshing. If I didn't know any better, I'd suspect you were trying to change my mind on the matter."

A small smile quirks my lips. "Is that such a bad thing?"

His hazel eyes give no hint of what he's thinking. Bypassing me, he crosses to a table in the corner and holds up a decanter. "Would you like a drink?"

"No, thank you." While he pours, I go back to wandering the room, then pause at the far end. An enormous painting hangs on the wall, and the longer I stare at the pepper-haired gentleman in a flowing black robe, the more my jaw drops. Why did I not notice this when I first entered? The green flecks flashing in brown eyes. The full lips. Granted, wrinkles crease the face of the man in the portrait and the nose is all wrong—much too distinctively hawk-like—but take away several decades, and I'd be staring at Oliver.

Narrowing my eyes, I look closer. Unspeakable power tilts his head, demanding attention, allegiance, full cooperation. I am naked before that gaze, as if he sees past my facade and beckons my soul to follow wherever he leads. He is a man not to be trifled with, one of intelligence and strong opinions. The hooked beak of his nose makes me feel as if I am but a mouse and he a raptor on the prowl.

Footsteps stop at my side, but I am too mesmerized to look away. "He looks rather formidable," I breathe. "Quite like—"

"Like an overbearing tyrant?"

"No." I turn away and smile at Oliver. "I was going to say like you."

"Oh?" His brows lift. "You think me formidable, do you?"

My grin grows. "I might have been cowed by you had you not come to me unconscious and bleeding."

"Yes, well. . ." He glances up at the portrait, and a black scowl darkens his brow. "I assure you I've made it a point to be *nothing* like my father." His words ring out, almost as loud as those that barrel in from the sitting room door.

"A pity, that, for you would not be in such a snarl of trouble right now if you were, hmm?"

Chapter Twenty-Two

The barrister strode into the room, and immediately Oliver stiffened. With one sweeping glance, his father's sharp green gaze calculated and stored information—information that could and would later be used against him. It always was.

"Father." Oliver bowed out of respect for the barrister's position, nothing more.

His father dipped his head in a curt nod. "Oliver."

Deep lines spidered out from the corners of his eyes. His hair, once black as jet, was now the colour of sun-bleached bones. His lips were thinner, the skin above his cravat wrinkled like a walnut, and there was a new slight bend to his shoulders—none of which made the man any less imposing. If anything, the years added more of an imperial tilt to his head.

"I would be lying if I did not admit surprise at seeing you." The barrister's face knotted into a scowl, his mouth a blade, cutting without further words. But as his gaze drifted to Maggie, his glower softened to a near smile. "I see you have not come alone."

Oliver reached towards her, stopping short of resting his hand on the small of her back, suddenly unsure of what she might think of such a show of possession. "Father, allow me to introduce Miss—"

"Daisy Lee." The barrister bowed over her hand with a gallant kiss to her fingers. "Your reputation precedes you, my dear. It is a pleasure to meet you."

She shot Oliver a glance, uncertainty quirking her brow, then broke into a smile and curtseyed, as if his father were nothing but an audience to woo. "The pleasure is mine, Mr. Ward."

"Please, have a seat." He swept his hand towards the sofa. "I hope my son has not been negligent in his hospitality." Looking past her shoulder, he frowned at Oliver, little folds of disapproval creasing the sides of his mouth.

"On the contrary. He's been nothing but a gentleman." Maggie's sweet voice filled the room, expanding to fill his heart. Was it her dulcet tone that flared heat in his chest or her stalwart defense of his character?

"I am happy to hear it. Shall we?" Quick to offer his arm, the barrister led Maggie to the sofa before Oliver could draw another breath.

He followed the pair, stifling a grudging gratitude when his father took the seat adjacent and left the cushion next to Maggie open for him. Once they were seated, the barrister's dark green eyes bored into him, imperial and disturbing. The man could see things, look beyond words, cast aside the inconsequential and expose the truth for what it was. A trait Oliver had inherited—yet one he abhorred when turned back on himself.

His mouth dried to bones, and he shifted uneasily. Sweet heavens! He could argue for days on end against his most prestigious opponents when it came to legislation. He could even tongue-wag the Speaker of the House into a corner without breaking a sweat. But here? Now? Suddenly he was a little boy again, unsure of himself, even though he knew he was in the right. Must it always be like this with his father?

"As I said, this is quite unexpected." His father ran his hand along the chair's arm as he spoke. "I had not heard you were released from Dartmoor."

"I wasn't."

"I see." His hand stopped, the abrupt stillness jarring. One side of his mouth curved into a sharp smile, like a hook floating in the water, waiting to snag an unwitting pike.

Oliver's gut clenched. The man was trolling for an opportunity to spear him through the heart. "No, Father, you don't see. You never have."

"Excuse me." Maggie edged forward on the cushion, blocking his view of his father. "But I think what your son would like to say, sir, is that despite past misunderstandings, he—*we*—need your help."

"Thank you for the clarification, Miss Lee. What kind of help, exactly, are you both hoping I might provide?"

Oliver snorted. A lawful inquiry could never be fully considered without a proper presentation of context, and his father was ever a stickler for details.

Oliver shoved to his feet, paced behind the sofa, and—hands clenched at his back—faced his father. "First, I think a little background is in order. Despite what you think of me, I did not steal the jewels for which I was accused. Miss Lee and I have proof—verbal—that Ambrose Corbin and Wendell Groat are the true criminals. They swapped Mrs. Corbin's ruby necklace with a paste replica, intending to sell the real gems. They expected to secret away not only the funds from that illegal sale but the insurance payout as well. Things didn't go as originally planned, yet Corbin—ever the opportunist—managed to charge me with theft and pocket the insurance money."

His father's eyes narrowed. "How do you know all this?"

"Mr. Groat said as much to Miss Lee—when he attacked her."

His father turned to Maggie. "Is this true, Miss Lee?"

"Yes."

For a moment, his father said nothing as he studied her face in silence, his gaze lingering at the slight swelling near the corner of her mouth. "So then, tell me." His voice deepened into his official barrister tone, the sort that pulled truth from criminals with nothing but its baritone boom. "Why would Mr. Groat threaten you so severely?"

"Because, I. . ." Maggie shifted on the seat, skirts rustling, like a bird who knew her wing was broken yet tried to hide it from a predator. "It is I who has the missing necklace."

"You?" Humourless laughter rumbled from his father's lips. "This just keeps getting better and better."

Of all the callous responses! Biting back a retort, Oliver side-stepped to stand directly behind Maggie, hoping to impart reassurance. "Miss Lee has been through quite enough today without your derision, Father."

One of his father's brows lifted. "Of course. My apologies, Miss Lee."

"No offense taken, sir."

Leaning back in his seat, his father folded his arms and once again skewered Oliver with a pointed look. "Well, Son, I must repeat, what is it you are hoping I can do for you and Miss Lee?"

Oliver pulled away from Maggie and paced the length of the sofa, then back again, fighting against unbidden memories. Once, shortly after his mother had died, before he knew better than to bare his soul to the barrister, he'd asked his father to defend the father of one of his friends from school. But the boy was from a lowly background, depending upon a scholarship for his education, not the sort of class with whom they associated. The barrister had refused to lend his legal aid, and the boy's father was transported. The scandal forced the school to withdraw his friend's funding, and the boy ended up in the workhouse with his mother. Both died within a matter of months. If only his father had helped the man, helped the boy, given more care to a request from his own son rather than societal strata.

Grinding his teeth, Oliver shoved down the black memory. Seeking his father, asking for his help, was a fool's errand. If the barrister wouldn't listen to a tearstained entreaty for justice from a ten-year-old, why should he heed an escaped convict?

Maggie's head lifted. Her big brown eyes gazed up at him, waiting.

He huffed a sigh. For her sake, he had to ask. There were no other options. He stopped and planted his feet. "All I ask for, Father, is sanctuary until I can figure out a way to serve justice to Corbin and Groat."

"Hmm." His father ambled over to the side table. He poured a drink without another word, his back towards them while he slowly sipped from his glass.

Maggie's teeth nibbled her lower lip. Each tick of the clock dug chinks into Oliver's confidence. Why did his father not answer?

Finally, the man refilled yet again, but this time turned and strode back to his seat, swirling the amber liquid around in the tumbler. "So I am to set aside my current missing-marquis case and house an escaped convict and a thief?"

"Miss Lee is no thief!" The words shot out like hot lava. "I will *not* have her character so maligned."

"Oliver, please." Maggie rose and joined his side, resting her fingers against his sleeve, then faced his father with a stiff spine. "The truth is I did not know the jewels in my possession belonged to Mrs. Corbin. I thought it was my stage necklace."

"Even if what you say is true, would the replica not technically belong to the theatre?"

"Yes." Her voice strangled, and she clenched her hands in front of her. "I suppose that it would."

Oliver advanced, this time blocking her from his father's view. "Stop bullying her. You have no idea what she's gone through, what she's suffered at the hands of Corbin and her manager."

"Corbin again?" His father set his drink down on the tea table then cocked his head. "What has he to do with Miss Lee?"

"Corbin is the reason she fled Bath with such haste, threatening her with untoward advances and the bankruptcy of her father's business. So now you know everything. Will you help us or not?"

Steepling his fingers, his father tapped them against his lips, mumbling all the while. "This is a very serious matter. Very serious. I should not think. . .no, that will never do."

After a few more indecipherable grunts, he strolled to the window, completely ignoring them.

"Fine," Oliver huffed and glanced at Maggie. "Come along. I was wrong to have brought you here."

Her lips parted, then closed, and she nodded. "Very well. But I should like to say goodbye to your father. He did receive us, after all."

"As you wish."

She left his side and crossed over to the window, but Oliver widened his stance, resolute. If his father was going to ignore him, he'd repay in kind.

"Mr. Ward?" She tapped the man on the shoulder. "Thank you for receiving us. It was a pleasure to have met you."

"Hmm?" He pivoted. "What's this?"

"I wanted to say goodbye," Maggie said sweetly.

"Goodbye?" His brows lowered into a straight line, and he looked from her to Oliver. "But you cannot think of leaving here."

For the love of God and country! The man was seriously ordering them about with no alternative whatsoever? The pressure inside his head spewed out his mouth. "Thunderation, Father! We cannot leave? Yet we also cannot stay? Then tell me, sir, what exactly *are* we to do?"

"I should think that quite obvious."

"What?"

"Why, hold a dinner party, of course. Tonight. Seven o'clock." Sidestepping Maggie, the barrister strode to the door and cast them a backward glance. "Do not be late."

⸺

Five hours is enough time to start a war, birth a child, perform a full-scale production of *Don Giovanni*, including dressing, cosmetics and voice warm-ups. But though I've had that many hours and more, I still cannot fathom the complex relationship between Oliver and the barrister. Not that the relationship with my father is any simpler. But this is different. The barrister is cryptically blunt—a concept I cannot grasp for it ought not even exist. And Oliver is a powder keg just waiting to blow. No wonder he fled this home as soon as he was able. Tension and strife are as much a part of the house as the paint and the draperies.

I pick up a hairpin and tilt my head. Coaxing a simple chignon is not so simple the way my fingers fumble and my mind wanders. A dinner party is the last thing I wish to attend tonight, especially as underwhelmingly dressed as I am in my simple grey gown—though at least I'd thought to pack it. Why had the barrister suggested such a thing? Who will be in attendance? Why so much veiled intrigue?

A small golden clock begins to chime, and before it strikes seven, a rap on the door is followed by Oliver's low voice. "Maggie? Ready for dinner?"

Tucking in a last wayward strand of hair, I cross to the door. "Yes, I—"

My mouth hangs open, but no more words come out. Oliver stands inches from me, clean shaven, raven hair slicked back save for a few rogue strands that curl at the ends in rebellion. A black tailcoat rides the lines of his body, sculpted against his broad shoulders, narrowing at the waist, then flaring long at his thighs. Sconce light brushes a pale glow along the curve of his cheeks, his straight, strong nose. . .his full lips. What would it feel like to brush my own against his? Heat blazes across my cheeks.

"Maggie?" Alarm flares in the green flecks in his eyes. "What is it? Are you ill?"

"Yes—I mean no! I—I mean, I am fine." I fan my face. What is wrong with me? I've seen attractive men before—frequently. Why such a visceral reaction now?

"I *am* fine," I repeat, convincing myself and hopefully Oliver. "I am just a little warm and quite a bit famished." I finish with what I can only pray is a convincing smile.

Little creases bunch on his brow, but then it clears, and he offers his arm. "I think I can remedy that. May I escort you?"

I rest my hand on his sleeve, glad for the support. The spicy scent of his aftershave weakens my knees as we walk down the corridor.

"My father may not be the easiest of men to get along with, but there is one thing he has in his favor."

I peek up at him. "This lovely manor home?"

"Even better." He glances at me with a smile that is half pirate, half king of the world. "His staff. Cook has been known to stir up party fare with naught more than four hours' notice. My mouth is already watering for her delicacies, though I must admit I am curious as to how many people she'll be serving tonight."

Apparently the same thoughts that have troubled me the past hours concern him as well. I peer up at him as we descend the grand stairway. "Speaking of guests, how ever does he manage to lure people here on such short notice?"

"Intimidation, I suppose. My father is known to be *very* persuasive. It's not just his nose that gives him the moniker the Hawk of Crown Court. If he sets about to do something, it will be done, no matter the means. But this evening will be a challenge even for him. I have no idea who he's invited or what he's up to, nor do I like it."

My step falters as we reach the ground-floor landing. What if the barrister has made some inquiries? Opened the door to Constable Barrow? Purposely invited those who could do Oliver or me great harm? Though Oliver's strong arm steadies me, I cannot help but ask, "You don't think it's a trap, do you?"

He shakes his head. "Subterfuge isn't usually my father's game. When he strikes, he strikes hard and fast. If he intended to trundle me back to prison, I'd be shackled by now."

I breathe freer. It could very well be that the barrister is truly willing to help us. I may have been too hasty in thinking ill of him, but mistrust is a hard habit to break.

Oliver directs me into the dining room. Chandeliers bounce light off rich walnut paneling. Ward ancestors stare down at us from gilt-framed portraits hung on the walls. At the center, a white linen–covered table is set with silver-rimmed china and crystal goblets—for four. Four? That's it? The tightness in my belly loosens. One guest besides ourselves oughtn't be too dangerous. Perhaps Oliver overplays his father's power of intimidation.

The man himself stands with a drink in hand, conversing with a thin lady in a blue silk gown. When they turn to us, both Oliver and

I stop dead. What kind of twisted jest is this?

Barrister Ward leads the woman towards us. She is plain-faced. The sort you might look at and then forget the second you turn away. Yet there is dignity in her mien, from the tip of her greying head to the beaded hem of her skirt. She is a mix of wealth and commonness. She is a contradiction of privilege and a certain timidity that comes with a lifetime of living in the shadow of the beautiful. She is Mrs. Corbin.

The very woman whose jewels are in my traveling bag.

"Adelia." The barrister looks to her, then gestures towards Oliver and me. "I believe you already know my son and Miss Lee."

Oliver's muscles tense beneath his sleeve. I blink. The barrister and Ambrose Corbin's wife are on a Christian name basis? How well do they know each other. . .and why?

"Indeed." Mrs. Corbin beams at me. "Miss Lee, the Theatre Royal has not been the same without you."

Though she smiles, a sadness hangs about her, a hint of desolate music in her tone, like the singing of a dirge on a very rainy day—and I suspect it has nothing whatsoever to do with my absence from the stage.

But more than that, she is far wispier than I remember. Her lovely gown hangs from her shoulders as loosely as a garment pegged to a line. Grey crescents curve beneath her eyes on skin that is sallow. She has aged years in the space of the past nine months.

Oliver clears his throat, pulling me from my observations. I immediately dip a curtsey. "Thank you."

"And Mr. Ward—" She turns to Oliver. "I must admit I have been looking forward to this."

Why would anyone anticipate a meeting with the thief accused of stealing a beloved heirloom? I peek up at Oliver, who flashes a glance at me before answering.

"I am intrigued, Mrs. Corbin."

The barrister rubs his hands together. "Now that we're all here, dinner awaits. Shall we?"

Dread roots me to the spot, but Oliver gently leads me to a chair and seats me next to him. The barrister holds out a chair for Mrs. Corbin, seating her diagonally across from me. Now that I am in the same room with the owner of the ruby necklace, the guilt of having it in my chamber cramps my belly again, and I press a hand to my stomach. I must confess to the lady, let her know her jewels are safely in my care, but how will she take it? Hysterical tears? An ugly confrontation? A run for the door to snag the first available constable?

I squirm in my seat as a bowl of beef consommé is set before me, then suck in a big breath and lift my face to hers. "Mrs. Corbin, I—"

"Tut, tut, my dear." The barrister waves his spoon like a baton. "Allow me to put your mind at ease. Adelia is aware her jewels are in your possession."

Oliver stiffens. "You told her?"

"Of course. It is her necklace, after all."

"So now what? You expect us to hand it over, call it a day, and allow her husband and Groat to continue on as if nothing ever happened?" Oliver's voice cracks along the edges. He shoves back his seat and shoots to his feet. "As if I was never shackled in a hole and left to rot? No, I will not have it!"

"Sit down at once." His father scowls. "You will dine like a civilized gentleman or I will ask you to leave."

Oliver says nothing, just stands there, clenching his hands so that his knuckles are white. I understand this raw-boned rage. This feeling of helplessness and frustration when life is unfair. But if he doesn't stop giving free rein to that fury, it will devour him.

"Please sit," I whisper for him alone.

He glances down at me, and I get a glimpse of that same rabid stranger staring out through his eyes. How long will that angry beast living inside him continue to override his good reason?

But then it's over, and he sinks to his chair, mumbling an apology.

Without even touching her spoon, Mrs. Corbin ignores her soup and leans forward. "I understand your apprehension, Mr. Ward, but perhaps you would hear me out? I assure you, your father and I want to see justice served every bit as much as you and Miss Lee."

Oliver heaves a great sigh. "Of course, madam. I regret that I have not yet mastered my anger for what your husband has done."

"Yes, well, I daresay Ambrose has that effect on people, always driving them beyond their limits. Which is why I came to your father shortly after you'd been sent to prison. You see, though I'd dearly wanted it to be, my marriage is not a happy one, as evidenced by the supreme insult of having a copy of my necklace made in the first place. It was a beautiful mockery, I'll give him that." A haunted look ghosts her face. Lines deepen. Shadows darken. Whatever she is about to say will cost her in ways I cannot begin to understand. "For quite some time now, I've suspected Ambrose of seeking affections other than mine. I believe this is something to which you can attest, Miss Lee?"

My throat closes, and I push away the soup. I do not wish to cause the lady any further angst, nor do I want to revisit that horrid evening nine months ago, but her gaze is direct, begging confirmation.

"Yes," I answer simply.

She nods, solemn, her bony shoulders sagging beneath the weight of my affirmation. "I appreciate your candor. But I am afraid my husband's infidelity is not limited to merely physical pleasures. He used the money I brought to the marriage to fund his degenerate lifestyle. But when I discovered my necklace—a gift given me by my mother on her deathbed—had been swapped for paste, he crossed a line."

She pushes back her chair. The barrister reaches for her, but she shakes her head and remains seated, far from the food, as if the smell sickens her. Yet it is not the broth that must surely be roiling in her gut.

Her gaze drifts to Oliver. "I didn't believe for one moment you were to blame, Mr. Ward, especially not when it was Ambrose's men who testified against you in court. Since then, your father and I have been working to gather evidence against my husband. You and Miss Lee could not have come at a more fortuitous time. The one thing I regret is that I did not confide in the barrister sooner. Perhaps this whole thing could have been avoided in the first place if I had."

Oliver's father leans aside and pats her hand. "You are not to blame, Adelia. That falls completely to your monstrous husband."

True. But he is not the only one. As soon as the footman swaps my hardly touched bowl of broth for a plate of lemon cod, I edge forward in my seat. "Your husband had some help with his skullduggery. My manager, Mr. Groat, did the actual swapping of your necklace. By rights, they should both be held to account."

Oliver picks up his knife and fork, yet pauses before stabbing a bite. "Which is what Maggie and I want to see happen."

"Good." The barrister waves off the footman now that the second course has been served. "We are all of one mind on the matter. Now, any ideas as to how to bring this about?"

"When Maggie and I first arrived, our plan was to plant the necklace on Mr. Corbin with Magistrate Hunter standing ready nearby, then accuse him and let nature take its course. It's a good plan, one that could work with two as well as with one." Oliver answers as if the matter is already decided.

I frown. "But how can a single necklace be found in the hands of two men at the same time?"

"Good point, but one that might not be so difficult to render," the barrister says. "I believe, by drawing from the wisdom of Solomon, it should be divided. Half for each. That is"—he faces Mrs. Corbin—"if you can bear to have your keepsake temporarily deconstructed?"

Her lips purse for a moment as she toys with a ring that rests far too large on her thin finger. Finally, she lets out a low breath and nods. "I admit I don't like the thought of my mother's necklace being tampered with, but if it serves to expose my husband and Mr. Groat's wickedness, then yes. I agree, as long as it is a professional who does the work."

"Of course. We will find the best," the barrister says.

Oliver pokes at his food, brow wrinkled in concentration. "But getting Groat and Corbin in the same place at the same time will take a fair bit of cunning. Miss Lee and I already contrived a meeting between Corbin and Magistrate Hunter. I don't think either of them will be too keen to accept another suspicious invitation."

"I know Hunter. He is a good man with a guileless mind, one who wouldn't suspect anything untoward about another solicitation."

Despite the barrister's optimism, I frown. The fiasco of earlier in the day barrels back with a wave of fresh danger. Thank God that waiter stopped me from making a groundless accusation. But Oliver is right. There is no way the cunning Ambrose Corbin will accept another curious invitation. I bite a forkful of flaky fish and, while chewing, mull on several possibilities—and then it hits me.

I set down my fork. "What if Mr. Corbin wasn't the one to *be* invited but *did* the inviting?"

Mrs. Corbin stops fiddling with the gold ring and looks up. "What do you mean?"

The barrister frowns. "I couldn't get Ambrose to grant me a five-minute conversation. How will you manage to persuade him to meet with Magistrate Hunter and Mr. Groat at the same time?"

"Just as you managed to get Mrs. Corbin here. A dinner party." I shift my gaze back to Mrs. Corbin. "Do you think you could arrange that? Host an event for which you draw up the guest list, invite a crowd, amongst whom will be Mr. Groat and Magistrate Hunter?"

"I suppose that could work." Her pale eyes seek out the barrister's and her shoulders rise a bit. She is still the same frail woman in sky-blue silk, but a fresh measure of strength lifts her chin as she angles it at me. "But I think I can do you one better, Miss Lee. It seems fitting to me that we re-create the night the jewels were stolen in the first place."

Re-create? Fling the door wide to memories I'd locked deep inside? I shake my head. "No, I don't—that's not at all what I meant."

But Mrs. Corbin grips on to the idea and the loose ring on her finger as if both are her salvation—as if *I* am her salvation. "I know it will be taxing, but don't you see? A dinner party with a surprise performance by you, Miss Lee, will be just the thing. The perfect distraction."

The fish in my stomach flips. No. Absolutely not. I cannot willingly relive that night of horror. "I really couldn't."

Oliver shoves away his plate. "You cannot seriously expect Miss Lee to walk into such danger. No offense, Mrs. Corbin, but your husband's threats drove Miss Lee away in the first place. I will not see her pressured all over again."

"Nor will she be, not by Ambrose." The barrister nods at us each in turn as he speaks. "With all of us in attendance, she'll never have a moment alone with the man." Then he looks directly at me, steely confidence in the set of his jaw. "I assure you, Miss Lee, your safety is of the utmost importance."

"We'll make sure of it, my dear," Mrs. Corbin adds.

I bite my lip, appetite completely gone. I've battled preperformance jitters before, but the churning in my belly is like nothing I've experienced. Can I really do this? Should I?

I peek at Oliver, whose eyes consume mine, and angst for myself fades in the next rising worry that nearly drowns me. What of him? What of his innocence? Even if I do pull off a stellar performance, what if Constable Barrow catches up with him before the evening is through?

I snap my gaze to Oliver's father. "Oliver is a hunted man. It's not safe for him to be seen in public."

The barrister opens his mouth to speak, but it is Oliver's voice that fills the room. "It's a risk worth taking if justice is served—and I *will* see it served, danger or not."

I don't know if Oliver sees it, but pride shines in his father's eyes. Could it be he is not the monster Oliver makes him out to be?

"I'm sure among the four of us we can think of some way to disguise you, Son. So then, it is settled." The barrister's gaze drifts to Mrs. Corbin. "Can you manage the affair in a week, or shall you need two?"

"Ambrose is currently home on leave to tend to some pressing business matter before Parliament reconvenes, and then he'll be gone again. It will have to be next Friday evening, but yes, I think I can manage."

That's only six days, and I'm supposed to meet with Mr. Groat in two. How on earth will I put him off? Still, this whole thing might work in my favor. I face Mrs. Corbin. "Do you think you could have the invitations drawn up and one given to me in two days?"

She hesitates, lips pursing for a moment. "Yes," she finally agrees. "But why? As the star performer, you won't need one to get in, you know."

"It's not for me. Have it addressed to Mr. Groat. I will deliver it to him myself."

"Are you out of your mind?" Oliver's voice strangles.

I smile. "Perhaps we all are, a little bit, to pull off this grand scheme."

Chapter Twenty-Three

Grasping the crisp invitation addressed to my manager, I stride out the front door of the barrister's home and approach a waiting carriage. Oliver tags my heels, grumbling. He's been protesting the past two days. His doubts are born of concern for my safety, and that both warms my heart and saddens me. Would that my father had cared as much. Though I've forgiven him for sending me off at a tender age with a conniving man who promised him riches, I still wish he hadn't. I wish he had cared enough to keep me close.

"I don't like this," Oliver growls behind me.

I don't either, but there's nothing to be done. The loathsome task must be performed. Hesitating at the side of the coach, I pluck at my reticule strings. Should I simply climb in and shut the door to Oliver's objections? Or tarry and have yet one more conversation that will hopefully ease his mind?

"Maggie, please. Reconsider. Let one of my father's men do it."

The haunting coo of a wood pigeon echoes from a copse of ash trees not far off. Another answers. A mournful exchange, earnest in its doleful sound, one that oddly gives incentive to try to communicate peace to Oliver.

Slowly, I turn and face him. "We've been over this. If I do not show up at the appointed time and place, Mr. Groat will hunt me down as doggedly as Constable Barrow pursues you, and that is no way to live, is it?"

He says nothing, but a vein pulses at his temple, giving away that my words have hit their mark.

A late-April breeze stirs, flopping a piece of Oliver's dark hair into his eyes. He tosses his head like a horse, flipping it away. "If anything happens to you, I. . ." He grimaces and shakes his head. "I won't be contained, and then I really will be guilty of a crime and sent back to Dartmoor."

His protectiveness wraps around me like a warm embrace. "I appreciate your concern, truly I do, but your father already has men in place to safeguard me should Mr. Groat try anything."

"They won't be close enough if he strikes you again." Something like sorrow tugs down the corners of his mouth, and he reaches to caress the curve of my cheek.

Unbidden, I lean into his touch. The heat of his bare palm against my skin surges through me, down to my toes. It's a startling feeling. Altogether dangerous and wildly addictive. My own traitorous hand rises to press against his, and I tell myself it is merely to reassure this man who's been through so much in the past nine months. But that's a lie. I *want* to feel his strong fingers, to give in to this foreign desire urging me to know more of him in ways I've never experienced.

And that scares me more than any meeting with Mr. Groat.

I pull away. "The Circus lawn is a very public place. My manager knows better than to make a scene that will draw attention. Besides"—I lift my chin—"I'm not that fragile. One blow will not break me."

Stillness spreads out from him. His throat bobs, and his words come out husky. "You are an amazing woman, Maggie Lee."

"You're not so bad yourself." I grin. "I'll see you when I get back."

He helps me into the carriage, and before he shuts the door, he pokes his head in with a last, grim-faced admonition. "Be careful."

"I usually am."

"Oh? Taking in a strange, bleeding man was careful?"

"Hmm, well. . ." He's got a point, but even so, I shoot him a direct stare. "I think that's turned out all right so far, don't you?"

A smirk quirks his mouth, and he shuts the door without further retort. The carriage lurches into movement. For the rest of the ride into Bath, I smooth my skirts with increasingly moist palms. Though I've done my best to calm Oliver's nerves, mine rattle as jarringly as the grind of the wheels.

The coach turns off Brock Street and onto the Circus. Three curved rows of large town houses form a circle. When I was a girl, the name always confused me, for there are no jugglers or monkeys, rope walkers or fortune tellers. It wasn't until my father pulled his nose out of a book long enough to explain to me that in Latin *circus* simply means ring or circle that I finally understood.

After the driver helps me out, I raise a quick prayer for courage, then skirt the carriage and cross the road to the vast lawn at center. Several nurses follow their young charges about. One young lad kicks a ball. Two little girls skip hand in hand. On the far side, a blanket is spread out in a square, a picnic basket being unloaded by a maid in a dark skirt. To my right, a man seated on a bench lowers his newspaper and dips a discreet nod at me. On my left, another man fiddles with some leather straps on a horse at the edge of the pavement. He also makes it a point to covertly tuck his chin my way. While I am grateful the barrister hired strong men to keep watch over the transaction, my stomach sinks. Oliver is right. They are not nearly close enough to rush to my defense should Mr. Groat turn violent.

Shoving aside the unsettling thought, I scan the area for my manager. Not far in front of me, Mr. Groat perches on a bench like a magpie peering about for something shiny to peck. The oily sheen of his black dress coat pulls in light and bounces it back.

As I approach, he rises, hand outstretched. "Let's have it."

I set a creamy white envelope on his palm.

"What's this?" Scowling, he rips it open, then jerks his face up to mine. "Where is the necklace?"

My heart hammers, and I swallow down a rising fear. "Safe."

"You're not." His dark brows sink, slashing an angry line below his hat. He advances.

I shoot up my hand, warding him off and stopping my guardians. There's no sense in creating a spectacle if I can talk my way out of this.

"You will have the necklace the night of that party." I nod towards the invitation. "And in exchange, you will introduce me before I sing, announcing that I am now a free agent, under no further contractual obligations to you or anyone else. Then—and *only* then—will I slip the rubies into your pocket."

He bares his teeth in a sickly smile and starts clapping, the white paper flapping with the movement. The noise turns the head of the boy with the ball.

"Well, well. That was quite a performance, Miss Lee. Perhaps I trained you too well." His hands drop. So does his grin. "Got yourself a backbone while you were gone, hmm?"

Mouth suddenly dry, I lick my lips, fighting the urge to summon one of the hired men. "It's a fair exchange. A business deal, that's all. I get my freedom. You get your valuables. We both walk away with what we want."

"I want it now." With a quick twitchy move, he shoves the invitation into his pocket and pulls out the ice pick. Low and close to his side as it is, no one glancing our way will know the weapon is pointed at my belly, not even my guardians. My pulse thrums wildly in my ears. I shoot a panicked look at the closest hired man, but just then a breeze lifts the paper he's used as cover and blocks his vision.

Panic tastes sour at the back of my mouth, but I ignore it and stiffen my shoulders. Fear is an aphrodisiac that will attract Mr. Groat instead of repelling him. "If you kill me now, you'll never see those jewels again."

His dark gaze bores into one of my eyes, then the other, probing in a way that crawls under my skin like tiny worms. I stifle a shiver.

"All right." He smiles and retreats a step.

My heart stutters to restart. Tension drains away.

Then Mr. Groat lunges, slicing the ice pick across my arm as he stalks past me. The sharpened tip tears open fabric and flesh. I grab the wound, a cry strangling in my throat, and both hired men rise and dash my way.

But it is too late. Mr. Groat casts a gloating look over his shoulder as he strides towards a waiting carriage. "Just a little reminder for you, Daisy. Public or not, I will have my way. See you Friday night. Oh and you might want to wear a long-sleeved gown to the event."

∞

Sebastian took a last drag on his cigarillo then dropped it to the ground and crushed it with his heel before swinging up onto his horse. He'd watched the meeting between Groat and Daisy Lee from a distance, like God. Keeping an eye on matters. Passing righteous judgment on the pair. The woman clearly needed discipline for her usurpation over man, as evidenced by the jaunty step with which she'd approached Groat and the stiff-necked way she held her shoulders. Groat, on the other hand, had crossed a line and needed to be put back in his own place. Intimidation of a woman to remind her of her subordination was one thing. Drawing blood another.

Clicking his tongue, Sebastian nudged his horse into motion and followed the woman's carriage at a distance, old rage surging up, and for one moment he was standing again over a dead man with a gun in his hand. It'd been a terrible bloodshed, but what man could stand by and watch his younger sister ravished?

His horse shook his head uneasily, jarring Sebastian back to the present. He blew out a breath and glanced up at the guileless blue sky. How much more justice would he be required to mete out before his own sin was atoned for? If he nabbed Ward, would he finally earn back God's favor? He scrubbed a hand over his face, and then froze as another thought struck him. In meting out God's judgment, attempting to compensate for his own evil, had he crossed a line like Groat? And if so, then how would he ever mend his relationship with his Creator? The thoughts nagged him all the way as the carriage left behind the city proper and ventured farther into the country.

A mile later, the coach turned off the main road onto a smaller lane, and finally swung into an estate where the gates stood wide open. Stupid owner. What was the purpose of a fortified entry if one did not close and lock it? Any manner of cutthroat or cully could enter.

He secured his horse to the side of one of the great pillars, then edged past the gates, hoofing it from tree to tree, shrub to shrub, following the gravel drive up to the manor house. Yet another security mistake. Providing this much cover for the sake of a genteel landscape was not only asking for prowlers but encouraging such trespassers.

But it gave him a great hiding spot and a view of the front entry.

Daisy Lee had already alighted from the carriage and was walking towards the door when out rushed Ward. His face contorted when he detected her injured arm. Sebastian frowned. Since when did a criminal care what happened to a woman? No, it was probably a ruse so that he could use her. Guilty men were notorious for their wiles.

Some sort of conversation ensued, but from this distance, the words were indistinguishable. Pursing his lips, Sebastian's gaze drifted from a line of sculptured boxwoods to a wide-trunked yew, both close enough to be able to hear. But were they too close? If he were discovered too soon, Ward would flee. Better to catch the scoundrel off guard rather than the other way around.

The carriage rattled off and the dialogue intensified. Perfect timing. He crouch-ran towards the tree, just in time to hear Oliver's heated words.

"No! I will not allow that man to torment you like this. Something has to be done. Now!"

"Oliver, please," Miss Lee entreated. "What's done is done. I'm hardly bleeding anymore. It is a superficial wound, nothing more."

"Go in the house, Maggie."

"Where are you going?"

"To stop Groat's madness."

Sebastian edged his face past the trunk. The woman's back was to him. Ward stalked away from her, towards the stables, and called over his shoulder, "Go inside and have Foster see to your arm. I'll be back shortly."

A disgusted groan issued from her, yet to her credit, she obeyed.

The woman dashed into the house.

Sebastian pulled out his gun. With the two separated, now was the time to strike. Still, it paid to be cautious. Snatching a convict always went better if civilians weren't involved. Curious servants and meddling gentry somehow managed to end up getting shot. He crept from tree to tree, calculating the merits of tackling Ward now or after he emerged from the stable. Probably better to wait. Yank the blackguard off his mount and, as soon as he hit the ground, crack him in the skull with the butt of his pistol.

The stable swallowed Ward. Sebastian made his move. Five yards from the door, he ducked behind a farm wagon. Once Ward passed, he'd spring. Listening hard, he waited for the thud of horse hooves. Several minutes later, the blessed sound pounded out the door.

He cocked his gun. Crept to the edge of the wagon. Trembled with anticipation. The hooves trotted closer.

But so did heels kicking up gravel, followed by a man's shout. "Stop right there!"

What the devil? Slowly, Sebastian peered around the corner of the wagon.

Ward glowered down at a grey-haired man who'd grabbed ahold of the headstall. "Get out of my way."

"You never learn, do you? Acting without thinking. Impetuous and proud. You are not God to mete out justice on a whim."

"Miss Lee's safety is not a *whim*!"

"You do her a better service to remain here and follow our plan as we all agreed. Be a man of your word despite how you feel. All of this will be settled in a matter of days. Stay the course."

A matter of days? Sebastian frowned. Something was afoot here. Something he needed to know about. He dared to lean just a bit closer.

Ward glowered at the man a moment longer, snorting as loudly as his horse. Then the sneer dissolved into a grimace, and he heeled the horse in a tight circle and returned to the stable.

The elder fellow watched him go, then turned.

Sebastian squinted as he studied him. High cheekbones. A broad mouth. A few dark hairs streaked in amongst the white. And a very distinct nose. It was hooked, a veritable beak. . .just like a hawk's. Sebastian lowered his gun as the ugly truth sank deep in his gut.

Cassius Ward. Oliver's father. All of Groat's warnings barreled back. The eminent Hawk of Crown Court was a man who could make snatching his son a miserable amount of paperwork at best, or worse, twist it sideways and have Barrow himself detained. Of all the wretched providence!

Tucking his gun away, Sebastian eased behind the wagon, deflated but not devastated. It was only a matter of time, now that he'd located Ward. A matter of days, apparently. Perhaps Groat knew more. And in the meantime, he'd watch. He'd wait. Patience wasn't usually one of his virtues, but perhaps God was testing him.

And this time he wouldn't fail.

Chapter Twenty-Four

Oliver crept downstairs and, out of habit, took care not to put his full weight on the center of the eighth stair. It creaked. Always had. Shortly after his mother had died, he'd learned that lesson as a ten-year-old on a midnight venture to pilfer some biscuits from the kitchen. Tonight's scheme, however, was much less nefarious. A book from the library ought to do the trick for wooing him to sleep. Hopefully. By all rights he should be bone weary without such a sleeping aid. His body was, but his mind would not shut down. Too many worries. Too many recurrent memories.

And far too many thoughts of Maggie.

Thankfully, all her arm had needed was a bandage. Her sleeve had borne the brunt of the attack. She'd chattered through dinner without so much as a wince. Even so, he couldn't stop thinking about it—about her—in ways he had no right to. She'd not yet given him leave to pursue her after this whole ugly affair was over. Perhaps she didn't intend to. And he wouldn't blame her. She'd seen him at his worst.

He cinched the banyan tie tighter at his waist, lest the hem catch and send him crashing the rest of the way down. The flame flickered in the oil lamp, casting a monstrous shadow of him against the wall when he descended the final step. As a lad, it would've frightened him. Now he had bigger dragons to slay. Groat and Corbin at the moment . . .then the possibility of Maggie walking out of his life forever.

Nearing the library, he slowed his pace and frowned at the golden light spilling out from the door opposite. His father's study. What was he doing up at this late hour? Hah. What a baseless question.

The barrister always had spent more time poring over law books to the detriment of all else—even his little boy.

Face forward, jaw set, Oliver strode past the door.

"Is that you, Oliver? A moment, if you don't mind."

He stopped. This was new. The barrister had actually noticed him? Pivoting, he retraced his steps and entered his father's sanctuary. The scent of ink and Grey's tea welcomed him. The Persian runner stretching the length of the room did not. How many times as a lad, an adolescent, a young man, had he stood there weathering a lecture or a reprimand?

Pulling his gaze from the spot, he faced his father, who sat ensconced behind his massive desk. "You're up late."

"Just organizing a few last-minute details for Friday evening." Gathering a sheaf of papers, he tapped them against the desk until each page lined up like a row of soldiers. He set them aside, then leaned back in his chair and folded his arms.

Oliver tensed. What sort of homily was he to endure tonight?

But his father said nothing. Outside, a gentle rain beat against the glass panes of the window. Gas hissed from the newfangled sconces on the wall. Other than that, all was silent.

Oliver set his lamp down on the man's desk, jarring them both with the rattle of the glass globe. "You wanted to speak with me?"

"Yes, I did. About Miss Lee."

He blinked. He'd heard stunning things from politicians and barmaids, but this one caught him off guard. What could his father possibly wish to discuss with him about her?

Once again the rain dripped, the lights softly fizzed, and his father's lips remained sealed.

"And?" he prompted.

Leaning forward in his seat, the barrister reached for his mug of tea, the leather chair creaking with the movement. "I am sorry about her arm. She is quite a brave lady."

Oliver shuffled his feet, suddenly unsteady. This was unfamiliar territory. His father didn't usually creep around the fringes of a topic. "Indeed, she is."

His father slurped a drink of tea, then continued to hold the mug in both hands, staring into the liquid. "Though I've only had the pleasure of Miss Lee's acquaintance for three days, I am of the opinion she is a remarkable woman."

Unease prickled across his shoulders. Where on earth was this conversation headed? Oliver shifted his weight from one foot to the other. "She is rather extraordinary."

His father grunted, then set down the mug and speared him with a direct gaze. "I wanted to apologize for my harshness earlier today. It was commendable of you to wish to see that scoundrel Groat pay for his maltreatment of her."

Oliver sucked in a breath, audibly, but it couldn't be helped. An apology *and* a compliment? Was this man truly his father or an imposter?

"Apology accepted," he conceded. "But you were right. I let my anger get the best of me."

Astonishment flickered in the man's green eyes. Oliver braced himself for the resultant about-time-you-learn-to-admit-your-shortcomings monologue.

The barrister rose and clenched his hands behind his back, a favored power stance when standing at the bar. "Tell me, Oliver, what are your intentions towards the lady after all of this is over?"

Instantly his hackles rose. Could the man never think well of him? What suspicions did the barrister have tucked away in a back pocket?

"What do you mean?" He measured out the words evenly.

"Come now, I may be getting on in years, but I am not blind." His father paced to the window and stared out at the black night. "I see the way you look at her, the way she looks at you."

"I don't know what you're talking about."

"Don't you?" He faced Oliver, one brow arched high in a knowing angle.

Oliver bristled. "Even so—which I'm not admitting to, mind—what concern is it of yours?"

His father merely sniffed. "As I've said, since getting to know her, I am struck by her intelligence, her beauty, her guarded heart."

"You sound as if you're the one who intends to pursue her."

"Don't be ridiculous. I'm old enough to be her father—and as such, I will not stand by and see that young woman's heart broken by you."

By *him*? White-hot rage burned through his veins. "Do you really know me so little?"

His father grimaced and sank back to his seat, aging years in front of him. "I hardly know you at all."

"Exactly!" Oliver planted his hands on the desk and leaned forward. "Which is why you do not get to have this conversation with me. You have not earned the right to be privy to the intent of my heart."

His father winced, and a spark of remorse for such harsh words squeezed Oliver's chest. Sighing, he straightened and planted his feet on the Persian runner. His father never failed to goad him to extremes.

"Fair enough, Son. Just. . ." The barrister's mouth twisted, whatever he'd intended to say trapped behind the barrier, until finally he blew out a long breath and peered at him. "Be careful. I would not like to see either of you hurt."

"Really?" A snort ripped out of him. "All of a sudden you actually care about my welfare?"

"I have always cared about you."

Of all the audacious statements! Oliver flung out his arms. "Is that so? Then tell me, Father, why did you not come the day I was unjustly condemned to prison? Why were you not there for me? Why did you not fight for me?" The questions flew like grapeshot, loud, sharp, hitting the walls—and his father—with blunt force.

"I didn't know about it," his father said quietly.

"You? The Hawk of Crown Court didn't know about his own son's trial?" Scoffing laughter rumbled in his throat. "Surely you don't expect me to believe that."

"I am many things." His father lifted his chin and stared down his hooked nose. "But I am not a liar."

No. He wasn't. Yet the dark side of that virtue often cut deep with its pointed barbs.

Oliver raked his fingers through his hair, tugging hard, wildly, wanting to run from the room but at the same time stay and discover what could have possibly kept his father from his trial.

He dropped his hand, helpless against a rising, morbid curiosity. "What was it, then, that was so important you sequestered yourself away from the biggest scandal in Bath? Why would you. . .ahh. Wait a minute. I should have known. A case. You were working on a case. Tell me, Father, who was it that was so important you didn't have time to keep abreast of your own son's disgraceful arrest?"

"Does it really matter?"

"Who!" He slammed both fists on the desk.

His father's eyes narrowed at the outburst, yet his tone remained placid. "I was unexpectedly called out of town—under false pretenses, I might add—to a manor home north of London. A storm arose, the bridge washed out, and I was essentially cut off from civilization. By the time I made it back to London to catch the next train, the line had shut down for repair. I resorted to hiring a coach, which added more time. But, I assure you, the second I heard of your incarceration, I began filing appeals. I've been working on your case ever since."

Like a burned hand held beneath cold water, the information soothed but wasn't permanent. Oh how he wanted to believe it. To trust that his welfare was utmost in his father's mind. But the barrister always had a plausible excuse, and this one neatly hid the fact that his father had not fully answered his question.

Oliver forced an even tone to his words. "Whose case were you working on?"

Without a flinch, his father met his gaze. "Lord Candlewood."

"Hah! *Lord* Candlewood?" The name soured in his gut. "An earl. Why am I not surprised?"

"Believe it or not, Oliver, the wealthy and titled deserve justice as much as the poor and downtrodden."

"Sure. Justice for the rich and privileged, but God help the poor, the needy, those of lesser value."

"Justice is not free. If it weren't for those 'rich and privileged,' I would have no means to help the poor, the needy, and those of lesser value, as you put it."

"Nice sentiment—except you never find enough time to help them, do you? Because even when your ten-year-old son begged for your assistance to help his best friend's father, you were too busy defending a viscount."

"Did you never stop to think that perhaps, through your childish eyes, you didn't see the full picture? The truth is I did look into the case, and found that the man you were so certain was a paragon of virtue was actually guilty of embezzlement."

Oliver reeled, completely off kilter. "Why did you never tell me this before?"

"At the time, you wouldn't have understood, and even if you had, I doubt it would've made a difference. You would've continued to argue for the sake of your friend. Your strong sense of protecting the innocent is a noble but sometimes misguided trait."

The weight of his father's words was too much to bear, and his knees nearly buckled. His father was right. On all accounts. Oliver braced himself against the desk. "Then later. Why didn't you tell me later?"

"Would you have heard me? You didn't even give me a chance tonight to explain I had been defending Lord Candlewood's first footman."

A servant? Oliver stared at his father as if he'd sprouted horns, everything he thought he knew about the man turned upside down and inside out. And as much as he wanted to protest he would have listened, would he have? Because in the end, it still didn't explain why a young boy was made to suffer the consequences of his father's sin.

"Oliver, please hear me—"

"No! You've said enough!" The words boomed in the small chamber, his whole body shaking. He was in no mood to endure a further

I-told-you-so from his father, and nothing would change the past. Nor would it change anything in the present, for here he was, a little boy in man's clothing, unable to understand why the world was so unjust.

He filled his lungs, held the air until he felt a burn, then slowly blew it all out and opened his eyes. "I appreciate you housing me and Maggie. I really do. It's a risk that could mar your sterling reputation, and I own I am a bit surprised you've bent so far as to allow the possibility. But once this is over, Father, I think it better if we part ways once and for all. Good night."

Snatching his lamp, he pivoted and strode to the door.

"Oliver, come back here."

He kept walking. After Friday night, he'd never come back here again.

∞

Rain cries down the windowpanes in a steady *pat-pat-pat*. I stand next to the glass, shivering in my nightgown, and all I see is the pale-faced reflection of a ghostly woman staring back at me. Dark eyes overlarge. Hair a tumbling mess. I angle my head. My cheeks are more rounded than I like. It's a morose waste of time, this scrutiny of my faults, but it's better than tossing about on the bed, which is how I've spent the last hour. . .and likely will the rest of the night.

Huffing a sigh, I turn away from the window. If I'm going to be awake, I should at least make the best of it, and the best thing to do in such a situation is to read a book. I collect my robe and take care while shoving in my injured arm. Truly, it doesn't hurt much, but it pays to be cautious. If infection sets in and a fever follows, I'll not be able to attend the great downfall of Mr. Groat and Mr. Corbin in three days.

I light a small lamp then venture into the corridor, padding on soft feet. At this late hour, everyone is abed. But as I tread down the staircase and turn into a broad passageway, I revise that opinion. A door opposite the library stands open. Heated words roar inside.

Two voices. I frown. As if Oliver and his father don't quarrel enough during the day, must they squabble into all hours of the night?

Holding my robe tight at the neck, I scurry past, praying not to be seen. But a few steps beyond the door, some of their words sink in, and my breath catches in my throat. I stop. Oliver's father hadn't attended his son's trial? A need to know the reason why overrides my sense of propriety. I back up, flatten against the wall, and blow out my lamp. Eavesdropping is wicked, but not nearly on par with a father—a powerful man of the law, no less—not being there for his son.

Though I strain my ears, the barrister's reply is too soft to distinguish. No matter, though. Oliver's voice booms loud enough for the both of them. "You? The Hawk of Crown Court didn't know about his own son's trial?"

My brow knits into fine knots as the conversation continues. I fear Oliver is too busy excoriating his father to really listen to the man. Does he notice the regret in his father's voice? The raggedness rasping with each word? Is he too focused on an injustice of the past to hear the pain and repentance in the present? Why does he not—

Then it hits me, and my shoulders sag. Who am I to cast judgment? How many years did it take me to let go of my own sense of rejection in order to not only listen to my father but forgive him for signing me away to Mr. Groat? Father felt he had no choice other than to do so for monetary reasons, but perhaps the barrister's motivations are just as valid, if only Oliver would consider them.

"I think it better if we part ways once and for all," Oliver growls. "Good night."

Good night?

My heart stutters, and I dash from the study door to the library. Footsteps thud in the corridor, headed my way. Sweet blessed heavens! How am I to explain myself standing in a dark room in the middle of the night? Turning in a wild circle, I scan from wall to wall, seeking a place to hide.

Across the room, draperies hang open in a bay window. Perfect.

I race to the spot and yank them shut just as pale yellow light seeps under the gap between hem and floor. My blood drains to my feet. Did I make it here in time or did Oliver glimpse the flash of my white robe?

Closing my eyes, I listen hard. With my pulse throbbing a primal beat, it's difficult to distinguish if shoes brush against carpet. So I hold my breath, hoping to still the crazed pounding, and. . .

Nothing. Only rain *tap-tap-taps* a steady patter against glass. I release a long, low breath, blowing out all the tension of what could've been a very sticky situation. Thank God I made it here in time.

And then curtain rings screech.

My eyes fly open.

Oliver stands a pace away, one brow arched high. "If you fancy to win at a game of sardines, you've chosen a very poor place to hide."

Chapter Twenty-Five

She was a vision, this woman. A dream. An enticing temptation no mortal man could resist. Forgetting everything about the harsh words with his father, Oliver lifted his lamp higher, desperate for a better look at Maggie.

Dark curls brushed against her neck, fallen free from the loosely tied coil atop her head. Her brown eyes were impossibly wide, little flecks of gold catching the light and bouncing it back. A man could get lost forever in that gaze.

So he looked lower, pausing ever so slightly on her full lips, then down further, along the creamy skin of her neck, past the chain of her mother's locket, to the shadowy depression where her robe rode low on her collarbone. Life pulsed vibrant there. How warm would that skin be? How soft?

Sweet heavens! What was he thinking?

He shook his head, praying the movement would jostle his common sense back into place. "What are you doing here?"

"I. . .well. . ." Her throat bobbed. "I couldn't sleep."

Colour spread over her cheeks in a most becoming shade. And though he really shouldn't, the urge to tease her welled all the more. He advanced a step—then immediately regretted the move. Her sweet rosewater scent nearly dropped him to his knees.

"And," he drawled. "Do you find this method of entombing yourself near a draughty window to be an effective sleep inducer?"

The dusky pink on her cheeks flared exotic. "Don't be silly."

Ignoring all reason, he leaned closer. A breath away. The slightest effort on his part and he'd be kissing those lips. "Silly? I'm not the one hiding behind a curtain in the dark of night." The words came out huskier than he intended, his teasing taking a turn into an intimacy he couldn't afford right now, one he wasn't sure she even wanted.

Panic flashed in her eyes. "But I. . .I—"

Instantly he retreated a step, thoroughly sobered. He was no better than the blackguards who pawed her after a performance.

"You'll catch your death here. Come." He swept his hand towards the sofa near the unlit hearth, allowing her to pass. Following close behind, he held the lamp aloft, lighting the way, and snagged a plaid woolen throw to drape over her shoulders as she sat.

"Shall I ring for warm milk?" he asked. "I find it to be a much more successful way to induce drowsiness."

"No, thank you. Let the servants rest. The truth is I came down to get a book, hoping to read myself into oblivion. On the way, I passed by the study and. . ." She bit her lip.

The implication dropped him into the seat across from her. Clearly her little nighttime prowl had turned into something darker for both of them. He set the lamp on the tea table between them. "You overheard?"

She peered directly at him, a small nod dipping her head. Her face was overly white in the light. "Forgive me?"

Muscles suddenly cramping, he massaged a knot at the base of his neck. What had she heard? How many of his father's lame excuses? How much of his own snipping and sniping in response? Now she'd not only seen him at his worst but heard him as well. Blast it! Why could he never control his tongue around the man?

"Forgiven and forgotten." Oliver fluttered his fingers in the air. "Think nothing of it."

If only it were that easy.

"Oh but I do think a great deal of it. I would not be a very good friend if I did not." She leaned forward, her robe rustling softly against the leather sofa cushion. "It pains me, this rift between you and your father."

"Please," he said, "do not trouble yourself. My father and I are two very different people, that's all."

"Actually, I suspect you are more alike than either of you believes, but it's more than that. If I may be so bold, might I share a few thoughts?"

He scrubbed his face before lowering his hand. He'd love to hear her thoughts, explore her mind, her imaginings, her theories on life and love and God and everything—everything *other* than his relationship with his father.

Chimes bonged from the grandfather clock in the corner, one after the other, breaking the silence and offering the perfect excuse. "It is late." He rose and offered his hand. "Shall I see you to your room?"

She sank back defiantly. "You cannot keep running."

"Clearly I am not." He lifted his arm towards the ceiling. "You find me beneath my father's roof, after all."

"That's not what I mean, and you know it." She jutted her jaw.

Determined little nymph! Ahh, but the way her nostrils flared, she was a beautiful nymph at that. Still, he would not—could not—let that sway him. He shook his head. "I will not have this conversation. Not with you. I like you too well for that."

In one swift movement, he swiped up the lamp and took a step towards the door. "Come along. I would not leave you here in the dark."

"Oliver, listen." Fabric swished and fingertips pressed into his sleeve. "You've made a difference in the lives of so many. The downtrodden. The forgotten. It is a noble thing you do in Parliament, fighting on behalf of those who have no voice."

A bitter chuckle rumbled in his throat, and he turned to face her. "You're talking to the wrong man. Perhaps you could enlighten my father on that account."

"Perhaps it is you who needs the enlightening."

"Me?" He choked on the word. She wasn't seriously taking his father's side in all this, was she? "In your own words, *I* am the one making a difference—or at least I was before I landed in prison. It is my father who hides behind his robes and wigs and lofty diatribes of rights and laws."

Pulling back her hand, she folded her arms. "Did you never stop to think that maybe—just maybe—you yourself left justice behind to focus on the violation of it instead?"

He gaped. "How so?"

"Without a fully complete vision of justice, there is no possible way you can fight against iniquity."

The lamp in his grasp shook, shooting macabre shadows across the room. Who was she to judge his understanding of all that was right and fair and good? How could she possibly assess the white-hot ember burning in his soul that drove him to champion the underprivileged? Why did she not accuse the barrister of lack of vision?

"A very pretty speech, Miss Lee," he rumbled. "But since you've decided to play this game with me, I expect you to defend your words."

"Very well." Unfolding her arms, she snugged the throw tighter at her neck. "I am no philosopher or great theologian, but I believe justice began in Eden. Not only were all the components good, they were *very* good. Righteousness reigned in that garden because all was in right relationship with each other—human and animal, male and female. That is the world God intended—a world of just relations. Do you agree with me thus far?"

His brows sank. "Agreed."

"So, then tell me, Oliver, how is your relationship with your father?"

The little vixen! Of all the circuitous logic. Disgusted, he shook his head. "That has nothing to do with my work, my purpose in fighting abuses of the law."

"Oh Oliver, it has everything to do with it. Please, hear me out." Slowly her hand dropped, and she took a timid step closer, blinking like a doe. "When the just world God created was spoiled by sin, He set out to restore it. The whole of scripture is dedicated to telling that story—how God works to set the world right. Through

Abraham, Isaac, and Jacob; through David; and ultimately through Jesus, the One who will bring perfect justice again someday. Until that day comes, He uses us, His followers. Don't you see? Through us—through you—God *is* setting the world right. Yet how can God bring the justice you so earnestly seek to the *whole* world if you refuse to seek the same restoration in your relationship with your earthly father?"

The anger simmering inside him flamed molten in his gut. "You have no idea of what you speak! The years. The pain. So many scars upon scars."

"Perhaps not, but I do know this... When you ask God for justice in this wicked world of ours, are you not really asking that His glory be vindicated against *every* sinner who defiles that glory—yourself included?"

Gripping the back of the chair, he planted his feet to keep from staggering. He wanted to stop up his ears. Run. Hide. Anything to get away from the terrible truth.

But still her words kept coming, her soft voice cutting sharp and deep. "Oh Oliver, don't you see? True justice starts with repentance. How can we ask God to show justice in the world while willfully nursing our own hidden prejudices, selfishness, lusts, greed...our own broken relationships?"

He gripped the sofa so tight, his knuckles cracked.

"And only the repentant can be justified in their hearts, for justice is not free. We have all done wrong, and someone must pay the cost. So God nailed those iniquities upon the only One who didn't deserve it, so that He might be both just and compassionate." Closing the distance between them, she peered up at his face, brown eyes alight with a strange glow—the fiery gaze of a true saint. "Think on that, as will I, for therein is the true path to peace that will offer us both rest tonight and forevermore."

They stood in silence then, save for the old clock ticking and the rain drip-drip-dripping. And his heart sank, bleeding out right there on the library carpet. Was she right? In failing to make amends with his father, had he shackled his own pursuit of justice? Like an old man with a withered arm, he slowly passed off the lamp to her. "Take this and see yourself to your chamber. I will—" Sudden emotion clogged his throat, and he cleared it. "I will remain here for a while."

Little creases drew shadowy lines on her forehead. "Are you certain?"

He nodded.

"Well, good night then, Oliver."

"Good night."

Liar! There'd be nothing good about the long black hours ahead of him. In truth, this just might prove to be the bleakest night of his whole existence, because Maggie—God love her—was utterly and totally correct. His view of justice had been small. Incomplete. Perhaps his father wasn't the blackest of sinners after all.

Perhaps it was time he took a good look at himself—a hypocrite of the worst sort.

⚭

Everyone knew that drunkards wouldn't inherit the kingdom, which meant the lost souls slugging back spirits inside the Pig & Pallor were doomed. Every last one of them. Sebastian sucked in a final drag of his cigarillo then flicked the stub towards the pub's open door. Who knew? Maybe the burning end of it would catch the whole structure on fire and the place would go up in hellish flames here and now.

But then he blew out a breath and reached for another smoke. The burning would have to come after he spoke with Groat, found out exactly what had transpired between him and Miss Lee, discover if the man knew anything about the cryptic "matter of days" of which the barrister had spoken. Fishing around, he poked his finger from one side of his pocket to another. Empty. And he hadn't thought to bring his pipe along. Scarping Groat! How much longer must he wait for the man?

He leaned back against the wall, sucking his teeth. Should he simply go inside and haul the devil out by his collar? Drinking was a sin. But so was immersing himself in a den of iniquity. Still, it wouldn't be by choice, but by need. He *needed* to speak with Groat, and God always helped those in need. In fact, he'd be doing Groat a favor by hauling him out of there and giving him a sharp reprimand. Some discipline. Yes. Perhaps it was time Groat received a corrective prod. A crack to the skull, maybe. Strike the fear of God back into him. Especially after the way he treated Miss Lee today.

He stepped away from the wall just as a dark shape scuttled out the door. The night was too black to see the man's face beneath the brim of his hat, but Sebastian didn't need to. Round body. Skinny arms and legs. Darting this way and that with jerky motions, like a crazed beetle trying to escape the crush of a heel about to slam down from above.

Groat.

Sebastian strode to the man's side and grabbed hold of his shoulders before the fellow listed sideways into the gutter.

"Wha's this?" Groat's black little eyes lifted to his, widening then narrowing, widening then narrowing, as if his vision must be adjusted in increments like the lens of a spyglass. "Barrow?"

Groat yanked away, then whirled to face him with a poke in the chest. "Don't touch." His last word stretched, the *chhh* sound spewing out a noxious waft of liquor fumes.

Sebastian fanned away the stench. "Your meeting with Miss Lee today. . . What did she say? What did she give you?"

"You were there?"

"Of course I was there. You're the one who said where the woman is, that's where I'll find my man. And you were right. I located Ward."

"Good for you." Groat teetered on his spindly legs, the pendulum arc of the movement growing ever wider. One more sway and—

Sebastian shot out his hand, shoring up the man before he passed out.

Once again, Groat wrenched away, staggering to keep upright. "I said don't touch!"

Another blast of cloying sourness hit him in the face. A man could only take so much of this. Sebastian reached for his truncheon, gripping the handle but leaving it attached to his belt. For now.

"So, what did Miss Lee say? What were you handed?"

"An invi—" Groat shot up his hand, hiccupped, then continued. "An invitation. A party."

"When? Where?"

"You"—Groat leaned in—"are not invited."

Sebastian reared his head back. "I don't need to attend. I just need the information."

"Days. Three." Groat stared at his fingers, lifting one, then another, until three digits finally stood tall. "Sunday?" he mumbled, then shook his head. "No. Friday."

Good. That was definitely a *matter of days.* "Where?"

"Armagnac."

"Armagnac?" He rolled the word around on his tongue, trying to make some sort of sense of it. Nothing came to mind. "Is that a street? A surname? An estate?"

Groat lifted only one finger this time, wagged it, then pulled out a flask and tipped back his head, pouring so much in his mouth that it leaked out the sides. The sound of the liquid guzzling down his throat was nauseating. Finally, he capped the thing and shoved it back into his pocket, then stared at Sebastian with a wobbly head. "It's a drink, you thick-headed. . .thick-headed. . .thick head!" A fine spray of saliva showered out with the exclamation.

Enough was enough.

Ignoring the stink of him, Sebastian grabbed the man by the collar and shook him hard. "Where is the blasted party going to be?"

Groat's eyes bulged and blazed, and with surprising strength, he shoved Sebastian in the chest, freeing himself. "I said don't touch!" The words were low, guttural, inhuman in an eerie way—and completely sober. Groat didn't so much as wobble a hair; he just stood there, black eyes burning holes through the night, through Sebastian.

Was that what he looked like when he said the same to others? An unbidden shiver skittered across his shoulders, and he backed

m the man, hands up. "All right. Fair enough. Just give me
... name of the place where the party will be, and I'll walk away."

Groat didn't move. That rankled. It was peculiarly unnatural. A
man in his condition should be tottering on his feet. His lips hardly
even moved when he spoke. "Corbin's. Ambrose Corbin's."

"Good." Sebastian let out a breath. "Very good. And a good night
to you, Mr. Groat."

Now was the time to strike, while Groat stood there like a statue,
completely unsuspecting. Sebastian turned slightly, intimating he was
about to leave, then whipped out his truncheon, ready to instill God's
discipline on the drunkard.

He spun, wood swinging, but his club whooshed through empty
air. What in the world?

Narrowing his eyes, Sebastian peered into the dark while turning
in a full circle. The pavement in front of the Pig & Pallor was vacant.
The whole street was unoccupied. No fleeing shadows. No sound of
scuttling footsteps. No Groat. The man was smoke and magic.

Slowly, Sebastian tucked away his weapon. He was good at what
he did, catching convicts, criminals, devious men of all sort. But there
was just no catching a demon.

And it was better not to try.

Chapter Twenty-Six

Pressing on through a cadenza gone bad is as excruciating as chewing on a piece of gristle with a rotted tooth. But it must be done. To stop midsong is not only the death of the piece but the end of a career. Not that my vocation is stellar at the moment. . .and neither are the last few notes I trill. With so little practice over the past several months, how will I ever make it through tomorrow night's performance?

Applause claps a staccato beat behind my back, echoing from wall to wall in the small sunroom. I whirl.

The barrister leans with his shoulder against the doorframe. Heat rises up my neck. How long has he been here? How many off-key notes and ruined rhythms has he heard?

A smile breaks wide across his face. "Well done, my dear. I daresay you'll be all the rage tomorrow evening."

"I wouldn't go so far as to say that, but thank you." I dip my head then spread my hands. "And thank you for allowing me this private place to practice."

"In truth, I'd all but forgotten this sunroom was even here, I so rarely venture from my study." He strolls inside, pacing the length of the room, his green gaze drifting about until it finally lands on me. "I hadn't realized just how unused and empty this house is until the past several days. It's been quite nice having you and Oliver here. More than I can say."

Just as I suspected, despite Oliver's words to the contrary, this great man of law really does have a heart. I angle my head. "Does your son know you are happy he came?"

"Oliver?" His brows rise, and a rueful chuckle follows. "No. Though we both make our livings giving speeches and swaying opinions, neither of us is very good at communicating."

"That doesn't mean you shouldn't try."

"He won't hear me. I'm afraid he's as set in his ways as I am in mine." Sadness tugs down the curve of his mouth, and he bypasses me, stopping in front of one of the mullioned windows. Weak sunlight paints him in a melancholy light, with his shoulders sloping like an unheard prayer fallen to the ground. The mighty Hawk of Crown Court is truly nothing more than a shell of an old man burdened by regrets.

My heart squeezes. This rift between him and Oliver is destroying them both. I pad softly to his side, desperate to impart some sort of encouragement. But then I press my lips closed. What a ludicrous thought. Who am I to speak words of supposed wisdom to this esteemed man of great intelligence?

I peek over at him, but he doesn't see me, not with that faraway glaze in his eyes. His jaw grinds, muscles moving in tight synchronization along his neck. Whatever he is thinking tortures him to a degree I cannot begin to fathom and, oddly enough, gives me courage to try to ease his pain.

"If I may be so bold, sir, you may be wrong, you know. While it's true Oliver is an angry man, and rightfully so, having suffered such hardship, that does not mean he cannot change. Nor are you so advanced in years and trapped in rigidity that you cannot alter your ways. I'd say there is much hope for you both, for God yet softens the hardest of hearts."

The barrister's jaw stills. His frock coat pulls taut against his steeled shoulders. He is tense. *I* am tense. Did I say too much?

His face swivels to mine. Like a kestrel poised to attack, his green gaze pins me in place. For an eternity he says nothing, nor do I. I can't. My throat is clogged.

At last, a small smile eases the strained lines on his face, and once again I breathe freely.

"You are good for Oliver, Miss Lee. For me as well. How much your own father must adore you, unless. . ." His smile fades. "Forgive me if I misspoke and he is no longer among the living."

I shake my head. "There is nothing to forgive, sir. My father is very much alive. He runs Rag and Bone Books down on Milsom Street."

"Oh? Have I so greedily consumed all your time that you've not had a moment with him?"

"It's not you. I'm afraid it's me. I've gotten so caught up in this whole affair of restoring justice since I've arrived, I own I haven't given my father much thought. So you see, before you give me too much credit, I am as rogue an offspring as your son. But rest assured that when this is all over, I shall call on my father straightaway."

"Why wait? Go now." He strides towards the door. "I'll have a carriage brought around."

I dash after him. "Oh, but I don't want to trouble you."

He flutters his fingers in the air. "No trouble at all."

It may be no trouble for him, but will it bring peril to my father? "I really think I should wait until after the party, when everything is settled."

He faces me, undeniable pain flashing in his eyes. "Do not make the same mistakes as Oliver and I. Trust me when I say there is nothing more important than seizing the present moment to mend relationships."

His words hit home, and I nod—then dash off to snag my coat and bonnet. In a trice, I climb into the carriage and rumble down the road to see a man I've not conversed with in nigh on a year. Though my father and I made peace with each other long ago, it's still generally awkward when I visit. He yet feels bad for being forced to send me away at such a tender age. I feel awful for having blamed him in the first place. But we both hold on to the truth that all worked for the good, being that neither of us ended up in the workhouse. Therein do we stand united.

The closer the carriage draws to Milsom Street, the lighter my heart. In witnessing Oliver and his father's relationship—troubled as it is—I am suddenly aware of how much I miss my own papa. Even if he's engrossed in a book, just to see him will be a balm to my soul. And I suspect that after nine months of no contact whatsoever, I just may be a balm to his as well.

As soon as the carriage stops, I open the door and descend to the pavement before the driver can assist. Though I doubt Mr. Groat will bother me before Friday, I cast a quick glance around me. Seeing nothing suspicious, I dash into the bookstore.

Wonderful scents take me back years. The somewhat greasy smell of ink. The slight mustiness of dust collecting on the highest shelves. The unique aroma of old books that comforts like a gentle spring rain, as ancient as time itself.

"Papa?" I call as I wander the familiar maze of shelving. "It's me. Maggie."

I run my finger along the spines while I search, greeting old friends. *Wuthering Heights*, *The Count of Monte Cristo*, *Barnaby Rudge*. A smile stretches across my lips. These titles and more are where I found my solace after endlessly long hours of waiting on customers, where I escaped to when Papa paid me no attention, where my little girl heart was mended after Mother died. The written word taught me I was not alone, that hardship comes to all, and connected me to the heroes and heroines who conquered those hardships, ultimately giving me courage. Indeed. Books are light and air.

Rounding the final corner before my father's office, I once again call out. "Papa? Are you—"

A man strides out the open door. Brass-framed spectacles draw circles around his eyes. His coarse brown hair is rather unkempt, sticking up in uneven patches like a lawn that needs a good mowing. He is tall. He is gangly.

He is not my father.

He nods towards me. "Can I help you, miss?"

"Yes. I am looking for the owner."

"Why, you're looking at him, miss. Mr. Wasterwell at your service."

He dips a polite bow.

My nose scrunches. He smells of kippers and brandywine, nothing at all like Papa's scent of warm tallow soap. Why is this man pretending to be that which he is not?

I advance a step and square my shoulders. "I'm sorry, Mr. Wasterwell, but you must be mistaken. Mr. Lee is the proprietor here. Mr. Theodore Lee. I should like to speak with him, so if you wouldn't mind stepping aside. . . ?"

"Hmm." His lips press together, and he doesn't move from blocking my way to the office door. "Apparently you've not heard."

If there is some sort of news, I prefer to hear it from my father, not this stranger. Still he doesn't budge, forcing me to ask, "Heard what?"

"I am sorry to say, miss, that Mr. Lee's been gone these past three months."

My frustration mixes with a rising alarm. I grip my reticule tight, trying to make sense of all this. "Where has he gone? Where is my father?"

His brows shoot skyward. "Am I to understand that you are—"

"Yes. I am Margaret Lee. Theodore's daughter."

Mr. Wasterwell's throat bobs and his voice comes out tight and thin. "I see. Please, wait here."

He disappears inside my father's office. My stomach knots. Either the man is eccentric, or there is a reason for his odd behaviour—a reason I'm not sure I want to know. When he returns, he holds out a paper-wrapped package, a book, judging by the feel of it.

"He wanted you to have this."

My grip turns icy. "Then why did he not give it to me himself?"

Mr. Wasterwell shakes his head. "I regret to inform you, Miss Lee, that your father is deceased. May God rest his soul."

∞

Picking oakum until his fingers bled. Breaking rocks with a small pickax until his muscles ached. Neither compared to crossing the servants' hall balancing a tray filled with champagne flutes on an upturned palm beneath the iron stare of James, the first footman. Sweat dotted Oliver's forehead as he peered at the quaking glasses. Liquid sloshed to the rims of each little devil. Sweet mercy! If he dropped yet another salver, he'd never again be able to look James in the eye, so complete would be his humiliation. The flagstones were already littered with broken glass and spilled water.

But four paces later, he reached the sideboard and gently—ever so gently—lowered the tray atop it. Victory! He spun to face James, satisfaction lifting the sides of his mouth. "There. How's that?"

"Well. . ." James pursed his lips, as imposing as any member of Parliament in his starched and ironed livery.

Smile wavering, Oliver's brow crumpled. "Well what?"

"At least you didn't spill anything."

"All right." His smile vanished. "Let's have it. What did I do wrong?"

"Above all, a footman must stand tall." James lengthened his neck, growing half an inch. "Shoulders back." His suit coat leveled to a razor-straight line at his shoulders. "And your gaze must always be fixed dead ahead." So focused was his stare, even if Oliver tossed a rock at the man, James wouldn't so much as blink.

Oliver frowned. "I thought that's what I was doing."

Like a soldier standing down, the footman's taut posture relaxed, and his gaze swung back to Oliver's. "I'm afraid you slouched, sir, and you spent more time peering at the glasses on your tray rather than to where you were going."

Blast. Guilty as charged. How would he ever pull off blending in with the rest of Corbin's serving staff tomorrow night? "I must admit, James"—he shook his head—"your job is harder than it appears."

"Thank you, sir. Not many gentlemen would say so." Pride gleamed in the man's blue eyes. "How about we work on opening champagne for now?"

Good. This should be a stroll through the park. He nodded. "Now that's something I can manage."

"We'll see."

The words were cryptic. So was the flash of a smirk slipping across James's usually stoic expression before he turned to retrieve one of several bottles in a nearby ewer. Doubt tried to elbow its way into Oliver's confidence, but he merely sniffed and crossed over to the man. He'd popped many a cork in his lifetime. This wouldn't be so hard.

With a white towel draped over his arm, James cradled the champagne like a baby. "In opening a new bottle, it is not necessary, and indeed not advisable, to allow the cork to pop loudly. If properly cooled—and make sure that it is at all times—the cork is easily extracted without exploding. Keep it at a forty-five degree angle, with your thumb atop the bottle. Don't think so much about removing the cork, but rather about easing the bottle away from it. A few twists, a small amount of gentle pressure, and. . ."

Hsst. The cork came away with a sigh.

"Immediately after opening," James continued, "wipe the mouth, thus." He swiped the hem of the towel against the opening, then lifted a brow towards Oliver. "Got it?"

It wasn't his usual flamboyant way of cracking open some bubbly, and not nearly as festive, but if it was a requirement, he really had no choice. He reached for a fresh bottle. "Yes, this I can do."

He unwired the cage, pressed his finger to the top, twisted, and—

Pop!

Champagne geysered out. The cork shot like a bullet, nicking the plaster near the doorframe, inches away from the butler's eyes, who happened to enter at a most inopportune moment.

Foster scowled at them both—and instantly Oliver was a lad of nine, wilting beneath the butler's glower. Strange how the little boy yet lived and breathed in the body of a thirty-year-old man. Shoving down a sudden unease, Oliver straightened as tall as he should've been whilst carrying a tray.

"Sorry to interrupt this. . ." Foster circled two fingers in the air, indicating the huge mess Oliver had created. "But there is someone here to see you, sir. In the sitting room."

"Thank you, Foster." He turned to James. "We'll have to practice more later tonight. It could be a late one. I'm afraid it might take longer than either of us will like."

James dipped his head. "Very good, sir. Oh, and sir? For what it's worth"—he leaned closer, lowering his voice for Oliver alone—"I wouldn't be too concerned if I were you. At the first dinner party I served, I dropped an entire tray of Bollinger and lived to tell the tale. It is politeness and civility towards guests that is of the utmost importance, not your grace or lack thereof. Don't let Foster's glower put you off too much."

"Thank you, James." He clapped the man on the back and, without giving the butler a second glance, strolled out of the servants' hall.

Fatigue tagged his heels, and he stifled a yawn as he ascended the stairs. After a late night considering all Maggie had said, then spending the better part of the day learning the finer points of being a footman, he was weary.

But fatigue faded as he entered the sitting room and spied a man in a tatty purple tailcoat. It paid to be on one's toes around Filcher. Though the fellow was a good asset for connecting discreetly with the shadier portion of society, you never could tell what a man in need might do with a fortune in his grasp. And now he stood with his back towards the door, hunched over one of the barrister's golden Chinese urns. So did a boy, dressed in a smaller version of Filcher's trademark tailcoat. Oliver frowned. As far as he knew, Filcher didn't have a son.

"I don't think that will fit beneath of either of your coats. Not without a noticeable bulge."

Both turned, eyes wide. Filcher fumbled with the urn, nearly dropping it. Oliver sighed. Was that how he'd looked when trying to balance that tray of flutes?

"What? Why, I'd never!" Filcher patted the vase as if it were his own wee babe. "Just admirin', tha's all." With great care, he lifted the urn to the mantel and tenderly eased it into place.

Oliver's gaze drifted to the boy. Face clean. Hair trimmed at the brow so that his brown eyes were unobstructed—eyes that looked familiar. Oliver peered closer until gears started clicking. Ahh. The boy. The one who'd helped him and Maggie escape Barrow's long arm.

"I see you've gained an assistant." He winked at the lad then faced Filcher.

"Aye. I discovered Bodger that day he escorted yer lady back to Avon Street. Right smart lad." He cuffed the boy on the back of the head. "I'm groomin' him."

Oliver bit back a snort. Grooming him? For what? A life of nefarious contacts and shady dealings?

Still, though he hated to admit it, the boy was cleaned up, the wan hollow of his cheeks not nearly as pronounced. At least Filcher wouldn't beat the lad and would keep him fed—a step up from life alone on the streets. And if—no!—*when* Oliver returned to his rightful place in Parliament, he'd see to it his housing legislation passed, which would better Bodger's lot even more.

The boy advanced, holding out the paper-wrapped package he'd been clutching to his chest. "I'd like to return this, sir. It were a fine coat, but Mr. Filcher here's got me a new one what fits much better."

After the boy handed off the parcel, he hooked his thumbs inside the lapels of his recently acquired coat and puffed out his skinny chest.

Oliver smiled. "And a very fine coat it is, Master Bodger. Thank you for returning this instead of selling it for a profit."

"Aye, he's an honest boy, God love him," Filcher rumbled. "Which might be a problem. . ."

Before Oliver could ask what he meant, Filcher pulled out a canvas case from inside his coat then opened it up atop the tea table, effectively silencing them all. Three identical ruby necklaces sparkled in the ray of sunshine angling in from the window.

"Caw!" Bodger breathed out.

Oliver didn't blame him. The jewels could steal the breath from the coldest of hearts.

"Ol' Billy did a right fine job of it, if I say so me'self." Bending close, Filcher huffed on one then buffed it shiny with the hem of his velvet sleeve.

Setting the package aside, Oliver closed in on the necklaces and studied each in turn. "It is quite good work. But which is which?"

"See here?" Filcher lifted the farthest necklace on the left and turned it over in his hand, then pointed to the clasp. "That engraved X means this is the all-paste necklace. The other two are half and half."

Once again, Oliver compared the three, then let out a long, low whistle. "That's amazing. Completely identical save for that etching. Had Groat originally gone to this Billy of yours, I fear Mrs. Corbin would've never known her jewels had been stolen in the first place. Once again, Filcher, your connections pay off. Literally. Wait here, please, while I fetch your money."

He strolled from the room, intending to collect the banknote from his father for Filcher's work, but as he neared the bottom of the main staircase, the front door flew open. In dashed a billow of skirts and the distinct sound of choppy breaths and sniffling. Maggie didn't even stop to remove her bonnet or wrap.

Oliver paused, one hand on the balustrade. Something wasn't right. "Maggie?"

She didn't so much as look up, just plowed ahead, chin tucked, face hidden by the brim of her hat. Clutching a paper-wrapped package, she gave him a wide berth and darted towards the other handrail.

Until he sidestepped her, blocking her way. "What's happened?"

She shook her head, still refusing to meet his gaze. Alarm snaked up his spine. She'd faced Groat, run from Barrow, dragged him broken and bleeding off the moor, and none of that had affected her so visibly. What the deuce had shaken her thus?

With the crook of his finger, he lifted her chin. Brown eyes puffy from crying finally looked into his. His gut clenched. Would to God that he could make right whatever it was that caused her so much anguish, but without knowing what that was exactly, he was helpless. "Do you feel ill? You're not hurt, are you? Have you had another run-in with Groat?"

He tensed, waiting an eternity for an answer—*any* answer.

"I'm fine," she finally clipped out.

"Clearly you are not. What is wrong?"

"Just. . ." She drew in a shaky breath, a world of hurt in the sound, one that punched him square in the gut.

"Just what?" He stroked her jaw with his thumb, hopefully coaxing some sort of explanation from her.

Her gaze burned into his. "Oliver, please, promise me you will make things right with your father."

He frowned. Her request didn't match the torment in her voice. He'd given her no reason since last night's quarrel for her to think he'd cleaved the rift any wider between him and his father.

"Why?" he asked.

She grabbed his arms, fingers digging into his sleeves. "Promise me!" The words spewed out, echoing in the hall. A lost little girl couldn't have sounded more desperate.

"Shh," he soothed. "Calm down. I promise I will try, all right?"

Her eyes filled, shimmering with a sorrow he couldn't begin to understand. Biting her lip, she slowly nodded—then burst into tears and burrowed her face into his shirt.

Speechless, he wrapped his arms around her, holding her. Just. . . holding. Each of her sobs cut deeper into his heart. Whatever had caused this outburst couldn't be good.

It couldn't be good at all.

Chapter Twenty-Seven

It is futile, this looking out a carriage window into the shadows of night. Even when the coach ventures into the gas-lit lanes of Bath, I still don't see anything but black. The darkness of grief filters everything. And no matter what I do, I cannot shake a deep foreboding that day or night, this gloomy view will be mine for quite some time.

My lower lip quivers, and I press my mouth into a tight line. My father left me a letter, tucked inside a copy of *Jane Eyre* of all things, assuring me of his love, but there is a hole in the world now. A hole in my heart. The vast emptiness of it catches me by surprise. Papa and I never had the closest of relationships, so why do I feel such a keen loss? Though I've pondered the question since I learned of my father's death yesterday, I have no answer. All I have is a heavy weight in my chest that will not easily be cast aside.

Leather creaks and warmth wraps around my folded hands. I pull my gaze from the glass and meet Oliver's concerned stare. He leans forward in his seat, his fingers infusing strength into mine. He is a shape-shifter, this man. First an escaped convict. Then a gentleman. Now a footman. His crisp black livery with the Corbin insignia on the lapel rides the strong lines of his shoulders. It is a stark contrast to my voluminous bloodred skirts. It's not the exact dress I wore on that fateful night, but it is close—thanks to Mrs. Corbin's resourcefulness.

"You don't have to do this, you know." His voice is low, a soothing accompaniment to the dull rumble of the wheels. "We'll figure out another way."

"Oliver is right." Next to him, his father shifts on the seat. His hawkish face turns towards mine. "You've taken a serious blow, my dear. There is no shame in backing out now."

I shake my head, willing the movement to dislodge some of my melancholy as well. "No, I want to do this. I *need* to do this. Had it not been for Ambrose Corbin driving me away, I'd have been here for my father. Maybe spent his last moments on earth at his side. Tonight, I sing for him. For his sake, and for yours." Turning my hand over, I grip Oliver's with an affirming squeeze, new strength unexpectedly filling me as my own words reach back inside me. My father is beyond Corbin's reach now. The threats that had bound me for the past nine months no longer wield any power. I lift my chin and breathe deeply for the first time since learning of my father's passing. "I will delight in exposing Mr. Corbin for the true villain he is."

As we turn onto the well-lit Corbin drive, light bathes half of Oliver's face. He pulls back and straightens on the seat, his expression a strange mix of admiration and trepidation.

Once again, I peer out the window, this time focusing on the task at hand. The carriage veers off the main drive, bypassing a lineup of other coaches, and circles the building until it finally stops at a side door. Once the three of us alight, a shrouded figure steps from the shadows and beckons us to follow.

Inside, we are immediately ushered into a storage closet that smells of muddied Wellingtons and waxed canvas that's been dampened one too many times. My nose tickles, and I press my fingers against it lest I sneeze.

The door closes. A lamp is lit. Mrs. Corbin removes a dark hood and mantle. Her pale green evening gown shimmers with hundreds of tiny seed pearls. Her silver-streaked hair is perfectly coiffed and curled, held in place by diamond-studded combs. Despite being a woman of middle age, she sparkles with elegance—a testament to the depravity of her husband, for any man ought to be proud to call her his wife and not seek to gratify himself with other females.

Her lips part—then suddenly close when her gaze lands on the ruby necklace resting on my collarbone. Little furrows crease her brow, but, though I try, I cannot figure out if it's sadness or anger that troubles her so.

Then her chin lifts, and the trance is over. "There is no time to waste." Her gaze drifts from me to Oliver and finally lands on the barrister. "The magistrate is here and already making noises that he shan't stay long."

Oliver's father grunts. "I was afraid of that. Old Hunter is a stickler for a pipe and his bed by ten o'clock. I shall have my work cut out for me to keep him within arm's length the whole evening. Well then, a quick rundown, shall we?" He claps his hands and rubs them together. "Miss Lee, have you the half-paste necklace to pass on to Mr. Groat?"

I nod. "It's in my bag."

Next to me, Oliver's deep voice rings out. "And I have the other, ready to slip into Mr. Corbin's pocket."

"Very good." The barrister nods.

Mrs. Corbin sweeps her hand towards me. "And I shall endeavor to match your performance tonight with as much flair as you, Miss Lee. As soon as you're finished singing and the applause dies down, I will accuse you of stealing my necklace."

"At which point I will refute you and point out the real thieves." And oh, how good that will feel!

"When all is accomplished, we shall meet back here. God-speed everyone." The barrister tips his head towards Oliver and me, then opens the door and holds it wide for Mrs. Corbin. "After you, Adelia."

They step out, but before I can follow, a light touch on my sleeve turns me around.

"Maggie, I . . ."

Oliver's words stall, yet hundreds more are birthed in his stare, none of which I can decipher. Like a book written in a foreign language, I can no more read what he was about to say than I can read Portuguese. But no words are needed. Somehow, some way, I understand this man as if he's poured out his heart to me. He is worried—and rightfully so—but it is more than that. Something deeper. He cares for me in a way that goes beyond a kiss or embrace, and that does strange things to my belly.

Leaning close, he presses his lips to my brow and whispers, "Be careful." Then pulls away.

The loss is staggering. Even so, I curve my mouth into a brave smile. "I will. And you as well."

With a last glance, I leave him behind and join Mrs. Corbin, who waits for me in the corridor. The barrister is already gone back to the carriage to make a grand entrance through the front door. Oliver will descend the servants' stair to join the ranks of the many who serve refreshments.

I follow Mrs. Corbin along a back passage. No plush carpets or golden sconces adorn this mean passage. Just oak planks and tin candle holders mounted on walls of somewhat cracked whitewashed plaster. What would the servants who use this corridor think to see me in my ruby gown trailing the sparkling skirts of Mrs. Corbin?

Before we run into any maids, Mrs. Corbin stops at a plain door. Strains of conversation and laughter crescendo as we enter. It is a small sitting area. A sofa. Two chairs. A tea table, fully stocked. And a ceiling-to-floor set of burgundy brocade draperies partitioning this area off from the rest of a great hall. A chill lifts gooseflesh on my arms. This is the same place where I stood nine months ago.

Mrs. Corbin turns to me and gathers my hands in hers. "May God bless you—bless us—on tonight's performance."

Before I can respond, she flees like a ghost in the night, slipping through a crack where the curtains meet the wall. Against all reason, I follow, driven by a compelling urge to see just how many and who are in attendance. There is only an inch gap, but it is enough for one eye to peer out.

Most of Bath's society mingles in their silk gowns and white cravats. Over in one corner, a small ensemble plays quiet music that underlays the chatter. All is familiar. My preperformance nerves begin to unspool—until a certain gentleman strolls into the room like a

Greek god. The crowd parts, allowing him passage. I shrink back and snug the curtain tight against the wall. My heart pounds in my chest like a caged sparrow mad to get out. Just the sight of Ambrose Corbin chokes me, and I lift both hands to my neck.

How on earth will I sing tonight?

∞

A London townhome. A country estate. An abbey, a castle, or hall. No matter the venue, every party was the same. As much as the wealthy liked to preen and prance, wearing bespoke suits and gowns in order to stand out, the lot of them looked identical. Oliver frowned. Picking out Corbin amidst the sea of black tails would be as tricky as keeping his tray balanced.

Weaving through the revelers, he donned a more placid mask as he searched for the scoundrel. Now and then guests signaled for him to stop and relieved him of yet another glass of champagne. Though he hated to slow his search, he had no choice but to comply.

Across the room, his father cornered Magistrate Hunter. Not a very dangerous assignment, but a difficult one, nonetheless. Oliver's gaze lingered a moment more, focusing on his father. As always he wore a mantle of power that demanded attention, but this time Oliver detected something more, a determination to set right a wrong, a stance he couldn't help but admire. Despite his promise to Maggie, he'd not yet had time to make amends with the man—but he would. Tonight, God willing. When this whole sordid affair was behind them all, he'd speak with his father and set things right, as much as it depended on him, then comfort Maggie, somehow, for the loss of hers.

Near the door, people suddenly parted. Steadying the tray, Oliver turned towards the movement. Long legs in perfectly tailored trousers strolled in, each step stoking another log onto Oliver's burning anger. Corbin. Just the sight of him twisted his gut.

The glasses on the salver rattled as Oliver upped his pace and reached into his pocket. A slight bump. A quick transfer. Justice would be served before the midnight buffet was fully stocked with platters.

But then a silver-haired matron stepped in front of him, blocking his path. Her eyes were pinched. No, her whole face was wrinkle upon wrinkle. A prune in an evening gown, clutching a small dog to her breast. She stroked the pup's head, rings glittering on her fingers, diamonds sparkling on the dog's collar. Oliver blinked.

"Portia here needs a drink." Each word snipped the air like a pair of scissors. The queen herself couldn't have commanded with any less authority.

Nodding, Oliver sidestepped her. Let some other hapless servant see to her Yorkshire's needs. Now was the perfect chance to pass off the necklace. Corbin stood with his back towards him. He might not even have to bump into the man from this angle. Just a quick pass-off and—

"I said Portia needs a drink. Now!" The shrill words turned heads—Corbin's included.

Oliver pivoted. If this demanding dowager exposed him before he could plant the jewels, all would be ruined. Forcing his lips into a smile, he dipped his head in a polite bow. "Of course, madam. I will return with some water posthaste."

"Which is what you should have done in the first place. Humph!" She sneered, her lips rippling like a clamshell. The little dog squirmed in her arms. "I should think the Corbins would not keep such ill-mannered help."

Ignoring the barb, Oliver clenched his teeth and made his way back to the sideboard. One glass tipped over as he set down the tray. Liquid spilled out in a bubbly stream. Blast! He cast about a covert glance, preparing for a dressing-down from the first footman, but miracles apparently still happened. No one noticed. Good, then they also wouldn't notice if he shoved the tray to the back of the table, picked up a small bowl, and dumped the nuts in it onto the mess. Working quickly, he reached for a crystal pitcher and filled the now-empty bowl halfway with water, then retraced his steps back to the woman.

"Here you are, madam." He held out the bowl with two hands.

"Finally," she barked and, ever so tenderly, extended the pooch so that its pink tongue could lap up a drink.

Degradation came in all forms. The crushing defeat of a prized piece of legislation. A stripped-bare beating in the prison yard. Standing amidst the wealthy, serving a dish of water to a dog that ranked higher than him by society's standards. Oh how far he'd fallen.

Finally the pup quit drinking. The woman curled her upper lip at Oliver and strolled away without so much as a thank you. Blowing out a long breath, Oliver once again donned the servant's face he'd practiced with James and returned the bowl to the sideboard, then started all over again to scan for Corbin.

Thankfully, the man hadn't moved far. Corbin yet stood somewhat near the door, engaged in a conversation with…Oliver squinted. Ahh. Lord Callahan. Of course. Corbin always made it a habit to woo the most influential, and Callahan was a high-ranking member of the House of Lords.

Shoving his hand into his pocket, Oliver fingered the necklace and edged his way over to the pair. Closer. Arm's length, now. A slight reach and—

Corbin turned his way.

So did the matron with the dog. "You there! Portia needs—"

Thunderation! It was now or never.

Averting his face, Oliver bumped into Corbin's shoulder, hopefully diverting the man's senses from detecting the necklace he slipped into his pocket. Without missing a step, Oliver kept on walking, straight for the door.

"Stop right there!" Corbin bellowed.

Oliver upped his pace, crossed the threshold, reached the front hall, and—

"I said stop." The words were a growl.

His step faltered. Causing a scene here and now would attract attention, possibly expose him, destroy everything before Maggie had a chance to pass off her necklace to Groat.

He halted and, though it galled him to do so, hung his head and sagged his shoulders in a display of submission. Every other muscle, though, knotted from the strain.

"Your pardon, sir," he mumbled.

Corbin's leather shoes clicked on the tiles, stopping just behind him. "Do not think you can so rudely assault me in front of my own guests. You're finished here. Take off that livery and get out of my house."

Slowly the tension ebbed. That was it? A simple dismissal? The man could have no idea the service he'd just rendered.

"As you wish, sir." Smiling, Oliver once again walked away.

"Wait!" Corbin's heels caught up with him. "I will have your name as well. Never again shall you work in a genteel home. I'll make certain of that."

Of course he would. Rotten powermonger. He should've known better. Corbin wouldn't let him—or any servant—off so easily.

He cleared his throat and pitched his tone lower than normal. "My name is—"

"Face me like a man when speaking!"

Fingers dug into his arm, jerking him around.

And then he was staring into the devil's eyes. Blue. Piercing. Rock hard—and flashing with recognition.

"Ward! What the deuce are *you* doing here? And in my livery, no less!" His gaze narrowed to slits. "How did you get out of gaol so soon?"

Inside the ballroom, chatter ceased. The clickety voice of Groat rang out. Oliver's hands clenched to hard balls. As much as he might like to thrash Corbin, that bit of justice was not his to mete out. He was only here to make sure that justice was indeed done.

In one swift move, he cranked Corbin's arm behind his back and snapped up his wrist towards his neck. One false move and Corbin would dislocate his shoulder. An effective hold. One Oliver knew well, for it was one of Barrow's signature pins.

He shoved the man forward, towards the gathering, and spoke low in his ear. "I'll explain later. I wouldn't want you to miss tonight's entertainment."

Chapter Twenty-Eight

I run my clammy palms along the smoothness of my red gown. This time, it is not my father's life that hangs in the balance but that of a man whom I've come to care about deeply.

Oh God, grant Your mercy on this night.

I pour hot water into a teacup and stir in a spoonful of honey. Bless Mrs. Corbin for remembering my preperformance penchant. The cup shakes in my grip as I lift it to my lips. It is not the fear of singing that trembles through me—just the usual amount of nerves in that respect. It is all the what-ifs that crawl over my skin like invisible spiders.

What if I drop the necklace instead of slipping it into Mr. Groat's pocket and the whole crowd sees?

What if the magistrate leaves before the true thieves are exposed, giving Mr. Corbin and Mr. Groat time to disappear? Or time to gather false witnesses and somehow turn the blame back on me or Oliver?

And—worst of all—what if none of this charade makes any difference and Oliver is once again locked away, perhaps for forever?

"Are you ready?"

The words click through the air, and my stomach sinks. I turn to face Mr. Groat. The curtain still sways behind him from where he shimmied between like a cockroach through a crevice.

I set down my cup. "I am."

"And the jewels?" His head angles, his black little eyes probing my face. "You have them?"

"I do."

"Then let us not tarry." He lunges, so that he's nose to nose, his moist breath dampening my cheek. "And do not think for one second to cross me again, hmm?"

It takes all my courage not to shrink back. "I will keep my word if you keep yours."

His dark gaze violates mine a moment more, then he's gone, the curtains swinging behind him.

Sharp clapping rings out. "Ladies and gentlemen. . .pardon me. . . your attention please."

The guests' droning fades to a hum, then disappears altogether.

"I am pleased to bring to you a talent that has not been seen since last year, here, at a gathering much like this." Mr. Groat's announcement click-clacks like sharp heels against a wooden floor. "Some of you may have even been fortunate enough to be in attendance that night."

A few oohs and ahhs filter through the room.

"This songbird," Groat continues, "is well known for her vocal capabilities. Most often she dazzles audiences at the Theatre Royal, but tonight marks a milestone in her career. After this evening, this famed soprano will fly on to other stages, other towns, other cities, for she is now a free agent, no longer tethered to Bath, and no longer mine alone to direct. This is a very special gathering, indeed."

He pauses for theatrical effect, and I inhale deeply, breathing in freedom. The bond is broken. He is no longer my manager. For the first time in my life, I am none but my own—a completely exhilarating and frightening thought.

"And so without further ado, I give you. . ."

When he pauses again, I palm the incriminating necklace and scoot close to the curtain.

"Miss Daisy Lee!"

Applause rings out. Mr. Groat pulls aside the draperies, takes a bow himself, then pivots and fixes his stare on me. I walk forward. He advances my way. As we pass, I slide the rubies into his pocket and continue walking until I am at the center of a half ring of guests. Only then do I smile brilliant and true. It's done. Mr. Groat carries his own doom.

Strains of music begin. The applause dies. Silently I count the beat, waiting for my cue.

And then I see Ambrose Corbin near the door. His nostrils flare, his eyes are wide, almost bulging, as his gaze fastens on me. My counting screeches to a halt. Though there are rows of guests between me and him, I shudder. He is as intimidating as the night he ran his finger along my bare neck and down my collarbone. His stare is fastened on the rubies at my throat.

My cue comes.

Goes.

And I stand mute.

∞

Every muscle Oliver owned quivered to wrench Corbin's arm just a tad harder. Apply a bit more pressure. Make the scoundrel cry out and experience in a small way the suffering he had borne the past nine months.

But then he'd be no better a man than Corbin himself. He reined in the urge and held the monster fast at the back of the crowd. Music started. Corbin stiffened. Grim satisfaction filled Oliver. It wouldn't be long now before manacles clapped tight against Corbin's wrists, justice finally served.

A few curious gazes drifted their way. One man edged towards them—then stopped, just as the music did, and snapped his gaze up front.

Alarm buzzed in Oliver's head. Why was Maggie's resonant voice not filling the room?

The music circled back to repeat the opening strains. Though risky, Oliver released his hold on Corbin and stepped aside to see what was going on. If Corbin made a move, he'd flatten him.

Peering over the heads of those in front, he spied Maggie standing beneath the dazzling light of a crystal chandelier, resplendent in her red gown—and a look of abject terror on her face. Her gaze was pinned on Corbin.

Oliver scowled. If he could run to her, he'd pull her into his arms and hide her eyes against his chest that she may never again have to look upon that beast.

But no time for that. He shot up his hand, and when her gaze startled to the movement and then darted to his own face, he infused every bit of encouragement and strength into the mouthing of a single word.

Sing.

Time stopped. He held his breath. Once again the music swelled. When it softened for her intro, would she open her mouth?

God, please, give Maggie the courage that I cannot.

Her chest rose and fell, frantic at first, then calming. A strange light blazed in her eyes. Had Corbin's spell been broken, or had *she* been broken?

Sing, Maggie. Sing!

As if she read his thoughts, her chin lifted, she parted her lips, and the sound of heaven came down to earth. The crowd sucked in a collective breath at the purity of her voice.

And then they were alone, just him and Maggie. Her brown eyes boring into his. Her sweet mouth moving for him and none other. Despite the distance and people and impossible circumstance, the space between them charged like the air before a lightning strike. She was his in that moment. He was hers. Joined as one in the ethereal music flowing from her lips.

Off to the side, a black shape scuttled against the wall. Though it killed Oliver to end the connection, he turned towards the movement to see the tails of Groat's suit coat flying out one of the other doors.

Blast! What to do? Stay here and make sure Corbin didn't flee? Or go after the known escapee?

He snuck a quick glance at Corbin, but just like the rest of the guests, the man was entranced by Maggie. Besides, he likely wouldn't rush away now that he'd seen the ruby necklace at her throat.

Oliver retreated the few steps to the nearest door, then broke into a dead run as Groat fled down the corridor. The man bypassed the main entrance and swung into another passageway, towards the servant stairs, apparently intent on exiting a back door.

Oliver pumped his legs harder. Snagging Groat at the rear of the house would be easier anyway. Fewer waiting carriages. Fewer coachmen to attract attention. A square courtyard bordered by outbuildings instead of a vast and open circular drive.

Taking the stairs two at a time, he gained on the man and landed on the ground floor just paces behind Groat. He might even tackle him before the man reached the door.

But then a scowling butler stepped out from a doorway and blocked him. "Get back to work!"

Ignoring him, Oliver veered aside—just as a scullery maid entered the corridor with a tray. He jerked sideways, praying to miss her as he tore past, but his shoulder caught the platter. The dish flew and shattered on the floor. The maid shrieked.

Oliver stumbled, balancing for a split second on one foot, then charged ahead. "Sorry!" he yelled.

Groat was already out the door.

"By all that's holy!" the butler boomed. "Where do you think you're—"

Oliver bolted outside, the door slamming against any further rebuke. To his left, Groat's top-heavy body skittered on long thin legs, straight towards a waiting horse tethered near a watering trough. Oliver sprinted, lungs heaving. Five yards to go. Four. The man was so close now that he could smell his sweat. Two more strides and he'd launch, ride Groat to the ground and—

Something shot out in front of him, shin level. Oliver flew. He whumped to the gravel, air knocked from his lungs. His chin drove hard into the rocky soil. Before he could gasp in a breath, a boot ground into the small of his back. His arms were pinioned behind. Rope cut into his wrists. By the time he could breathe, he was yanked to his feet.

And Groat was riding away.

Chapter Twenty-Nine

My final note hovers on the air. The musicians capture it and skill-fully bring the aria to a bittersweet ending. Face uplifted, I smile and blink back tears. It is this thin space before applause that satisfies the most. The magical part when I am caught up in the worship of the moment, just God and me and the breathless wonder of the human voice He so graciously gives. No matter that I stumbled through the cadenza and barely hit the highest octave, it is enough for Him—and for me—that I gave it my all.

A thunder of clapping breaks loud and strong, and I grieve the split second of holy silence just passed. Had the audience heard it? *Felt* it?

Dipping my head in gratitude, I give in to the crowd's approval before my nerves fray at the edges. In the grand scheme of things, tonight's performance wasn't about me or my singing, but about righting a wrong. Everything hinges on the next few minutes.

I lift my face as a few guests shout, "Brava!" and curtsey my appre-ciation, taking care not to allow my gaze to slip to the corner where Ambrose Corbin stands—for then I really will lose my nerve. Instead, I meet Mrs. Corbin's gaze and give a tiny nod.

She screams.

A collective gasp follows.

Mrs. Corbin darts from the crowd, her finger aimed at my neck. "Those are my jewels. My *stolen* necklace! You are a thief!"

Those behind her cannot see the slight wince that crinkles the sides of her eyes. Though we preplanned her exact words, it is touching that she hesitates to bring such a false accusation against me.

Slapping my hand to my chest, I feign surprise—which hushes the entire room. Blood is in the water and all wish to see the circling shark attack its prey.

But none expect that I am the shark.

Instead of shrinking back, I advance. Every eye fixes upon me. This will have to be my finest performance ever. "I'm afraid you're mistaken, Mrs. Corbin. These are naught but a bit of paste. As far as I am aware, your husband and Mr. Groat are the last ones to have your jewels."

"Preposterous!" Ambrose Corbin shoves through the gaping onlookers and stalks straight towards me. "You will give me my wife's rubies, and you will give them to me now."

He springs, arm outstretched, fingers extended. I recoil.

Too late.

The clasp bites into the back of my neck as he yanks. The chain gives. Gems fly everywhere.

"Now see what you've done!" Corbin roars and wheels about, madly scrambling to pick up the fallen rubies. Several other guests do the same. It is a macabre scene, silks and suits grasping about like blind beggars after thrown pennies.

"What is the meaning of this?" Magistrate Hunter breaks through the circle of onlookers. Though he is roughly the same age as Oliver's father, a tired air hovers about him, with his silvery wisps of thin hair sliding over the top of his head, a vague memory of what used to be sandy waves. This close, he looks older than I first credited him at the hotel restaurant.

Mr. Corbin snatches the rest of the jewels from the hands of his hapless guests. One man frowns. Another lady sticks out her lip in a full-blown pout. Did they seriously think Ambrose Corbin would allow them to leave with such a priceless party favor?

Once the gems are collected, he wheels about, a feral glaze in his eyes. A cornered rat couldn't look fiercer. "That woman"—he hitches his thumb at me—"is in league with Oliver Ward. Both are criminals.

Arrest her this minute!"

"That is a strong accusation, Mr. Corbin." The barrister pushes through the crowd and pulls up next to the magistrate. He seeks out my gaze, his green eyes calming and strong. "The magistrate would be remiss to issue any warrants without further investigation."

Mr. Hunter nods. "Mr. Ward speaks true." He shoves out his palm. "Hand over the evidence, Mr. Corbin, so that we may get to the bottom of this."

Mr. Corbin clutches his handful of broken necklace to his chest. "I'll do nothing of the sort. These belong to me! To my wife."

Oliver's father stretches to his full height and looks down his nose at Mr. Corbin. Though his imposing stance is not directed at me, I stiffen. I cannot imagine facing such a nemesis were I the accused in a court of law.

"Refusing to comply with a magistrate's request is a punishable offense, sir." The barrister doles out each word like a crack of thunder.

The crowd draws closer. I hold my breath.

Mr. Corbin sneers, then slams his handful of jewels into the magistrate's waiting fingers.

With them occupied, the barrister dips me a little nod. It's time.

I draw in a breath, then speak so the entire room may hear. "Mr. Hunter, perhaps you should check Mr. Corbin's pockets. As I said, he and Mr. Groat are the last ones to have the real jewels. It was Mr. Corbin's original idea and Mr. Groat's complicity to fashion my paste replication based on Mrs. Corbin's."

The magistrate's eyebrows crawl up to his hint of a hairline. "Is that so?"

Mr. Corbin's gaze burns holes through me. "What game is this, Miss Lee?"

Mrs. Corbin steps closer to me. How many times has she had to fend off her husband's rage? The thought of his bullying her, his unfaithfulness and lechery, surges fresh courage through my veins.

I wave to his suit coat. "If I am lying, then you should have no problem showing the magistrate the contents of your pockets, sir."

His face reddens to a murderous shade. "I will not have some light skirt ordering me about in my own home. Mr. Hunter, if you do not put a stop to this charade at once, I will—"

"If you've nothing to hide, sir, then show me your empty pockets." The magistrate shifts the broken necklace to his other hand.

Strange how a room once so alive with chatter and laughter can suddenly sound like the grave. No one speaks. No one breathes— save for Mr. Corbin. His chest heaves as he finally digs into his right pocket and turns it inside out. "See? Nothing!"

My chest tightens. Had Oliver insufficient time to plant the necklace?

But the magistrate does not move. "And the left?"

Mr. Corbin shoves his hand into that pocket—and pulls out the half-paste, half-real necklace. He lifts it high, blustering. A murmur runs through the crowd like an unholy wind.

Magistrate Hunter swipes the rubies from the man's hand. "I'll take that also, Mr. Corbin."

Mr. Corbin growls and shoots me an icy glare. "What are you up to, you little witch?"

The crowd shuffles ever closer—but this time Ambrose notices the movement, for the dark scowl etched into his face smooths into a placid smile that he directs towards the magistrate and barrister. A small chuckle rumbles in his chest. "Why, I am sure this is nothing but a small misunderstanding. Let us adjourn to the sitting room and sort it out there." Swinging his arms wide, he faces his guests. Truly, the man ought to be onstage himself.

"Friends, please. Enjoy the evening. A repast will be served shortly, whereupon Mrs. Corbin and myself shall rejoin this happy gathering. So drink, dance, and make merry." He retreats several steps and snags his wife's arm. "Come, darling."

Skirting the crowd, he pulls her along with long-legged steps.

The barrister turns to Magistrate Hunter. "Will it aid you, sir, if I retrieve Mr. Groat for your questioning, since he was handling the jewels as well?"

Mr. Hunter nods. "Very helpful. Oh and Ward, the jeweler, Mr. Flaversham, the one we spoke with earlier? Bring him too, if you please."

"As you wish, sir." Once again Oliver's father seeks out my gaze just before he turns away. The crowd cannot see his face, neither can the magistrate, but I do. The wink he gives me shores up and fortifies my flagging bravery—and I'll need every bit of it as the magistrate guides me out of the ballroom and into the sitting room.

We barely cross the threshold when Ambrose Corbin slams the door shut. I jump. So does Mrs. Corbin. Mr. Hunter merely raises a brow.

Ambrose circles me, then flicks his fingers at my face and scowls at Mr. Hunter. "There is foul play afoot this night, and it begins and ends with this woman and Oliver Ward."

I edge away from him until I bump up against a window. Mrs. Corbin joins my side.

"Now, now, sir." The magistrate speaks as if to a fretting toddler. "If I recall correctly, Mr. Ward resides at Dartmoor Prison. I fail to see how—"

"He's here! In this very house." Mr. Corbin's face deepens to the shade of a freshly dug beetroot. He spins towards his wife and me. "And the two of you have arranged for this whole charade, have you not?"

Every muscle in me screams to run away and hide from the awful rage that pulses strong in the vein standing out on his neck. But I force my chin high and will my voice not to squeak. "I am here at the request of your wife."

He snorts. "And you just so happened to wear the same costume as your last performance?"

"Again"—I shrug—"at the request of your wife."

He hurls his full fury at Mrs. Corbin. "Do not tell me you ally yourself with them as well."

"Mr. Corbin." The magistrate steps between us and him. "I suggest you sit down and leave the questioning to me. We will see who is truly in possession of the missing jewels."

"Bah!" he roars, then strides to a side table, where he pours a tumbler full of brandy and gulps it down.

Beside me, Mrs. Corbin draws in a deep breath. "Mr. Hunter, I wish to state for the record that the necklace in question is mine, not my husband's. It was bequeathed to me alone at the demise of my mother. She, being a dowager countess, was in full legal possession of the rubies and signed them over to me. So you see, sir, anyone who is found to be holding those jewels other than myself truly is the thief."

Ambrose spews a mouthful of liquor as he pivots to face her. "You conniving little vixen! You would accuse me? Your own husband?"

Though she trembles beside me, her voice rings out pure. "You ceased to be my husband the day you sought affections elsewhere."

I want to shout, "Brava!" for her bold truth, but just then the door opens. The barrister and a squat little man, all podgy and perspiring, stroll in, drawing everyone's attention.

Mr. Hunter dips his head in greeting. "Thank you for coming, Mr. Flaversham. I am certain you can clear this whole thing up with your expert opinion." The magistrate's gaze shifts to the barrister. "And Mr. Groat?"

A grim frown wrinkles the barrister's brow. "I am afraid, sir, that Mr. Groat is nowhere to be found."

∽

Oliver lunged against his bindings, against Barrow's hot breath hitting the back of his neck, against the world and all the unfairness of the universe. A beast raged inside of him. Snapping. Snarling. Straining to get out. A primal howl roared past his lips.

"You've got the wrong man!"

Barrow's truncheon dug into the small of his back. "All liars will burn in the pit of hell. Now move."

Barrow laid his weight into the club, shoving him forward.

Oliver stumbled a few steps, then spun. The brim of Barrow's hat hid his face in shadows. The rest of him was cloaked in black.

The man truly was a fiend of the night—*his* fiend. His own personal demon from the abyss.

"Listen to me!" Oliver's voice bounced off the courtyard walls. Were there not a party going on inside, the whole of the house would hear him. "That man on the horse, Groat, the one who just rode off, he's got the rubies in his pocket. He is the real thief, not me. So is Corbin, inside. You're making a mistake, Barrow! You're letting the true criminal get away."

A mirthless chuckle rumbled up from deep inside the man's chest. "Every deceiver shall swim in the lake of fire, Ward. Repent now before it's too late."

Sweet blessed heavens! There'd be no convincing this hard-headed pretend saint, leastwise not with words.

Ducking his head like a battering ram, Oliver charged. The top of his skull hit full on Barrow's nose. Cartilage crunched. Barrow staggered, cussing oaths that would make a pirate blush. But before Oliver could run free, the man snagged the fleshy part of his upper arm.

"Now you've gone and done it, haven't you?" Barrow roared.

The chill in his voice instantly froze the hot fury in Oliver's belly. He'd heard that tone only once, the night before the man from the cell opposite his was found beaten in the yard. Bludgeoned until his face was unrecognizable. More than likely from a truncheon.

Like the one in Barrow's hand.

With every bit of muscle he could muster, Oliver wrenched from Barrow's grip. But the momentum was too much with his hands pinioned at his back. He lurched sideways and fell, his shoulder grinding into the ground. Hard.

But not as hard as Barrow's club. Oliver's head jerked aside as the wood smacked into his jaw. He rolled. Yet the blows kept coming. Raining down faster than he could move, until he finally curled into the fetal position to keep from having his guts battered into the gravel.

"What would you do without a shepherd, Ward? Hmm?" Barrow bellowed, then hoisted him up by a handful of hair. Holding him at eye level, he shouted into his face. "You'd get yourself into more trouble than you're already in. Maybe even get yourself killed. Why, it's you who ought to be thanking me, that's what. Keeping you from harm. Bringing you back to the fold. It's God's work that I do. Aye, you ought to be real thankful to God and to me."

In one swift movement, Barrow released him and cracked the heel of his hand into Oliver's forehead. Off balance, Oliver whumped backwards onto the ground. Warm blood spilled from his nose, his mouth, one of his ears. Every bone ached. Every muscle screamed. But even so, he rolled with a groan and staggered to his knees. "You're mad!"

"Maybe." Barrow squatted, face to face. "But at least I'm free."

The words hit like a sledgehammer to his chest, driving the air from his lungs. Barrow was right. Here he was, bound again, at the mercy of a maniacal lawman. Was he to relive the same hellish nightmare?

No, not if he could help it.

While Barrow stomped towards a horse tethered nearby, Oliver shoved to his feet. If he could make it inside, get help, maybe he might stave off Barrow's single-minded obsession to haul him back to prison.

He staggered like a tosspot, knees threatening to buckle with each step. Four yards to the door. Three. Two more and—

Laughter barked at his back. "You never quit, do you?"

Barrow grabbed him from behind. The world flipped. Despite his violent wrenching, more rope bit into his flesh as he was tied down to the back end of a horse.

Barrow swung up on the saddle, leather creaking, then he clicked his tongue and the horse walked on. Oliver writhed, straining to break loose. He couldn't leave now. What would his father think of him disappearing this way? Any chance of making amends would be gone, and his father would forever be disappointed in him. Oliver wrenched again, but the more he wriggled, the deeper the bindings cut.

He jerked up his head, desperate to spy anyone who could help him—and then he froze. The sweat on his brow turned to icy beads. In the window they passed, a red gown swayed near the glass.

Maggie.

His heart stopped. *God, no. Please!* If Barrow succeeded in hauling him away, not only would his father not know what happened to him—*she'd* never know. Any hope he'd ever had of making her his own would be shattered if he disappeared like this into the night. Even should he get free again, she wouldn't dare trust him. He strained his neck higher, memorizing her outline, until the flash of red moved away and disappeared.

The horse rounded the side of the house. Oliver cast about a wild glance. Several coachmen huddled together in the shadows. The scarlet glow of a cigarette passed between them.

"Hey! This man is taking me against my will!"

Barrow shifted on the saddle. "Shut your gob or I'll give you what for."

"Help! This man is—"

A loud thwack smacked against his temple.

And everything went black.

Chapter Thirty

Except for periodic outbursts from Ambrose Corbin, the sitting room is deathly quiet. The magistrate, the barrister, Mrs. Corbin, and I all lean towards the jeweler, Mr. Flaversham. He's already examined the loose jewels broken free from the necklace I'd worn and declared them to be paste. He's also run the rubies found in Mr. Corbin's pocket through a gamut of tests. Now, he holds what's left of the necklace in question up to a gas lamp, giving it a final look through a magnifier that makes one of his eyes the size of a platter.

Finally, he lowers the thing and turns to us. "It is my expert opinion that the necklace found in Mr. Corbin's pocket is made up of half paste and half rubies."

Ambrose slams down his tumbler with a curse. He's already drunk a third of the decanter, so it is no wonder he lists to the side as he strides over to our gathering. "Someone put that thing into my pocket. I am not to be blamed for whatever hellish scam is afoot this night."

The magistrate eyes him for a moment, then turns to me. "And you say Mr. Groat was working with Mr. Corbin?"

I nod. "Yes, sir."

The magistrate rubs his chin. "Since Mr. Corbin possesses only half of the real gems, it seems probable Mr. Groat has the other half."

I bite the inside of my cheek to keep from smiling too broadly at the very conclusion we hoped he would draw. "That does seem quite likely, sir."

Mr. Corbin flings out his arm, grabbing hold of the magistrate's sleeve. "For the love of queen and country, man! You don't really believe that little she-devil, do you?"

"Watch your language, Mr. Corbin." Oliver's father steps to my side. "Miss Lee is not the villain here."

The magistrate plucks off Ambrose's hand and frowns into the man's face. "Until all the facts are laid bare, I will not adhere to any belief whatsoever. In the meantime, I think it best if you come along with me, sir, where I can keep an eye on you."

"I will do no such thing!" With a sneer, Mr. Corbin charges back to the liquor cabinet and splashes more brandy into his cup. Most of it spills. Amber liquid pools on the shiny wood, drips down the side, and stains the carpet beneath.

The barrister dips his head close to Mr. Hunter's. "Corbin won't go easy. I've rounded up a few men who wait outside the door in preparation for such an outcome as this. Shall I call on them?"

The magistrate cocks a brow at him. "Always one step ahead, eh, Ward?"

"I try, Mr. Hunter."

The magistrate nods his approval, and Oliver's father strides away.

"Ladies." Mr. Hunter's gaze shifts between Mrs. Corbin and me. "If you'll be so kind as to wait outside."

"Wait for what?" Once again Ambrose charges towards us, reeking of cognac and rage. "Do not think for one minute, Hunter, that you and your station are beyond Parliament's reach." He stabs his finger into the magistrate's chest. "Continue down this road and I have the power to make your life very uncomfortable."

"I should think, sir, comfort might be more of your concern than mine. I hear the holding cell at the gaol is a bit damp this time of year." He lifts his chin at the men the barrister ushers in. "Constrain Mr. Corbin, gentlemen, and have him brought to my coach, if you please."

"You cannot take me from my own house! You traitorous—"

Before any filthy language gushes from his mouth, I hook my arm through Mrs. Corbin's and usher her from the room. I do not stop until we are beyond earshot, where I guide her to one side of the wide corridor and study her face for any signs of swooning. She's been through a lot, not only this evening but in all the years she spent with such a heinous man.

Though she is as thin as ever and once again twirls the overlarge ring on her bony finger, her colour looks healthy. Her eyes are bright. She doesn't tremble or waver on her feet. Good signs, all.

Even so, I query, "How are you faring?"

"I should ask the same of you." Her lips arc into a small smile. "Still, I thank you for your concern. I am better than I expected, actually. I knew this evening would be taxing, but honestly, it is a relief that Ambrose will finally have to account for his sins."

I smile in full. "You are a strong woman, Mrs. Corbin."

Little flecks of silver gleam in her pale blue eyes. "There is iron in your spine as well, Miss Lee."

Footsteps clap against the tile, and we both turn to see Oliver's father approach. He stops in front of us, a pillar of strength we both naturally gravitate towards.

"The magistrate will see to Ambrose, locking him up until a trial is arranged. He's also sent for several men to pursue Mr. Groat. I'd say, ladies, that our job here is finished. Adelia"—his gaze seeks out Mrs. Corbin's—"would you like me to dismiss your guests for the evening?"

"Thank you, but no." She stops fiddling with her ring and smooths her hands along her skirt. "I owe them some sort of explanation, or who knows what will appear in tomorrow's papers."

"As you wish." He offers me his arm. "Miss Lee, shall we go meet up with a certain footman and call it a night?"

"I would like nothing better—"

"Pardon me, but if I may have a word with Miss Lee?"

We all turn to face a dandy of a fellow. From the tips of his glossy Italian leather shoes to the pristine top hat he holds in his white-gloved hands, the man is the epitome of a high society gent. His face is somewhat familiar, yet I cannot place him. Not surprising, really. Over the course of the years, I've been introduced to more people than can be accounted for.

The barrister slips me a sideways glance. "Do you know this man?"

"No, I..." But as the stranger's brown eyes hold my gaze, a memory surfaces. An outing to London where I'd sung a few years back. A soiree for the elite. Had he been there? Was he...? Ahh.

"Why, yes. Indeed I do." I dip a small curtsey at the newcomer. "Good evening, Mr. Lamb. I didn't realize you were in town." Then I smile at Oliver's father. "It's all right. Mr. Lamb is a theatre manager in London. I'll join you and your son in a moment."

Mr. Ward eyes the man, then gives an imperial sniff. "Very well. If you say so." Then he pulls away from me and offers Mrs. Corbin his arm instead. "Come, Adelia. I'll see you to the ballroom on my way downstairs."

As their footsteps fade down the passageway, Mr. Lamb's tenor voice fills the void. "That was quite a performance tonight. I mean, other than what happened with Mr. Corbin. In light of your recent absence from the stage, your aria was surprisingly divine."

I cannot help but grin. Coming from the manager of the most prestigious opera venue in all of England, his words are high praise indeed. "Thank you."

He fingers his hat, edging it in a circle as he speaks. "Allow me to be blunt, Miss Lee. Your former manager, Mr. Groat, made it quite clear that you are on your own now. Which means you are free to accept any offer you like."

Curious, I nod. "That is true."

"Brilliant!" He advances a step, then straightens his shoulders. I catch a waft of bergamot and Turkish tobacco.

"I have a proposition for your consideration. A contract for two years, with me. Think of it. The Royal Opera House. Covent Garden." He waves his hand through the air as if underscoring a freshly painted signboard with my name on it. "It can be yours. *All* yours. 'Daisy Lee' will be on the lips of London's wealthiest and most powerful. And from there, who knows? It's only the beginning."

I gape like a landed halibut, unprofessional and downright unladylike, but completely unstoppable. "Oh. . .I. . .well—"

La! I sound like a lunatic. I snap my lips shut before the man has me committed to an asylum.

"Allow me to be clear." He smiles, his teeth a flash of white in the sconce light. "If you want it, the Royal Opera House is yours. You may set the terms of the contract, within reason."

My heart skips a beat. I reach for the wall, seeking something solid lest my weak knees give way. This is it. The opportunity of a lifetime—of a hundred lifetimes. There is no more prestigious stage in England. Mr. Lamb's offer would not only restart my career, it would launch me into the upper realms of the entire music world. Glory. Wealth. Fame. And most of all, the chance to sing unfettered, according to my heart's desire, free of others' dictates, sharing the gift of beautiful music with even more people. It's all within my grasp with the utterance of a single *yes*.

My gaze drifts past the man who holds my future, skims down the corridor, and stops at the entrance to the ballroom—the last place I'd seen Oliver. Surely he'll understand if I jump at this chance. He is a politician, after all. An opportunist. How many open doors has he run through in order to gain his standing in the House of Commons? And it's not like I need his permission. I am finally and fully my own woman. I'd be a fool to turn down Mr. Lamb's generous offer.

But then I remember that singular moment when my eyes locked with Oliver's as I sang. The way everyone and everything ceased to exist, and we were the only two souls in the universe. Just thinking of it now rushes a surge of warmth from my head to my toes.

And then I know.

As much as I want to continue sharing the gift God gave me, the joy of singing for strangers pales in comparison to the love of a good man in a quiet home. God gifted me with music to share with

Him first of all, and I can do that as well out on the vast expanse of Dartmoor as upon London's finest stage. Indeed, that *is* the stage I now yearn for most—a house at the end of a moor where dogs and children can roam free. My children.

Oliver's children.

I pull away from the wall and snap my gaze back to Mr. Lamb. "I appreciate your offer, sir. It is no small thing that you propose. Trust me when I say I am deeply honored. Were I to sing anywhere, I would covet a position as resident soprano at your theatre."

"Pretty words, Miss Lee." He frowns. "Yet I get the feeling you are about to turn me down."

"I am."

"Well." He dons his hat and straightens his sleeves, then looks me full in the face. "Whoever he is, I hope he is worth it."

I blink. "What makes you think it's a man?"

"Only a woman befuddled by love could turn down so magnificent an offer." He smiles and withdraws a small calling card, offering it to me. "Look me up next time you're in London. I think I can manage to get you a few tickets. And whoever this beguiling man is who's stolen your heart, I hope to meet him someday."

"Thank you." I pluck the card from his gloved fingers. "Would that I had signed with you at the start of my career."

"Would that you had as well. Good evening, Miss Lee."

He bows then strides down the corridor, taking my golden opportunity along with him. Inwardly I search for the slightest hint of regret, for the niggling feeling in my feet that I should run after him. But all I feel is a desire to dash down the passageway in the opposite direction and throw myself into Oliver's strong arms.

So I do. My slippers fly across the carpet. I know the way to the back staircase as if I am skipping down a corridor at Morden Hall. It is the same escape route I used last year, only this time as I scamper down the steps, I am not running from a man but towards one.

I swing into the small storage closet, breathless with hope for an even brighter future than that promised by Mr. Lamb. The barrister faces me as I enter—but he is alone. I glance back out the door on the off chance that Oliver is even now coming down the corridor.

He is not.

I face his father. "Where is Oliver?"

"Actually, my dear." The barrister frowns. "I was hoping you could tell me."

Chapter Thirty-One

Early the next morning, I fold up my red gown and lay it in my travel bag. The fabric pools like spilled blood, and I shiver. It is a forlorn sight, so final and bittersweet. Never again will I grace a stage in such a fine costume. Though I am ready to be done with my public life, it still comes with an emotional cost now that it is officially ended. This sorrow, however, is nothing compared to the sharp ache in my heart for my father. Two loves lost in as many days. I only hope I do not lose a third. As far as I know, Oliver is still unaccounted for. . .unless he intends to surprise both the barrister and me at breakfast.

I snap the bag shut and hurry out the bedroom door. Eggs and toast are the last things on my mind. I am hungry for a dark-haired, hazel-eyed man.

As I near the dining room, I slow my steps, tuck in a last stray curl, and swirl into the room with a smile, ready to greet the man who owns my heart.

But the curl flops back onto my brow, and my smile fades. I stop at the head of the unoccupied table. The barrister is not here.

Neither is Oliver.

I approach the sideboard with a frown. Snubbing the covered dishes and urn of coffee, I pour a cup of tea. For now, it is all I can stomach. Holding the cup in two hands, I survey the empty room.

Doubt scalds as hot as my first sip. I thought Oliver cared for me. After all, he'd asked to call on me once his name was cleared. But am I deceived? Had he only used me to get Corbin arrested and then when he got what he wanted, left both me and his father? Lord knows it wouldn't be the first time I'd been betrayed by a man.

The cup shakes. Tea dribbles over the rim. I set it on the table, half-drunk. No. I will not believe Oliver capable of such a duplicitous act. I cannot. The pain would be too great. He will show up. He will! And he'll know where to find me. It shouldn't take me but a few minutes to pack up my belongings and begin the trek back to Morden Hall. With my career officially ended and my father gone, there is nothing more for me here in Bath.

I stride towards the door—just as the barrister rounds the corner and nearly bumps into me.

With a quick reach of his hand, he steadies my arm. "Pardon me, Miss Lee, but you are just the person I was hoping to see."

He wears his black riding cloak, smelling of leather and horses. Mud flecks spatter the fabric, especially near the hem. Though he's doffed his hat, his silver hair is wild, as if he jumped from his bed without a thought to pomading it back. Had he?

I look past him, into the corridor, hoping to see Oliver's strong outline, for surely that's what the barrister has been about this morning. What else could possibly coax him out for a robust ride at such an early hour?

"Is Oliver with you?"

"No, my dear. Perhaps you ought to sit down."

His admonition drapes over me like a burial shroud. Nothing good ever follows such a caution. I shove down a rising wave of alarm and retreat a few steps, then stiffen my shoulders and my resolve. I am far beyond quailing like a frightened schoolgirl.

"I am no frail flower, Mr. Ward. I may hear whatever you have to say as well on my feet as on a chair."

Something flashes in his greenish eyes, though it is hard to tell if it is pity or admiration. I pray for the latter. Pity would mean something is terribly, horribly wrong.

A small chuckle rumbles in his throat, and he swipes some grit off his brow with the back of his hand. "You are a rare one."

His words squeeze my heart, so familiar are they. "Your son has said the same, several times."

"Yes, well, I am afraid we are more alike than he cares to admit. Do you mind?" Lifting a finger, he points to the coffee urn. "It's been a long morning."

Hah! It's been a long night. A long week. A longer year. I want to scream at him to explain where he's been and why he'd told me to sit down, but the haggard lines on his face quiet that urge. The weary bend of his shoulders affirms his request. Who am I to refuse him?

"It is your house, sir. You do not need my permission."

Without another word, he crosses to the sideboard and pours a cup. After his first drink, relief sighs out of him, and he turns back to me. "Thank you for your indulgence. I am not accustomed to hard riding so early in the morning."

Not wishing to appear a vulture pecking for information, I pick up my tepid cup of tea and take a sip. It goes down like lead, but it at least gives me some semblance of restraint before I ask, "Where have you been?"

"Mr. Hunter sent one of his men here to fetch me just before dawn."

"For what purpose?"

"To identify a body."

My cup crashes to the floor, shattering into a hundred pieces along with my heart. Have I lost Oliver before I've even gained him? I sway and reach for the table, negating all my flimsy words of bravado. I gape at the barrister. "Please don't tell me. . ." I choke. I cannot even finish the words.

The barrister slams down his cup. In two long-legged strides, he guides me into the nearest chair.

"Take heart, Miss Lee. It was Mr. Groat. Apparently he'd made such haste in fleeing with his newly found wealth, he was thrown from his horse."

I sag against the back of the chair. Thank God! But then shame charges through me. The death of any man ought not be so callously dismissed, even a greedy blackguard such as Mr. Groat. "And the jewels?"

"Recovered." The barrister pulls a chair close to mine and sinks into it. "That leaves Mr. Corbin alone to take the blame for the theft of his wife's ruby necklace. He admitted as much to me and signed an affidavit."

Once again I gape. Is this morning to be nothing but surprise after surprise? "Why on earth would he do such a thing?"

A rogue smile curves his lips. "Somehow he got the idea his sentence would be lightened if he confessed. He provided me with the names of the two witnesses and the judge he bribed to have Oliver convicted, along with the messenger he paid off to call me out of town that week." Something dark flashes through his eyes.

Hmm. Had the Hawk of Crown Court struck again? I eye the man. "An idea planted by you, perhaps?"

"A lesson in the law, Miss Lee. Never directly answer a question when you can avoid it altogether." He winks—and my heart stops. He looks entirely too much like Oliver.

"Last I saw Mr. Corbin," he continues, "the man was bound and headed for prison."

"I am happy to hear it." I am. Truly. Justice will finally be served to a man who deserves shackles and a cold, cold cell. But it is an empty victory without Oliver to share it. "Thank you for telling me, yet what news of Oliver? Have you any word of him?"

"I do." He scrubs his hand over his face, aging five years in a blink of an eye. "I fear, Miss Lee, that he's met the same fate as Ambrose. And in light of such, there is no time to lose."

∞

After three days in the saddle, Sebastian Barrow was finally home. So why didn't he feel elated to see the stark walls of Dartmoor Prison? He was free of the stench of the city. Free of the press of crowds. Free of the devilish Groat. Better yet, he was returning the guilty to the pit. Life didn't get any better than this. But the smile that stretched his lips as he closed in on the gates felt thin, pinched.

A side door opened and out popped Hoff with a "Ho, ho!" and a jagged smile. Half his teeth were missing on the left side, lost in a tussle with a red-raged ox. A fearsome enough sight, but even more unsettling when combined with the mis-sewn scar that reached from his jaw to clear over the top of his head.

"Well, well! If it isn't Barrow," he crowed. "We been taking bets on when you'd be back, and if you'd get your man." Hoff craned his neck past the horse's rump to where Ward stumbled behind. A loop of rope around his neck connected him to the saddle, and his hands were bound behind his back. It was always better to make an escaped convict walk the final ten miles so that he'd remember every last step. Yet Sebastian shifted uneasily in the saddle. After having spent so much time with the wicked Groat, it seemed too much like something he would have done.

With a huff, he refocused on Hoff. "Don't know why anyone would be foolish enough to wager against me. Besides, gambling's a sin."

"Only if you lose—which I didn't. Looks like I just earned myself a pint at the pub tonight." Hoff's laughter was as ragged as his face. With a jangle of keys, he unlocked the gate and swung it wide enough for the horse and prisoner to pass through. "Cutter won't be so happy to see you, though. But Cutter be hanged! Stop by the Plume of Feathers tonight and tell us yer tale, eh?"

He gave another grunt, this one noncommittal. Sharing the victory with his fellow officers would be a fine way to end this mission, but doing so in a den of iniquitous drunkards might taint his triumph.

With a click of his tongue, he urged the horse onward. Once past the gate, he glanced back at Ward. Dirt flecks covered him like the pox. His trousers gaped open at the knees, torn from hitting the gravel so many times. Stubble, blood, and dirt darkened his face—but not nearly as black as the fury burning in his eyes. He hobbled along, careful to keep pace lest the rope bite into the raw skin at the back of his neck, but never once did his ferocious stare lose strength.

Blast the man! This would be so much easier if Ward just would show a little penitence. Barrow jabbed his heels in the horse's side, upping the pace. By the time he cantered across the parade ground and reached cellblock A, Ward breathed hard behind him.

Sebastian's boots hit the ground and he winced as sharp pain stabbed the pad of his foot. Blast! He *still* needed new boots, and all because of Ward. He yanked on the rope, pulling the man close to him. "You've been nothing but trouble, you know that? You're a worthless excuse for a man."

Ward's jaw worked, the bruises riding up and down with the movement. Then he closed his eyes, releasing a slow breath. "No man is worthless in God's eyes. Every soul holds value." His face hardened. "Even one possessed by a demon."

A tremor shot through Sebastian. How dare Ward lump him together with the likes of Groat. He backhanded the man, the smack of it bouncing off the rock walls of the gaol, then jerked Ward toward him, face to face. The stench of him was enough to gag an elephant. "Mind your manners, Ward, or I'll have to mind them for you."

Loosening some slack, he stalked to the door and pounded his fist against it.

A slidey hole scraped open. Two bloodshot eyes peered out, widening as recognition flickered. The hole slammed shut, and the door opened. Smyth, the doorkeep, cuffed him on the shoulder. "Flying carps, Barrow! Yer a sight. Welcome back, man."

Sebastian clenched every muscle, readying to flatten the addle-pated fool yet again for touching him. Then the image of Groat in front of the pub, his black eyes burning holes, froze him. He wasn't Groat, being that he worked for God, not the devil. Yet the image was enough to anchor his fist to his side. He dipped his head at the man and yanked Ward along, not stopping until he reached the front desk.

"Warden in?" he asked.

"No, and I didn't figure you'd be either." As predicted by Hoff, Mr. Cutter, the turnkey on duty, folded his brow into a magnificent scowl.

Sebastian peered at the man from beneath his hat brim. "Don't go pretending you didn't miss me."

Cutter spit out a few inglorious profanities. "You think your boys in the cell are going to be any happier to see you than I am?"

"I'll have them smiling in no time." A faint smile lifted his own lips, then vanished. "Now, where's the warden?"

Cutter leaned back in his chair. "Over in cellblock B. Ought to return by the time you lock up your man." His gaze slid to Ward, and a low whistle followed. "That one's a little rough. Give you some trouble, did he?"

Something in Cutter's reaction made his gut clench, but he held his gaze steady. "Nothing I couldn't handle. Ward's cell ready and waiting?"

"All nice and cozy like." Cutter reached into a drawer and tossed a key in the air.

Sebastian caught it and set off again, now and then jerking the rope to be sure Ward knew who was in charge. It always paid to assert one's authority, especially over a convict who'd managed an escape. He couldn't have the man thinking he'd ever accomplish that mistake again.

Most of the cell doors were open, the prisoners being employed for the day. Not Ward's. Barrow shoved the key into the lock and, after an accompanying click, flung the door wide. He tucked the key into his pocket, removed the loop of rope from around Ward's neck, then pulled out his knife and yanked Ward close. "Turn around."

Ward's nostrils flared. "You brought me all this way just to stab me in the back?"

"I said turn around."

Ward stared him down a moment longer, something flickering in his eyes before he faced the gaping maw of his cell, muttering about justice and repentance. Sebastian began sawing through the man's bindings. While not sharp, the back end of the blade still drew blood from the thin skin where the rope had chafed, yet Ward didn't so much as gasp. The man had fortitude, he'd give him that. Much more than that weasely Groat. Were he not a convict, why, Ward might have been a man he would have felt proud to call a friend.

The bindings fell. Sebastian lifted his knife, then smacked the butt of the hilt square between Ward's shoulder blades. The man hurtled into his cell.

And it was finished. The captive brought home. The prodigal returned. He could only imagine what was going on in Ward's head right about now. As for him, the victory of the moment warmed through him like a sweet August afternoon.

Sebastian reached for the door. But before he could shut it, Ward spun, a strange light in his eyes. What was this? Sebastian paused and peered closer.

All the fury in Ward's stare was gone. Not one shred of anger flared in his gaze. Instead, pity welled. An entire flood of foreign compassion—and Sebastian got the distinct impression that it took Ward as much by surprise as it did him.

"Go ahead, Barrow. Lock me up. But know this." He straightened, though it must've cost him after being forced to walk so far. "For all your talk of right and wrong, sins and salvation, you don't know the first thing about God or mercy."

With a mighty shove, Sebastian slammed the door so hard, the reverberation echoed throughout the gaol. "I'm not the guilty one in a cage."

Wheeling about, he strolled down the passageway toward the stairs. *You don't know the first thing about God.* No, Ward had it wrong. Must be. Because he had brought another sinner to justice just for Him. God surely was smiling upon him.

Wasn't He?

Chapter Thirty-Two

"You don't know the first thing about God or mercy."

Oliver ground his teeth as he paced circles in his cell, his words from several days ago yet plaguing him. He'd meant for Barrow to wrestle with the accusation, but an ugly twisting of fate turned the indictment right back on him. Being locked in isolation had given him more than enough time to ponder his own charge. Was it a mistake or a mercy that he was back in this hole?

Growling, he dropped to his knees and lifted a ragged prayer.

Why, God? Why the shackles when You know I am innocent? What sort of justice confines a man for a crime he did not commit?

His throat closed. Captivity, loss, every right and dignity stripped from him—all choked the very air from his lungs. It took several deep breaths before he could even think of continuing.

I assume that You have placed me here for a reason, Lord. But I cannot fathom why. What good can come from ruining me in every way possible? Please let me see, glimpse what You are doing. Grant mercy, for me, for Jarney, and...

He gritted his teeth a moment more, the thought of Maggie almost too much to bear. If Groat had gotten away, how awry had the rest of the evening gone? Had they succeeded in getting Corbin locked up, or had he once again bribed his way out of culpability? And if the man were still on the loose... He squeezed his eyes tight.

Keep Your watchful eye upon Maggie and protect her as I am unable to. Comfort her as she grieves the loss of her father.

Father. The very word gouged his own wound deeper. Was his father thinking of him too? Or had his disappearance been the last straw, and his father decided to give him no more thought at all? If only he had made amends sooner!

How, God? How am I supposed to keep my promise and make things right if I'm locked up here?

Out in the passageway feet shuffled. Doors slammed. The fading light filtering in through the window high up in his cell confirmed the sounds. Another day spent. Or rather another day wasted. Thunderation! At this point his whole life was wasted. There'd be no recovering his political career, no chance of getting his legislation passed, not with the added stain of being a recaptured escapee. Not even the precinct rat catcher would listen to a convict, let alone the prime minister. Without his leadership in the House, it would be up to the other few men who fought for underprivileged souls like Filcher and Bodger. Clearly there was nothing more he could do. Ever.

His hands curled into fists, but this time he stopped short of punching the wall. What was the point? His knuckles were already scabbed over, with nothing to show for the blood but the continual latent rage simmering inside him.

So he bowed his head instead.

God, I surrender, for I can do nothing else. If not me, Lord, then raise up another to fight against Corbin, for Your people's sake. For Your sake.

Blowing out a weary sigh, he rose and crossed to the wall between his and Jarney's cell, then slid to the cold stone floor. He may not be able to do anything for the poor on Avon Street, but he could yet offer encouragement to his friend. He turned his face to the barrier between them, speaking loud enough for Jarney to hear. "How are you holding up, my friend?"

"I have lived another day—" A fit of coughing barked rough and phlegmy, severing Jarney's words.

"Blast! You need a doctor!" This time Oliver did punch the wall. Though he couldn't see his friend, the man's reedy voice boded ill. Truly, it was a miracle Jarney yet lived.

The barking continued. There was nothing for it but to wait—and pray—that his friend would ride the wave of his lung fever and not get dragged under.

Finally, the storm ceased, and Jarney's weak voice started and stopped in spurts, his already throaty accent made even thicker by his condition. "God knows. . .my needs. . .my friend. He will provide. . .at the right time. He's kept me and you alive for a reason."

A bitter chuckle welled, and Oliver leaned his head against the wall, speaking more to himself than to Jarney. "If I had half as much faith as you, I'd be a saint."

"It only takes. . .a mustard seed."

Footsteps thudded down the corridor. Oliver clamped his mouth shut. If Barrow caught them talking, there'd be yet another bruise to purple his flesh. When the steps stopped outside his door and keys jangled, his gut clenched even tighter than his jaw. Had Barrow heard him?

Oliver shoved to his feet. Facing the man while seated was just asking for a kick in the teeth.

The door screeched open. Barrow stood grim-faced, truncheon in hand, a dark god bent on meting out crooked justice. Did the man never go home? It was late. Why was he still here?

"You've got a visitor," he growled.

Oliver tensed, wary of taking his eyes off Barrow. Was this some kind of trick?

Barrow stepped aside and another man swept past him, ducking lest his skull crack against the low header. Before the man even straightened, Barrow slammed the door shut. When the fellow did finally stand tall, Oliver sucked in a breath.

His visitor was his father?

"Oliver?" In three long strides, the barrister closed the distance between them and held his lantern higher. The longer he stared at Oliver, the deeper grief carved lines into his face, aging him well beyond his fifty-seven years. Oliver shrank back, his stench, his grime, the weight of the manacles assaulting him afresh. But God had heard his prayers. Here was his chance to make at least one thing right. He opened his mouth, but nothing would come out.

His father moved closer, eyes narrowing as he scanned every bruise and each cut. "Who did this to you?"

Oliver bit back a maniacal laugh. For all the years his father had worked to send offenders to gaol, did he really have no idea to what sort of hell he condemned them? He shook his head, evading his father's question. The truth would do no good anyway. He turned partially away, fists clenched against the tremor trying to tear him apart. "Why are you here?"

Reaching into an inside pocket, the barrister retrieved a rolled parchment and offered it to him. Oliver's breath hitched. An official stamp marked the top edge in blue ink. Either this was the written documentation of the complete term of years he was to serve or. . . Dare he hope?

His fingers shook as he grasped the thing and unrolled the paper, then the whole world trembled as he read, the words blurring together.

Sentence revoked.

Full release.

Effective immediately.

He crushed the paper to his chest. "Am I to understand that I am free?"

The barrister's throat bobbed, yet he didn't speak—and when he finally did, the voice was foreign. Only once had Oliver heard such thick emotion, such raw brokenness from the man. . .the day his mother died.

"Would to God, my son, that I had been at your trial to begin with and this had never happened in the first place. But yes, you are free." Reaching out, he squeezed Oliver's shoulder. "You are well and truly free."

Oliver closed his eyes, cherishing the words, allowing them to sink low and begin to heal all the wounds he'd suffered. *Well and truly free.* He was well and truly free! He drank the phrase deeply.

"Thank God," he breathed out.

Then he blinked his eyes open and stared at the man he'd so long resented. The man who'd secured his release, despite his disappearance, despite the rift still between them. "And thank you, Father. All these years, I. . ." He swallowed against the lump in his throat. "Well, I was wrong to dishonor you in my thoughts, in my words. But no more. Let us both leave our transgressions here. All of them. Shackled. Forgotten."

"And forgiven?"

A smile stretched his lips wide. "Yes, forgiven. It is high time we start over." His breath hitched as a new thought struck him. Just because he was ready to make amends didn't mean his father was. "That is. . .if you're willing?"

"Willing?" His father's voice broke. His face contorted. Several breaths later, he lowered the lantern to the floor, then lifted his arms and held them out strong and steady.

Eyes stinging, throat impossibly tight, Oliver flung himself into his father's embrace. His chains rattled and the shackles bit into his wrists, but he didn't care. God love them both, the iron bindings just didn't matter anymore. His father on earth and in heaven had set him completely free.

How long they stood there, father and son at long last one, Oliver couldn't say. He'd stand there a hundred years more, so right did it feel.

But then Barrow banged on the door, his gruff voice rumbling from outside. "I've not got all night. I'm to take you both to the warden's office. Let's move."

After a final clap on the back, his father released him and scooped up the lantern. "Are you ready to leave?"

Oliver laughed. "Since the day I arrived. But what of Corbin? And Groat? Are they—"

"A tale to be told at another time. For now, let us shake the prison dust from our feet, hmm?"

As curious as he was, the urge to leave behind this place of torment welled even stronger. Allowing his father to lead the way, he followed the barrister to the door, and after a rap and a "Ready!" Barrow let them out. Oliver ignored the man's sneer as they passed. Barrow's imposing hulk was hardly worth thinking about, not when freedom was mere steps away.

But so was a barking cough. Oliver stopped dead in his tracks in front of Jarney's door. "Father, wait."

The barrister turned, one eyebrow arched high—and no wonder. Who in their right mind would wish to tarry in the bowels of a prison?

Oliver gestured towards his friend's door. "I cannot leave here without seeing to Jarney. Not only is he as innocent as I, but he's sick, nearly unto death. Is there nothing you can do for him?"

His father frowned.

So did Barrow, truncheon at the ready. "My directions are to bring you to the warden's office, Ward. No one else. Now move."

It was a risk but one worth taking. Maybe this was even the very reason God had brought him back here. Oliver turned away from Barrow and spread his hands wide, chains grating in a high-pitched cadence. "Father, please!"

He held his breath. So did the ten-year-old boy inside him. All the years between then and now folded into nothingness. Would his father come to his friend's aid this time? And if he didn't, despite his own words of forgiveness, would some hidden remnant of old bitterness rage up stronger than before?

Something moved behind his father's eyes, shadowy, indistinct, then dawned into a burst of brilliant compassion. He reached out and clamped a hand onto Oliver's shoulder. "I can do nothing for him now, Son, but I promise I shall look into his case."

Oliver nodded, relieved more than he could account for. It wasn't instant help for Jarney, but it was a beginning—more than his friend had hope of before.

But another bout of coughing once again leached out Jarney's door. Time was a commodity his friend just didn't own. Oliver speared his father with a determined stare. "While I appreciate your offer, can you not at least get him into the infirmary until you look into his case?"

"Now that I think I can manage." He looked past Oliver to Barrow. "Open the door, guard, if you please."

Barrow planted his feet wider, slapping his truncheon against his open palm. "I don't answer to you."

A muscle on his father's jaw twitched. Not a good sign. Neither was the steely tone of his voice. "Officer Barrow, you will answer to the master at the workhouse when I see you stripped of your position if you do not open that door. Now!"

"As obstinate as your son, are you?" His bushy brows drew into a sullen line. "Fine. I'll open the door, but I am not to blame if the likes of you catch his fever."

Barrow swooped over and made short work of the door, then stood aside, glowering.

Oliver rushed in, but he didn't have far to go. Jarney lay curled in the fetal position near the threshold. Sweet mercy! Were they too late?

"Jarney!" He dropped to his knees beside him, praying, hoping, straining to hear a response—any response.

A slight moan wheezed out.

Carefully, Oliver eased him up to sit, while behind them both, the barrister bellowed at Officer Barrow. "Get some water for the man. Can you not see he is in need?"

Jarney's eyes gleamed abnormally bright in the dim light. His skin burned, and the stench of him nearly choked Oliver. But oh, how sweet the moment when his friend's gaze finally fixated on Oliver's face. "Ward? How did you. . . Is this a dream?"

"No, friend." Biting back a sob, he brushed the man's stringy hair from his brow. "I am here. Just like you said, it looks like God's watching out for you. You're finally going to get the medical attention you need."

Feet clipped a few steps behind them, and then the barrister crouched with a cup of water in hand. "Here is some—"

His father sucked a sharp breath and the cup clattered to the floor. "Henri? Can it be?"

Jarney's yellowed eyes drifted to Oliver's father, then widened. "Cassius?"

Oliver looked from one to the other, completely taken off guard. "Father, you know this man? You know Jarney?"

"Know him?" The barrister gaped, then lowered his voice. "He is the missing Marquis of Lambesc, Henri J'Arney. Help me get him to his feet."

Oliver stumbled, as wobbly as his friend as he helped his father hoist the man upward. Once standing, he stared at Jarney—no, J'Arney, if he were to believe it. "Is it true, my friend? You are a marquis? Why did you not tell me?"

Leaning heavily on the barrister, J'Arney looked past them both to where Barrow hulked outside the door, then issued a raspy whisper, "The walls have ears. . .and I have many enemies. For my safety and yours. . .it was best to be an English Jarney instead of a French J'Arney."

But it was too much. The speaking. The standing. J'Arney's eyes rolled back into his head and he collapsed fully against the barrister.

"Guard!" his father roared. "Help me get this man to the infirmary."

Oliver shook his head. "Father, I am well able to—"

"No." Securing his hold beneath J'Arney's arms, his father lifted his face to Oliver's. "I'll see Henri to the doctor. You report to the warden's office."

"But Father—"

"Oliver, trust me in this. I will not let you down. Now go!"

He hesitated, debating, then wheeled about. His father wanted to help—*was* helping. The miracle of it all left him breathless. And God was not done working wonders, for Oliver was also striding past Barrow for the last time.

But two steps past the man, Barrow's hand clamped on his shoulder and hot breath hit the back of his neck. "If you're not in the warden's office when I get there, Ward, I promise I'll hunt you down like the rat you are."

Waiting alone in a warden's office is a peculiar sentence in and of itself. I dare not wander out the door to inquire how much longer I need wait. Just the thought of asking the turnkey at the front desk raises gooseflesh on my arms. His nose and ears look as if he's been punched too many times, and his left eye has a perpetual squint. How often has he leapt off his stool to scrap with anyone who chances by?

Unease prickles down my spine. I assume the warden, the barrister, and Oliver will appear shortly, but I don't know—and not knowing raises all sorts of uglier questions that I don't want answered.

What if a convict straggles in here while I'm alone?

What if a new prisoner arrives before the warden returns?

What if there's been a mistake and Oliver will not be released after all?

I pace the small room, trying to outrun my fears and angst and deep, deep yearning to press my cheek against Oliver's chest and hear him rumble, "All is well." But it's not. Not yet. And I cannot keep my gaze from straying to the rack of rifles behind the warden's desk or the shelf of wooden clubs lined up and at the ready next to them. How awful it must've been for Oliver on the day he first arrived, knowing those weapons could be used against him for no fault of his own.

A knock raps at the door. I press my hands against my stomach. The warden wouldn't submit to such a formality to enter his own office. What if it's that horrid, hairy guard Mr. Barrow? The voice I've depended upon for the past ten years packs its bags and moves away, leaving nothing but a squeak to pass my lips.

Another knock, this time followed by a deep tone. "Warden Cawsey?" The doorknob turns. The wood inches open. "Your pardon, sir, but—?"

Oliver stands on the threshold, mouth dropping. He takes a step. Then two. Then rasps, "Maggie?"

Chains jingle from the shackles on his wrists. His left eye

swells at the center of an ugly purple bruise. There is a cut on his jaw and his forehead, and his right cheek is scraped as if his face has been slammed against a wall.

My heart breaks. Despite the brutality he's suffered, I've never seen such a handsome man in all my life. I rush to him and tenderly cup his uninjured cheek with my hand. "You're hurt."

He smirks. "Not as badly as the first time we met, remember?"

"I will never forget." My voice breaks, bent beneath thick emotion. He'd have died that day had Nora and I not taken him in. He looks half-dead now.

"What are you doing here?" He frowns.

Biting my lip, I lower my hand. There is no possible way I can tell him how frantic I was to see him, touch him, drink him in without sounding like a desperate woman. No doubt he'd rather hear of the intricacies of his release than endure the nonsensical pledges of a woman in love.

Deciding on a safer route, I peer up at him. "How much has your father told you?"

"Only that I am free. And as such, I assume Groat and Corbin now wear beauties such as these." He holds up his wrists, and for the first time, I see the raw skin where the metal has chafed.

I bite back a wince and will my words to come out even and unaffected. "Mr. Corbin yet awaits trial, but yes, your father assures me there is no way he will escape justice this time. The false witnesses he hired to accuse you revealed the full truth in a formal deposition, as did the judge whom he'd bribed to put you away. Ambrose himself even signed a statement bearing responsibility for the unlawful way he schemed to collect insurance money and sales profit by selling his wife's ruby necklace."

Oliver sucks in a breath. "Why on earth would any of them do that?"

"Apparently the Hawk of Crown Court is every bit as persuasive as you once told me."

His brows rise. "Indeed. And Groat? What of him?"

It's my turn to shrug. "That is for God to decide."

Oliver's face visibly pales beneath the dark stubble of a sprouting beard. "Don't tell me he's still at large."

"No. He was found the morning after your abduction, his neck broken from a fall."

"I see." Oliver blows out a breath and turns from me, wandering across the room and back again. I don't blame him. It is a lot to take in.

Finally he faces me. "And Mrs. Corbin? How is she faring through all this?"

"She's holding up well. I know it's hard on her, but she's not as gaunt as she was, and I even spied a bit of colour in her cheeks the day she saw your father and me off."

"I am happy to hear it." He nods, and a hank of his dark hair falls forward, hiding his purpled eye. He flicks it back with a jerk of his head. "I suppose this whole sordid affair is at a close then, eh?"

"Not quite."

"What else?"

I pad closer to him, then stop a breath away. I cannot begin to predict what his reaction will be nor if I'll even have the courage to expose my heart in such a vulnerable fashion, but I do know this: if I do not tell him what I came here to say, I will regret it the rest of my life.

"There is still a piece of unfinished business, one for which I finally have an answer." I lift my face to his and meet his gaze. "Yes."

A small smile ghosts his lips. "I like the sound of that, but to what are you agreeing?"

"You once inquired if, when you were free, you might call upon me."

He goes suddenly still. The green flecks in his eyes darken to moss. I cannot read what he thinks, how he feels, if he is repulsed or deeply moved. Nor does he say anything. I am left alone at the edge of this cliff.

"That is, *if* your offer still stands." My resolution falters, and I retreat a step. "Perhaps I presume too much."

"You presume too little, but you are correct. I do not wish to court you anymore."

My world tips, until he lifts his arms and encircles me, chains and all, in his embrace. "I wish for more, Maggie. So much more."

His husky words hardly register before his mouth comes down warm and soft on mine. Many a time men have stolen kisses from me, but this is different. This I welcome, cherish, *need*. I grasp handfuls of his shirt and press against him. All the years of fearing men, shying from them and closing myself off ends now. Here. With this man. This brave, justice-loving convict who smells of dirt and filth and musky promise.

Oliver pulls back, not far, just enough for his eyes to ask permission for more. Bruises or not, I reach up and guide his lips back to mine. The next kiss surpasses the first, but I cannot tell if it is he or I who searches and seeks with such hunger. It doesn't matter. My heart is his. He is mine. There is nothing more I want than to be one with him.

"What's this?"

Startled, we pull away from each other, but with Oliver's chains wrapped around me, we both stumble.

Near the now-open door, the barrister glances at the warden and snorts. "I've seen restraints used in many ways, Warden, but I think this is a first."

∞

First lugging Jarney to the infirmary. Then getting stuck helping Hoff with a jammed cell door and pinching his thumb in the process. Now this. Barrow pulled out his gun and sighted down the barrel at the beat-up pile of rags between the lady and the barrister, all of whom were steps away from the front door, walking out as if they owned the place. Did the barrister and that woman really think this little ruse would work? That he wouldn't notice them making off with a prisoner who rightly belonged in a cell?

"Stop right there, Ward."

All three halted. Ahh, but this would be good. Not only would he lock up Ward once again but his father as well for trying to help the man escape right in front of his eyes. As for the woman, well, he supposed she could go ahead and leave. Everyone knew women were easily deceived through no fault of their own.

"Stand down, Mr. Barrow." The command came from behind him.

He ignored it and clicked open the hammer.

"I said stand down, man!"

He frowned. Why would the warden order such a heinous breach of justice? Even so, he lowered the gun. Authority must be respected, or the world would be chaos.

A few clipped steps later and the warden drew up beside him, speaking to the three shapes yet frozen. "My apologies, Miss Lee, Barrister, Mr. Ward. You are free to leave." Then he turned to Sebastian. "A word, Mr. Barrow. In my office. Now."

What was this? Though it provoked him in every possible way, he reholstered his gun and followed the warden into the office.

The warden sank into his seat and lifted his face. "The case of Mr. Oliver Ward is no longer your concern or mine. It turns out he was wrongfully accused."

Sebastian jiggled his finger in his ear. The words might as well have been gibberish, so little sense did they make. "Come again?"

Warden Cawsey leaned forward, chair creaking, and folded his hands on his desk. "The truth is, Mr. Barrow, that Mr. Ward is as innocent as Adam before he bit the apple."

Preposterous! Could the warden speak nothing but garbled nonsense? Sebastian narrowed his eyes. "How can that be?"

"Men make mistakes. Only God's justice is infallible."

God's justice? What of his justice? What of weeks spent traipsing across the country with a hole in his boot and hardly enough coins to spare for his cigarillos? He was doing his job. His duty! But then a horrible thought hit him sideways.

Had he been doing it wrongly?

The thought stunned, igniting a firestorm in his gut. He slammed his hands down on the tabletop and stared into the warden's eyes. "Do you mean to tell me I hunted down and gaoled a blameless man?"

"In a word, yes. But that's not all I mean to say—"

The warden continued talking, yet it was all a swarm of bees, buzzing and buzzing. Rather the barrister's words to his son barreled back. *You are not God to mete out justice on a whim.* Slowly, Sebastian straightened and pressed his hands to the sides of his head. He'd captured and incarcerated an innocent man? What kind of monster did that? Why, he was no better than that devilish Groat, no better than the filthy lecher who'd tried to ravish his innocent sister! The world spun. Nausea crawled up to the back of his throat. No, he was worse than that. He was like the Romans who'd hung the innocent God-man on a tree. How the devil would he ever atone for this? For the first time ever, he was out of answers.

God, what do I do now?

"—well, Mr. Barrow?"

The words were muffled. He lowered his hands, shaking his head slightly. "Sorry, sir. What did you say?"

"I said you're a fine officer, but I fear you take your job far too seriously, to an extent that is not now nor ever shall be sanctioned by my office. Either you mend your ways or find yourself another career. Which will it be?"

He wavered on his feet. Or maybe the room moved. Mend or find? Those were his only choices? Wait a minute. . .what about find *and* mend?

He sucked in air, everything suddenly becoming clearer. Sharper. Why had he never thought of that before? All this time he'd been trying so hard to mend his relationship with God—done everything in his power to remedy that single moment when he'd taken a man's life for attacking his sister—that he'd not given one minute to actually *finding* God. Sweet, beautiful mercy! Ward was right. His pulse hammered loud in his ears. He didn't know the first thing about God because he needed to *find* God first.

And there was only one place to do that.

"Thank you, Warden. I think, perhaps, it is time I do both." Sebastian unpinned the badge on his lapel and laid it on the desk. Then he pivoted and stalked out the door, following in Ward's footsteps.

To freedom.

Chapter Thirty-Three

March 1862
St. Petroc Church, Lydford, Dartmoor

There are moments in life that are surreal. A fiery sunset. The first cry of a newborn babe. Looking deep into the eyes of the one you love while standing at the altar of a country church. As Oliver reaches for my hand and slides a gold ring on my finger, I cannot help but wonder if this is all a dream and at any moment I might awaken in my cold and lonely bed in the house at the end of the moor.

But his touch is warm and real. So is the passion in his voice. "With this ring, I thee wed." Both his hands wrap around mine, skin to skin, flesh to flesh. "With my body, I thee worship."

A thrill charges through me. There is no mistaking the desire in his gaze or the craving that burns low in my belly.

"And with all my worldly goods I thee endow, in the name of the Father, and of the Son, and of the Holy Ghost. Amen." He raises my fingers to his lips and kisses a benediction soft and sweet.

The vicar clears his throat at Oliver's breach of etiquette. I hide a shameless smile. The clergyman is notorious for his strict traditional ways.

"For as much as Oliver and Margaret have consented together in holy wedlock, and have witnessed the same before God and this company, and thereto have given and pledged their troth either to other, and have declared the same by giving and receiving of a ring, and by joining of hands; I pronounce that they be man and wife together, in the name of the Father, and of the Son, and of the Holy Ghost. Amen."

Oliver leans towards me. I bite my lip. If he kisses me full on the mouth here in front of the Reverend Mr. Mollet, I shall never be able to attend another service without my face turning red.

But instead, he whispers for me alone, "I love you, Maggie Ward."

The more the name sinks in, the deeper I stare into Oliver's eyes, the larger my grin. It seems forever ago I lamented never having a Mr. Rochester to love me—and now Jane Eyre's words have become my own.

Reader, I married him.

The next several minutes blur together. Nora smiles her congratulations as she hands me my primrose bouquet. Oliver's father claps him on the back. The vicar mumbles something about the parish register. Next thing I know, Oliver and I stand in the vestry and I sign my name next to my husband's.

My husband's!

Oliver pulls out an envelope and passes it to the vicar. "Our thanks to you."

As if on cue, church bells start ringing, announcing to the world a new union has formed. Oliver reaches for my hand, and though we've entwined our fingers many times over the past nine months, the gesture still sends tingles up my arm.

He nods towards the envelope. "There's a little extra in there for the sexton as well."

"Ahh yes, the ghost of the church, eh?" Mr. Mollet chuckles. "No doubt he'll appreciate it, but allow me to be the one to thank you in his stead. He's a hard worker but a bit skittish around others. Prefers his solitude."

"Then we shall respect that and leave before he is finished ringing the bells. Good day, Vicar."

"God's blessing on you both."

Oliver dons his hat and guides me outside—where a shower of grain rains on our heads.

"There's the happy couple!" The barrister tosses another handful, as does Nora, who stands at his side. The two are the sum of our small wedding party. It took some bargaining with Oliver's father to keep this event so intimate, yet as Oliver helps me into the carriage draped with white bunting, a wry smile twists my lips. No doubt next month's reception at the barrister's manor home will be crawling with well-wishers.

Dobbs, all cleaned up and freshly shaven, glances over his shoulder from the driver's seat. There is a scar near his eye where Mr. Groat gouged him with the ice pick, but by God's grace alone, he yet has his vision.

"Congratulations, missus," he says.

I grin. For the first time, his name for me fits. I am well and truly a missus now. "Thank you, Dobbs."

Oliver climbs up next to me, hardly sitting before he pulls me into his arms. "Are you happy, Mrs. Ward?"

"More than I have a right to be."

"Then I guess you don't need this, hmm?" Oliver waves a folded paper in front of me.

I try to snatch it from him, but he holds it out of my reach. "What is it?"

"My gift to you." He finally allows me to snag the paper.

And as I read, I gasp at the words. It is a contract for the Royal Opera House signed by Mr. Lamb—with a blank signature line just waiting for my name.

I look from the paper to Oliver. "How. . .what?" I stammer.

"After our engagement was announced, I was paid a visit by one Mr. Lamb, whereupon I learned that a certain famous opera singer had turned him down flat."

I shake my head. "But Oliver—"

"He was quite insistent that the world deserves to hear this songbird's voice." He leans closer, his tone husky. "And I quite agree."

"But I am a wife now. *Your* wife."

"There is no reason you can't do both. When Parliament's in session, I have to go to London anyway, and Mr. Lamb was quite amenable to having you sing even on a limited basis. But it is up to you. Only if you want it."

How am I so fortunate to get such an understanding husband? "Yes—yes! Thank you so much." I clutch the paper to me. Gift upon gift. "I mean, only if you're sure."

"Quite sure, my love." He gathers my hand and lifts the finger ensconced with gold to eye level. "I would that my wife sing wherever she pleases."

His words warm my heart and I smile at the ring. His ring. The metal feels foreign yet so right against my skin. . . Wait a minute. My bare skin? I frown. "My gloves! I forgot them on the table at the back of the church."

"Never fear." Oliver releases me and taps me on the nose. "If you'll recall, I'm a champion at returning lost gloves to absentminded ladies."

The memory of him disguised as an old woman on our covert trek to Bath rises up. I smirk. "At least this time you're not in a gown."

"Ahh, but a groom should never outshine his bride." He winks then calls to Dobbs. "Hold up a moment. It seems the lady's forgotten something."

He hops out of the carriage, waves for his father and Nora to pass us, then turns back to me, his head just clearing the low side of the barouche. Late-morning sun rests brilliantly on his broad shoulders. His head tips to a jaunty angle. "Did I mention there is a retrieval fee that must be paid up front?"

"Such as?"

"A kiss from my wife."

Willingly I lean forward, cherishing the way we blend so perfectly into one. By the time he pulls away, I am breathless.

"Well." I arch a brow. "From now on, I shall remember to lose things more often."

∽

Strange how a pair of lacy gloves, so petite and frail, could represent such a strong woman—*his* woman. No. . .his wife. Oliver pressed the white fabric against his chest. There might come a time when he stopped smiling about his good fortune, but not this day.

His grin widened even further as he glanced down the aisle to the wooden cross atop the altar. So much light and gratitude flooded his soul, he couldn't stop from bowing his head.

How kind You are, God. How merciful. Thank You for setting this prisoner free.

Then he wheeled about and strode towards the door. The sooner the wedding breakfast was over, the sooner he could make Maggie his in every possible way. But just before he reached the entryway, the bell tower door flung open and a demon stepped out.

Oliver froze, every sense on high alert. The old scars on his back prickled, and the smile he thought he'd never lose slipped off his lips. He blinked, but that didn't make the hairy man in front of him disappear.

"Barrow?" he choked. "Can it be?"

The man's bushy brows sank. So did his shoulders. "Yes, Mr. Ward. Indeed it can."

"*You're* the sexton?" He shook his head, hoping the movement would assemble his jumbled thoughts into a coherent line. It didn't. "I—I don't understand."

"God's ways are mysterious—and so is life."

Oliver scanned the man. There was no truncheon clenched in his meaty fist. No snarl or threatening stance. He just stood there in a simple sack coat, hair combed back, beard trimmed to a manageable length. But the most noticeable difference was in his eyes. The man's brown gaze was clear. Peaceful. The driven constable bent on executing twisted justice no longer stared out at a world gone wrong.

Oliver nearly dropped Maggie's gloves. "What happened to you?"

Half a smile curved Barrow's lips. "Do you believe in the power of words, Mr. Ward?"

"As a politician, I should hope so."

"Well. . ." Barrow scratched his jaw, his eyes drifting up to the rafters. This was new. Never once had the man been at a loss for something to say.

After a few moments, Barrow's hand lowered and his brown eyes bored into Oliver's. "Two words changed my life that day you walked free, changed me every bit as much as the 'I do' you shared here with your bride today. God used Warden Cawsey to call me back to Him, and believe it or not, He even used Groat."

His brows sank and deep lines folded in the whiskers at the sides of his mouth. "Listen, Ward." He stepped away from the bell tower door and advanced.

Oliver stiffened. Could be Barrow's avowed redemption was true—or it could be a ploy. Some kind of ruse to get close to him, to slap on shackles and steal him away. But no. He was free! There was no possible way Barrow could haul him back to prison. Not anymore. So. . .perchance his words were true? The humble dip of the man's head certainly attested to it. Even so, Oliver shifted his weight, prepared to fight or flee.

"I know I wronged you. Beat you. Tortured you." He paused, his jaw working, then he jerked up his face and met Oliver's gaze head-on. "Still, if there's any way you can find it in your heart to forgive me, I would be ever grateful."

Oliver's grip tightened on the gloves as memory after memory surfaced. Barrow cracking him in the skull with a club. The man's iron fist pounding into his nose. The tip of Barrow's boot crunching into his ribs or the relentless cross-country pursuit that nearly killed him. All the blood and pain cried out for redress—and then his gaze drifted past Barrow's shoulder to the sun shining through the stained glass window, illuminating an image of the Good Shepherd hefting a ragged sheep on his shoulders. Maggie's gloves fell to the floor.

He was that sheep.

And so was Barrow.

Both of them had done things, said things, grieved the One who'd bled and suffered in their stead—and yet God never once turned away His compassion. How could he refuse a fellow sheep, even one as gruff and undeserving as Barrow?

With a sigh, he scooped up the gloves and faced the man. "Yes, Mr. Barrow. By God's grace and great mercy alone do I forgive you."

The swell of Barrow's throat bobbed, and miracle of miracles, tears welled in the man's eyes. "Thank you, Mr. Ward."

"Thank God, Mr. Barrow. Not me." Oliver's smile returned. "Now then, good day. I have a wife that must be attended."

Light of step, Oliver bounded out to the carriage and hoisted himself up, marveling the whole way at the Paul that God had made of Barrow's Saul.

"Onward, Dobbs," he called as he shut the door and sank into the seat, then handed Maggie her gloves.

She frowned at them. "That took quite a bit of time. Were they terribly hard to find?"

"Terribly. So difficult that I fear I must charge you more for the retrieval."

Her lips parted, but before she could speak, he pulled her into his arms and kissed her soundly. Ahh, but he could get used to this!

She snuggled against him, head on his shoulder, and oh, how right it felt. How right the day. How right the world. Without a word, the contented sigh breathing out from Maggie concurred. By the time the carriage rounded the last curve and Morden Hall came into sight, Oliver was sure of one thing.

He was the most blessed man to walk the planet.

"We're home, love." He gently set her from him and hopped out of the carriage, then turned to help her down. Together, they neared the door, just as his father stepped out. Inside, Malcolm woofed his greeting at a nearby window.

"Before we partake of Nora's wedding feast, allow me to give you my wedding gift." The barrister swept out his hand. "And here it is."

Oliver looked from his father's empty fingers to Maggie, who looked as perplexed as him.

"Where?" she asked.

"Right in front of you." The barrister chuckled. "You are no longer the tenants of Morden Hall but the owners."

"Father!" Oliver gasped. "It is too much. We cannot possibly accept—"

"Humour me, Son." His father clapped him on the back. "It's not every day my boy marries the most beautiful woman in all of Dartmoor."

Red warmed Maggie's face to a rosy hue. "Thank you, sir."

"Tut, tut! It's Father now, my dear."

"Very well. Thank you, Father." Leaving Oliver's side, she stood on tiptoe and kissed the barrister's cheek.

Oliver smiled at the sight. Were it not for Maggie, would he have reconciled with the man? "Indeed, Father. We are very grateful."

"And I am very hungry." Turning, his father yanked open the door and shouted, "Let the feasting begin!"

With a light touch to the small of Maggie's back, Oliver guided her to follow—until the sound of pounding hooves stopped him flat. They both turned.

A man in a brown riding cloak reined a magnificent bay to a stop just in front of them. Winded and dusty, Henri J'Arney dismounted with a lopsided smile, still thin but not the cadaverous sack of bones that he had been. "Looks like I arrived just in time."

While the sight of his hale and hearty friend did Oliver's heart good, still... What was he doing here? The grand reception was weeks away. Oliver cocked his head. "In time for what?"

A rogue smile curved the Frenchman's mouth. "A wedding gift." He held out an envelope.

Maggie scooted closer to Oliver's side as he unfolded the paper.

25 April, 2:45 p.m.

Though he read it three times over, the writing made no sense. Judging by the way Maggie peeked up at him with an arched brow, she didn't understand it either. Was this how it was to be with wedding gifts? Each one a puzzle to be solved?

He refolded the paper and speared J'Arney with narrowed eyes. "What's this?"

"Your appointment with the prime minister."

Oliver gaped. Impossible! He'd tried valiantly to meet with the viscount and, despite his best efforts, hadn't been able to gain an audience with the fellow's shoeblack let alone the man himself.

"How the deuce did you manage this?" he spluttered.

"Without shackles, the sky is the limit." J'Arney waved his hand at the clouds. "Not to mention there are many privileges to being a diplomat, access being chief amongst them. Now, are you going to invite me to your wedding breakfast or not?"

Oliver shook his head, mumbling under his breath. "I can hardly believe it. Perhaps my legislation isn't dead after all." He turned to Maggie. "Do you know what this means? Boys like Bodger will no longer have to live in squalor."

"If you can persuade the prime minister, that is. But knowing you, that shouldn't be a problem." Her brilliant smile shifted from him to J'Arney. "Pardon my husband, Mr. J'Arney. It may take him a moment to get over his shock. Please, go inside."

"Oui, madam. Merci." Doffing his hat, J'Arney bypassed them and entered the house.

No sooner did he go than Maggie turned to Oliver—and all thoughts of politics and lawmaking fled, cast out by the love shining in her eyes. "Will you mind it very much, do you think?"

Grabbing her hands, he pulled her close. "Mind what?"

"Living here, in this house at the end of the moor, away from dinners and dances and society? Except for when Parliament is in session and we are in London, it will be a quiet life this far out."

"It won't be for long, not if I have my way."

"Oh? And what way would that be, Husband?"

Tipping her face, he tasted her sweetness, kissing her lips and the curve of her neck until she weakened and leaned into him. Satisfied, he set her from him. "We'll have this countryside ringing with children's laughter in no time—*our* children. Would you like that?"

A wide smile flashed. "Very much."

"Well then, Wife." Bending, he swept her off her feet then straightened. "Let us begin our new life."

Historical Notes

Dartmoor Prison

Situating a prison at the center of an unforgiving landscape really is a brilliant idea. So thought the creators of Dartmoor Prison—and they were right. Even after two hundred years, this fortress still houses convicts. The institution was originally built in 1806 to detain French prisoners of war, but with the breakout of the War of 1812 against the United States, the walls confined American prisoners as well. When things simmered down, the prison closed in 1816 but then reopened in 1850, coinciding with the passage of legislation against transportation. Since then it has and still does imprison a range of offenders such as gangsters, killers, and political prisoners.

Whist Hounds and Pixies

No, I'm not talking about card-playing dogs or sweet transparent-winged cherubs who fly around in tutus. These two creatures of folklore are a shade darker than that. A whist hound is a mythical red-eyed beast, doglike in movement, and about the size of a small calf. If you happen to see this black animal prowling the moor, run the opposite direction, for it's said if you follow one, you'll be led to your death with an accompaniment of sinister laughter and mournful baying. This hellhound legend inspired Sir Arthur Conan Doyle to write *The Hound of the Baskervilles*.

Pixies, or fairies as they're sometimes called, are mischievous to the point of causing harm. If you happen to get lost on the moor, especially in a mist, you can bet it was the pixies that turned you about.

Moors, Tors, and Quaking Bogs
A moor is a vast expanse of open, infertile land with low-growing vegetation that often contains rolling hills and outcroppings of rock, which are called tors. Bray Tor is a free-standing pile of rocks and is a real place located near Lydford, Devon. Dotting the Dartmoor countryside are quaking bogs. Think of them as great sphagnum moss and peat sponges, usually in the higher, central parts of the north moor. Those that are deep can be impossible to escape, so while hiking about in a moor, it's best to carry a walking stick to test the ground when you see a suspicious patch of what could be a bog.

Lock-Up Keepers and Constables
Mr. Barrow's position is a fictional mix of a constable and a lock-up keeper, but for the sake of modern sensibilities, I merely refer to him as constable because that's a term most people recognize. A lock-up keeper guarded prisoners in a correctional institution, but other duties included transporting convicts between gaols (which is the British term historically used for jails), courtrooms, prisons, or any other number of places. Armed with this information and for the sake of continuity in the story, I took the liberty of extending Mr. Barrow's duties to tracking down one of the prisoners for whom he was responsible.

The Theatre Royal in Bath
The Theatre Royal is one of Britain's oldest venues that still offers quality entertainment today—plus it's absolutely gorgeous inside. The building was originally constructed in 1805 but was rebuilt after a fire in 1863. . .from one of Wendell Groat's vigil lanterns, perhaps? But no, Wendell Groat is a fictional character. The real manager at the time was James Henry Chute.

Victorian Weddings

Maggie and Oliver celebrate their wedding in much the same style as their peers. A traditional wedding kiss wasn't so traditional back then, hence the omission of "you may now kiss the bride." In fact, in the opening of chapter thirty-three, Oliver and Maggie's wedding vows and the vicar's prayer are taken directly from the Church of England's *Book of Common Prayer*. A change in this story is the church bells ringing after the ceremony. Traditionally they rang as the couple entered the church to make the villagers aware a ceremony was taking place and to scare away any lurking evil forces. It was an English custom to hold a noon ceremony with breakfast thirty minutes later at the bride's home.

Sexton

Sextons are often thought of as grave diggers, but first and foremost they were employees or officers of the church. Their main responsibility is for the care and upkeep of church property. In smaller parishes their duties can and do stretch to ringing bells and digging graves. It was not necessary or traditional that Oliver left a small compensation for the sexton, but that's just the nice kind of guy he is.

Bibliography

Amphlett, D. C. *The Bath Book of Days*. Cheltenham: The History Press, 2014.

Andrews, Robert. *The Rough Guide to Devon and Cornwall*. London: Rough Guides Ltd., 2017.

James, Trevor. *Breakout! Escapes from Dartmoor Prison*. Cornwall: Orchard (Tor Mark), 2015.

Knight, Jenny. *Bath through Time*. Stroud: Amberley Publishing, 2012.

Steedman, Carolyn. *Policing the Victorian Community: The Formation of English Provincial Police*. Vol. 9, *Routledge Library Editions: The History of Crime and Punishment*. New York: Routledge, 2017.

Tames, Richard, and Sheila Tames. *A Traveller's History of Bath*. Moreton-in-Marsh: Chastleton Travel, an imprint of Arris Publishing Ltd., 2009.

Thomson, Basil. *The Story of Dartmoor Prison*. London: Forgotten Books, 2018.

Acknowledgments

So many people are instrumental in the birth of a new book baby. Though most of my time is spent shut in a room by myself, I am never alone in the storytelling journey. My list to thank everyone involved would be a novel in itself, so let these few mentions suffice as a small glimpse of who my team is. . .

Chawna & Jim Schroeder are the dynamic father–daughter duo who are indispensable when it comes to hatching intricate plot details, not to mention Chawna's opera star sister-in-law, Barbara Quintiliani, who was willing to give me insight into a world with which I am not familiar.

Though I research like crazy, I couldn't do without a final historically accurate once-over read from my author buddy Julie Klassen.

Speaking of author buddies, it's Elizabeth Ludwig, Ane Mulligan, Shannon McNear, Sharon Hinck, and Tara Johnson who bear the brunt of my weeping and gnashing of teeth while I craft a story.

My books would never be on the shelf if it weren't for publishing professionals Annie Tipton and Wendy Lawton. Plus a shout-out to editor Reagen Reed who catches my lapses in logic or repeated words.

My cheerleading friends Stephanie Gustafson, Cheryl & Grant Higgins, Linda Ahlmann, and Maria Nelson always stand at the ready with an encouraging word. So do my many readers, who make this writing gig all worthwhile and keep me going when I want to give up.

Last, but not least, I wouldn't be doing this without the support of my long-suffering husband, who puts up with me day in and day out. Mark is my real-life hero.

About the Author

Michelle Griep's been writing since she first discovered blank wall space and Crayolas. She is the Christy Award–winning author of historical romances: *Once Upon a Dickens Christmas, The Noble Guardian, A Tale of Two Hearts, The Captured Bride, The Innkeeper's Daughter, 12 Days at Bleakly Manor, The Captive Heart, Brentwood's Ward, A Heart Deceived,* and *Gallimore;* but also leaped the historical fence into the realm of the contemporary with the zany romantic mystery *Out of the Frying Pan.* If you'd like to keep up with her escapades, find her at www.michellegriep.com or stalk her on Facebook, Twitter, and Pinterest.

And guess what? She loves to hear from readers! Feel free to drop her a note at michellegriep@gmail.com.

Other Books by Michelle

12 Days at Bleakly Manor
Brentwood's Ward
The Innkeeper's Daughter
The Noble Guardian
A Tale of Two Hearts
A Heart Deceived
Gallimore
The Captive Heart
The Captured Bride
Once Upon a Dickens Christmas
Out of the Frying Pan